To Weave

A Tangled Web

of Love

A novel by
Dr. Gloria A. Preston

All Characters and Events are Fictitious

Order this book online at www.trafford.com
or email orders@trafford.com

Most Trafford titles are also available at major online book retailers.

Printed in the United States of America.

ISBN: 978-1-4269-0217-8 (sc)
ISBN: 978-1-4269-0218-5 (hc)
ISBN: 978-1-4269-0219-2 (e)

Trafford rev. 03/16/2011

 www.trafford.com

North America & international
toll-free: 1 888 232 4444 (USA & Canada)
phone: 250 383 6864 ♦ fax: 812 355 4082

To Marijoan and David,

for their loving support, patience and advice.

Forward...

Maggie sat tapping the Tarot card. The Magician's face stared at her. Her red-rimmed, green eyes stared back.

"Is he supposed to represent Harry?" Maggie's normally calm voice went high-pitched without warning.

To Shadow and Daisy it sounded more like a distress signal. The terriers, who had been cozily curled by her side, leaped at once to her rescue covering her face with their cold noses and wet kisses.

"It's okay my poor darlings. Mommy's just got a bad case of the jitters," she explained, stroking them generously until the threat of danger was forgotten and the cairns settled back into their well-worn grooves in the overstuffed couch.

"It's no wonder your dogs are nervous, honey, what with all the worrying you've done these past weeks. Why you've hardly slept a wink in all that time and besides," Maggie's mother shook her head, "the only card that could represent Harry would be the Devil."

"I guess Harry could have been a warlock or a sorcerer if he had wanted to. One would only have had to look into his eyes." Maggie shuffled through the deck searching for the image of the hooved creature. "Half goat, half god, got that right." She quickly turned over the next card. It was the Lovers. A spot of color crept over her cheeks. She tossed the card back onto the table. "How appropriate, that's all I need."

"Maggie dear, Harry's got his own book of shadows rooted in who knows what intrigues."

"Illusions can bedevil any human being, Mom, and Harry's no exception."

Maggie ran her fingers through her jet black hair, loosening a few shoulder length strands from the French twist she had created that morning. She walked to the hall mirror and smoothed her hair in a quick attempt at repair. Wrapped in a new, blue Armani pantsuit, her tall, willowy frame exuded a look of competency. She never wore make-up but today she had made an exception and wore lip gloss and eyeliner. Now she shook her head, displeased with the results.

"Mom, do I look too severe in these tailored clothes? Perhaps if I wore something…" Maggie's voice trailed off despairingly.

"Honey, you look great; quite the professional."

"The cab's here. I've got to get going."

"Call me, dear, as soon as it's over. I'll be sitting here on pins and needles until I hear from you."

"Don't worry, Mom." The anxiety in her mother's face was almost too much to bear and Maggie wrapped her arms around her, hugging her tightly. "Got any last words for the condemned?" She asked wanly, somberly buttoning her coat and wishing she was small enough to fit inside her mother's bathrobe pocket.

"Tell the story, Maggie. It sounds crazy but it's the truth. Who can argue with the truth?"

"You're right, Mom, and like they say, truth is sometimes stranger than fiction."

Maggie had not trusted herself to drive into work and hoped that being a passenger for the hour and a half ride into the city would calm her nerves.

"Where to, lady?" The pokerfaced cabbie inquired impassively.

"The WordTech building." She gave the driver the address and wished it was as easy in life to go from point A to point B.

As the taxicab merged into traffic, she stared out the window at the large, green freeway signs posted clearly along the highway. When had her roadway signs become indistinct? Her goals once plain and simple were now splintered into a misleading maze of tangled webs.

"It's a trip without a destination," she said to no one in particular.

"What was that, lady?" The driver questioned impatiently.

"Nothing," Maggie muttered, "I guess I was just thinking out loud."

The cabbie shook his head and looked away from the rear view mirror.

"Thump, thump, thump," she mimicked as she listened to the taxi's wheels hitting against the rough asphalt, "it sounds a lot like my heart."

Maggie wanted the problem to right itself. She desperately tried to make sense of what was happening in her life as haphazard thoughts whirled through her mind.

By noon the whole business will be history and possibly my job, too. I just wish the whole thing were over and our lives were back to normal. Harry, how could you have let this happen? I should have realized that what you asked me to do would create an upheaval in our lives. My only excuse is that I did it for you. A lot of good hindsight is when the catalyst of destruction has already exploded.

Thump, thump, thump. Maggie listened as the sound grew louder. Hypnotically time began to melt away. She felt herself giving into the rhythm of the rapidly moving car and watched through the window as the fleeting images merged into indecipherable, colorless forms. She tried to fight the sleep that began overtaking her but it was useless and she finally surrendered to quiet nothingness.

Chapter 1

"Hey lady, wake up. Here's your address." The taxi driver's voice sounded as though it were coming from a far away place.

Maggie found waking up terribly difficult. "I'm sorry, I must have dozed off," she apologized as she forced open her eyes.

While her fingers fumbled for the fare, Maggie stared at the WordTech building unwittingly imagining the worst-case scenario. However, once inside the massive steel and glass building, she was amazed at how calm she felt.

"No more looking back," she promised as she stepped out of the corporate elevator and resolutely walked toward the CEO's office.

"Hello, Maggie," Irene Parks cheerfully greeted her as she entered the reception area.

"Hi, Irene. Are they ready for me yet?" Maggie hoped the straightforwardness of the inquiry concealed her nervousness.

Irene got up from her desk and hugged Maggie. "Not yet, would like some tea or something?"

"No thanks, Irene. I'll just sit here until they call me." Maggie smiled at Irene. They were good friends and had served together on several committees.

"Maggie, did Harry really have you type that material for him?" Irene asked coyly.

As the CEO's administrative assistant, Irene prepared all agenda items and Maggie knew she was well aware of the situation.

"Irene, I didn't type anything for Harry that wasn't confidential and necessary."

"Maggie, you're the soul of discretion," Irene whispered as she eyed Maggie discreetly from across her desk.

The door of the CEO's office opened slowly and Alan Cummings stood in the doorway. "Come on in, Maggie. Thanks for joining us."

Maggie smiled warmly as she took his outstretched hand in hers. "Thank you, Mr. Cummings."

Maggie knew she had no choice in the matter but Cummings, a stickler for procedure, expected his staff to observe the proprieties. Nicknamed "Santee" by the WordTech employees, the rotund little man with twinkling blue eyes and white goatee jovially escorted her into his vast office.

Ed Granger, WordTech's corporate attorney, was sitting in one of the two chairs juxtaposed to the CEO's mahogany desk. He stood up as she entered the room.

"Hello, Ms. Reynolds."

"Good morning, Mr. Granger," Maggie said, taking the chair next to him.

"For legal purposes, Ms. Reynolds, do you affirm that you are granting this deposition of your own volition?"

"Yes, I do, Mr. Granger," Maggie nodded at the tall, gaunt looking man.

Although only in his early forties, Granger appeared much older. Suffering from some type of nervous disorder his wizened face was a mass of premature, craggy furrows and his habit of combing the dozen or so long strands of hair atop his balding head unflatteringly forward only added to his aged appearance. It was common knowledge throughout the company that the crusty lawyer was in fact the primary legal power for the WordTech organization and as such savored a well deserved reputation. His cold and calculating manner served to intimidate all those with whom he came in contact, and seeing him, rather than one of the other attorneys, slightly unnerved Maggie but she was determined to remain composed.

"Ed, this is an informal meeting. Don't sound so stuffy. After all, Maggie's here of her own accord." Mr. Cummings looked directly at Maggie and smiled.

"Ms. Reynolds, to maintain legality," Granger's gravelly voice continued on in spite of the CEO's reproof,"Mrs. Parks will take your statement verbatim during this meeting. You'll have ample opportunity to review it before signing. Are those terms acceptable?"

"Yes, I'm in agreement, Mr. Granger." Maggie insinuated herself deeper into the soft leather chair and hoped her response had not revealed the rancor she felt at the formality of the proceedings.

Mr. Granger, who had a habit of continually putting on and taking off his glasses, had barely begun to lift them off his nose when the door opened and Irene came in and took a chair at the back of the room.

"Let's get right to the point, shall we?" As his pudgy fingers leafed through the large file, Alan Cummings grew increasingly agitated. "There seems to be some problem in Harry's, Mr. Cooke's department." He stopped reading and looked at Granger. "What's it all about, Ed?"

"It's been reported by Paul Keating of the Accounting department that Mr. Cooke had Ms. Reynolds type some non-business related material during business hours on a company computer." Granger, holding tight to his copy of the file, glanced back at Mr. Cummings.

"Maggie," Mr. Cummings said in a soft but firm tone,"I find this whole thing hard to believe. I hardly think a professional of your caliber would be involved in anything unethical. And we all know Harry. He's got his finger on the pulse of his department. Everything's always shipshape. Isn't that true, Ed?"

"Very true A.C.," Granger confirmed without hesitation.

Mr. Cummings took a deep breath and continued on. "I don't mind telling you that a report of this kind disturbs me. To have to interrupt business for something of this nature is totally unacceptable. However, seeing that you're involved, I know there must be some reasonable explanation for this perturbing incident. Maggie, tell us, is there any truth to Mr. Keating's accusations? Can you shed any light on this matter?" The irritation in Mr. Cummings' voice was unmistakable.

"I don't want to say much in view of the fact that Mr. Cooke isn't present," Maggie replied, knowing that both men could very well have done without any mention of Harry's involvement in what they considered a petty disruption of their busy activities.

"Don't concern yourself with that matter, Ms. Reynolds. Mr. Cooke will speak for himself later," Granger interrupted sternly.

"Yes, Maggie, we can all understand and appreciate your sense of loyalty but you'll have to explain exactly what Mr. Keating means when he accuses you of the use of WordTech property, particularly your computer, for unwarranted, non-business related purposes. What could possibly be construed as non-business material?" Then, almost as an afterthought, he asked, "Ed, isn't this the incident you and I discussed last week?" Mr. Cummings, his anger escalating, looked intently at Maggie without waiting for Granger's response. "I'll ask you again, Maggie, is there any truth to this report?"

"Yes, in fact it is true, Mr. Cummings." Maggie stopped and waited for the startled expression to leave Cummings' face.

"Explain that please," he insisted sharply.

Maggie continued, "For some time now, Mr. Cooke has been

suffering from acute anxiety. About two months ago he asked me to type material that he planned on presenting to his doctor. The material was a journal that Mr. Cooke hoped would help during his therapy sessions. Since the material was extremely confidential, he asked me to type it during business hours and I agreed after I learned the reason for his request."

"What in fact was the journal material related to?" Granger, whose glasses now seemed suspended in midair, kept his eyes on Cummings after having asked the question.

"Ed, is it necessary for Ms. Reynolds to describe the journal's content?" Mr. Cummings, whose chubby pink cheeks were now crimson, persisted in spite of his apparent discomfort. "After all, you've provided us with a typed summation of the CD which we have on file. It would seem superfluous to have Ms. Reynolds elaborate on what we already know. I'm sure you agree with me, Ed." Having had his say, Mr. Cummings summarily closed the file on his desk ostensibly intent on avoiding any further reference to material he apparently viewed as inappropriate.

"I think, A.C., if Ms. Reynolds were to give us a periphery description that would serve our purposes here today. As you say, we have the said material on file." Ed Granger's tone was resoundingly solicitous.

"Thank you, Ed." The older man eyed Granger fixedly before turning his attention to Maggie. "Maggie, could you tell us a little about what Mr. Cooke had you type? Mind you, we don't expect garish specifics." His tone advised Maggie to tread cautiously.

"Yes, of course, sir. The majority of the text reflected his sexual activities," Maggie hesitated momentarily and then resumed, "and the writings had to do with his impulsive behavior and the actions that behavior brought about." Maggie colored slightly as she recalled Harry's depictions of his perverted escapades.

"Ed, I'm sure that's sufficient information. After all, Maggie, Ms. Reynolds, has added an entirely new dimension to this situation, one I'm sure HR will want to hear about." Mr. Cummings seemed relieved that the revelation was at an end.

"Are you aware that using company time for personal business is grounds for immediate termination, Ms. Reynolds?" Granger's sonorous voice pierced the silence of the room.

"Yes, I am, Mr. Granger. I gave the matter serious consideration before agreeing to take on the task. Since it had to do with my boss, his health and the betterment of both the department and WordTech, I felt it was a necessary assignment. As I told Mr. Cooke, if I had believed it was merely a personal task he was asking me to undertake, I would have refused for the exact reason you have just mentioned. However, due to the serious nature of his request and the ramifications involved, I felt it was my duty to help Mr. Cooke."

"Well said young lady. I heartily agree. The whole matter is extremely distasteful and was brought on, as you say, by Mr. Cooke's illness. I would think, Ed, that sufficient motivation and completely understandable in light of what Ms. Reynolds has told us." Mr. Cummings obviously wanted to end the discussion and remove the unsuitable topic from the corporate agenda as quickly as possible.

"Regrettably A.C., the seriousness of such a claim from a co-worker's standpoint must be thoroughly investigated before we can close this matter. For that reason it will be necessary to meet with Mr. Cooke and Mr. Keating prior to submitting our findings to the committee."

Mr. Granger's response seemed to pain Mr. Cummings who openly grimaced.

"Ms. Reynolds, you will be informed of any further proceedings requiring your presence, and, as I mentioned, we will need your signature on the deposition as soon as possible."

"Thank you, Maggie, for your candor and truthfulness." Mr. Cummings, who seemed genuinely pleased with her testimony, smiled broadly. "We appreciate your unfaltering determination to do the best for both your department and WordTech in what could have been construed as an embarrassing situation. Your continued dedication is much appreciated. I'm sure that after we talk to Harry, Mr. Cooke, we will be able to bring this matter to a prompt and positive conclusion." Mr. Cummings rose and walked over to her chair and grasped her hand in both of his. "Thank you for coming, Maggie."

"Thank you, Mr. Cummings," Maggie said, relieved that the meeting was over.

"Ms. Reynolds, I'll walk you to the elevator," Granger offered dryly.

"Thank you, Mr. Granger," Maggie replied without looking in his direction.

Only after having pressed the down button did Granger break his stony silence. "It goes without saying, Ms. Reynolds, that nothing of this matter may be discussed with anyone outside of this office, including both Mr. Cooke and Mr. Keating. You have an excellent reputation and we know you wouldn't want to jeopardize your position with any further violations of WordTech's code of ethics." His speech completed, Granger waited only until the doors opened before turning his back and walking away.

Coming down in the elevator, Maggie wasn't sure if she had been vindicated or merely granted a stay of execution. Although torn between pride and frustration, she felt somewhat reassured by Corporate's decision to allow her veracity to go unchallenged having presumably accepted her decision to have assisted Harry in his predicament but whether she would be exonerated was still unclear.

"Well, what the hell happened?" Leeann asked, gaping at Maggie.

"Talk about unpleasant experiences," Maggie groaned loudly as she caved into her office chair. She could tell from the look on her assistant's face that Leeann had anticipated the worse.

"Is it over? Are you still employed?"

"Yes to both of your questions for the time being. I can't go into detail but suffice to say the uproar hasn't been quelled. Granger's getting ready for round two," Maggie said, her edginess dissipating as she shuffled through a wad of messages on her desk.

"In other words you're still in hot water. Just a lot of soggy talk and after all you've done for this place…"

"Don't Leeann. I'm playing this by the book."

"Okay, okay, Maggie. By the way, here are a couple of new messages. I marked them both urgent. Harry sounded nervous as hell and wanted you to get back to him right away. You can draw your own conclusions about the other."

"Thanks, Leeann." Maggie saw that the other was from Paul and tossed it into the wastebasket before calling Harry's cell number.

"Good riddance," Leeann muttered under her breath as she walked back to her desk.

"Harry, what's so urgent?"

"Maggie, I know you just came down from Corporate. I need to see you right away." Harry sounded anxious. "Can you meet me after work?"

"Sure, Harry, but…"

Harry interrupted. "Do you remember the Spanish bistro?"

"Yes."

"Can you be there about eight?"

"Harry, it may not be a good idea to… ." But the call had ended and Maggie decided it was probably better to see Harry rather than talk with him on the phone, particularly after Granger's warning.

Leeann came back into her office waving another message

slip. "It's urgent from you know who. How long do you intend on putting Paul off?"

"Indefinitely," Maggie said rigidly.

"Why don't you just tell him where to go?"

"Leeann, I appreciate your advice but I need time to think."

If anyone could help her sort through this mess, Maggie knew it would be Leeann. She was the only person who knew the entire situation, and as far as Maggie was concerned, the only one she trusted to keep it confidential.

"If you ask me this whole thing smells."

"It hurts too much, Leeann. I can't even talk about it. When I've had time to decide how I'm going to handle it, as usual, you'll be the first one I tell."

"Sure, Mag," Leeann shot her a sisterly smile and added, "just don't let 'em get you down."

"I'll survive."

Maggie had learned years ago that her assistant was an indispensable branch on the WordTech grapevine. Leeann knew just about everyone at the telecommunications company and was usually aware of new developments long before they were officially announced.

Having initially been hired as point person for the department, Leeann discovered early on how to procure supplies for the staff. Through the years her ingenious requisitioning skills had gained considerable fame and were deemed extraordinary throughout the company. Always on top of every situation, the petite five foot-two, long-haired, wily blonde acknowledged all requests immediately in a distinctive Brooklyn twang emitted in decibels that more often than not turned people's heads. Her savvy experience and practical, earthy outlook made her seem wise beyond her years. She had a unique sense of humor, could be brutally candid and wielded an acerbic wit like a sword. Married and divorced twice, she had no children, and as she liked to say it, "no fucking regrets." She was extremely proud of her popularity with the opposite sex and enjoyed regaling the department with her dating adventures. Although only twelve years older than Maggie, she was fiercely loyal having taken the younger woman under her wing the moment they met.

"Face it, Maggie, he did you dirt. If he had been my boyfriend and done to me what he did to you, I'd kill him."

"Leeann, the problem is I'm partly responsible for Paul's actions."

"For once in your life, Maggie, try to accept the facts without analyzing them."

"That's easier said than done. I know Paul and to a certain extent I can understand where he was coming from. After all, he did warn me."

"Making excuses for him won't take the pain away, Maggie. Don't forget, I've known you since you were a wet-behind-the-ears kid dropped into WordTech's world of movers and shakers, and you've never been one to shirk responsibility. Even in the beginning, remember?"

"Funny, I was just thinking about that on the ride in this morning," Maggie said, recalling her first days on the job. "It was both hectic and terrific, and thanks to you I kept my head above water and…"

"Parlayed your assets into a career," Leeann said, grinning broadly.

"They say you're as good as the best thing you've ever done, and I'd like to think I've done a good job here at WordTech."

"Damn straight! You were purpose driven the day you walked through the door."

"Let's not kid ourselves, Leeann. I hung onto Harry's coattails every step of the way. Even though I was eager and optimistic, without Harry I'd never have gotten initiated into WordTech's hallowed echelons."

"You've got guts, Maggie. You were the quickest study I ever saw but you worked like hell to get the job down pat in a few months. No one gave you anything."

"I was tempted into loyalty by the boss's job."

"What do you mean?"

"Harry Cooke, Director of Marketing; when I saw that title I knew the job was my ticket into an apprenticeship of power. He was the kind of boss I had always wanted."

"So, Harry was on the top rung of the corporate ladder, so what? Lots of people are in positions of power but that doesn't make those who climb with them any less enterprising."

"Yes, I know, but if it wasn't for Harry giving me the chance to prove myself I don't believe I'd be up here now."

"If you don't mind my saying it, that's the kind of thinking that got you into this mess in the first place."

"What are you talking about?"

"I'm talking about the way you feel about Harry, and his asking you to do that stupid piece of shit, and you feeling so beholding to him that you did it."

"He needed my help, Leeann."

"Uh huh, but of course you never once thought about how much you owed the guy for handing you the job like it was on some fricken, golden platter?" Leeann gave Maggie a hardnosed look.

"Okay, okay, Leeann, but he's more than a boss; he's my mentor whose friendship I value."

"You just can't accept getting lucky and grabbing the brass ring."

"I don't believe in luck."

"Okay, call it circumstances. You were in the right place at the right time. After all Maggie, you were savvy enough to learn the ins and outs of this business, and like I said before, parlayed the job into more than it was when you first started. You've got brains, kid. I've seen 'em come and I've seen 'em go, and you earn every penny they pay you. You don't owe anybody anything, least of all Harry."

"No, Leeann, you're wrong. Harry gave wings to my goals and ambitions. I won't ever forget that. He groomed me in the management process, and even when I made mistakes, and I made some big ones, he prodded me on and kept me believing in myself. How many bosses do you know who would do that?"

"I still say it's just a job."

"Listen, until Harry, all the execs I ever knew were so busy looking out for number one they couldn't be bothered with mentoring a new kid on the block. He was special, he had faith in me," Maggie recounted, a look of passionate frankness upon her face.

"Okay, so you got on well together. He liked you and you liked him. Believe me, it was no match made in heaven."

"What's that suppose to mean?"

"Harry's a bastard. The very fact you could hold your own with him says something for your own intelligence."

"He's tough that's true and I admire that trait in him but hitting it off doesn't mean a step up on the career ladder."

"You're right," Leeann nodded affirmatively, "and you've got to be one hell of a smart cookie to make the grade in this company."

"But you'll have to admit that having someone in your corner who wants you to excel is more than half the battle. And if it happens to be your boss, well, what can I say? In my case, it was Harry."

"Okay, but maybe you didn't know he was a tyrant who drove everybody crazy until you came on board. He went through assistants like wet paper towels. You can't imagine how we all held our breath until you went permanent after your first year of probation."

"Harry's taken a bad rap simply because he's a bold decision maker."

"I'll give him that much. He's fast, instinctive but so are sharks. It's that very trust in the moment that makes Harry recognize talent in others. He can smell it."

"Leeann, it's a whole lot more than just seeing a person's potential. It's taking responsibility for the training, coaching and teaching of that individual. It's also support and understanding without equivocation. It goes way beyond the job description. It's hard to explain unless you've had a boss like that. Believe me, they're rare."

"Maggie, can it be that you don't know it was you who helped Harry keep the ship afloat? You're thorough and methodical and you get a kick out of planning and organizing every minute detail. That's what Harry needed. The surprising thing is that you were successful together in spite of being so different. Your work styles complemented the best in both of you but there's no one on the staff that doesn't credit you with making Harry a happy camper which translated into cohesive teamwork and bonus money for our department."

"Leeann, you make it sound like Harry had nothing to do with growing me into the professional I've become today."

"Oh bullcrap, Maggie. You believed in yourself and you grew into an inveterate member of the WordTech team by using your skills and abilities."

"You're entitled to your opinion, Leeann, but you'll never convince me. This job has taken me to heights I never thought possible and I know it's all due to Harry's guidance."

"That's your one strong weakness, my friend."

"What is?"

"Men with lean, good looking bodies."

"Leeann, are we still having the same conversation?"

"Remember what you told me when you first started? You said you fell in love with Harry the moment you saw him."

"My God, Leeann, I was twenty-three years old."

"Like they say in the movies, tall, dark and handsome and to you he could do no wrong."

"That's crazy. So, Harry's good looking, but that doesn't mean I'm in love with him."

"Uh huh, and I suppose that lean, strong body and square-jawed sculptured face of his doesn't still turn you on."

"Hardly a reason to work my butt off, Leeann; I happen to love this job. It's as simple as that," but Maggie couldn't help smiling as she recalled how she had drawn a sharp intake of breath when she had first stared into Harry's uncommonly attractive face.

"Who are you trying to convince, Maggie?"

"Leeann, don't confuse my philosophy with yours. You're the eternal romantic and you'll never understand why my job is just as important to me as my relationships. And it's not about money either. It's a part of both men and women's fundamental nature, a fulfillment of our need to be of service."

"Not my fundamental nature, girl. As I see it, men have a duty to perform and women should be grateful for the service."

"Oh, Leeann, this isn't about sex."

"Can I help it if I have a healthy sexual appetite?"

"I didn't say we were saints, but… ."

"Then stop making the job and Harry sound so noble."

"Yes, but that's exactly how I do see it. It's the discipline; a selfless giving back to a society that expects people to be productive. That's why it's so important to find a job that makes you feel good about yourself. Work is not only therapeutic but it helps people to value themselves."

"And how does Harry fit into all that?"

"Harry's a man of principle who believes in the same values I do, and that means more to me than looks or anything else for that matter."

"Oh, brother, do you really believe that schmaltz?"

"Bottom line, Leeann, I believe in Harry and after all he's done for me I'm not going to let him down when he needs my help."

"I swear, Mag, sometimes I don't get you at all. It's like you're afraid to accept success on your own merits. Don't forget Harry has a lot invested in you, too. You both pooled your resources together but face it, half the credit belongs to you."

"Leeann, we're arguing at cross purposes."

"Maggie, mind if I give you a little advice?"

"No, go ahead, Leeann, you will anyway."

"Don't go putting Harry on any pedestal. Greek gods have a habit of disappointing us ordinary folks."

"Leeann, he's my boss and he's a human being. He's also been my friend and instructor for seven years."

"Maggie, all I can say is that for a smart girl you've certainly surrounded yourself with jerks." Leeann turned and walked out.

After she left, Maggie sat back in her chair and stared out the window. Even the breathtaking view of the city from her nineteenth floor office couldn't uplift her today. Where had it all begun? Was Leeann right? Could she possibly have put too much faith in Harry? And what about Paul; what did he expect to gain from all this?

It's hard to believe, Maggie old girl, that this all started with that simple want ad in the classifieds. I answered the ad for an administrative assistant and got more than I bargained for. Not only did I get a great job but I got Harry for a boss. I also met Paul. How could such a little pronouncement have had such a profound impact? If I had been aware of the far-reaching effects this job would have on my life, would I have concentrated all my efforts on achieving it? Yes, without a doubt I'd do it all again. Perhaps now is a good time to sort through the bits and pieces and come up with some answers. Unraveling the tangled webs will take time but my memories are all there, neat and tidy, just as I left them.

Maggie bent down and retrieved the crumpled message from

out of the trash. The pain of Paul's betrayal cut into her like a knife and she involuntarily shuddered. She sat gripping the paper as tears welled up in her eyes.

Staring out the window it almost seemed as if it were raining, raining as hard as it had been that day three years ago when she first met Paul. Maggie closed her eyes as her mind began rewinding, turning time backwards.

Chapter 2

Orientation at WordTech was a big part of the employment process. During a series of indoctrinating courses new employees learned that re-education was the prime directive of the corporation. To that end, old ideas were promptly replaced with organizational ideals and value tenets that were intended for immediate on-the-job utilization.

Mandatory adherence to policy was strictly enforced. Skeptical first-timers were given a checklist that included a-what-to-do set of regulations in which security measures were a priority. With so many areas off-limits to most personnel, learning to navigate the building was difficult. WordTech guards maintained constant vigils predominantly on certain floors where dedicated workforces, housed in highly secured laboratories and think tanks, designed and produced the communication products for which the company was famous.

It took Maggie five years to land her dream job at WordTech but after four years with the company, and an A-2 security clearance, she had yet to make a complete tour of inspection. She opted instead to familiarize herself with the huge international firm by using her research skills along with the company's virtual tours to gain an in-depth view of the corporation.

WordTech Incorporated was a thirty-seven floor microcosm whose employees could spend days inside the colossal building without having to emerge for any of the necessities of life. In addition to three five-star restaurants and dozens of fast food eateries, the glass and steel edifice boasted a gym that held an oversized swimming pool, and both indoor and outdoor tracks. The latter, located on the roof, was surrounded by a green belt park one city-block long, and gave employees access to a nature retreat on a daily basis.

The monstrous megaplex was one of three identical buildings, the other two having been built in Hong Kong and Dubai respectively. Each contained a movie theater, a fully staffed day nursery and clinic, a company credit union, several uni-sex hair salons, a combination dry-cleaner and laundry, a bookstore, a non-denominational chapel, and an underground parking facility which accommodated every WordTech employees' vehicle.

There was even a lavish hotel on the twenty-seventh floor which provided accommodations not only for company clients but employees whose job or personal life necessitated its use. One could virtually remain at the job for weeks without ever leaving the building. It was a standing joke that many of the employees had met, dated, married and had children while at the company without interrupting their work schedules.

One rainy afternoon Maggie stood reading a small book of poems at the borrow-a-book counter in the back of the company bookstore. With her wire-rimmed reading glasses perched precariously on the tip of her nose, she was completely absorbed and unaware of being studied by a young man from across the aisle. She stopped reading and looked up, however, when his throat clearing became so pronounced she could no longer concentrate.

"That book must really be something. I've been trying to get your attention for the past ten minutes. Are you researching for your department or are you on personal time?"

"Elizabeth Barrett Browning, don't you just love her?" Maggie said, pushing her glasses on top of her head. "I usually take a late lunch and avoid the crowds. Besides, it's too wet outside to do much of anything else."

"Really." He gave a sudden broad smile. "I'm Paul Keating, Accounting."

"I'm Maggie Reynolds, Marketing."

"Yes, I know. If you have time for a cup of coffee, I'll explain."

"Make that a cup of tea and you've got yourself a deal."

Although only a few inches taller than she was, Maggie could see that Paul's five foot, ten inch frame sported a well muscled physique. His long face had strong aquiline features and his dark brown eyes contrasted nicely with his sandy colored hair. His friendly manner, coupled with humorous ways, made him easy to talk to and Maggie found herself liking him at once.

"So tell me, how did you know my name?" Maggie asked, settling herself comfortably into one of the small booths at the yogurt shop.

"I asked Mrs. Allwedd in HR." Paul nibbled at the sprinkles in his yogurt cup while giving Maggie an exaggerated look of seriousness. "I told her it was imperative that I meet you."

"And what did Gwen say?"

"She laughed and told me that she wasn't a matchmaker. She also said you were a real nice person."

"Gwen's a charming lady and one of my favorite people."

"Mine too. As a matter of fact, it was because of her name that she and I got more acquainted."

"How was that?"

"Genealogy's a hobby of mine and I was intrigued by her last name. When I asked her about it she told me that Allwedd was an old Welsh word for key."

"I had no idea." Maggie felt the hairs on the back of her neck stand up as she fingered the charm around her neck and thought about that first meeting she had had with the director of Human Resources.

"Did you know I had my first interview with Gwen in the fifth floor ladies' lounge?"

"I've heard of some strange places for interviews but that beats all. How did that happen?"

"I had just dropped off my resume in HR and was headed back down to the main floor in what turned out to be a terribly crowded express elevator. When it stopped for no apparent reason everyone just stood there quietly staring at the doors. Then there was this huge sigh of relief as they suddenly opened. We were all waiting for someone to either get on or off when I felt someone or something push me from behind. I wound up outside the elevator and stood there like a dummy as the doors closed."

"You're kidding? Who could have pushed you?" Paul questioned.

"I don't know exactly. It felt like a force against my back but somehow it didn't quite seem human. It wasn't painful or anything but more like a gust of wind lifting me up and out. I know it sounds crazy."

"How did Gwen figure in all this?"

"Sure you want to hear?"

"Yes, go ahead," Paul said excitedly. "It sounds like a mystery thriller."

"Well, I saw this woman headed to the ladies' lounge with a company key in her hand. You know the kind that looks like it's attached to a big piece of plywood or something so it doesn't get lost."

Paul nodded.

"Anyway, I knew once the door shut I'd be locked out, so, like an idiot I raced down the corridor and caught the door just as it was closing."

"What happened then?"

"Nothing, I just sat down on one of the lounge chairs and tried to make sense out of what had just happened. Gwen came out of one of the stalls and watched me as she washed her hands in front of the mirror. She must have figured something was wrong because she was very sympathetic and asked me if everything was all right. It was then she noticed this." Maggie lifted the charm from off her neck and held it up for Paul's scrutiny. "She really admired it and said it was quite beautiful."

"It is beautiful. It's a miniature key, isn't it? Hey, do you realize we've mentioned the word key three or four times in this conversation."

"Yes, and after you told me the meaning of Gwen's last name, I knew it wasn't just a coincidence. I get goose bumps just thinking of it."

"What did Gwen say then?"

"She asked me what the key represented."

"And… ?"

"I hate to do this, Paul, but it's too long of a story and I've got to get back to work."

"That's not fair, Maggie. When do I hear the rest of it?"

"When do you want to?"

"How about tonight over dinner?"

"Sounds good. Where would you like to meet?"

"The Almanac on the fifteenth floor has great food," Paul suggested readily.

"Seven o'clock okay with you?"

"Great, I'll make a reservation. See you then, Maggie."

After that first meeting, Maggie discovered that Paul knew a great many people at WordTech. Unlike her, he was an extrovert by nature and his friendly, out-going personality endeared him to both management and staff. Maggie found him an indispensable resource, introducing her to people not only involved in the marketing side of the company but those who knew the inner workings of the huge conglomerate as well.

Schedules permitting, they took time for occasional coffee breaks and fast food lunches where Paul, although a diehard fitness pro dedicated to nutrition, usually capitulated to Maggie's tastes for tuna sandwiches, chocolate shakes and curly fries.

Paul always had tickets for this or that show and they usually treated themselves ahead of time to dinner at one of their favorite restaurants. After three years they were more than best friends and enjoyed a satisfying yet undemanding relationship that allowed them both their independence. Although they had continued dating others for awhile, their mutual interests in dancing, physical fitness and the theater offered a comfortable and convenient lifestyle that gradually graduated to exclusivity.

"Hey, Maggie, how about a seven a.m. run tomorrow?" Paul shouted over the crowd as the express elevator made its way down to the garage.

"Listen, Mr. K., I'm not getting out of bed one hour earlier for you or anyone else," Maggie said, her flippancy causing heads to turn.

"Come on Maggie, it'll do you good. I promise just once around the track," Paul continued to plead as they walked to their cars.

"Okay, but why do I always let you talk me into it? I'll meet you on the track at seven thirty," she smiled, knowing Paul's persuasive techniques were actually excuses to spend more time together.

"I thought we said seven?"

"No, you said seven but if we're only going around once, I can sleep a little longer and meet you at seven thirty," Maggie corrected wryly.

"Are we still on for tomorrow night?"

"Sure, but don't forget starting next week I'm back to volunteering at the community center a couple of nights a week. The kids have been sending me the cutest tweets every day since they found out I'm coaching the swim meets again this year."

"You only go through life once, and once is enough if you do it right. I say skip all that volunteer business, Maggie, and spend more time with me."

"If we're not careful people will start thinking we're going through it together." Maggie realized she and Paul had slipped into a familiar pattern, seeing each other almost every night of the week.

"That's fine with me." Paul squeezed her hand tightly.

"Paul, I was kidding. You know that's not something either of us wants. I like my life the way it is."

"I know, without commitment," he shook his head at her. Let's talk about it tomorrow, Maggie. There's a new club opening on the east side. They say the band's fantastic. I've got to run, but I'll call you tonight," Paul said, sprinting toward his parking space.

∼✻∽

Maggie was glad that Paul was as mad about music and dancing as she was. Their lives revolved around the downtown clubs that offered both the activity they enjoyed and the awesome sounds of first rate bands. That evening they rushed through dinner and made their way across town checking out a few of the trendy nightspots before deciding on one of the more popular groups.

"Great band," Maggie whispered as she nestled her head on Paul's shoulder. "These guys even know how to mellow the slow numbers."

"You're a sentimentalist, Maggie, but I like it for an altogether different reason." Paul squeezed her tightly.

"Where did you learn to dance so well, Paul?"

"I took lessons when I was about twenty-two years old. I was in the service and stationed in a one-horse town in Mississippi. The only thing going on Friday nights was either drinking at one of the local bars, or a dance class taught by a husband and wife team; they were old but in great shape. They were like the Fred Astaire and Ginger Rogers of their day. I think they were on Broadway or something. Anyway, they taught us guys the steps and since there weren't enough women, we had to take turns leading and following."

"Sounds like fun," Maggie teased.

"What I remember mostly is how following really got on my nerves. Sue Davis, that was her name, and Mike, that was her husband, they were always after me to quit leading. No sooner would I stop, than I'd start again. I think they were glad when I got reassigned to San Diego. I know I sure was."

"The Marines?"

"Yep, I didn't make the Corp a career but I did a four year stint. I got lucky and did the rest in sunny Diego."

"You've got a great smile, Paul. Did I ever tell you that it was your smile that attracted me to you the first time we met?"

"Could I interest you in any of my other virtues? I'd make a great husband in case you were thinking along those lines."

"I thought we both agreed marriage wasn't for us."

"That was in the beginning. We've gotten to know one another a lot better since then." He hugged her closely.

"Is that enough to start a marriage on?"

"Some people have less."

"Who for instance?"

"My mom and dad for instance. They only knew each other for two weeks before they got hitched. My dad said he knew right off mom was the one by the way she looked at him when he sang off key."

"How did your dad find that out?"

"The way he tells it they met in a bar and he was with some friends and she was with some guy. The band was playing one of dad's favorite songs and, feeling no pain, he belted out the tune. He was giving it his all when he noticed this attractive brunette at the end of the bar. She was nibbling on her lower lip and shaking her head. He said he knew in that instant."

"How did he get her phone number?"

"Mom must have known too because dad gave his business card to the bartender after putting a question mark on the back and mom just wrote her number down along with her name. Like dad says, the rest is history."

"What a romantic story."

"How did your parents meet?"

"To tell the truth, I don't really know. My dad died when I was ten and mom doesn't like talking about the past." Maggie lifted her shoulders and shrugged.

"Do you remember your dad?"

"Yes, I do, vividly. I loved him so much. He was a magician of sorts."

"Was he in show business?"

"Not that kind of magic. He taught me the power of positive thinking. He told me that if I wanted anything in my life all I had to do was close my eyes and picture it, here." Maggie put her index finger on Paul's forehead. "The magic's in the mind."

"Does it work?"

"Sure it does. The trick is in convincing your mind that what you want you already have."

"I don't get it."

"It's pretty involved but a simple explanation would be to close your eyes and see a big, white screen. You picture yourself having or doing the thing you want most in the world. If it doesn't go against the laws of nature, and you keep visualizing the picture again and again, eventually the deep mind brings it to you."

"That's an incredible theory."

"It's been around for a while, like affirmation cards."

"What are those?"

"You write positive thoughts, always in the past tense, like I aced that test with flying colors, or we had a great date, but you need to put in some details, you get it, on three by five cards and put them where you can see them. Then you read them out loud everyday. Your mind believes what you say has already happened so it manifests your ideas into reality."

"Is it like hypnosis?"

"No, it's more than that. If you want something you have to work to get it. It isn't going to just show up on your doorstep. You've got to listen for clues or as my dad liked to call them hunches. You get signals and it triggers the mind that you're on the right track."

"What kind of signals?"

"Oh, ideas that pop up for you when you least expect it. For instance, I was sure what I wanted to do after high school but because my mom kept insisting I go to college I was frustrated. I had done my affirmation work by seeing myself successfully working at a job and then one day I was sitting in class and this girl walked past me and dropped her book. It fell open to the page on secretarial positions. I handed it back to her and noticed the title. It was called, *What Color Is Your Parachute?*"

"That's a pretty popular book on careers, isn't it?"

"Yes, and it happened, just like that," Maggie snapped her fingers,"and my hunch and purpose were linked. After that I just followed the yellow brick road. It eventually led me to WordTech."

"What happened to your dad, Maggie?"

"When he found out my grandmother, his mother, was dying, he wanted to go back to Italy to see her. He wanted all of us to go but it was too expensive. On his way back, he was in a car accident and killed. We got a telegram and I remember my mom crying and crying. She couldn't even tell me at first, and when she finally did I couldn't believe I'd never see him again. But I was wrong, I still see him in my dreams."

"I would have liked to have known him."

"He would have liked you, Paul."

"You said he went to Italy. Reynolds doesn't sound Italian."

"Our family name was Renoldazzi but my father changed it when he came to America. He said we needed a name people could pronounce." Maggie laughed.

"Maggie Renoldazzi. So you're really a sexy Italian lady. What part of Italy were your folks from?"

"My father met my mother here. She's Irish. My father's parents were from a small town outside of Rome called Palombara Sabina. I went back to see my dad's grave a while ago. He's buried in a family plot in a small cemetery on the outskirts of the town."

"I'm sorry, Maggie. Hey, do you remember when we first met and you told me how you had run into Gwen Allwedd? We got so interested in talking about other things that night you never got a chance to finish the story. Does that key you wear have something to do with your father?"

"You've got a good memory, Paul. Yes, the key I wear was given to me in a dream by my father. I copied it from memory as soon as I woke up. My mother had the design made into a charm."

"It's unique and very beautiful, like you." Paul touched the key lightly as it rested in the small hollow of Maggie's neck. "Why three prongs? What do they represent?"

"It's the philosophy my father taught me to believe in. It's what I value most in life. My faith in a higher power, my loving relationships and the work I've chosen to do in this life."

"Simple but effective. What did Gwen think about it?"

"She asked me which one I valued most."

"And which do you, Maggie?"

"The first is foundational and the other two the supporting

beams. All three must have value to give purpose to your life. In that way, each works in harmony with the others, equally, so that one does not take precedence over the other."

"I get it, separate but whole," he murmured brightly. "A structurally sound idea, Maggie, but I bet it's why you shy away when I get serious?"

"No, Paul. Power comes when life has meaning. My life now is balanced and I'm content knowing that the key has opened all three areas of my life."

"You could still maintain that balance after marriage."

"Of course, but the point is that you and I both agreed we wanted an uncomplicated relationship. It was a mutual decision that's allowed us a well-adjusted lifestyle. "

"A rather compartmentalized lifestyle if you ask me. Life doesn't always work that way."

"You've missed the point entirely. It's not compartmentalization but synchronization."

"Anyway, there's no use arguing with you, Maggie. I'll just write my own affirmation card and picture the whole thing, right here." Paul kissed his finger and touched her forehead. "I know exactly what I'll write on it."

"Paul, don't get serious."

"Why not, Maggie? I'm like my dad. I knew the moment I met you."

"What about our promise not to make any demands on one another?"

"I know I said I'd be content with our relationship the way it is but I think I've got to let you know how I feel. You've become the most important person in my life. You mean the world to me."

"Paul, I'm not going to feel guilty because I can't reciprocate that feeling."

"Don't. I'm over twenty-one and I know there were no promises between us. Just because you can't return my feelings doesn't mean I have to stop loving you, and I do love you, Maggie."

"I don't love you, Paul, not like that, not enough to build a marriage on. The reason has nothing to do with you but everything to do with me."

"I can't help thinking it's because of Harry that you feel that way."

"Paul, that's not true," Maggie said indignantly.

"No? How would you know when you spend your days catering to him?"

"Paul, please don't go there. My business relationship with Harry has nothing to do with us."

"Well, okay, but nothing is going to stop my feeling the way I do about you. I don't think I could live without you, Maggie, and I'm willing to wait until you feel the same as I do."

"Why do you have to spoil what we have with one another? Why can't we just be friends and go on the way we have been?" Maggie asked irritably.

"For how long? It's getting harder for me to love you without thinking about our future together." Paul put his lips to her ear and whispered, "Marry me, Maggie. We'll make it work."

"No, Paul, I don't want complications in my personal life or at work. If you're going to turn serious then there's no point in our seeing each other as often as we have been. It would be unfair to both of us."

"I won't say I'm not glad it happened. I wanted you to know how I feel about you but I'll respect your wishes."

Maggie's frown spread into a smile.

"That's what I get for falling in love with a career woman." Paul fingered the charm at her neck. "I wish I had the key to unlock your heart, Maggie Renoldazzi."

Maybe it was odd but on the drive home although she found

herself growing increasing impatient with Paul she did not object when he suggested they drive to Windy Point and park. The sounds of the sea stirred her as much as his gentle hands and graceful kisses and she was moved to kiss him back. He smelled of spearmint and aftershave and the scents commingled irresistibly, sparking a sense of longing that had always made giving into him easy. This time was different. Her mood had changed and she could find no comfort in his arms. She wanted to mask her irritation and let his words sway her into making love but it was useless.

"Let's go to my place, Maggie," Paul entreated.

"Not tonight, Paul." Maggie begged off, avoiding his eyes.

"Don't tell me you're still hurt?" Paul asked disbelievingly.

"I don't know what I am, Paul. All I know is that I can't be with you like I am."

"Oh come on, honey, you're just tired. We'll have the whole weekend to ourselves," Paul said, his arms reaching out to embrace her.

"No, Paul, not tonight. It doesn't feel right."

"Don't sound so damn sensible, Maggie," Paul winced in anger. "Make up some lousy excuse, like PMS or something."

"Drive me home, Paul, please." She pulled back sharply, insistently, and the spell was broken.

"What's wrong with me? I wanted to feel the touch of his body against mine but even my craving the pleasure of his company isn't enough to change my mind. I can't explain this feeling of emptiness and it would be senseless to try.

"I don't get it. Why the hell are you punishing me?"

She saw his eyes as he moved away from her. Their look saddened her but she said nothing.

The air was cold and silent on the drive home. He walked her to the door and pecked her lightly on the cheek. She let him drive away without a word.

Chapter 3

They remained quietly at odds over the weekend but by Monday Paul was back to being his old self. For the first time, however, Maggie noticed that he began coming to her office on a more systematic basis. Where before they had kept each other in the loop via text messaging and cell calls, she now found him waiting in the reception area reading newspapers or talking to other employees. Other times he'd come back from an early run on some pretext or another and walk into her office unexpectedly. Despite the fact he made it seem as though he had been waiting for her, there were moments when she got the distinct impression it wasn't her he had come down to see.

On one such occasion after a hurried excuse to get back to work, Maggie walked him out to the reception area and noticed the door to Harry's office was ajar. This was highly irregular considering that whenever Harry was out of the building she made certain to keep his office door closed.

"Denise, did you see anyone go into Harry's office?" Maggie waited until Paul was out of earshot before inquiring with the receptionist.

Although she hadn't noticed anything out of the ordinary, Denise explained that it had been an especially busy morning with everyone, including Maggie's assistant Leeann, away from the office for one reason or another and that she had been unable to monitor the comings and goings of visitors to the department.

Even though Maggie was uneasy about the situation she did not want to sound confrontational. After all, it would be easy to make a mountain out of a molehill, something she had witnessed Harry doing when he had found Paul waiting in his office earlier that month.

"That guy's a sonofabitch. Keep him out of my way," Harry had screamed good and loud to everyone within shouting distance making it plain that he wanted Paul to stay away from him.

Except in meetings they attended together, each man went out of his way to avoid contact with the other and she was acutely aware that this last incident had made the circumstances all the more serious. Harry's vehement reaction coupled with Paul's peculiar behavior decided Maggie on an investigative quest to find out exactly what was going on. If she were to get any answers as to why the two men were so antagonistic toward each other, she knew she'd have to ask one of them and Paul seemed the logical candidate.

In the meantime, she had been waiting for an opportune moment to discuss several urgent issues with Harry who had been extremely busy since returning from an out-of-town conference. She had not wanted to burden him with matters easily handled on her own but Production's need for an immediate solution coincided with his calendar being free for the next half hour and she decided this was as good a time as any to interrupt him.

Totally immersed in his current project, Harry didn't look up when she came into his office. Rather than disturb his concentration, Maggie sat back and quietly watched him work. She found herself studying him almost as if she were an artist about to paint his portrait.

His dark, wavy hair usually well kept was tousled in frustration. One defiant strand curled stubbornly across his brow giving him, she thought, a look of boyish vulnerability. His face, although partly obscured by his large glasses, was a mass of scowls but nothing, not even the hint of a five o'clock shadow, could detract from his masculinity. He was, as she had told Leeann, uncommonly handsome.

Sitting in his rolled-up shirt sleeves, an image Maggie found particularly appealing, Harry reminded her of an old-time, struggling newspaper editor championing lost causes. Etched into his face was the gruff look of a rugged, hard-hitting reporter whose early days had been spent searching out crime stories but who now nailed down deadlines with scathing editorials. Amid an imaginary haze of swirling pipe-smoke, she watched his bare, sinewy arms and large expressive hands. She recalled how masterfully he used them during meetings to make his points as though they were an extension of his vocal prowess.

"Maggie, how long have you been sitting there?" Harry asked as he removed his glasses and looked over at her.

"I didn't want to interrupt you," Maggie said sheepishly.

"No, please go ahead. What's up?"

"Things are reaching a crisis level in Production. They need to know which way to go in the presentation tomorrow. Also, I put together a list of the major issues involved in the Toller negotiations and I'll need you to review it before they sign the contracts on Friday." Maggie stood and laid several files on Harry's desk.

"Browbeater. Now I know where I got all my wrinkles," Harry teased lightheartedly.

"Incidentally, I've double checked the data base info and it's ready to go. We'll get the marketing surveys out by noon tomorrow."

"What would I do without you, Maggie?"

"I like hearing that, boss."

"You know, Maggie, working with you these past six …"

"Seven next month, Harry. It's gone rather quickly, don't you think?" Maggie added pensively.

"Seven years. That's quite a long time together. You've been good for me, Maggie. Kept me on track and even made me look like a well-oiled spring with the guys upstairs. Remind me to take you to lunch one of these days."

"Deal."

"You still like working for me, Maggie?" He gave her a studied glance.

"If it's a mutual admiration society you're looking for, chief, I qualify. As far as I'm concerned, working with you is everything I'd ever hoped a job could be. I couldn't have designed a better position nor had a better teacher."

"Well, I like hearing that. Maggie, do you think we're still the perfect team?"

"I don't know about perfect, but we're good. Sounds like you have some doubts."

"No, it's just that I'm tired. I've decided that after we finish the Marshall proposal next week, I'll take a month off and go fishing, maybe to Mexico. Ellen and I … well… I guess it's no secret … we've been having problems lately."

"I didn't want to say anything."

"Oh, it's okay. I thought maybe I could save the ship before it goes down for the third time. Anyway, you'll be glad to know that I've put your name in to look after things while I'm away."

"What, as acting manager?" Maggie's voice went an octave higher.

"Well, no official title but I told them I wouldn't have anyone else in the job. You know it better than I do and you're good at it. You'll get the bonus money and who knows, we may even wangle a promotion out of those guys upstairs."

"Thanks, Harry." Maggie was truly pleased with Harry's confidence in her.

"Just promise me you won't get any ideas about leaving the department while I'm away. I know of two department heads that would kill to get you on their teams."

"Don't worry, boss. I'll never leave you." Although she had said it half in jest, Maggie felt herself blush at the comment.

"Promise, light of my life?" Harry's smile practically lit up the room.

"Sure, Harry, you're the only one to whom I owe my allegiance… you and WordTech."

"Listen, when I get back, let's get the Silverstein project into Environmental," Harry said, changing the subject.

"Right, I'll work up the numbers and have them ready for you."

"Well, let's see if we can't put out some of these fires," Harry said as he casually brushed back the wayward wisp from off his forehead and put back on his glasses.

Afterwards, with a notebook full of resolutions, Maggie went back to her desk and sipped at her tea which had grown cold. She sat back in her chair, shoved her glasses on top of her head and thought about her relationship with Harry.

She did love Harry. Not the sexual kind of loving, but loving in an altruistic fashion. Her respect for him had grown through the years, and her opinion of him as a human being, not just a boss, bordered on the reverential. Paul was probably right; she did spend a great deal of time doting on him.

Harry's just celebrated his fortieth birthday and even if he tries to hide it I know he feels down. Physically he's changed very little in all the years I've known him. Maybe slightly gray around the temples but that only gives him an air of distinction. Of course he had to get those big black horn-rimmed glasses to correct his astigmatism, but that couldn't be helped. On the whole he's still as handsome as ever. I do notice though there's been a subtle change in his personality.

I think it coincided with the problems he and Ellen have had with their marriage. Poor Ellen, she was so possessive of him, and then suddenly she began to distance herself from all of us, especially the folks that have known them for the past eleven years. The rumors are flying and although I hate to hear them it seems the devoted wife and amorous husband have come to a parting of the way. I wonder who wanted out of the nuptials. Maybe that's why Harry was so depressed. Poor Harry, he's feeling the full effects of a failed marriage and although I know he doesn't like to speak of his personal problems in the office, I can see that his buoyant personality has sure taken a beating and left him looking tired and rundown.

"I hate to intrude but how about a cup of tea?"

"Paul, you do sneak up on people." Maggie, jolted out of her reverie, hoped Paul wouldn't detect the friction in her voice. Lately she found herself resenting his interruptions regarding her thoughts about Harry.

"No quick lunches for us today, honey. I've got an eight o'clock reservation at Dominic's. What do you say to pasta, lobster and gobs of butter?"

"Paul, I…"

"I know Maggie, no complications. We'll just enjoy each other's company? What do you say?"

"Okay, Paul, but right now I've got work to do."

"I'll pick you up at seven."

"Okay." Maggie put her glasses back on and swung her chair toward her computer.

"Hey, don't get tied up with that boss of yours working overtime tonight. I'm hungry already," Paul shouted from outside her office door.

The remark made Maggie cringe. She knew he had deliberately said it, and it wouldn't have surprised her if he had hoped Harry was within hearing range. She was glad no one could see her face redden but she felt a myriad of intrusive eyes staring at her back. Paul had already disappeared into the elevator but somehow the act of getting up and closing her office door gave her a feeling of satisfaction and she continued her thoughts in private.

I hope I'm not transparent. I could kill Paul for being so callous. He's deliberately using our relationship to antagonize Harry. It's no business of his what I do for Harry. I'd hate to think that Paul was becoming possessive, especially since our relationship has been built on both of us being free without commitment. Now with Harry so blatantly angry at Paul, and Paul obviously up to some subterfuge, there's bound to be trouble.

❧

After dinner, she and Paul went back to WordTech anticipating the grand opening of one of the chicest clubs in the building. The Whistlestop's dance floor was a crush of people gyrating to the electrifying sounds blasted from the bandstand.

"What a wild group! Don't you just love it?" Maggie found herself yelling at the top of her lungs as she and Paul left the crowded floor after the set.

"Great, but I need a cold towel. I'll be right back, Maggie. Hey, I'll order a fresh round on the way out." Paul, drenched in perspiration, headed off to the men's room.

"Hey Maggie, how's it going?"

Maggie put down her drink and turned to see Harry standing behind her. "Harry, this is a surprise! What are you doing here?"

"Same as you I imagine, enjoying the festivities of opening night."

"It's great isn't it? The band's fantastic."

"I haven't danced yet. Would you like to?"

"No thanks, I'm waiting for Paul and I'm trying to cool down before the next set."

"Paul Keating?" Harry asked, obviously irritated.

"Why yes. He just stepped away for a minute."

"That's one guy I wouldn't want to run into. If you'll excuse me, Maggie, I'll be seeing you." Maggie watched as Harry sauntered toward the bar and sat down next to a striking brunette in a bright pink dress.

"Was that Harry Cooke?"

"Yes, he just dropped by to say hi."

"That guy's the biggest skirt chaser in town. Don't get involved with him outside the office, Maggie. It's bad enough you see him on a professional level but believe me everyone's on to him."

"Oh, Paul, you're such an exaggerator."

"No I'm not. Why do you think his wife is divorcing him? She's had it with that playboy."

"What do you mean?"

"Harry's sex crazy."

"That's ridiculous," Maggie shrieked as she fought back a sharp-edged need to lambast Paul.

"You don't want to believe it about your precious Harry. But don't forget, I've known him longer than you and that smooth operator style of his doesn't change the rotten things he's done. Sure, some women will say he's a great guy but that doesn't change the leopard's spots."

"He's my boss, Paul, and I feel an obligation to him. I also don't like talking about him behind his back. Could we change the subject?"

"I don't like him hanging around you. You always say that he doesn't act anyway out of the ordinary in the office but I saw him leering at you a few minutes ago, and I suppose you're flattered by his attentions?"

"I thought you said you weren't going to act like a jealous lover? For heavens sake, he only asked me to dance."

"Maggie, could you stop believing he's the most wonderful man in the world and face facts."

"I don't know what you're talking about."

"Don't you? Everyone in your office thinks you're sleeping with him."

"Stop it, Paul, right now or I'll walk out of here."

"All right, all right, I should know better but I'm crazy about you, Maggie. What am I to think when you tell me you're not interested in making our relationship permanent but you go out of your way to protect him?"

"Frankly, Paul, I don't care what you think. I'm sick to death of the rumor mills and everyone's interest in someone else's sex life. I thought you and I had a good relationship. We've never talked about changing our lifestyle and I thought we were both content."

"It's my fault. I've moved forward and you haven't. When we're together you've made me think you felt the same way. I couldn't help falling in love with you."

"Paul, don't you see what you've done?"

"Yes, I've run the risk of ending our relationship."

"I've been honest with you, Paul, and I trusted you had with me."

"No regrets, Maggie. It could just as easily have gone the other way. We both knew what we were getting into from the beginning."

"I'm not ready for commitment, Paul, and I won't be forced into something that I'm not ready for. I can't make it any clearer than that, and I'm tired of having this discussion every time we go out."

"That's clear enough, Maggie. I won't jeopardize the relationship any further but until you tell me differently, I'd like us to go on seeing one another."

"I think we need to give ourselves some time, a couple of weeks, maybe? What do you think, Paul?"

"You wouldn't want to hear what I think, Maggie, but if it's what you want."

"Would you mind, Paul, if we called it a night? I've suddenly gotten very tired."

Maggie stood up and allowed Paul to help her with her coat. They walked in silence down to the parking lot.

Chapter 4

"Hey, sleepyhead, wake up." The call woke her at eight in the morning.

"Paul?"

"No, it's Harry."

"Harry? What's wrong?" Still suffering the effects of the late night on the town with Paul, Maggie sat up rubbing the sleep from her eyes.

"Maggie, I've got something to ask you?"

"What is it? Anything go wrong at the office? I did send the contracts out by special messenger." Maggie's mind raced over yesterday's task list.

"No, no, nothing like that."

"Harry, now that I'm in meltdown mode at five minutes after eight," Maggie said sarcastically reaching for her alarm, "what is it you want? You've never called me on a Saturday morning before."

"Take it easy, will you. I need a favor. That's the reason I'm calling."

"Harry, please tell me what you're talking about."

"I need a date."

"You need a what?"

"Yes, you heard right, a date. I'm expected to attend Corporate's award program this evening, and I know it's the last minute but could you help me out?"

"Well, that's a relief. For a moment I thought it was something really serious."

"This is serious, Maggie. I need your help," Harry sounded contrite.

"I suppose it's a formal occasion?"

"Yes, it's a black tie dinner dance at Maxims in the WordTech building. You know most of the folks. I'll be honest with you, Maggie, I don't want to go alone and since you're taking on my job, so to speak, it would give you an opportunity to schmooze with Corporate."

"Well, sure. I guess I'm okay with that. Where shall I meet you?"

"No Maggie, you're helping me out on this one. I'll pick you up. Just give me the directions and I'll see you at seven-thirty, and Maggie…"

"Yes, Harry?"

"Thanks a lot!"

❧

"I can't believe you said yes." Maggie's mom was furious when she told her about Harry's request.

"Don't worry, Mom. I don't mind. It'll give me a chance to get to know the corporate big wigs on a more informal basis."

"Is there anything that man could do that you'd object to? He takes such advantage of you, it's shameful."

"Oh, Mother, please. It's really no big deal."

"He's certainly got you in his hip pocket. I suppose I should be happy that he makes you feel that way. Why just the way you light up hearing his voice says it all."

"Mom, you sound like Paul. It's only a business function and one that I hope will do me a lot of good."

❧

"I hope I'm not too early?"

"Not if you're Harry Cooke, Maggie's boss." Mrs. Reynolds, her face cross with resentment, pointed Harry in the direction of the living room.

"To the lady of the house, a breath of springtime," Harry said, holding out an enormous bouquet of white daisies. "Now I know where Maggie got her looks."

"You've got a bit of the blarney in you, Mr. Cooke, but it's a nice thing you've done." Mrs. Reynolds, her expression suddenly radiant, timorously reached for the flowers.

"Harry. Please call me Harry."

"Thank you so much, Harry. Please sit down and make yourself comfortable. Maggie will be down in a minute."

With a sense of humor exaggerated by an Irish brogue, Harry's genuine attentiveness made an instant convert of Maggie's mom. From her vantage point on the upstairs' landing, Maggie could see her mother was visibly moved by Harry's gift. She watched as the two sat and chatted like old friends. Her mother, relaxed and less reserved, laughed delightedly as her eyes occasionally drifted toward the mantle and the large vase of blooms.

When the downstairs went suddenly quiet, Maggie was forced to leave her dressing table and take a second look. This time it was Shadow and Daisy who were having their way with Harry. She almost laughed out loud seeing the dogs bounding across the room, devotion in every leap as they jumped into his lap and covered his tuxedo with hair. Harry, totally at home with their frolicsome behavior, sat on the couch giving each doggie a good rub.

Maggie had to will herself back to her room to finish dressing. She would have much preferred joining the party below but Harry's last minute invitation still required a show of elegance. She had gone shopping earlier in the day searching for exactly the right dress for the occasion, but now, looking at herself in the form fitting, strapless white evening gown, she suddenly had pangs of doubt. The taut brocade bodice seemed too revealing, and her decision to wear her hair long and unrestrained now vied with an earlier decision to wear it up.

"Probably much too formal. Oh, what the heck," she said in mock vexation as she sprayed herself with perfume and installed the simple pair of diamond studs into her ears. "I'm out of here." She gave herself one last glance in the mirror before pronouncing the results finished.

Harry rose from the couch as Maggie descended the staircase. "My God, Maggie, no one has any right to look like that."

"Harry, after the last few hours I needed to hear you say that."

"You don't need anything but I did bring you this." Harry's eyes remained on Maggie as he handed her a gilt-edged box.

"Why, Harry, how did you know I loved yellow roses?"

"I don't know…I, I…," Harry stammered as he watched Maggie affix one of the rosebuds to his lapel.

"Your boutonnière, sir," Maggie said, cocking her head sideways and eyeing Harry from a distance. "Now you're perfect."

"Thanks, Maggie."

"For what, Harry?"

"For looking the way you do tonight."

"That was nice, boss," Maggie said, touched by Harry's sincerity.

She handed him her satin rap and lifted her hair as he put it across her shoulders, feeling his fingers slowly yet gently brush against her back. The impression lasted only a second but she turned abruptly and met his penetrating gaze.

They stood in silence until he asked, "Ready, Maggie?"

"Ready," she answered softly, pinning the corsage to her small beaded bag. "Good night, Mom."

"Good night, Mom," Harry echoed.

"Good night, children," Mrs. Reynolds laughed, "have a good time."

Maggie watched her mother standing in the doorway as Harry started the car. "You made a hit with my mom, Harry. I haven't heard her laugh so much in years."

"I like her. She's a lot like you," Harry remarked thoughtfully as he threw the silver Jaguar into gear and pulled away from the curb.

It was a quiet drive on a relatively uncongested freeway and Maggie noticed that both she and Harry seemed reluctant to break the comfortable silence. Harry was a fast but competent driver, and within the hour they were pulling into the valet parking section at WordTech's downtown garage.

"What a crowd," Harry shouted as he led the way, elbowing through the throng.

The Club Maxim was an extremely popular nightclub, and although many of WordTech's parties were held there, Maggie noted the staff's deference to Harry as they greeted him by name.

"Looks like you're pretty well known here, Harry," Maggie observed wryly.

"It goes with the territory, luv, as you will soon find out."

While smartly dressed waiters roamed the room with large trays of canapés and tall, fluted glasses of champagne, Maggie followed Harry's lead as he smoothly mixed and mingled with senior management. He lost no time in making sure her name was a buzz word among the division directors and then maneuvered her in front of the CEO. Alan Cummings, who had been talking to Ed Granger and Rod Tierney, two of WordTech's high-powered attorneys, seemed happy with the interruption and Harry used the opportunity to verbally position Maggie alongside the corporate forefront.

"Here's one man's number you've got to have programmed into your cell phone, Maggie," Harry said by way of introduction to the corporate head.

"Delighted, Ms. Reynolds." Mr. Cummings' eyes twinkled approvingly in Maggie's direction. "You and I must have a one-on-one quite soon. As Harry can attest, it's a prerequisite for all my managers."

"I look forward to it, Mr. Cummings." Maggie took the pudgy, outstretched hand and squeezed it lightly in a return gesture.

"Call Irene on Monday morning and have her put you on my calendar."

"I will, and thank you, Mr. Cummings." Maggie noticed Mr. Cummings seemed hard pressed to relinquish her hand and it wasn't until she actively pumped his several more times before he surrendered.

"Gentleman and Ms. Reynolds, I believe we're being signaled to be seated." Mr. Cummings looked directly at Harry and winked before he proceeded to walk to his table.

"Thanks for the schmooze opportunity, Harry, but what was that all about?" Maggie felt Harry's hand on her elbow as he deftly directed her across the room.

"The CEO just told me in no uncertain terms that you've made quite an impression with him. That's called securing support in this business, Maggie, my dear."

There were many sizable tables with large parties already seated but Harry and Maggie were shown to a smaller table where they joined Ted Halsey, Director of Purchasing and his wife Barbara. After a brief round of niceties the food was served and as each course made its appearance, a different vintage of wine was generously poured, keeping the partygoers in a resplendent mood. Harry and Ted talked business while Maggie listened attentively to Barbara's exchange of ideas on a variety of household issues, not the least of which were the couple's two young children.

"I hope you don't mind our making an early night of it," Barbara Halsey informed them soon after the awards program concluded. "I'm rather worried about my son, Josh. He has a slight fever and we're anxious to get home."

"Well, we couldn't have planned that any better." Harry filled their wine glasses as soon as the Halseys had departed. "Now, what shall we talk about, Maggie?"

"It's funny, we've worked together all these years and now we can't even make small talk," Maggie said jokingly. "I hope you don't mind my asking but was Ellen supposed to come with you tonight?"

"You're definitely entitled to an answer, and yes she was, but since she and I are no longer seeing eye-to-eye, she declined the invitation."

"I'm sorry, Harry."

"Don't be. I'm still hoping we can salvage something but so far she's not buying."

"I hope it works out for the two of you. Ellen's a wonderful woman."

"No use fooling you, Maggie. You probably already know I've a reputation as a lady's man, among other things. I'd better watch it or with a few more drinks I'll be telling you the story of my life."

"I wouldn't mind listening."

"Thanks, Maggie, but I don't want to disenchant you. You're the one person in my life who I hope thinks I'm a good person. I don't know if I ever told you but your respect is something I value highly. It's funny, when we're young we don't seem to care as much but as we get older we worry about what people think about us, especially the people who matter most," Harry said, his eyes fixed on Maggie's.

"Harry, I'm flattered. It's nice to know we feel the same about one another."

"Like you said, we have a mutual admiration society."

"You seem so down lately. Is it because of Ellen or is something else bothering you?"

"Maggie, let's not talk about me. It would spoil the evening. I'd rather talk about you. Anyway, I think you know more about me than I do about you. Don't you think I'm owed some equal time?"

"Sure, as long as I retain the prerogative of asking you questions later on."

"Deal. Let's start with what I do know. You're smart, professional and quite beautiful. Now, what else would I like to know about my favorite assistant?"

"Your only assistant, Harry, and tonight you're positively gushing with compliments. Aren't you overdoing it a bit?" For no reason she could think of Maggie was suddenly restive by what she perceived as Harry's lack of sincerity. "What are you trying to do, kill me with kindness or just set me up to play "Truth or Dare"?"

"Neither one, Maggie, and besides I don't believe you have anything to hide."

"Meaning you do, Harry?"

"Oh, no you don't, Maggie. It's not your turn, yet." Harry shook his head with laughter.

"Okay boss, shoot."

"This is a three-part question."

"Hey, what are the rules of this game?" Maggie asked insolently.

"Sh, don't interrupt your elders. Who was your first love, where did you meet him and how did the relationship end, if it has?"

Maggie slowly sipped at her drink as she gave serious thought to the questions. "Tony Rossi, a college art course, and yes, mutually," she answered succinctly.

"Well, that didn't get us anywhere."

Maggie looked across the table at Harry who looked crestfallen. Not wanting to spoil his happy mood, she added, "Okay, the details, but I warn you this material is boring and would be of interest to no one."

"Let me be the judge of that. So, what was it that attracted you to this Tony fellow?"

"At heart I'm a pretty old fashion girl and I liked him the moment we met. He talked and acted a lot like my dad. He and I had more of an alliance than a love affair."

"Meaning what exactly?"

"It's kind of hard to explain but we inhabited time together and appreciated everything in the moment, kind of like opening a window on a spring morning. Life poured in on me. I had never felt so alive. It was a wonderful period of my life. The emotional and physical part of our lives became an extension of our commitment to one another. Besides being the love of my life, Tony was a good teacher and a great friend."

"Sounds like you care a great deal about him. Is he still part of your life?"

"Not like it was. He's working in an altogether different vineyard these days."

"What happened?"

"Let's just say Tony found someone else who mattered more than I did."

"I find that hard to believe."

"No, he had good reason and I understood completely."

"Don't tell me you don't even have a jealous bone in your body?"

"Not in this case." Maggie smiled knowingly.

"How did you meet him?"

"I enrolled in Tony's college art class right after high school graduation. He was working on his thesis and was planning to live in Italy for the summer. He invited me to go along with him. It was quite a holiday and to a naïve eighteen year old it was bliss. We immersed ourselves in art, culture and the Italian life style. I was never happier."

"And now…?"

"Harry, this may seem hard for you to believe but I lead a pretty well ordered life. If you're asking the obvious I don't believe in using sex as a carte blanche invitation to promiscuity. It doesn't fit into my plans. I'm self-directed and I put a lot of thought into the kind of guy I want in my life."

"Is that guy Paul Keating?"

"Harry, I don't know you well enough to answer that question."

"Well, so far I know you're not a player and you're one of those rare people who have a moral code which you pretty much stick to. You're also an independent thinker who believes in achieving success on your own terms. You're ambitious but not for ambition's sake. What I'd like to know is what makes you tick, Maggie?"

"We have a lot of sides to our personalities, Harry. We exist in varying relationships and what we are is the sum total of our emotions and our own self-estimation."

"What about how others perceive us?"

"That's where a strong sense of self and a simple act of faith come in."

"I guess I asked for that." Harry looked deflated.

"Don't take it too hard; after all, you asked the question."

"You're right, go ahead and explain."

"It's really pretty simple. I have faith in myself and in my God-given creative powers."

"With what objective?"

"Leading a good life."

"Are we talking religion?"

"Not that I feel the need to qualify, but I think it's more of a personal code of ethics. It's relying on my own power and moral responsibility and realizing nothing happens by accident or chance."

"How do you explain meeting me?"

"Harry, I wrote your description long before I ever met you. You were the caring teacher and mentor I was looking for. You were no chance meeting."

"You mean you lost Tony and got me?"

"Hardly boss, you're in a category all by yourself."

"So what's your secret?"

"No secret, just purpose. I work toward achieving what I need to give meaning to my life. And that equates to a strong sense of self."

"I think we're getting much too philosophical, which I don't mind as long as it doesn't lead to an examination of one another's moral character."

"For my part I'm a firm believer in leaving each person to focus on their own moral responsibilities."

"Good, I may remind you of that conviction someday."

"You won't have to. Involvement in other people's emotions can be totally destructive."

"How's that?" Harry finished his glass of wine and poured another.

"Taking on the emotional baggage of another person can damage one's sense of reason."

"That sounds awful," Harry mocked.

"I shouldn't scoff if I were you."

"Could you allow yourself to become emotionally involved with someone who went against your code of ethics?"

"Unlikely."

"Under no circumstances?"

"I guess it would be like giving money to a beggar."

"Are you kidding me?" Harry asked incredulously.

"Stop interrupting and listen. In the first place, you'd have to understand why you're doing it. Is it for pity or are you hoping that the person might rise above the situation. Once you determine that, your motives become clear."

"So you'd have to analyze your motives before your emotions could come into play?"

"Yes, do you find that difficult to believe?"

"I don't believe anyone has that much self-control, pardon my skepticism."

"Is that because you distrust people?"

"Partly, but mostly it's because I believe the old moral codes just didn't survive modern life. Besides a lot of people would think you were taking a great deal of fun out of life with such a well ordered existence."

"People still need a social code to navigate the unchartered waters in today's world," Maggie said heatedly, "possibly more so now than ever before."

"The problem with that is most members of society are hostile toward any type of control. The world today celebrates individualism and encourages the liberation of personal feelings. The idea of restraining their passions and putting personal interests aside would be unacceptable in today's culture."

"That doesn't negate the need for character."

"Come off it, Maggie. Our forefathers continually complained of our country's lack of character and the dissolution of our principles yet we've managed to survive bloody well."

"That's exactly my point, Harry. The rules haven't been discarded. People still admire dignity."

"I'm surprised you still believe that. The media publicly promotes corruption from every corner on earth. Manners are a thing of the past. Our conduct has virtually disintegrated into depravity and there isn't a culture on earth that hasn't been affected. What more proof do you need that the ethical system is dead?"

"Wow, talk about cynical. But don't worry, Harry, dignity won't die. It may hibernate for a while but people, whatever their differences, still recognize and celebrate the traits associated with nobility and pride. Indulging in every whim and fancy doesn't bring happiness. You can't build on superficiality and hope to feel good inside."

"Careful, old girl, you're close to proselytizing."

"I'll go you one better. I believe that each of us has the obligation to contribute something, no matter how small, to the welfare and progress of mankind."

"A noble cause, Maggie, but don't you think you're being unrealistic?"

"I didn't say the contribution had to be world shaking. It can be as little as going to the aid of a friend or helping out a homeless person."

"How do you reconcile not having the things you want? Suppose the person you love doesn't love you? That would probably make life suck, big time."

"Sure it would but life doesn't come with a guarantee, Harry. We can only do our best and make the effort. It's the struggle that defines us and gives us hope."

"So what is it you want? To throw down the gauntlet and face combat just to hold your head up high? Don't you know chivalry's dead?"

"We have to be true to ourselves. It's the only thing we really possess."

"I don't hold mankind in such high esteem as you apparently do. I'm a fatalist. I think things happen, irrespective of moral codes, conscience or personal direction. Most of the human race just drags itself along one day at a time and doesn't give a damn about the other guy. We're born alone and we die alone."

"I wouldn't have thought you were that pessimistic. I've always seen you as someone who takes life by the horns and directs yourself every step of the way. And I see you as a very caring individual."

"In the eye of the beholder?" Harry shot Maggie a curious look.

"Some of us have more sides than others." Maggie held his gaze.

"I've lived my life by taking things as they come. The difference between you and me is that you think about the future while I'm only interested in what's happening now."

"You just didn't walk into WordTech. You finished school and had ideas on how you were going to make a living. Maybe it wasn't long range planning but to some extent you had to be thinking about what you wanted out of life."

"Not as much as you apparently."

"I think about my goals like an architect thinks about building plans. It takes time to accomplish what we want in life. Anything goes is not an option for me."

"Isn't there an element of spirituality connected with it?"

"Yes, but don't be put off by that. It's all about faith and the priceless ability to believe in oneself and in others."

"Some people make complete messes of their lives. It's like quicksand, there's no getting out."

"Then the consequences should come as no surprise."

"Like they say, shit happens."

"No, choices happen."

"You don't believe that things happen in spite of us?"

"That kind of trouble happens only when people are too close to their own problems to see any value in them. It's like any business. You've got to take stock of the inventory and make do with whatever inner strengths you can develop."

"Oh, I get it. Never give up on yourself, etcetera, etcetera. Did you study psychology or something? It sounds to me as though your high-mindedness has got you fighting windmills."

"Introspection is always hard. It's the truth about ourselves we fear the most."

Harry's mood suddenly changed. He stared out across the room with a look of remorse in his eyes. "Somehow talking with you like this makes me feel as though I've let you down. You can't possibly know how undeserving I am of your loyalty."

"Harry, like I said, everyone makes choices. Yours have nothing to do with me but everything to do with you."

"I'm one of those don't-give-a-damn guys who pretty much run roughshod over people. I've always hated looking at the future and I despise the past."

"I'm learning a great deal about you tonight. You never struck me as that kind of person."

"I'm spontaneous. I don't think about it, I just do it. I don't care what the repercussions are."

"That's a destructive style."

"For whom?" Harry seemed particularly interested.

"For you or anyone else who gets in your way."

"Are you afraid of getting in my way, Maggie?"

"Should I be?" Maggie felt challenged.

"Like I said, I'm not much of a caring man. Values, ideals, trusting in someone, they're all difficult for me. I guess somewhere along the line they were pretty much burned out of me. With you it's different."

"Harry, nothing ever comes easy. I keep working at it like everyone else."

"Funny, but I've always trusted you." Harry took her hand and searched her palm. "One of these days we'll have to compare lifelines. Anyway, Maggie, it's your turn. What do you want to know?"

"Harry, give me a rain-check. I'd rather dance with you now."

"Sure." Harry stood up and extended his hand, "Mademoiselle, s'il vous plait."

"Merci, Monsieur." Maggie took his hand and followed him out onto the dance floor.

"You're quite a lady, Maggie Reynolds," Harry affirmed softly as he took her in his arms and pressed his hand to the small of her back.

"You've got great technique, Harry, but then I'm sure you've heard that before."

"Maggie, I'm good at whatever I do," he admitted with a

husky laugh.

"Harry, of that I have no doubt."

That evening Maggie sat in bed with a glass of warm milk and her journal and jotted down the memories that were fresh in her mind.

I never realized how little I know about the man I've worked for all these years. I feel differently about him, almost as if he were a complete stranger who I met for the first time tonight. He's such a lonely, disillusioned man. He's hidden his fears and insecurities all these years. It's going to be hard seeing him as a boss but thinking about him on a personal level.

Chapter 5

A dozen yellow roses greeted Maggie when she walked into her office on Monday. She quickly pulled out the small envelope that was tucked between the vase and the long-stemmed beauties but was surprised that it had already been torn open. She removed the card and read,

Maggie,

Thank you for an inspirational evening.

~H.

When Harry came in she thanked him for the flowers; particularly for remembering they were her favorites.

"They're a sincere thank you, Maggie, for making a dull business function more enjoyable for me than it's been in years. And let me tell you, it didn't hurt you to make those connections, either." Harry gave her a knowing wink.

"You're right about that, Harry. Irene's already called and calendared my meeting with Mr. Cummings."

It was a hectic day and Maggie did her best to make sure the regular work schedules were implemented as quickly as possible. She didn't want the upcoming changes to interfere with Harry getting his office in order before departing on his long awaited vacation. Her own impatience to begin work on her newly augmented responsibilities made her jittery but she managed to handle the stress with her usual aplomb. The day went by in a flurry of last minute activities and although physically drained she looked forward to meeting Paul and relaxing over dinner.

They dined at their favorite haunt, Cher Sheri's. Located in the old Bohemian district, the tiny restaurant catered to young romantics and served superb French cuisine for which Paul and Maggie were passionate. Recognized as regular patrons, the owner enticed them to try one of Chef Louie's divine desserts but the decadent concoction, shared in the midst of candle glow and soft music, could not lift the pall that had settled over their evening.

"A penny for them," Paul broke the silence.

"They're not worth it, Paul. I guess I'm just tired."

"You forget how well I know you. Something's bothering you."

Maggie looked away. "I don't lie very well, do I?"

"Somehow I feel there's a third party at this table."

"What are you talking about?"

"All this has something to do with Harry, doesn't it?"

"Paul, is this conversation leading to another one of our ill-timed quarrels?"

"Okay, let's get it out in the open. Why were you out with him on Saturday night?"

"There's no need to raise your voice, Paul. I only went with Harry to an awards dinner."

"And I suppose he sent you flowers just for doing him the honor of attending the function. Of all the gall that guy's got. Inspirational evening my ..."

"Paul, I might have known it was you who opened the card."

"Yes, and I'm not making any apologies for it either. Don't you think you should have told me about it before accepting the invitation?"

"How dare you go into my office and read my mail?" Maggie was livid.

"Now who's shouting? Besides, it wasn't mail and don't evade the question, Maggie."

"How pathetic is that? We're not married, not even engaged. We're friends, plain and simple; at least I thought we were but you've shown me nothing but disrespect. We agreed at the beginning to live independent lives without strings or attachments and you've broken that bond."

"Then maybe it's time we made a more serious commitment, Maggie."

"No, Paul. You don't get it."

"Maggie, don't you think you're overreacting a bit?"

"This constant sparring has become painful, Paul. Right now, I'd like nothing better than to walk out of here."

"You're making way too much of this. What's the real reason?"

"You seem to know everything. Tell me what you think the reason is."

"We've been in this relationship for a long time and now suddenly Harry enters the picture and things fall apart. What am I to think?"

"Think what you want to Paul, you will anyway. You're so worried about my relationship with Harry, what about your relationship with him?"

"Now what are you talking about?"

"What goes on between you and Harry? Every time he sees you he goes ballistic. You're like two bulls ready to tear each other to pieces. Both of you are pretty level-headed guys but not when you're in each other's sights."

"If you must know, we hate each other's guts. And now it appears he's given me even more reason."

"What's it all about, Paul?"

"It was long before I met you. Harry and I used to be good friends."

"I would never have guessed."

"It all started when I got assigned to do Marketing's expense accounts. I happened to discover a few discrepancies on some of Harry's business trips."

"What kind of discrepancies?"

"Nothing serious but I wanted some backup data and I began asking the marketing consultants about the conferences they attended."

"What happened?"

"They told me there were times when consultants were slated to go but Harry would cancel somebody at the last minute and take their place. He usually went with his wife. When I pieced the stories together I found out Harry never attended any of the sessions at the conference but relied on feedback from the consultants who did."

"What's new? It happens all the time. That's why busy department heads have other consultants in attendance. It's not a big deal."

"I agree, but I went after more backup information. I wanted to know why Harry always waited till the last minute to cancel the consultant's trip and replace the name with his."

"Was there an explanation? Lots of execs find they don't have to do a meeting or something and then make arrangements to do the conference instead."

"Like you said, it wasn't that big a deal but when I rechecked previous budgets I learned Harry had been playing the game for years. He consistently changed the names at the last minute and even padded his expense accounts with people that he felt it was necessary to wine and dine, people from companies whose association with WordTech I considered negligible."

"I'm not minimizing it, Paul, but it certainly not what WordTech would consider a crime. And personally speaking, I'm surprised at your presumption in deciding who should or should not be on Harry's expense account."

"I admit I was nervy but he blew it all out of proportion. When I mentioned the discrepancies to him and asked for additional backup information everything hit the proverbial fan. He went nuts. He told me that as Director of Marketing he could run his department as he saw fit and didn't need a clerk telling him what he could or couldn't do, particularly as Accounting had already authorized his trips."

"Why didn't you just ask Harry instead of sneaking behind his back?"

"I don't know, maybe I thought he was hiding something. Anyway, he told me that I wouldn't be doing the Marketing accounts anymore and that anyone who wasted so much time on unnecessary research would probably not be at WordTech much longer. He wrote me up leaving my supervisor to note my actions on my next PA and told me to stay the hell away from him."

"You certainly couldn't blame him. Did you submit the paperwork to your supervisor?"

"I did more than that. I actually took the report directly to Corporate. I personally handed it to the CEO's secretary. I believed what he was doing was wrong, but in hindsight, it wasn't something I'd do if it happened today. Like you said, other directors were doing it but the dressing down he gave me put me into a tailspin and my pride was hurt. I was particularly hurt because we had been such good friends."

"Did Corporate get back to you?"

"No, but something must have gone down because Harry didn't plan any more last minute trips and the conferences he attends are all by the book. Other departments have followed suit and it's a

WordTech policy now."

"Congratulations."

"Thanks, but Corporate probably just slapped his wrists."

"What happened to you?"

"I was relieved of my Marketing tasks but not before Harry wrote me up. Then I was put on pro for not going through channels. My supervisor told me to stay below the radar for awhile."

"Why are you smiling?" Maggie looked puzzled.

"Ever since the incident, Harry knows I don't bluff. He steers clear of me. He doesn't trust me and I sure as hell don't trust him. He knows I have ways of finding things out and that kills him. That dictatorial attitude of his has made enemies of a lot of people."

"And that gives you some kind of satisfaction?" Maggie shook her head glumly.

"Yes it does, and don't bother looking so smug. Harry is a dishonest person in a position of authority and I intend to continually remind Corporate of that fact until they do something about him."

"Could he get you fired?"

"No, I know too much about Harry Cooke."

"What's there to know about Harry Cooke? Granted he's a maverick but he heads up a well-managed department and produces a ton of revenue with a staff that adores him."

"Do they, Maggie? No one knows when Harry might call them on the carpet for a poor job performance or some trumped up act of disobedience. You just haven't run into that Harry, yet."

"Paul, in my opinion you've got a pretty weak case. People with axes to grind within the business industry are legion and that's one of the reasons HR departments exist. Everybody believes he or she is in the right but that's why there has to be a department head to make decisions."

"Well said, Maggie, for a corporate clone."

"Paul, please don't go into Harry's office when he isn't in there."

"Are you accusing me?"

"No, I'm telling you," Maggie glowered.

"If I were to tell you what I know about Harry…"

"Paul, please, you know I despise gossip."

"Sure, Maggie, but remember Harry isn't all he pretends to be. Anyone could wind up being one of his victims."

"Meaning me I suppose?"

"If you want to tell him I was in his office, go ahead. I'm one person who's not afraid of old Harry."

"Paul, let's forget the whole incident. Harry's on vacation for a month and I'll be occupying his office. I'm sure you'll respect my position and override any hidden agendas that may come up. I'd prefer not to keep the door locked but if necessary…"

"Okay, okay, I'll call a truce while Harry's away."

"No, Paul, you've got to promise to stay out of our offices permanently. What you're doing isn't right."

"But it's all right if Harry just steps in and steals my girl."

"Paul, Harry has done no such thing. He's my boss and nothing more."

"Is that the truth, Maggie?"

"Yes, of course it is. This is getting old, Paul."

"Okay, I'm sorry. It's just that I care a great deal for you and for him to …"

"Stop it, Paul," Maggie said crossly.

"All right, you win. You've got my word on it." Paul kissed her hand. "Forgive me?"

"Sure, but how about a rain-check on our dance plans tonight?"

"No, let's go, Maggie. You'll feel better once we're there," Paul protested.

But she didn't feel better. Her head ached so badly she had to pull away from Paul and leave the dance floor to get some air.

"I'm all right, Paul. I felt sick and it was so hot in there," Maggie explained when Paul caught up with her. She was sorry she had let him talk her into making a late night of it.

"Why don't we stay out here and enjoy the evening, Maggie. I'll get us some drinks. Hey, is that what they call a lovers' moon?" Paul seemed determined to avoid any serious exchange.

"Paul, I'm not good company tonight. Please …"Maggie begged, her long pause signaling an unspoken understanding.

"Okay, home it is. But I know you're angry with me, and I just wish you'd let your hair down and say what you really mean. Rant and rave, give me hell because that's something I could deal with."

"For me, that would be a waste of time and energy. Besides, you've got enough anger for both of us."

"True friends agree to disagree. We used to be able to talk through things like this but that's gone I guess."

"Gone like a lot of things," Maggie agreed sadly.

"This isn't working, is it, Maggie? Maybe you're right. Why don't we take a vacation from each other while Harry's on his?"

"That's not a bad idea, Paul. It might help both of us see things more clearly."

Chapter 6

Harry's one month hiatus turned into two. The extra time allowed Maggie to complete two new proposals that were readily approved by the planning committee and finish an exhaustive list of tasks she had put on hold. However, when Harry called in to let her know he would be back in the office on Monday, she was glad. She was looking forward to seeing him and hadn't realized how much she had missed him.

The morning started innocuously enough. Later, when she recalled the events of that day, except for the change in Harry, there had been nothing remarkably special about it. Harry, although somewhat preoccupied, appeared healthy and relaxed but when Maggie went into his office to welcome him back she could sense his evasiveness. At one point he seemed to deliberately go out of his way to avoid her. Even the small talk about his trip lacked warmth and it obviously made their reunion all the more strained.

"Is everything all right, Harry?"

"Sure, what do you mean?"

"You seem so distant. I thought perhaps I had done something you disapproved of."

"No, nothing like that, Maggie; let's talk later. I've got to get the feel of the place again." He literally waved her from the room.

"Okay, Harry, I've left an outline of the major issues we need to discuss before tomorrow's board meeting and… ."

"Maggie, I said later." Harry was abrupt and dismissive.

"Let me know when you want to review the material, Harry." Maggie, although disheartened by Harry's brusque behavior, knew better than to let an irritable executive get her down.

He'll come around to his old self once he's had time.

Maggie was getting ready to leave for lunch when the intercom buzzed. "Yes, Harry."

"Maggie, come in for a few moments." Harry clicked off before she could respond.

She put her purse back in her desk drawer and grabbed a pencil and pad, making the few steps from her office to his in a single stride. She sat down and was instantly swallowed by the cavernous armchair.

"Let's play devil's advocate, Maggie." Harry sat leering at her from across the desk. His voice had taken on a surreal quality.

"What do you mean, Harry?"

"What do you, mean, Harry?" he mimicked. "What do you think I mean, Maggie? We need to stop fucking around and get down to business."

Maggie tried to conceal her look of astonishment. "What's the matter with you, Harry?"

"You and I need to come to an understanding," he said between his teeth.

"I knew you were displeased. Which one of the projects did I mess up on?"

"Maggie, I've made sure the entire staff's out to lunch so we won't be disturbed." Harry's face was wet with perspiration and he seemed breathless as though he had run up a flight of stairs.

"Harry, let me get you some water." Maggie jumped out of the chair, knowing something was terribly wrong.

"Stop glaring at me," he bellowed "and sit the hell down."

"What is it you want to discuss, Harry?" Maggie looked down at her notebook, trying desperately to sound calm and reassuring.

"Everything can be measured," Harry began, "and given the time and the resources it is possible to quantify economic values by any type of marketing company." Harry rambled on as though he were giving a seminar. "Do you agree? I said, do you agree?" It was Harry who was now staring at her.

"Harry, if you're talking about the Silverstein report, I've already done the initial research and compiled the numbers specific to the demographics we discussed earlier. We were right on. The relevant strategy supports our original theory and I think Corporate will be surprised by the figures and…"

"Shut up, Maggie. Stop prattling. Fuck the reports and figures and the company," he said savagely.

"What's wrong, Harry? Are you sick? Maggie could no longer contain the alarm in her voice. Harry had never spoken to her like this before.

"Sure, everything is just fine, just dandy," he growled, brandishing his hand in the air and knocking off some of the yellow notepads that sat stacked on his desk.

"Harry, what's happened?" Maggie wanted to rush to him, loosen his tie and call the clinic. She was sure he was having an attack of some sort.

"Maggie, you've been working for me for seven years. I trust you. Do you trust me?"

"Yes, Harry." Maggie felt close to tears. She wanted to run but was too frightened to move not for herself but for Harry.

"Good, because there is something I need you to do for me." Harry began to flip through the notepads on his desk in a desultory, half-hearted fashion.

"Do what, Harry?" Maggie asked tremulously.

"Just listen to what I have to say," he snapped.

Maggie looked into Harry's eyes and they were vacant blue pools. With his chest heaving and his shoulders caved in, his body language seemed to be telegraphing a short-circuiting crisis. Harry disappeared into a haze. Just as Maggie reached for the phone, the mood lifted.

Harry was suddenly apologetic and commenced to regale her with compliments. "Maggie, you did a great job while I was gone. I've got to hand it to you, the projects look great! Corporate is very pleased."

"Thanks, Harry, I enjoyed the work," Maggie said, growing suspicious of Harry's motives.

"I take it you love your job, Maggie? Now I'm going to need your help on another project."

"Harry, you're stressing me out. Can you get to the point?"

"I've got way too much of a workload, Maggie, you know that. Taking this vacation has made me realize how much time I spend here at WordTech. I'm on overload." Harry looked down at the mound of material strewn across his desk and shoved the paperwork aside.

"Do you want me to take over a few more projects until you feel better?" Maggie was intent on diffusing the situation.

"I hope you mean that because I do have a project in mind." Harry's eyes were riveted to the stacks of notebooks on his desk. "This is it. I want you to approach this assignment just like any other. I particularly value your ability to be objective and unbiased, no matter that my life's blood is poured into this crap."

"What are you talking about, Harry?" Maggie decided that Harry was suffering the effects of some sort of breakdown. She couldn't fathom what direction his talk was taking but it was clear he needed her to do something. Harry, however, was taking his own sweet time about telling her what it was he wanted her to do.

"This is altogether a very hush, hush assignment. I don't want you talking about it to anyone. Is that understood?"

Maggie nodded, her eyes averting Harry's glassy stare. Instead, she focused her attention on his office.

She had always found Harry's office a quiet haven. What appeared to most people to be random disarray was in fact a methodical, complex system of organization. It was, she had often thought, a lot like Harry. His office had always given her the feeling of imminent discovery, as though hidden in an ancient temple were dusty manuscripts stacked to the ceiling containing the lost secrets of civilization.

Now she found herself blinking back tears as she sat in the cozy library-like niche and tried to focus on the bookshelves lined with books and binders of every color and size dating back years. Harry was quite proud of his collection and it was used as a resource by several of the other departments.

She searched Harry's walls, eyeing each of the familiar promotional flyers he had designed, expensively matted, framed and hung with pride. Finally, her eyes came to rest on the gilt oval frame that sat ensconced on his desk revealing a strikingly attractive woman whose natural attributes dominated the picture.

"Are you listening?" Harry's voice was shrill and demanding.

"I'm listening, Harry."

"I need you to discreetly type up these notes." Harry again indicated the legal pads.

"Is that all, Harry?" Maggie sighed with relief. "I'll be glad to take them home and do the job." The simplicity of the project in the aftermath of the bizarre buildup made her almost want to laugh out loud.

"No, I don't want this material out of the office. It's very personal. I need this project done neatly and efficiently. I need you to keep up with it on a daily basis. That means doing it on your computer and doing it during your working hours here in the office."

"Harry, couldn't I hire a typist or contact an agency? No one would have to know anything about you. I'd say they were my thoughts for a thesis or something."

"No, that wouldn't work." Harry's smile was cruel. "These are the notes of a mad man. You are the only one I'd trust to do them." Harry's complexion was becoming mottled and his voice a whisper. The shift in his personality was evident.

"Harry, have you taken leave of your senses? You must have taken an overdose of medication. What you've asked me to do is against Corporate's policy. It's the kind of stuff terminations are made of. I can't and won't do it."

"Don't be ridiculous. I can't stand it when you get so dramatic. You have a way of exaggerating everything out of proportion. My request is simple and you're making a fucking federal case out of it."

"Harry, you've known me long enough to know that I won't condone anything that goes against my principles."

"Even if it means my life?"

"Your life, what do you mean? You're scaring me, Harry." Maggie realized that anyone watching the scenario wouldn't be the least fazed by either Harry's or her appearance. She remained self-contained while Harry looked as though he were dictating a letter rather than a list of brazen demands. No one could know that her icy composure veiled her growing fears.

"Not my physical life but my mental well being."

"Harry, I knew something was wrong with you."

"I wouldn't ask you unless I was in a spot. You already know my personal life is in shambles, what with the divorce and all. Without Ellen I'm nothing." Harry was good at playing with emotion and switching tactics in midstream.

"Now who is being dramatic, Harry?"

"I'm going to tell you the truth, Maggie."

"That's refreshing, Harry. I was getting worried."

"I'm doing this for medical reasons. I'm seeing a psychiatrist. He wants me to journal my thoughts before I go into therapy. That's the reason for all this."

"Harry, I'm glad you're seeing a doctor."

"Maggie, you're the only person who'd understand why I've written such disgusting revelations. I hated writing them down, they're vile and sickening. Just getting up enough courage to ask you to type this trash made me crazy and I had to take a few extra tranquilizers. This is as bad as it gets and if you don't help me, I don't know what I'll do."

"What a crazy thing to do, Harry. Surely you know that your doctor will understand what you've written. That's the whole point to therapy. The doctor would probably prefer your own notes. Why should you have to have someone retype them?"

"Don't second guess me on this, Maggie. Just believe me when I tell you I need to have this degrading garbage in some semblance of order and ready to present at my initial session. You're about the only person on earth who can decipher my scrawl."

"Harry, why should we risk both our reputations, not to mention our jobs, for something that can be handled without resorting to dishonesty?"

"Maggie, my job is on the line. I'm at the end of my rope." Harry began to moan, rocking back and forth in his chair.

"Harry, Harry." Maggie pulled herself up out of the chair and moved to Harry's side. She put her hands on his shoulders and massaged the muscles through his sweat-soaked shirt.

"Maggie, I'm counting on you. For God's sake, help me!" His chest heaved up and down and he seemed near collapse.

"Okay, Harry, okay, I'll do it. How soon do you need them typed?" Maggie felt sickened by her capitulation but the sight of

71

Harry, fragmented and panicky, was worse.

"I'll give you several notepads each day. I'd like them typed before the end of the day. I want you to edit them for clarity and change the names. The ones I used were real and after thinking about it I don't want to get anyone into trouble."

"Then what? Put them in a plain manila envelope and drop them in some secret drawer?"

"Maggie, that's a great idea."

"You're not serious?" Maggie realized that Harry was unaware she was being facetious.

"You've got to keep this our secret, Maggie. No one will be looking for my notes on your computer. No one else has your password. No one must know." Harry was remarkably composed and detailed.

"Harry, if it weren't for your medical treatment, I wouldn't do this." Maggie watched Harry's face. She was worried about irritating him.

"That's right, Maggie, doctor's orders." His request, fanatical as it was, and her acquiescence, seemed to pacify him. He was soon his old self and seemed to have forgotten the entire astounding occurrence.

"You're the boss, Harry."

"Don't be so sensitive, Maggie. Things like this get done in corporate America every day and no one's the wiser. It's no big deal."

"That doesn't make it right. Pressure is a dangerous thing; once it begins it can't be controlled."

"Maggie, I'm not coercing you, I'm asking you to help me out here. Consider it one of your noble causes."

Maggie flinched at his words. At that moment she hated Harry and his hypocritical two-facedness. "When this is finished, I never want to discuss it with you again. Agreed?"

"Agreed."

"Let me have the first group." Maggie snatched at the two

notebooks Harry doled out in her direction.

"Maggie, why are you taking this so hard? Lighten up. After all, you are my administrative assistant."

"Thanks for your vote of confidence, boss."

Harry's stinging words reverberated in her mind as she recalled what Paul had said about the staff's feelings toward Harry's exacting attitude. It crossed her mind that she might well be Harry's next victim whether she helped him or not. She hastily discarded the notion realizing that now, more than ever, she needed to trust him.

"Like I said, Maggie, you're taking this all too seriously."

"Harry, I feel totally flattened. In half an hour you've managed to undo what we as a team accomplished in seven years. But don't worry, like you said, I'll get over it."

Maggie returned to her office emotionally distressed and tried to put the situation into perspective.

I've suddenly become his task-oriented secretary, dutifully handling a daunting chore. He's not the least bit concerned about my feelings. True, he's not in full control of his senses, but to act in such a dictatorial fashion shocks me to the core. I wonder what this will do to the relationship we've shared all this time. He's my boss and he's never before asked me to do anything that would in any way have jeopardized either one of us. What could he possibly have written that he wants no one else to see? If it detracts from him, would I want to know? If he is suffering from a nervous breakdown which I believe he is who would I contact? Corporate? Ellen?

Maggie took the notepads and locked them in her drawer.

I've got to get hold of myself or my imagination will run wild. I'm in control. First things first, Harry is entitled to my trust. He's earned it. We've got history together and it's got to count for something. You just don't throw away seven years of friendship. I don't think he'd ask me to do this unless he was truly under excessive stress. I'll give him the benefit of the doubt. After I see what it is he wants me to type I'll let him know whether or not I'll do the job. I'll take it one step at a time and go cautiously toward a decision. Right now, I've got to get out of here. I need some fresh air.

Maggie grabbed her purse and headed toward the elevators. She had promised to meet Paul for lunch.

Chapter 7

It had been Paul's idea to celebrate their mini reunion over lunch and he was already seated when Maggie walked into the restaurant.

"Hi, Maggie," Paul stood up and hugged her before she had time to sit down at the table. "You look tired, everything okay?"

"As usual, Paul, you look healthy and fit."

"I hope you've missed me as much as I've missed you, Maggie."

"Paul, did you know Harry was back in town?"

"You avoided my question nicely, Maggie, so you obviously didn't come here to talk about us. But to answer your question, yes, I heard he was due back today."

"Paul, maybe lunch wasn't such a good idea. Do you mind if I just have a cup of tea?"

"Has something happened?" Paul's eyes darkened.

"No, it's just that my workload's heavy. I'm behind on everything and I've really got to get back to the office."

"Oh, I get it. Harry's back and you're slaving over him already."

"That's not true, Paul. I'm on deadline for several projects that I created while Harry was away and I've got to finish them." For a moment Maggie thought of telling Paul the truth but then remembered her promise to Harry.

"Sorry, Maggie, I didn't realize you were under the gun."

"It's all right, Paul." Maggie sipped her tea and tried to keep her hand steady.

"Maggie, I can't help it if I'm a bulldog about certain things."

"What was that, Paul?" Maggie tried to focus on what Paul was saying.

"I'm talking about my investigating Harry. I've done a lot of thinking about this while we were apart and I've come to the conclusion that you'll just have to trust me on this. I know you're logical enough not to let my dealings with Harry have anything to do with us."

"I thought we had finished that discussion weeks ago. Most people get on with their lives, Paul, but not you."

"Maybe you don't want to know what Harry's done."

"Paul, must you be so cryptic? It's annoying."

"I'm not just drudging up a lot of old wives' tales. Harry is in this deeper than you can imagine."

"Paul, my advice is to forgive and forget."

"No, I can't just forgive and forget it. And if he had done to you what he's done to me and others, you wouldn't be so quick to use the old forgive and forget adage. He hasn't hurt you yet, but lookout when he does. We'll see if you're so high-minded then."

"Paul, I really can't sit here and listen to this." Maggie was becoming increasingly antagonized by Paul's presence.

"The king's back, long live the king."

"Paul, you've picked an inopportune moment for this discussion. Do whatever you have to do, but leave me out of it." Maggie, feeling Paul's scrutiny, wanted to distance herself from him.

"Sorry, Maggie, do you want to take a walk or something?"

"No, Paul, I've got to get back."

"It seems lately you're always rushing away, Maggie. I know you're keeping something from me. Anyone can see it's bottled up inside you and you're ready to explode. Can't you talk to me?"

"No, Paul. I can't." Maggie stood up brusquely, inadvertently knocking over her cup.

"Maggie, what's wrong?" Paul asked anxiously.

"It's all this crazy talk, Paul, that's what. Don't you get it?"

"Maggie, I…"

She didn't wait to hear Paul's response but made a hasty retreat toward the elevators. Unable to shake the oppressive mood, she decided to take Paul's advice and walk. She needed to be alone, and hoped the quietness of nature would restore her enough to take on Harry's request with a more open mind.

The rooftop park was crowded with lunchtime employees who were eating at picnic tables or sitting around the fountains, laughing, talking and enjoying the warm summer day. Maggie, caught up in her own world, was oblivious to the noise as she strolled along soaking up sunshine and wading through her own private thoughts.

Maybe I have blown this all out of proportion. Maybe Paul's right. Perhaps I should have confided in him. No, it's better to keep my word to Harry and tell no one right now. This is probably not a big deal. In all the time I've known Harry he's been above board. He has never asked me to do something deceitful before, and although my gut instincts tell me it's wrong, I've got to help him out if I can. His erratic behavior is a warning sign. He's sick, that's pretty much certain. In my heart of hearts I believe he's earned my friendship and trust. Until he proves himself differently, I'll have to consent to his demands. I wish I could stop worrying about how WordTech will view my decision.

It was late afternoon before she could bring herself to look at the first draft. She didn't know what to expect but the hairs on the back of her neck were already standing end to end, a sure sign that something was wrong. She opened the notebook and began to type what appeared to be a series of crudely written sexual vignettes.

"Oh, great stuff, Harry," she mocked reproachfully as she

read what sounded like a boring bedroom romp written by an unskilled writer.

She didn't like editing the jumbled phrases and structural inconsistencies but at Harry's behest she made the changes and corrections hoping the material would be more readable for his doctor. Although she was used to Harry's handwriting there were moments when even she couldn't decipher his scribblings and had to muddle through as best she could.

Worried she'd be unable to continue the task if the shoddy material should grow bolder, Maggie typed quickly trying to avoid any mental pictures Harry's sizzling stories conjured up in her mind. With the completion of the first half of the notebook her initial fears seemed unwarranted and she began to warm to the task. Harry apparently had the prowess of a sophomoric Casanova, a fact substantiated by his lurid imagination. His soap opera descriptions of the floozies in his life and the temptations of which he took full advantage were second-rate and straight out of a Hollywood script.

Guiltily she admitted to herself that satiating her curiosity about Harry had more to do with this than anything else and, she reasoned, his gossipy scandal sheet might offer some insight into his personality.

"Anyone can see this is plain, unadulterated drivel," she snickered to herself. "It's like reading a cheap romance novel."

However, two hours passed and she found herself unwilling to end the task. Harry's tainted vocabulary evoked memories of heated emotion and within a short time she was caught up in his gaudy saga. She was both surprised and appalled that his crude words had the power to stir her sensually. It was only through an act of shear will-power that she forced herself to stop typing. She stared fixedly at the page and exhaled noisily. Having underestimated the allure of his inferior but absorbing tales, Maggie now realized she had become an unwitting spectator to an assortment of trashy escapades.

Good heavens, if the situation wasn't so deplorable it would be hilarious. Here I am a grown woman, on the job, typing a paper that is stupidly lewd for a boss who is obviously ill. To top it all, I could very well achieve an orgasm right here in the privacy of my office. I'd better quit joking around but I can't help thinking this belongs in Ripley's. Secretary types scintillating review for boss and inadvertently gets caught up in imaginary liaisons. I must be crazy to be doing this. Is it because of Harry? Am I jealous? I can almost picture him there with those women. Whether he's made these wishful scenes up in his head or whether they really happened doesn't matter. What does matter is that I get hold of myself and keep this tripe in perspective. Who knows if Harry has an alternative plan up his sleeve and this is some type of diversionary tactic. Whatever, I won't get any more involved than I am already. Type the stuff and forget about it, Maggie.

Maggie, however, couldn't bring herself to type any further. It was way past seven and she felt exhausted. Saving the material under the code name "HICChronicles" she exited the file and left for home.

That evening after walking her dogs, Maggie sat down next to her mother who was channel-surfing with the TV remote.

"Got a minute, Mom?"

"Certainly, darling, is everything all right? You seemed unusually quiet at dinner. How are things at the office?"

"Everything was going well until this afternoon." Maggie gave her mother a detailed description of Harry's unusual request.

"Dear God, what are you going to do?"

"Do, why I've already done it. I started typing the stuff this afternoon."

"Maggie, remember when I was doing the cards and... ."

"Yes, they showed transition in the spread. How true that was."

"Maggie, the cards don't predict the future but they can offer insight into your unconscious mind. Once you know what you're up against, volatile excesses and disillusionment, you'll be able to deal with it," she said, touching Maggie's hand reassuringly.

"Mom, there's something else. This afternoon when I was typing Harry's notes I suddenly felt the need to be with him. Not like we've been as boss and assistant but more like, well, I can't explain it," Maggie said, suddenly feeling like an adolescent embarrassed by her own admission.

"No need to my dear. Your impulses are only human and from what you told me about his writings you couldn't help but be sensually provoked. It's like reading a titillating book or seeing a pornographic movie, one does get aroused. And at the office yet, what could he be thinking? I'm afraid Harry's put you in a very compromising position."

"What can I do? I just can't quit. That would be running away. You should have heard him, Mom. He was so miserable. This is terribly important to him and obviously to his doctor."

Maggie took the Tarot deck off the coffee table and shuffled the cards. She cut them and put them face down in the center of the table.

"Oh, Maggie, what a terrible predicament," Mrs. Reynolds shook her head as she watched her daughter lay upright the first card.

"The Fool. That's okay, Mom, to me that card means new beginnings."

"That may be, dear, but it also means you have lessons to learn through your own folly. You must be ready to make the right choice."

Maggie went to bed that night filled with fury over having to do Harry's bidding. She had been angry before but now her anger was a fulminating denunciation against the man who had represented so much good in her life and who she now felt had violated that trust. She tossed and turned and finally allowed herself to sleep.

The dream came sometime toward morning. It seemed to be

a continuation of Harry's writings and her inescapable desires. In the nightmare, she lay covered in reams and reams of beautifully handwritten scrolls. A giant hand held a pen aloft and dribbled red ink onto her skin.

In her dream, Maggie knew the ink was blistering her flesh, yet there was no pain. She fought to release herself but was pinioned to the page like a butterfly in a science laboratory. She could feel herself giving way to a new sensation. Stirred with emotion, her blood turned hot, creating pain so tormenting it hurt her heart. Pouring out of her body, it moved of its own accord toward the red ink. She watched in horror as the crimson fluid merged with the ruby-colored ink igniting a fire whose flames she knew would ultimately engulf her. Fighting for control, she woke with a start.

Well, no need to ask Dr. Freud what that was about.

Maggie pounded her pillow and closed her eyes in anticipation of a sequel but it was a dreamless sleep that finally overtook her.

✿

Although hard pressed to admit it, Maggie found herself anxious to return to Harry's writings. She opened mail, finished corporate marketing reports and worked on deadline projects always with the thought that toward the end of the day it would be time to take up the task. She become quite cunning at making sure no one was watching as she opened her desk drawer and retrieved the notebooks. She also made sure to delete the material from the hard drive after putting it onto an external drive for Harry's perusal.

Now I've taken to acting like a spy in some B movie. Lord knows where this escapade will end. Well, in for a penny in for a pound. Poor Harry, if any of this is true, his life is without discretion and his soul must be crying out in agony. He's risked his very reason, his sanity, to embark on this endless journey of torment. How can I save him from this perilous trap? His fidelity, his honor, his decency are all at stake. He worships sexual pleasure and he's unaware the price it will cost him. I best finish the work and hopefully the sooner I do the quicker he'll be able to get psychological help.

Trying to distance herself from the content, Maggie typed quickly. She stopped however, when she saw her name appear in the text...

Lately I can't keep Maggie out of my mind. She is such a beautiful woman but too professional and too cold for my tastes. Still, one wonders what it would be like to be with her...a stunning woman and oh, that delicious ass...

Maggie could hardly believe her eyes as she tried to read through the passage. Her first thought was that surely it wasn't her Harry was referring to in his story. When she realized he had dared to bring her into his vulgar sexual exploits, her emotions ran the gamut from sadness to infuriation and finally threatened to boil over. Not wanting anyone to see her in such a state of agitation, she closed the document, put the book away and hurried to the ladies' lounge as her thoughts raced out of control.

Wasn't it bad enough Harry that you had the gall, the audacity to force me to type such garbage in the first place? Now you've alluded to me in the grossest, most unimaginable way possible. Not only do I feel outraged but I feel betrayed. How could you Harry? I believed you and I was willing to do whatever it took to get you better. Now it seems as though you're determined to bring me down to your level but I'm stronger than you Harry and I'll prove it.

Maggie ran cold water over a paper towel and pressed it against her burning forehead. She felt physically and mentally exhausted. Stretching out on the couch, she hoped that a few minutes of relaxation would restore her energy but her thoughts were unstoppable and recklessly rocketed through her mind.

Why do I feel as though Harry has sullied my reputation and defiled me as a person? Why do I hate the poison he writes, yet feel drawn to it like a firefly to a flame? It has nothing to do with me regardless of what he's written. I've got to keep this whole issue in containment. Harry's sick and I'm only in this to help him. He can never do anything to me that I don't allow him to do. Harry, I swear I'll get you well and if I'm going to be of any help to you I've got to stop overreacting. Why am I so angry with those words he wrote? Am I really angry? I better keep all this at a distance and concentrate on the important things like remembering to change my own name.

"Maggie, Maggie, you okay?" Leeann was shaking her awake.

"I'm fine. I got tired and laid down for a minute," Maggie said groggily as she slowly regained her senses.

"Gee, kid, you scared me. You were sleeping so soundly I thought you were dead. Aren't you feeling well? You've been gone for over an hour. I thought you'd gone home."

"An hour! I've got to get back to work. I've got to put some overtime in tonight."

"It's after five, Maggie, get out of here. You've been putting in way too much overtime as it is."

"Thanks, Leeann, but it's important."

Maggie's legs felt like petrified stumps as she dragged herself back to her office completely drained of strength. She'd promised Harry she'd have the next notebook finished tonight and she resigned herself to the task.

The words on the page had taken on a confidential tone that had not materialized before. Maggie stopped typing and began to read in earnest. This was a side of Harry that he had managed to keep obscure.

I think I'm a manic depressive. I'm sure I'm a manic something or other. The junk I'm writing could be the diary of a mad man,

no, on second thought it is the diary of a mad man. There are moments when I'm higher than a kite and then there are moments when I'm so low only the promise of suicide keeps me going. It's funny but it's the highs that make me want a woman.

The lows make me want to keep to myself. They're like big blankets that threaten to smother me and yet I want to wrap myself up and be totally alone. I'm lying in a big cocoon, hanging on an empty branch of a tree frozen in the dead of winter. When do I get to hold the promise of transformation—even butterflies get a chance at metamorphosis. What I wouldn't give for such a spring. Dear God, how I wish I could change and be someone else but it's too late for me. I'm in it for the duration of the ride - a one way ticket to Hell.

When I was a kid and read Hemingway I really got into that "movable feast" crap. I thought it all related to sex; like eating and drinking, it was all about stirring the desires of women. In exchange these lovely creatures would caress you to their bodies and hold you against their breasts, keeping away the loneliness. I never got enough. Like a guy in the desert, I was constantly quenching my thirst. When I was young I was scared that I was really sick, but now I'm just one of many sicko slobs.

I hate having to think of the future. It's almost as bad as the past. I want only the present. This is what counts. Make it happen now. Sex is a game. Who cares what the consequences are. I like the feeling of debasing myself because it means that I have no respect for any human relationship. I fear personal commitment, I always have. I can't afford to have any emotional ties. That would be dangerous. Lucky for me no one has ever come really close to knowing Harry Cooke. What would I do if it ever happened? I think I'd have to kill the person or myself or both of us. KM knows how I feel about that. Oh what tangled

webs I've woven.

Maggie was surprised by the depth of Harry's revelations and his personal insights. For the first time since she had begun this project she felt he was being honest about his feelings and his fears. She had been drawn into this house of mirrors by a sideshow huckster and without warning a shard of glass revealed a strange glimmer of hope.

Then, just as she was beginning to believe he was finally revealing snippets of his real self, Harry was back at being the same old Harry. The tedious, repetitive stock phrases were again laid out in the manuscript in full vigor of Harry's prowess as the all American man and Maggie had no recourse but to diligently type the driveling rubbish.

When I'm in the mists of this heinous project, I wonder if it's worth continuing. I could take it to HR and they'd insure Harry would get the help he needs. No, I've determined my course of action and I'm committed to squarely standing behind my decision. Perhaps it's not the wisest decision I've made and if others knew of it they would certainly misunderstand my intentions and might even condemn me. I'll stop vacillating. I've made a judgment and I'll see it to the end.

Maggie took a sip of water and opened the next notebook.

Harry, it's my faith in you that keeps me going. Your words tonight remind me of how sick you are and how desperately you need help. How anyone could possibly live such a wearisome and monotonous lifestyle is beyond me. Obviously you've never learned that the really worthwhile things in life are not gained by external means but through commitment to that which has value.

Typing the endless nonsense began to weigh on Maggie's nerves and although no longer embarrassed at having to peep into Harry's bedroom to observe his sexual workouts it was his male ego she found hard to take.

Harry, not for one moment do I believe any of this tripe. You're a wishful thinker. These scenarios are figments of your overactive imagination. No guy could have that much stamina. This only proves that you do need to see a shrink, at least to help you understand why you've written what you have. I only hope I have the strength to type one more of your silly tales.

What was of interest, however, was the fact that Harry continually used the initials KM in his writings. Although he seemed to have nothing to do with KM sexually, the fact that he mentioned the KM individual in scenarios which suggested a connection of some kind struck Maggie as curious and she began to watch for them, making personal notes regarding the connotation in which the initials were used.

KM, KM. Who is KM? There they are again those same initials. I don't recognize them as anyone Harry knows, yet he constantly refers to this person only as KM. Maybe he will reveal it down the line.

As she completed the last line of the notebook she was working on, Maggie decided it would be a good idea to quit for the night. She was tired and didn't want to risk making any errors.

I've had it with your true romance novel for the week, Harry. My intentions to finish another book were good, but I'm too, too tired. Besides, boss, I don't think you have the foggiest notion that typing this hogwash has caused me a great deal of stress and emotional fatigue. What I want now is a hot bath and a cool glass of Chablis. Best that I get out of here while the getting is good but I'd better keep focused. Then it's off to a happy weekend, girl.

Maggie copied the file and then erased it from the hard drive. She turned off the computer, shut off the lights and locked her office door.

Chapter 8

Leeann was in the boardroom arranging the agenda folders next to each manager's chair when Maggie arrived on Monday morning.

"Everything's ready for the meeting, Maggie. There's just one snag." Leeann nodded in the direction of Harry's office.

"He's not in yet? This is the third monthly planning meeting he's missed. It's getting to be a habit." Maggie began reviewing the agenda items in case Harry didn't show up.

Harry had always been the epitome of punctuality but soon after his divorce she noticed his frequent bouts of tardiness and eventually absences. There were even a few mornings he arrived in his office wearing rumpled clothes and smelling of stale liquor.

After the first incident, Maggie made sure there was plenty of hot, strong coffee, and freshly laundered shirts available. She even went as far as securing the dry cleaner's assistance in having his suits sponge pressed at a moment's notice. Harry, she knew, made light of everything without any show of concern, whereas she on the other hand was unnerved at the slightest provocation regarding his reputation and, in spite of his negligence, was determined to safeguard it.

"Cover for me, Maggie" was all he'd say if he called in late for an appointment or missed a meeting, but when he started excusing himself altogether because he was working on projects from home

Maggie began worrying in earnest. She had gleaned from Harry's journaled notes the definition of working at home and she was committed to getting him back on track.

She facilitated the meetings but steered clear of making unnecessary excuses for him. Some of the managers were annoyed by Harry's nonattendance but the majority seemed comfortable knowing she was in charge.

The more involved Maggie got into the task of typing Harry's sexual dalliances, the more concerned she became about his mental health. His disheveled thoughts, although sexual in nature, had an underlying ambiguity as though Harry himself were growing less sure of his own sensibilities. Maggie found scrawled at the end of one of the notebooks a short description which again painted Harry in a different light. She read with renewed interest how he felt about himself and his world of promiscuous depravity.

I am corrupt. My lust has finally turned my inner being into a perverted degenerate. Am I reprobate, a piece of garbage that no one wants? I suddenly realize that if I were to die tomorrow no one would really care. I would die unloved because I am incapable of loving.

I sit for hours in lonely hotel rooms afterwards, holding my head in my hands. It's dark outside but lately I'm getting afraid of the dark. I want to get up and go home but I can't bring myself to move. The fear gnaws at my insides and even another drink doesn't give me release or courage. My life—what have I done with my life? Could it be that there is something in me after all? I'm like the dark. I keep myself covered with the blackness. Now, suddenly, I crave light. God where is the light?

It was this particular account that forced Maggie to reassess Harry's mental acuity. She wondered just how important these notes would be to his doctor and if by waiting for the finished product Harry was endangering his own welfare. His lifestyle was taking a toll on his work ethic and he was growing more distant. Increasingly disconcerted with the entire project, and fearing for Harry's sanity, Maggie felt as though she were on both ends of a teeter-totter.

I'm angry at being drawn into this scandalous enterprise but I'm also frightened that Harry is getting sicker. I can no longer ignore my mounting apprehensions. I've got to confront Harry to get him back in balance before he deteriorates further into his obsessive illness. I need to know how much longer before he presents the material to his doctor.

Maggie tried repeatedly to bring up the subject but Harry continually ignored her on some pretext or another until she finally had enough.

"Harry, I can't do this anymore," she shouted, barging into his office and flinging the envelope onto his desk.

"What's the matter with you, Maggie?" Harry asked, perplexed by her uncharacteristic behavior.

"Don't pretend you don't know, Harry. I've been waiting to speak to you for over two weeks and you've conveniently managed to evade the issue."

"I'm busy, Maggie, and you know it. It can't be all that important." Harry, his forehead cupped in his hand, continued writing.

"It's very important, Harry. So important, that we either talk now or you find yourself another stooge to do this so called job."

"Okay, okay. Why didn't you just say so in the first place? I didn't realize it was all that serious but I honestly don't have time right now, Maggie. Could we talk about it after work?"

"That's fine, Harry."

"I'd rather it be someplace offsite if you don't mind?" Harry sounded irritated.

"Where do you suggest?" Maggie, irked by Harry's wily machinations, made no attempt to disguise the frustration in her voice either.

"There's a little Spanish restaurant, Su Casa, in Hillsborough. It's off Tenth Street. How about seven thirty? I'll buy."

"Let's make it Dutch, Harry. I'd rather this be strictly business if you don't mind."

"Whatever you say, Maggie. Boy you're touchy today," he said condescendingly.

As if dealing with Harry wasn't enough, Maggie found herself in just the opposite straits with Paul. It seemed to her that he was going out of his way to pry into her affairs, using one ruse or another. He was particularly interested in her office activities and the more she tried to sidestep his inquisitiveness the bolder his tactics got. She was still fuming over this morning's exchange which had started after Leeann told her about the phony invoices.

"Hey, Maggie, Paul brought these in for your signature but I know you signed these billing invoices last month. This is useless paper." Leeann leafed through the stack of forms irritably. "What's up with him?"

"He's got a lot on his mind, Leeann, and probably forgot." Maggie made light of the error but knew Paul was up to something.

"By the way, he was here just a few minutes ago."

"Really?" Maggie went over to Harry's empty office and made sure the door was locked before going back into hers.

"Hi Maggie, what's happening?" Paul had insinuated himself into her chair and was studying her computer screen.

"Nothing whatsoever to do with you, Mr. Keating," she said, trying to sound unruffled, "but I thought you weren't going to come into our offices unannounced any more." By the look on his face the barb had hit home and she watched him grudgingly get up and walk to the door.

"I thought that was only while Harry was away. If I didn't know better I'd think you were hiding something from me, Maggie. Don't you trust me?" Paul narrowed his eyes as he searched her face.

"Paul, I have an A-2 confidential security clearance and you, of all people, should know better."

"So sorrrrry, Ms. Reynolds. Please forgive my trespassing," he sneered.

Infuriated by Paul's attitude, she spun around in her chair, deliberately ignoring him as he walked toward the elevators. As spiteful as the episode had been, she was glad she had spared herself further questioning. She had enough problems of her own to worry about.

Am I becoming paranoid? I'm suspicious of Paul and edgy about Harry. In the meantime, I'm having trouble focusing on my own tasks. It'd be funny if I'd wind up being the department's Employee Assistance Program's candidate for psychological counseling. The way I feel, maybe checking out what the EAP has to offer wouldn't be such a bad idea.

❧

"Well, I'm off, Mom, see you tonight."

"Be careful, Maggie. Don't let that good looking Irishman talk you into doing anything you don't want to do."

"Don't worry so much, Mother. I'm not a little girl anymore."

Having gone home to change her clothes, Maggie was wearing what she referred to as her "power outfit." The casual jeans and cashmere pullover made her feel equal to any situation.

The taxi made good time and she arrived early. The tiny café, shimmering in candlelight, was warm and inviting, as was the old waiter, who, wearing a colorful serape over his shoulder, smiled courteously as he led her to a charming, little table.

"Senor Harry will be here shortly, Senorita Reynolds. I will leave the menu, yes?"

"Yes, thank you, Senor," she smiled graciously.

Maggie was surprised the Maître d' had acknowledged her by name but guessed that Harry had arranged it. She pretended to look over the menu but her heart was pounding. She wanted this to be a business meeting but Harry's journaled words kept getting in the way. She resorted to a stern and unsympathetic approach to reprimand herself.

If you don't get hold of yourself, Harry will fly off the handle and you'll lose the momentum of this meeting. Take a firm stand and charge headlong into whatever this turns out to be. Easy girl, remember he's your boss. You need to be there for him. Stop thinking about yourself and start thinking about him. He needs help and he needs it now.

She was still scolding herself when Harry interrupted.

"Helloooo, Maggie! Been waiting long?" He was smiling that broad Irish grin and she felt her self-confidence begin to melt.

"Not long."

"Looks like we both had the same idea." Harry, dressed in a sporty black polo shirt and slacks, pointed to her attire. "Green's your color, Maggie. It suits you."

"Thanks Harry, you look good, too. This is a nice little hideaway you've found."

"Come into my web said the spider to the fly."

"Harry, now that we've gotten the preliminaries out of the way, can we please get seriously down to business."

"Serious the lady says. That calls for a drink. What will you have, Maggie, me darlin?" He waved at the waiter.

"Nothing for me, thanks. You promised me time to talk and that's all I came here to do."

"Well, I won't get serious unless you have a drink with me."

"For heaven's sake, Harry. All right, I'll have a glass of Chablis."

He ordered the wine and a scotch and soda and then sat looking at her. "Well, what's on your mind?"

"Harry, I don't know any way of putting this delicately except to tell it as I see it."

"Fine, go ahead. I'm listening."

"Don't you think you've been acting pretty strange lately?"

"What are you getting at?"

"I'm talking about this new cavalier attitude of yours."

"What attitude might that be?"

"Oh come on, as though you don't know. What about coming in late and missing meetings? Don't you call that kind of behavior strange?"

"Just because I missed a few meetings doesn't mean something's wrong. Why, has anyone said anything?"

"No one has said anything, but that doesn't answer my question." Maggie thought Harry's response indicated she had hit a nerve.

"Get to the point, Maggie."

"Harry, it's not just about the meetings. It's the whole picture. You come in late looking like a drowned rat, if you come in at all. You've left me to handle the meetings, you've missed appointments, and worst of all your behavior in the office has changed."

"What are you referring to?"

"Harry, you rant and rave so much the department doesn't know what to make of it."

"You don't suppose you could be exaggerating just a little. I admit I've had a rough couple of months but I'm getting better now. I've always run a taut ship and my staff knows it. That's no secret but I expected more from you."

"And while we're at it, what about that crazy, sick journal of yours? The things you write in it, Harry. They're perverse."

"Now we're getting to the crux of the situation." Harry shook his head and laughed.

"Don't laugh, Harry. You don't know how serious this is. I can't believe your life is based on such narrow self-interests."

"It's not that I don't appreciate your comments, Maggie, but I warned you the content was X-rated. I'm a man of excess. What can I say? Anyway, I thought we had a deal. You weren't going to bring the project up." Harry waved for another drink.

"That was after we finished it which by the way I hope is soon."

"A raw deal, that's what I'm getting from you. You see me in those wicked scenarios and you think I'm going down the drain."

"Harry, the journal is just the tip of the iceberg. You've changed, and not for the better. I'm worried about you. What headway have you made with your doctor? Whether you believe it or not, I'm in your corner and I want you to get help. What you need is a shot of raw courage, not another drink."

"What's this, some kind of tactical ploy you're using on me?"

"Harry, don't start playing now you see it, now you don't."

"What do you mean, Maggie?"

"Sounds like you're getting ready to buy time by making up one of your stories."

"Whoa, I give up. You've gotten to know me pretty well, Maggie. To answer your question, I haven't seen the doctor yet. He wants to wait until my journal's finished."

"What? You can't be serious. Whose idea of therapy is that? I only volunteered for this madness because you said you were seeing a doctor."

"Do you think there is something wrong with my head?"

"Yes, Harry, I do think you need help and the sooner the better."

"Maggie, for one thing, you're not a doctor. For another, you're building this whole thing out of proportion. All I asked from you was help in typing up my notes and now you're getting your Irish temper up."

"Harry, don't patronize me." Maggie shoved her glass across the table and stood up to leave. Harry grabbed her arm and she sat back down.

"Okay, okay. I'm sorry."

"I need answers, Harry, not the run-a-round."

"What do you want me to do, admit I'm shaky? Okay, I admit it. People go through good times and bad times and right now it's a bad time for me. I can't seem to get on solid ground. Maybe I have gone a bit overboard." Harry ordered another drink. "Half the time I don't know why I do the things I do."

"Harry, you drink too much."

"I'm lonely."

"So, a lot of us are lonely. That's not a rare disease."

"I don't know what happens to me but it's like I'm afraid that if I stop in the middle, I won't get to the end."

"The end of what?"

"I don't know, the end of the game, I guess."

"Something's happened to change you, Harry. You've gone from being disciplined and focused to unkempt and uncaring, unless that wasn't the real you I've worked with these past seven years and you've managed to hide from me who you really are."

"The past years were good but you're right, I am different. It's as though I woke up from a deep sleep. I want something more out of life."

"Harry, you've got a tremendous amount of responsibility and I realize there are times when you need to relax and get away from it all but to chuck it for this fast and loose lifestyle is just plain crazy."

"I like living on the edge, Maggie. I always have. It's not that I've changed into someone else, it's that I've gone back to being what I always was."

"What were you? A debauched drunk bent on self-destruction. I don't for one minute believe that you'd compromise your principles for a few thrills. You probably think you're getting old and you're worried about death. You can't drink yourself back to your youth. Drinking isn't a solution, its dissolution."

Harry smiled indulgently. "You don't know me, Maggie."

"Well, help me get to know you."

"You should have been put off by now with what you already know about me. Hasn't my journal convinced you I'm hopeless? Besides, this has nothing to do with getting older, or getting divorced."

"That's your male vanity talking, Harry. You can't be so unrealistic that you believe only alcohol and sexual fantasies make life palatable."

"I control my drinking, it doesn't control me."

"Where have I heard that before? Harry, drinking doesn't make the problems go away. It only exaggerates the character flaws."

"Hell, if I believed that I'd kill myself."

"No, because even drunk you're a caring person who wants to do the right thing."

"How do you know that?"

"Let's just say I read it somewhere."

"I thought you said it was sick and perverse?"

"Yes, but it has some redeeming qualities."

"Like what."

"Like the parts where you're honest with yourself."

"You're an understanding person, Maggie, and a mighty attractive one I might add." Harry reached for her hand but she pulled it back.

"Easy, Harry. This is not one of your scenarios."

"Ouch, that was cruel, Maggie."

"Alcohol and emotion don't mix."

"Ever hear of the dark night of the soul? I think my soul has been kneeling in perpetual darkness since I was born. Ever wonder what eternity might be like, Maggie? I think it might be the absence of light. Even dying in a blaze of glory wouldn't help me because I'd still be faced with a black eternity."

"You were right the first time, Harry, I'm no doctor, but you certainly can't fix your own wound. You're bleeding to death and you don't even know it."

"I know I've got to get through this on my own, Maggie, but you're the only real person in my life right now. You and I are more of a married couple than a lot of married folks I know. Somehow when I talk with you I feel patient and hopeful as though there was a light at the end of the tunnel."

"Harry, you've got to find the light for yourself."

"Sounds like something my old man used to say. When I was very small, I must have been about two, I remember crying in the dark and he came in and put me on his knee. He lit a match and told me to blow it out. I did it, and he said something about my having the power within me to do it. Funny, I haven't thought of that in years."

"How did that moment make you feel?"

"It was like I was strong enough to take on anything that made me afraid."

"Harry, the light's all around you. All you need to do is let it penetrate into the heart of your being. Your dad left you that legacy."

"But nothing else, not even a soul," Harry said in abject misery.

"What about your family, Harry. Where are they?"

"My dad and mom are both gone. I was an only child."

"What was your father like?"

"He was a compulsive gambler. He wasn't home very much so I can't say anything good about him. He never did anything for me and I don't spend much time thinking about him."

"Were you close to your mother?"

"No I wasn't. She was too close to the bottle to worry about me. Let's not talk about my parents. Suffice to say they didn't know me and they sure as hell didn't care about me," Harry said, suddenly angry.

"You had Ellen in your life."

"Ellen," Harry repeated the name reverently.

"You love her very much."

"I loved her, but you can put that in the past tense."

"What happened?"

"We had ten great years together."

"Then what happened?"

"I messed up. She caught me playing around a few times and then I caught her playing around a few times. Next thing I know we're married in what's called name only. You know, the separate bedroom routine, she going her way and I going mine. Five months ago she finally pulled the plug. The divorce was final just before I came back from vacation."

"And no kids?"

"Nope, we wanted to wait and then Ellen didn't want any. She was right. You can't count on kids to save a marriage. I'm living proof of that."

"Don't paint yourself as such a bad guy, Harry."

"Why not, bad guys are always more interesting."

"You think so?"

"Enough about me, let's hear about you."

"No Harry, this time it's my turn to ask the questions."

"Why bother, I'm no good. I'm an awful good-for-nothing and I've done some awful things. You're the kind of gal who needs principled and upstanding people like your dad and that Tony fellow in your life."

"Funny you should remember that."

"I never forget anything about you, Maggie."

"Harry, I think you're just a guy blinded by your own testosterone."

"Maggie, you're relentless. You sure know how to put a guy in his place. I need another drink."

"Harry, how about some food? The chicken and rice special sounds delicious and you need something more nutritious than scotch."

They talked quietly over dinner and Maggie was glad the hot coffee had a sobering affect on Harry who talked about his past with a surprising openness.

"Maggie, you remind me of a painting I once saw in Spain. It was of a beautiful woman whose features seemed to change from one minute to the next, revealing aspects I had not noticed previously. I began to spend hours, and eventually days, studying the canvas. She was a fascinating study and it was almost as though I could reach into the depths of her soul and retrieve her very essence. Her eyes, those magnificent eyes, I can still remember them. They penetrated every waking hour of my day and then haunted my dreams. I felt as if she held a secret and I was young enough to believe I could fathom it. I became passionate about her, loving every moment I spent with her, until I realized that like every woman she was determined to keep the mystery to herself."

"Not every woman is like that, Harry."

"No, you're right, and I'm just beginning to find that out."

"What do you mean?"

"You for instance. I've known you for years and I still find you a contradiction. You're an aggressive, resourceful, no nonsense individual on the one hand, but you're also a sentimental, intelligent, straight-from-the-heart schoolgirl who'd forgive the devil if he asked. You're a good person, Maggie, but like the painting, I keep wondering what secrets you're hiding."

"Harry, I am what I am."

"Maybe you're too good to be true."

"Harry, goodness is an equal opportunity enterprise available to anyone at anytime, and there are a great many people in the world like me who practice what we preach. But it's too late to talk philosophy tonight. I've got to get going."

"Maggie, have an after dinner liqueur with me?"

"Harry, I've got to get up early."

"I promise, just one. It's Chartreuse, but the gods call it ambrosia."

Maggie nodded in agreement and Harry ordered two glasses.

"Mummm…it's good but awfully strong," Maggie said, sipping the green liquid.

"A lot like you."

"Harry, one has to be careful not to take you seriously."

"I want you to take me seriously, Maggie."

Maggie lowered her eyes and reached for the check. "I thought we agreed to pay our own way?"

"You buy next time," Harry said, taking hold of her hand.

Maggie looked up and into his eyes. "Harry, promise me you'll talk to the doctor and give him the completed parts of the journal. If you do, I'll finish typing the project without hassling you further."

"You strike a hard bargain, Maggie." He stood and offered her his hand. As he drew her up from the chair he kissed her mouth.

"Like I said, pure ambrosia." He licked his lips and winked impishly.

Outside, the moonlit street was empty. As they stood in silence waiting for her cab, Harry put his arms around her waist. She could feel them tighten as he pulled her close to his body. The kiss was gentle, but unyielding. It drew her breath away and sent her spiraling. When he released his hold they stood for a moment soul searching each other's eyes. Then, as though daring the fates to replicate the upheaval, Maggie leaned into him and let it happen again.

His tongue found its way inside her mouth and she quivered uncontrollably. The shear force of his appetite sent her reeling, coursing through her depths until it seemingly spilled out the very soles of her feet. Her tongue, craving reciprocity, tore its way greedily into his mouth, until awestruck, they fell against each other. As though time were suspended they hung together embraced by their own vulnerabilities.

"Harry, that shouldn't have happened," Maggie was breathless against his ear.

"It had to happen, Maggie."

"No, Harry. Not to us."

"It will go on happening if we see each other again."

"I won't let it, Harry."

The cab pulled up along side them, quiet but insistent, shattering the interlude. As she got in Harry surrendered his hold on her hand and shut the door. The car lurched forward and Maggie watched out the window as Harry walked back into the restaurant.

Chapter 9

"Hi, Mom, it's after twelve. You didn't have to wait up." Maggie kissed her mother who had been watching television in the den.

"You seem especially happy, honey. What's Harry up to now?"

"He's promised to see his doctor. I think he's sincere about working things out." Maggie sat down on the couch and scratched behind the ears of her sleeping terriers.

"I don't believe it. He's up to something, mark my words."

"Mom, he told me things tonight that make me think there's hope for him. He can be so real at times. We talked about his life and I understand him more. He's a troubled man who really needs help."

"Maggie, when you talk like that I'm frightened for you."

"Mom, if it would make you feel better, let's look at the cards and see what they say."

It was a balmy night and Maggie had envisioned herself alone on the patio with a glass of wine and her memories of the evening. Instead, she heard the desperation in her mother's voice and decided that only by pacifying her would they both enjoy a good night's sleep.

"If you want to, it's okay with me." Her mother anxiously sat down at the table with the card deck.

Maggie cut the cards and pulled the first one toward her. She turned it over. It was the Tower.

"Oh, Maggie, what bedevilment have you gotten yourself into?"

"Mom, you know I'm as good at reading the Tarot as you are."

"It's the devil leading you by the nose."

"Oh, Mom, it means change, disruption of an old way of life, a moment of truth." Maggie regarded the card with a smile.

"It also represents a shocking revelation of some nature, and for you dear girl it can only mean trouble with Harry. It's the end of something you value unless you stop all these shenanigans."

"Mother, you're beginning to sound like Paul."

"And why not? Paul's a good man. He's someone who knows the difference between good and evil. He's not one to get you into trouble."

"Paul's my friend, Mother, nothing more."

"You've got a nice boyfriend and a nice job, Maggie, and the cards say you're jeopardizing it all for that scoundrel Harry."

"Mother, they say nothing of the sort. I've known Harry for seven years. Something's happened to change him. He's my boss but he's also a friend who needs help."

"You're typing his trash and acting like a voyeur, peeping into his vile world and Lord knows what else."

"Mom, it's not like a crime I can go to jail for. For heaven's sake I'm only doing a project for my boss."

"Don't try to justify your actions, Margaret Marie."

"What would you have me do? Leave him in the lurch?"

"Maggie, what's happened to Harry is not something that happened to him overnight. It's something that's been coming on for a long time but he hasn't paid any attention to it and a slip of a girl like you, who is both naïve and idealistic, can't possibly help him."

"Mom, you don't know him like I do. Since I started at WordTech it's been Harry who's trained me and supported my efforts. I won't deny I care a great deal about him," Maggie said, turning over another card. It was the Sun but inverted.

"There you are. If you weren't so smitten you'd be able to think clearly, Maggie. You're in for some dark days, my dearest."

"Mom, I hope you don't think I'm in love with Harry?"

"Aren't you? Look in the mirror."

"Let's finish the reading, Mom." Maggie turned over another card. "Strength, now there's a power card."

"And you'll need it to deal with him. He's underhanded, Maggie, and he's hiding something."

"Mom, he's tough like most business men today but no one will ever convince me that he's unethical."

"I don't know what more proof you need. You think you can help him get out of the black forest of his mind but he'll bedevil you before you even try."

"You know that card says I have the power to tame his wild nature," Maggie giggled.

"Maggie, stop joking. You're a good person but Harry's taking advantage of you. Even when you were little you went out of your way to pick up strays."

"Mother, Harry wouldn't use me. He needs me and besides he trusts me and I trust him."

"Dear God, you are in love with that jaded no account. He's nothing but a gigolo whose sated life has brought him nothing but misery, and misery loves company."

"Mom, you don't know anything about Harry. He's not like that."

"What do you really know about him, Maggie? You only work with him."

"That's right, Mom, and I'm his secretary, not his mistress."

"Must you talk like that? You're everything he's not, strong, principled and with a heart of gold. He's using you, mark my words. He sees you with Paul and he's determined to take you from him."

"Mom, my relationship with Harry isn't going to jeopardize my principles. And Harry has nothing to do with how I handle my love life. It's just that Paul and I are drifting apart."

"Be careful, dear, you're not just drifting, you're already treading into murky waters."

"Mom, I sincerely want to help Harry and I believe that deep within him there is a core of nobility. If I didn't know that for sure, I'd have given up on him long ago."

"It's a crime what a woman will do for love."

"Oh, Mother, I can't listen to this any longer. You're making this into a farcical melodrama. Harry's my friend and I won't let him down."

"Women and men can't be friends, Maggie. It always ends up with one or the other wanting more. You know what I mean."

"Mom, I'm getting upset and I don't want to say anything I'll be sorry for."

"All right, dear, just remember that I love you. Sweet dreams."

Maggie managed to keep her mother from seeing the tears spill down her checks as she climbed the stairs to her room. She needed a friend desperately. She needed to talk to someone who might understand her predicament. She punched in Leeann's cell number.

"Hi Leeann, it's Maggie, do you have a minute?" She sniffed into the phone as tears gush down her cheeks.

"What's going on with you, kid? Are you okay?"

"Listen, I don't want to talk on the phone. I know it's late but could we meet somewhere?"

"This sounds important. How about the Bella Luna, the coffee shop on Cedar Avenue off of Fourth Street? It's open all night."

"Yes, I've been there. Can we meet in half an hour?"

"Okay, I'll leave right now."

Bella Luna's dark interior was a throwback to the old coffeehouse era of the sixties. Great stuffed chairs and settees, mix-matched in paisley prints and wild colors, made for ample sitting room in the now smoke free building which still retained an intellectual atmosphere.

A colorful group of late night characters sat talking in far off corners while a few played chess or worked diligently on their laptops.

Maggie saw Leeann the moment she walked in. Reclining on an extra-large leather couch, she was propped up by a mauve pillow bigger than she was as she lounged at a table near the rear door.

"Hi, Leeann, you look comfortable." Maggie sat down and took off her coat as the waiter put down two steaming mugs and a basket of hot muffins.

"Maggie, I ordered you tea. The muffins are for me but go ahead and indulge."

"Great. Thanks for coming, Leeann. I needed to talk tonight. I don't know where else to turn." Maggie sipped at her hot tea after she buttered her muffin.

"What's happened? Is it Harry?"

"Why did you ask that?"

"Oh come on, Maggie. The way you two have been acting lately everyone knows something's up."

"I can't believe it."

"Listen, something sure has changed you in the last couple of months."

"What do you mean?" Maggie stopped eating and fixed her eyes on Leeann.

"Do you mind if I ask you a direct question?"

"Of course not, go ahead."

"Are you sleeping with Harry?"

"Sleeping with …no I'm not," Maggie retorted indignantly. "It has nothing to do with that."

"I'm sorry I asked. No, on second thought I'm not. At least it's out in the open."

"What's out in the open? What are you talking about?"

"It's just that everyone thought that you and Harry… ." Leeann's voice trailed off.

"He's my boss and I'm his assistant. There's nothing more to it."

"Okay, I believe you. What's the problem then?"

"I think Harry's having a nervous breakdown. I'm afraid for his mental health."

"Oh, is that all."

"Leeann, is that all you can say?"

"Listen, kid, Harry's crazy and it's about time you knew it."

"What are you talking about?"

"You poor thing, it's the executive assistants who are always the last to know. I tried to tell you about him so many times."

"Leeann, I can't tell you everything but Harry's in trouble."

"He's crazy like a fox and gets what he wants. Now he's got you."

"I don't believe you."

"That's your prerogative, Maggie. Just be careful. I don't know what Harry has gotten you to do for him but you're just a number in a long line of people. I hoped the day would never come when he turned on you but for some reason I kind of get the idea that it's happened."

"Harry isn't like that."

"Have you asked Paul?"

"You know about that?"

"Everyone at WordTech knows what Harry did to Paul."

"Are you talking about the budget scandal Paul accused Harry of?"

"No. It happened before that. I don't want to be an office gossip but Paul is a square guy who a lot of us think got a raw deal from Harry. Now it's Paul who's out for Harry's blood."

"Paul didn't tell me about anything except the budget situation."

"He didn't tell you about the stationery?"

"No."

"Paul used to worship Harry. You know Harry was his mentor. The two of them were like brothers."

"Paul told me they were friends."

"Sure, Harry hired Paul. Then for some reason Harry got suspicious of Paul. Paul was always playing cards with his cronies up in the lunch room and Harry heard something from someone about Paul talking out of turn about the department. Paul denied it but Harry wasn't buying. He wanted him to transfer out but Paul was stubborn so Harry rigged up a scheme to get him out."

"I don't believe it."

"You know the WordTech ruling on stationery?"

"Sure, Corporate's paranoid about it. It's not to be used for any purpose except WordTech business correspondence."

"That's it, and most managers and directors inform staff members early on, even warning them against using it for scratch paper."

"Yes, I'm aware of that."

"Paul was asked to do a report for Accounting listing marketing contacts whose bills were due in the next business cycle. According to Paul, Harry directed him to make all his notes on WordTech stationery because Harry wanted to see what info he was taking out of the department."

"So? What happened?"

"Hold on, I'm getting there. Paul, without thinking, keeps the notes instead of giving them to Harry and takes them out of the department. Inadvertently, one of the accountants found them and considered them suspicious. He showed them to his supervisor and they called Paul in. It was an innocent mistake."

"Why didn't Paul ask Harry to explain what happened?"

"He did. He went to Harry and asked him to clarify the situation to Accounting."

"What happened then?"

"Harry wrote Paul up for not following procedures. That was it."

"In other words he didn't stand up for him?"

"Well, let's put it this way. It didn't get Paul fired but it put him at odds with Harry. He was lucky when a spot opened up in Accounting and he transferred. That's when he started researching Harry's travel budget."

"So Paul survived."

"Yes, but to hear Paul tell it, it was in no way thanks to Harry. Paul never forgave him."

"Paul took a petty grievance and built it into a big grudge against Harry?"

"Paul's smart and supervisors like him. He's been careful ever since and has made friends in high places, which annoys the hell out of Harry. They hate each other's guts. When Paul took Harry to the carpet for the Marketing expense accounts, that blew Harry's mind."

"Yes, he told me."

"Paul wants to destroy Harry and Harry wants to do the same thing to him."

"They act like two overgrown school boys. What about you, Leeann? How's your relationship with Harry?"

"Oh, Harry and I have had our ins and outs through the years. He made life pretty miserable for me at one point but then I forgave Harry and moved on."

"If you don't mind my asking, what did Harry do to you?"

"It sounds trivial now but when it first happened I was devastated. First of all, before I tell you this story, I've got to tell you that I play the ponies."

"Yes, Leeann, word's got around," Maggie smiled reassuringly.

"With that said, about ten years ago I had to take time off to get some medical attention. I don't want to go into details but it was a woman thing. My doctor decided that Fridays would be good days for the procedure and I was to take a couple hours off in the afternoon. I had plenty of sick time so I put through all the paperwork. Harry signed off and HR approved it. Well, to make a long story short, it was painful and for three Friday afternoons I didn't come back into the office but added the sick time to my timecard. Harry called me in and asked why I hadn't returned. He told me that someone had reported seeing me at the track on those Friday afternoons."

"Of course it wasn't true."

"No it wasn't, and I denied it but Harry told me he'd prefer that I take sick time in the morning on another day. He said it would look better for the department and for me. He told me not to make further trouble and if I didn't do as he requested he as much as said he wouldn't keep me in the department. He told me to let him know when the appointment had been changed and when I asked him who had told him that story, he said he wasn't at liberty to say. I asked him why he didn't believe me and he said he didn't want to get into it. He dismissed me like it had been my fault."

"Then what happened?"

"For awhile he watched he like a hawk, waiting I think for me to trip up. When I didn't, he turned pretty cool toward me but kept his distance. That was better than being on my case."

"Why didn't you go to HR and tell them?"

"What could I have said? Harry was in the right. I've seen what happens when you go behind his back. He's like Velcro. He sticks to you and watches everything you do. That's what happened to Paul. He couldn't talk to anyone or do anything without Harry knowing what he was up to. Harry used it for a write up on his PA and he does it to anyone he thinks has crossed him. Paul was just lucky to get out from underneath him."

"You're saying Harry acts like an Orwellian big brother."

"I am? Well, anyway, I let go of the situation and decided not to make a big deal out of it. I like my job and I want my retirement. Since I could change the appointment, I did. I'm okay with Harry because I know that what he believed was a lie about me but it hurts that he believed it. He didn't trust me anymore but then I don't trust him either."

"Who do you suppose told him such a ghastly lie? And why would they do it?"

"It was obviously someone in the department he did trust but I could never figure out who it was."

"You said he's done things to other people?"

"Yes, if you go back far enough into the department's history you can rake up a lot of dirt. Things happened back then. They were probably similar to what happened to me. Whoever was his snitch really caused a lot of trouble and Harry went along with it, never bothering to unearth the truth."

"In other words, he had the last word." Maggie looked dejected.

"Yes and still does. Maggie, don't let Harry paint you into a corner. He's good at that. There are those of us who experienced it first hand."

"Are you telling me not to trust Harry?"

"No not exactly. I know you and Harry have a good relationship. I know you're above board and very professional. Everybody respects you. Harry counts on you for so many things and that puts you in an important position at WordTech. I just wanted you to know."

"My mother said something tonight about my not really knowing Harry. Perhaps she's right. What you and Paul have told me makes me even more curious about Harry. I've got to find out more about him."

"Geez Maggie, why would you want to do that?"

"I can't explain it, Leeann, but it's something I've got to do."

"If I can help just let me know."

"Thanks, Leeann. I may take you up on that offer."

Maggie looked into her cup and inhaled the fragrance of the herbal tea. She drank the brew, grateful for the chance to finally unwind.

"I bet you'd love to have your tea leaves read right about now, huh, Mag?" Leeann laughed as she finished off another muffin.

Chapter 10

The next morning Maggie waited anxiously for Harry to come into the office. When he didn't show up and hadn't telephoned, she called his cell phone. There was no answer and she didn't leave a message. She arranged his schedule and made a few appointments for later in the week. She was about to sit down and begin a new marketing proposal when Paul walked into her office and placed a cup of tea on her desk.

"Hi, I'm bringing you a peace offering."

"Paul, you're a lifesaver. I can really use this right now."

"Where's Harry?"

"Working as usual," Maggie's voice was guarded.

"Covering for him, again?"

"What are you talking about, Paul?"

"I think you know."

"Listen, Paul, maybe you don't have anything to do, but I have. You'll excuse me if I cut this conversation short."

"I'm glad someone's working."

"Really, Paul, that's how ugly rumors get started. After all Harry's my boss and deserves respect."

"Boss, respect, somehow I don't associate those words with Harry."

"You know, Paul, poison is a funny thing. It attacks the entity who premeditates the revenge."

"There you go getting on your high horse again. Revenge is a strong word, Maggie. Now who's starting ugly rumors?"

"I had tea with Leeann last night and she told me about the stationery incident."

"So what? I'm not the only one Harry's hammered on. I'm just looking for the skeletons in his closet."

"Doesn't that take time out of your work day?"

"You're starting to sound like Harry. Don't let him drag you down with him, Maggie. He'll destroy anyone that gets in his way, even someone as lovely as you."

"Paul, I realize you had trouble with Harry but projecting what happened to you onto others isn't fair."

"Not to change the subject but I guess our date's off Saturday?"

"Our date's on but only if we don't talk about Harry."

"Okay, from now on the subject's taboo. Pick you up at seven?"

Maggie nodded and headed into Harry's office but turned back just in time to see Paul walking over to the water cooler. He didn't take a drink but stood there waiting, almost as though he were watching her reflection in the glass framed picture hanging above the machine.

Is it my imagination or is he deliberately stalling and taking time to watch me? I won't have these doubts and menacing suspicions creeping into my mind, especially since Leeann's conversation added a new twist to the situation.

She unlocked Harry's desk drawer. There were only two more notebooks left. Did this mean the project was nearing completion or had Harry taken the day off to fill up a few more intimately suggestive narratives. She waited for late afternoon to begin typing. She had to force herself to start. She wished the whole thing were over, or that Harry had at least taken a partial copy of the iniquitous manual to his doctor.

Once she began to work, however, she noticed how quickly

she was in the thick of it again. Harry's writing held a strange fascination and her involvement in his intriguing descriptions won out, particularly with his again mentioning KM.

Everything I do, I do too much. Therefore, it goes without saying that a man of excess needs a woman of excess. Together they can scale the walls of pleasure to new heights. KM called tonight. It's on again.

The KM reference, what could it mean? That's a puzzle I'd like to solve. I've checked his e-mail address list without any luck. Harry, if any of your friends realized you were writing about them they'd have a fit and don't think I don't recognize the names of some of your old acquaintances. I hope I don't run out of name changes. Even I'm an alias. Oh boy, another entry on me? Harry, can't you leave me alone. These sidebar excursions are wearing me down.

Even as she said it, Maggie could not stop her eyes from scouring the passage.

In prayer one remembers. I worry what these thoughts will do to Maggie. Lately I can't keep her out of my mind. I've succumbed to her charms. She has reawakened my temptations. She is such a beautiful woman and I wonder what it would be like to be with her. Agonizing bliss; both forbidden and fully indulged.

My Madonna; my woman of desire, you are beyond the likes of me. It's best I keep you on a pedestal rather than debase you with the crudeness of longing from one such as myself. You are principled and above reproach and I fear destroying our relationship if I degrade it. Will you see me as the evil one? With you, could I become Dr. Jeckel and destroy Mr. Hyde? Can people change? Perhaps not, especially when they have gone too far over the edge and no one hears them calling out in their frightened loneliness. Please don't hate me forever my Maggie. I kiss below your breast, and one lower down, and still another, much lower!

Should I laugh or cry? This ruse isn't going to work Harry. These entries are simply pushing me away. It's not fair or right of you to bring me into your sexually exploitive fantasies. I need to remain objective and not allow myself to steep like a teabag in a pot of emotional hot water. The curtain has rung down on you Harry, old boy, and you haven't missed a cue but my survival means distancing myself from your lurid imaginings and wishful desires.

Maggie heard the phone ringing on Harry's private line and went into his office to pick up the receiver.

"WordTech, Mr. Cooke's office."

"Hello, Maggie. You always sound so professional, dear. It's Ellen. Is Harry there?"

"No, Ellen. He isn't in. Is there anything I can do?"

There was a long silence at the other end.

"Is everything all right, Ellen?"

"Yes, of course, Maggie. I need to speak to Harry. Do you have any idea when he'll be returning?"

"He should be in first thing in the morning."

"Could you ask him to ring me?"

"Of course, Ellen. Is there anything I can do to help?"

"No, dear, but…wait a minute. Is it possible you could meet me for lunch tomorrow?"

"Sure Ellen, if you'd like to."

"Can we meet at twelve? Do you know the Trocadero? It's downtown on Quince Street."

"Yes, Ellen. I'll see you there at noon."

By anyone's standards, the ex-Mrs. Harry Cooke was a beauty. Her peaches and cream complexion was crowned by a shock of carrot-colored hair piled high on top of her head. Petite and regally adorned in expensive jewelry, she stood out in a dusty-gold silk pantsuit that clung to her like eel skin. She was holding court with the Maître d' and a waiter when Maggie arrived.

"Maggie, darling, I hope you like vichyssoise. It's to die for here at Trocadero's." Ellen's smile was radiant with anticipation.

"It sounds delicious, Ellen." Maggie, her hopes for a small Cobb salad having faded with Ellen's revelation of cold potato-leek soup, lied outright.

"What kind of wine would you like, Maggie?" Ellen perused the wine list under the guidance of the Maître d' and eventually decided on a bottle of Pinot Noir.

"None for me, Ellen, I'd be asleep before I got back to my office. A glass of ice tea, please."

After the Maître d' left the table Ellen went right on with a conversation she had apparently started with herself before Maggie arrived. "Depression can be a terrible thing and I've exacerbated mine with alcohol. It's positively tormenting, darling. Why does poor Ellen do it? Because as painful as it may be indulging in the hair of the dog, it does make one feel better, doesn't it?"

"Self-prescribing can be unwise, Ellen," Maggie cautioned.

"Maggie dear, there are times when you can be so tiresome. Let's get down to brass tacks. I know you didn't want to get together for lunch to discuss the whys and wherefores of how I numb my pain. Suffice to say I know you're as anxious to talk about Harry as I am. I could hear it in your voice when I called the office."

"Harry didn't come in this morning. It's the third time in two weeks. I'm worried about him, Ellen. He's been acting strange lately."

"Harry is strange. He's a wonderful guy, but he's also a rat, a strange rat but a rat just the same."

"You don't sound very concerned, Ellen."

"Frankly, Maggie, I'm not."

The Maître d' brought Ellen the wine, displayed the label and opened the bottle in front of them. Ellen tasted the small amount he put into her wine glass and nodded approvingly. As he poured the wine Ellen reached over and held his hand down on the bottle. The wine glass was filled to the brim within seconds.

"Superb, as usual, Maurice," Ellen gave the Maître d' a long, sensual smile.

Maggie turned over her wine glass when he carried the bottle to her side of the table smiling flirtatiously.

"No thank you."

"Is there anything more the Mesdames wish?" The Maître d's decidedly French accent gave him a continental charm that Maggie was sure most women found very attractive.

"Yes, Maurice." Ellen gulped her wine glass empty and batted her eyes playfully while he refilled it.

"Very good, Madam," Maurice intoned as he corked the bottle and placed it back on the table in front of Ellen before departing.

"There's no use chilling it—I prefer it at arm's length and I tip him handsomely for the personal service," Ellen gushed.

"Ellen, I only have an hour. What is it you want to discuss?"

"If you're thinking this will loosen old Ellen's tongue, you're correct." Ellen poured more wine into her glass. "I always feel better talking about Harry when I'm intoxicated. Let's get down to facts. How long has Harry gone missing this time?"

"Missing?" Maggie looked down at the tablecloth and fiddled with her fork.

"Don't be cagy, Maggie. Stalling for time will do you absolutely no good. It doesn't become you. You're much too honest for that kind of reticence."

"Ellen, I have reason to believe that Harry is suffering from nervous exhaustion. Lately, he's hardly ever in the office and when he does come in he can barely work. His mood vacillates from that of a tyrant to a wishy-washy schoolboy."

"Have you been covering for him?"

"Yes, but it can't go on indefinitely. Do you have any idea what's going on with him?"

"Harry is a complex person to begin with and the combination of alcohol and sex can send anyone over the edge."

"Is Harry into sex?"

"All men are into sex, darling."

"I mean more so than most."

"Maggie, Harry has always been into sex, big time. If you're asking me has he a sexual addiction, I'd have to say I don't know for sure. Harry has a compulsive, driving need for sexual contact. It destroyed our marriage. By the look of it I'd say it was destroying his work life and his ability to function. However, I'd think a doctor would be a better judge than I."

"Strange you should say that, Ellen. Harry has told me he is seeing a doctor. Well, not exactly seeing a doctor but in the process of seeking therapy."

"That doesn't sound like Harry. Even when we had trouble with our relationship, Harry refused to see a counselor. He wanted highs every time we had sex and that was something I couldn't provide. When he started using his seven inches of heaven to seek out other havens of refuge, our sex life eventually became nonexistent, ending what had been a grand relationship. Yes, I can honestly say we had it all, anger, communication problems and a total lack of trust, particularly on my part. Everything combined to sever the connection and I filed for divorce."

"If you don't mind my asking, why did you divorce Harry?"

"Why, I just told you. Harry's a cheat."

"Yes, but he cheated on you before you ever considered divorce."

"Very discerning of you, sweets, and my how rumors get around. It's true though, but I will say in Harry's defense that even when he was cheating he was more man than a lot of others. There's something innately soft and gentle about Harry, as though, hidden under that rough exterior of his, there's a guy that wants to understand."

"There's nothing stronger in the world than gentleness."

"You're right, Maggie. It was that quality of Harry's that stood out amongst all the others. God knows he had his faults but every now and then there were flashes of what I thought was the real Harry. Poor guy though, he couldn't sustain it, at least not in that area." Ellen laughed at her own joke.

"Perhaps he made those decisions out of loneliness." Maggie couldn't think of any words that would make Ellen's pain less hurtful.

"Well, whatever it was, in the end he went back to being a bastard. I was left to my own devices to find meaning in my life. A girl can only hope for so long. When he didn't or couldn't change, I did. I wasn't the faithful little wife any longer. Harry probably told you that it was my fault. I was the one who wanted us to live different lives. My only excuse is that I got tired of waiting for him to change back into the Harry I married."

"Ellen, perhaps we better eat our lunch."

"You eat, Maggie. I'm taking in my own sustenance. Besides, the soup's cold." Ellen snorted loudly.

"It's delicious," Maggie said, genuinely impressed.

"Told you it was good, but anyway, where were we...," Ellen slurred but continued on unabated. "Oh yes, Maggie, suffice to say it would be impossible to maintain the levels of excitement Harry demanded and get anything else done. Harry wanted the all consuming sexual intimacy we had when we were first married. With my biological clock ticking like crazy, I wanted a relationship on a deeper level of commitment. I wanted children. Unfortunately, Harry didn't."

"You wanted children?"

"Yes, I wanted a home, not a brothel."

"You make it sound as though Harry was interested in you for only one reason."

"Oh, then let me make it very clear. It finally got to where Harry wasn't interested in me as a person at all. It took me a long time but I finally figured it out. Harry was only interested in his own satisfaction." Ellen's slurring was getting worse.

"Are you saying Harry's not capable of loving?"

"No, I'm just saying it's not his main interest."

"But you said he loved you."

"It was so long ago I'm really not sure anymore if it was ever really love," Ellen sipped at her drink. "Why the personal questions, Maggie? Oh, no, don't tell me Harry's done the unthinkable and made a pass at you, the stalwart and loyal Ms. Reynolds?" Ellen put her hand over her mouth and giggled uncontrollably.

"Ellen, regardless of what you think, I believe Harry needs help. Any addiction warrants assistance."

"You're a braver girl than I, Maggie. I put up with Harry's whims and indiscretions for far too long. Now I've got to get my own ship seaworthy." Ellen hiccupped. "As you can see, it's no easy task. But don't count old Ellen out yet. I may be having a devil of a time, but eventually I'll get over him."

"Is there any chance you and Harry could get back together?"

"Are you kidding? As a matter of fact, I've petitioned my church to have the marriage annulled."

"Ellen, I know he loves you very much."

"You're sweet, Maggie. Passion, however, rides a mad horse and although I am still madly in love with Harry I realize that my only salvation lies in getting as far away from him as I can."

"Knowing how you feel about him, Ellen, why did you want to see Harry?"

"Because my dear, some habits are hard to break."

Chapter 11

"Maggie, have I got news for you!"

"I hope it's good, Leeann. I could sure use some after our swim team lost tonight," Maggie reported as she lay sprawled across her bed.

"Sorry to hear that Mag and after your little guys worked so hard but I think I can cheer you up. I ran across an old WordTech retiree list and a name from the past popped out at me. Hoppy Dixon. He was Harry's supervisor at WordTech years ago."

"Harry's supervisor," Maggie repeated, sitting up. "Do you have any idea where he is now?"

"He's living at the Valley View Retirement Home in Mount Abby."

"Is he that old?"

"Well, he's got to be at least seventy or seventy-five."

"Talk about timing, Leeann. I was just hoping to find a lead on Harry and you come up with this windfall."

"Glad to be of help, kid."

"I'll call up there and see if I can visit with Mr. Dixon tomorrow. Maybe he can answer some questions I have about Harry's past."

"Good luck, Maggie. Keep me posted."

"Thanks, Leeann. See you Monday."

Maggie drove out of town early Saturday morning. She ignored a call from Paul. He sounded enthusiastic and invited her to an early morning run but she didn't feel like making excuses. It was a perfect fall day and Maggie rolled down the windows and breathed in the country air. The wind rushed across her face and tousled her hair as the car sped northward. Tiny wisps of memory floated pleasantly into her mind and she allowed them to linger, savoring the moments as they bubbled to the surface.

For the longest time I thought I was in love with Paul but now I think I was in love with the idea. Paul and I have taken a long time to consider committing to a relationship of any permanence and now I know it's something I don't want. Why is it every time I close my eyes Harry's always there. I guess it's because he's so much in my life. I'm not even sure how I feel about him. He's reawakened my longing heart and I want those delicious stirrings but that's not something you can build a relationship on. He's not someone I can give in to and I'll have to be satisfied to linger in memory on the edge of ecstasy. Poor Paul, I'm being so unfair to him. Paul is peace and Harry is chaos. My feelings for Harry need sorting out. Until I can understand, I will not allow my emotions to make decisions for me.

Abruptly the sign indicating Mount Abbey came into view and Maggie refocused. Concentrating on her mission, she watched for the road signs that signaled the home's approach following the directions she had been given earlier that morning by Mrs. Kemper, the cordial administrator of Valley View. She seemed happy to arrange a visit for Mr. Dixon who apparently hadn't had a visitor for quite some time.

Crossing the old Santucket Bridge, Maggie saw the entrance as promised. She turned off the road and onto a mile long curvy drive which meandered up an incline past a pine grove. Through the trees she saw the massive three-story red brick home. It was surrounded by broad avenues of lawn, clipped shrubbery and a profusion of flowers in neatly tended beds. Two mature oak trees stood guard in front of the gracious, white shuttered manor house that was clearly the center of the property. It was a beautiful place in a park-like setting, replete with benches, tables and over-sized umbrellas.

As Maggie parked in the visitors' area she was aware that there was no one outside to enjoy the beauty of the facility's gardens. She walked up the steps and noticed the sign hanging above the great, wooden double doors, "Please ring for service." The brilliantly colored stained glass windows had obscured the figure that came into the entryway but within a few minutes a tall, pleasant faced matron dressed in a white, crisply-starched uniform opened the door.

"Miss Reynolds, I presume? I'm Mrs. Kemper, Director of Valley View," her voice a virtual whisper.

"Thank you for allowing my visit, Mrs. Kemper."

"Why of course, my dear. We're happy our guests have visitors. Mr. Dixon is expecting you. We told him of your visit and he was quite happy. He's on the back veranda and has just finished his snack. Please come with me."

Maggie followed Mrs. Kemper through the house which was tastefully furnished in early American furniture. Historical paintings hung from the walls and expensive statuary depicting important events in American history was in evidence along the carpeted hallways. It was unlike any nursing home Maggie had ever seen and she thought that to be old and retired at Valley View would not be an unpleasant experience.

"We have only a select group of guests here at Valley View. We like to think of it as a vacation retreat rather than a retirement home."

"It's beautiful. It's so quiet and restful."

"Yes, our guests' needs are our first priority. They want a home that offers all the amenities but caters to an environment of privacy and peacefulness." For a moment it sounded as though Mrs. Kemper was offering a tour to a perspective client.

Outside on the tiled patio a variety of potted plants and

meandering morning glory created an attractive convergence around and up the portico. Large blue umbrellas sheltered a dozen round tables and chairs that were occupied by a variety of well-dressed senior citizens. An old gentleman, dwarfed under a huge, white Stetson, eyed them from across the pool. He struggled to sit up straight as they approached his chair.

"Hoppy, Miss Reynolds is here to see you." Mrs. Kemper fluffed the pillow behind Mr. Dixon's back.

"Thank you, Mabel." Hoppy grinned at Mrs. Kemper.

"Miss Reynolds, would you like a refreshment, coffee or tea?" Mrs. Kemper removed a tray with half empty dishes from the table but left the glass of ice tea in front of Mr. Dixon.

"No thank you, Mrs. Kemper." Maggie sat down next to Hoppy and watched as Mrs. Kemper made her way to several of the other tables.

"Hi Mr. Dixon, I'm Maggie Reynolds." Maggie took the feeble hand in hers and held it for a few minutes.

"Howdy, and welcome to the ranch, young lady." Hoppy doffed his hat revealing a remarkably shiny bald head. "Call me Hoppy."

"Hi, Hoppy," Maggie dutifully complied.

"Know how I got the moniker Hoppy?" The small, squinting eyes beneath the brim of the cowboy hat were surprisingly animated.

"Are you any relation to the cowboy star, Hopalong Cassidy?"

"Well dag nabbit, if that don't beat all. You're quite a surprise, Miss Reynolds."

"Please, call me Maggie."

"Well, how would someone as young as you know about an old timer like Hopalong? That's before your time, young lady." Hoppy's laugh was interrupted by a coughing spell.

"My father was a great fan of westerns. I grew up knowing names like Roy Rogers, Bill Elliott and Lash LaRue. I still watch cowboy movies on the western channel."

"Doggone it if that ain't something. My first name is Boyd and William Boyd was the original Hopalong Cassidy. My dad bought me a white cowboy hat when I was twelve years old. I kept the tradition and always wore a white hat. People got to calling me Hoppy." He rambled on, smiling through a perfect set of dentures.

"I work at WordTech, Hoppy and …"

"WordTech, Inc.," Hoppy interrupted. "Boy, does that name bring up old memories. It was a great company. I put in thirty-five years there. I retired as the Marketing Director. Yep, that was a great place to work. I started as a salesman when I was twenty-four but the one thing about WordTech was that if you knew your stuff they promoted you fast. What department do you work in, Maggie?"

"I'm an executive assistant in Marketing. I work for Harry Cooke."

"Harry? Do you mean Harry Cooke is still at WordTech?"

"Yes, he's the Marketing Director." Maggie was impressed with the old gentleman's memory.

"Why that son-of-a-gun." He slapped his thigh and laughed. "Do you like working for Harry, Maggie?"

"Yes, I do. He's a great boss. He's taught me so much and has given me a great deal of responsibility."

"Yep, that sounds like old Harry. He's a great guy. A little heavy handed with the bottle but only on weekends mind you. I never knew him to drink during the work week. On Mondays he'd come in ready and rare'n to work."

"Do you suppose his drinking had anything to do with his mother being an alcoholic and his father a gambler?"

"Shucks, as I recollect it Harry's father was a highly respected engineer but he was killed in some kind of accident. His mother, God bless her, couldn't hardly stand it and I think she died soon after."

"Really," Maggie was stunned.

"His maiden aunt, a real teetotaler, raised him. The house was prohibitionist dry and he told me he used to sneak drinks with his friends. Harry made it tough on anyone he felt had wronged him and from what I gather he was pretty rough on the old lady."

"Do you mean to say Harry was an orphan?"

"Harry's quite a liar, isn't he? I can tell by the sound of your voice and the look on your pretty face. I'd say you're just now finding that out." Hoppy snickered. "He's good though, you've got to give him that. You never know how Harry'll twist a story. I use to get a kick out of hearing him wangle his way out of something by making up a yarn. You'd know he was lying but you'd wonder just where he was go'in, and what he would make up along the way. By golly, he was good."

"I'm just beginning to realize how good."

"But, I can see in your eyes it won't make one bit of difference to you."

"Hoppy didn't Harry's storytelling affect his reputation at WordTech?" Maggie wished she had brought her notebook.

"Nope, Harry never let anyone or anything bother him, in particular the higher-ups at WordTech. If he heard that someone had spread something about him, he'd let it roll like water off a duck's back. It didn't matter what anyone said, he'd ignore it. Anyway, most everyone liked Harry. He had a way about him, you know what I mean?"

"Yes, I think I do."

"Don't get me wrong. Harry did get into some kind of sticky situation and a few people knew about it."

"Was there anyone you'd remember back then who would have been involved in the incident you're talking about?"

"Well, even though mostly everybody liked him they still got angry with the big guy. That's how it works in business. You make a lot of friends but a whole lot more enemies. There was a woman who worked at WordTech for a couple of years in our department. She had some sort of run-in with Harry. I think she worked for him but it's been so long I don't remember the details."

"What was she like?"

"She was pretty but down-right sassy and that changed her look if you know what I mean. She wasn't friendly to anyone but Harry. There was something about her I didn't like. I don't remember too much but I know she left not long after the skirmish started."

"Do you recall her name?"

"What was her name?" Hoppy seemed to draw his memories from a distant database. "Kate something... . Kate, my memory ain't as good as it used to be. She was something though."

"What do you mean?"

"You know, independent, outspoken. A lot like Harry."

"Didn't they get on?"

"I never said that. In my opinion they were in cahoots. Harry was just about the brightest kid I ever saw but he was inclined to be over imaginative, you know, way out in left field. There were times when I think he had trouble focusing on reality. Off the wall I think the kids say. On one or two occasions I got worried about him. I think that Kate woman had something to do with Harry's acting out."

"I don't understand. What was going on between them?"

"Maggie, you'd have to talk to her or ask Harry. I don't sweat the small stuff anymore. Besides, we all knew Harry was quirky. We just thought it was because of his drinking. He wasn't the only guy to overwork and over drink. That combination is lethal. It was probably what wrecked his marriages, at least the first one."

"Marriages?" Maggie thought she had misunderstood.

"From what I heard he walked out on his first wife. Nobody knew much about her. Her name was Jenny and I think they were just too young to get married, especially Harry, who was a born ladies' man. Women just naturally wanted to protect him but I guess

Jenny finally had enough and left him. I think they had a daughter, yep, I'm sure they did. Then there was Ellen Carstairs. I don't know how he got a great gal like Ellen to marry him but then Harry's a real likable guy. They sure loved each other."

"Unfortunately they've just divorced."

"It would be just like Harry to do that to Ellen but I bet she still loves him."

"What do you mean, Hoppy?"

"Well, even after he put the screws to me, I still liked him, and do to this very day."

"Hoppy, what did Harry do to you?"

"Harry was always in a hurry. He wanted my job so badly he couldn't wait for me to retire."

"Hoppy, did Harry force you out of your job?"

"Well, let's put it this way. I was planning on retirement in a year or two but Harry hurried the process. Me and the Mrs. planned on going down to Florida early and as it turned out I was on the links a couple years before I planned it. But it worked out seeing that she died not long after. I have to thank old Harry for those extra years we had together."

"How did Harry get you out early?"

"One day I got a call from Corporate to come upstairs. Who do you suppose was sitting in the office with Bert Conroy, the CEO of WordTech at the time?"

"Harry?"

"Yep, big as life, the two of them, sitting together real chummy like, laughing and talking. I didn't think anything of it at first but when Bert showed me a stack of contracts with my signature and told me I had overestimated several projects, I looked at Harry. He looked at me and smiled. We both knew whose projects they were but it was my signature that counted. Harry sure as hell wasn't taking the fall. I was expendable. I got the golden handshake."

"Did Harry set you up?"

"Not really. It was my responsibility. Harry was right about that. I had overestimated the costs and made the mistakes but instead of coming to me he went upstairs. That's what hurt."

"Why did he do it?"

"Harry was always looking out for number one. He's tenacious like a spider weaving a web. He takes his time and adds the threads slowly. He doesn't make mistakes. Once you get caught in Harry's web it's pretty much over. Besides, Harry was next in line for promotion. After all, I hired him. He just got tired of waiting."

"What was he like when you hired him?"

"Boy, howdy, he was nothing but a youngster who'd just graduated from college. No real experience except for the gift of gab and a knack for making money. He could sure tell a tale, a lot like me. I guess that's why I took a liking to him. I trained him in every aspect of the business. He'd absorbed information like a sponge and could apply it to business deals like a wheeler-dealer. He was good at making money for the company. I loved him like a son. Even after it happened I still couldn't be angry with him. That's why I can't understand why he doesn't visit me once in a while."

"Hoppy, couldn't you have spoken to the CEO?"

"What would have been the point? It would only have meant a lot of ugly words, corporate lawyers, personnel issues and deposition meetings to determine culpability. I didn't want any of it. It was time for me to step down and it was time for Harry to step up. Corporate wanted him in that position. He was well trained. I saw to that. Besides, it just meant more time for relaxation and I was ready to get out."

"Do you think Harry should be in a position of such responsibility?"

"Oh, Harry's okay. People expect that sort of thing in the

corporate world. He's no different than a lot of other guys. Big fish eat little fish. Harry's a climber even if it's over dead bodies. He's like a velvet glove; you don't even realize he's screwing you until it's over. Sorry if that sounds crude, Maggie, but it's the truth."

"That doesn't make it right."

"No, but the business world can be pretty cut-throaty."

"Yes, Hoppy, I've already found that out. It's seems to be the old question of does the end justify the means? Some of today's executives are as unethical as those in the past."

"Judging by the media and newspapers maybe even more so," Hoppy chuckled.

"I'm beginning to feel that strength of character is no longer an attribute for a great many people. It's a shame the world cannot see that honesty never produces bad results."

"Greed's a pretty hard vice to stifle, Maggie. And now days, men and women have to search harder for the hidden justice that regulates their lives. Most of them become just finger pointers, blaming others for their failures. You only have to look at the politicians to see they don't give a hoot about the people they represent. They're more concerned about their individual parties and who's going to win what election. They don't respect the president and they sure don't want to work together for the good of the majority. I'd sure like to see them come together and make a difference for a change. But don't get me started on politics," Hoppy laughed.

"You're a man after my own heart, Hoppy. It's getting late though and I'd better say good-bye. Thanks for letting me come and talk with you." Maggie got up to leave but Hoppy touched her hand.

"You be careful, young lady, it's a jungle out there."

"I'll remember, Hoppy."

"Maggie, come visit me again, won't you? You've been a real tonic to an old geezer. Harry's lucky to have you on his team. Be careful of that whippersnapper though. Harry has a way about him and it kind of sneaks up on you. Before you know it you either hate him or love him." Hoppy winked in Maggie's direction.

"I'll watch my back, partner." Maggie bent down and kissed Hoppy on the cheek.

"Hey, when you see Harry, tell him to visit me. Tell him I still love him and anything that happened is water under the bridge. Tell him the old man misses him and the good-old days."

"I'll tell him, Hoppy."

Hoppy lifted his glass toward Maggie. "Here's my special toast to you, pretty lady. Course you understand I used to have a lot more than tea in my glass, but anyway, here's to an eagle in your pocket, an old crow in your glass and a turkey on your plate."

"I liked that, Hoppy, and I'll remember it. Thank you."

"Till I see you again, Miss Maggie, take care."

Chapter 12

Driving back to the city Maggie's thoughts were of Harry. Hoppy's revelations about him had unearthed information that for the first time fostered doubts about the man she held in such high regard.

I've never had any reason to distrust Harry. I believed him to be principled and above-board. Ever since I started at WordTech he's been the person I've looked up to. I hate having these misgiving, but Harry's behavior on a whole is disturbing. Just hearing what Hoppy had to say makes me suspicious. That's why I need to find out everything before I draw any conclusions. I'm starting to act like a private detective. I hope I don't run into any trouble but I could sure use a clue or two. I remember Ellen saying that only a physician would be able to offer a diagnosis on Harry's condition. The first place to start is with a qualified specialist and I know just the person, Dr. Clare Sebastian.

Maggie first met Clare after registering for evening classes at the local community college. That was the year she graduated from high school and got her first secretarial job. Although her plan did not include returning to school on a full time basis, she liked the idea of taking courses that either piqued her interest or moved her closer to her goal of administrative assistant in a Fortune 500 company.

There were two courses that fall fitting the first criteria. One in art history taught by a young graduate student and the other an advanced psychology class, 'Literature and the Abnormal Personality' with Clare as the instructor. Maggie decided on both classes.

Clare Sebastian had been a practicing psychiatric physician in Europe years before she came to the college but as both faculty and students acknowledged she was a born teacher. Speaking with a modest German accent, Clare projected a deep resonating voice that clearly and dramatically described obsessive compulsive, schizophrenic and other disorders. The stocky-framed professor had no problem holding the attention of the class as she detailed the characteristics of each disorder, identifying the different types of abnormalities and the psychological implications associated with each disease, exhaustively comparing them to the portraits drawn in literature by Dostoevsky, Balzac, Hugo and others. Her zealous students, fascinated by the stories of human relationships and the havoc mental illness created in the life of each character, monopolized her time both in and out of the classroom.

Maggie recalled how on one particular evening she had seen the professor sitting alone in the cafeteria correcting papers and realized it was a perfect opportunity to talk to Dr. Sebastian personally. Looking back, she realized that neither she nor Clare was aware that the little exchange they shared that night would grow into a firm and steadfast friendship.

"Good evening, Dr. Sebastian, I'm Maggie Reynolds. I'm in your Psychology 310 class. Would it be all right to talk to you for a few minutes?" Maggie knew she was gushing but was unable to prevent her nervousness from showing.

"Yes, of course, Maggie, please sit down. I know very well who you are. I find your observations quite insightful and I appreciate the comments you make during class. We are outside the classroom, so please, call me Clare."

"Thank you, Professor, Clare, ... I know I'm not the only student who sits riveted to my chair when you describe those hidden areas of the mind but I wanted you to know how much I enjoy the class and how much I'm benefitting from your lectures."

"Thank you for your feedback. A teacher always appreciates hearing from one's students."

"Dr. Clare, you're so gifted. You're a practicing physician in your own clinic and a teacher here at the college. I envy your giving so much of yourself to mankind; healing patients and sharing your knowledge with us college kids. You inspire people with courage, confidence and ideals, something I'd love to do. I think it's so very important to use one's talents to help others."

"That is nice of you to say, Maggie. I find your candor refreshing but don't make me sound so magnanimous. After all, I am only putting my principles into practice. As my late husband Frederick used to say, it's the kind of giving that keeps boredom out and satisfaction in," Clare said, smiling at the memory.

"Professor Clare, that's exactly my point. I believe we have an obligation to leave this world a better place than we found it and you're doing just that." Maggie's praise was unrestrained with youthful exuberance.

"That is quite an observation and between the two of us I admit it is true." Clare smiled unassumingly.

"My father told me that our principles are driven by our purpose in life and it's up to us to hold them firm."

"Your father sounds like a very wise man."

"Yes, he was a teacher, too. He died when I was ten."

"I am sorry to hear of your loss but you were fortunate to have had such guidance. Now, what is it you wish to discuss this evening?"

"Professor, I've a strong belief in affirmations which has led me to an interest in Alfred Adler's philosophy. It seems to me that Adler's belief in the intrinsic motivation of the individual coincides with our life's objectives. The readings I've done on his theory regarding creative power convince me that affirmations achieve power in the same way."

"I'm impressed with your research but your use of the word affirmations is from a source other than Adler, yes?"

"Yes, but I believe his philosophy dovetails into the positive use of affirmations."

"I would be interested in seeing some of the sources you used to form that hypothesis. It is true that Adler believed that creative power was affected by the individual who then made certain ends come about by way of the will. Do you see affirmations in light of that definition?"

"Yes I do because the individual then moves toward the goal using that personal power."

"It's conceivable. Adler had a genius for living wholly, fully, warmly and wittily. In many ways he was more individualistic than either Freud or Jung. Keep in mind, however, that Adler cautioned that social interest must always take precedence to considerations of the self."

"Exactly, and doesn't that explain why he strongly believed in the work ethic and why he was certain that a great deal of human happiness came from job satisfaction." Maggie could barely contain her enthusiasm.

"You are correct, Maggie. Adler believed that both were critical to society and coupled with one's interest in the good of others he believed the individual could achieve a sense of personal power and completion."

"Clare, I've been fascinated by personal power since I learned creative visualization techniques from my father and I've used the process to become more goal-oriented."

"This is very good, Maggie. You have realized a high level of understanding. You are no doubt familiar with Abraham Maslow's theories on the hierarchy of needs, yes? Introspection leading to self-actualization is not easily achieved but it is the only avenue to the truth about who we are in life. If I may ask, how do you see yourself utilizing this knowledge?"

"It probably sounds mundane but I'm looking to get a job that is both satisfying and inwardly rewarding. Of course, I also hope to continue my studies."

"In other words, if I'm hearing you correctly, you want more than a job. You want a position that offers you an opportunity to feel a sense of completion based on your inner motivation."

"Yes, yes that's exactly what I mean!" Hearing the professor's summation of her dream gave Maggie a feeling of confidence.

"And what is your personal basis for this motivation?"

"I'd feel that working altruistically, tirelessly and totally for one individual would allow me to develop my own driving force. With that I can begin creating balance in my life."

"A commendable goal, Maggie, however, I fear that many in the corporate arena will not be able to acknowledge or comprehend such an uplifting ideal."

"That's true, Clare. I've only worked for one company so far but I can tell you the management doesn't measure up. They fall short because they're interested only in their selfish ends. They say they're looking for individuals who think outside the box but when it comes right down to it very few are willing or capable of seeing beyond their noses."

"Maggie, don't judge them too harshly. They are casualties of their own design. Their attitude should in no way effect your beliefs."

"I hope I don't get jaded, Clare. There is so much negativity out there."

"Guard your enthusiasms jealously, Maggie, for they are easily crushed by others less discerning. You are internally motivated and extremely optimistic. However, with those gifts you also feel a moral responsibility to craft a better working environment through empathy and social contributions."

"Somehow when you say it, Clare, I feel that my goal is achievable."

"Of course it is. The honesty of your affirmation based objectives is a core value that will serve you well and give you wings to soar."

"Clare, you can't imagine how important your words of encouragement and support are to me. I know I've got to work in a great many positions before I find the particular career I want but you're right, believing in myself gives me courage. I have no intentions of leaving to chance what I regard as most important to me. That's why I've been working on sharpening my skills."

"I have no doubt, Maggie, that when the right opportunity presents itself you will be more than ready."

"I do know one thing, Clare. The opportunity will be offered by an individual who will be willing to believe in me. When I find him or her I shall live up to my obligations as both coworker and friend."

"I cannot tell you what a pleasure I have had conversing with you this evening. You have an interesting mindset that promotes discussion."

"I appreciate the compliment, Professor." Maggie said, satisfied she had cogently conveyed her ideas.

"Many of your peers do not have even the slightest awareness of what you are seeking. You already know where you are going, and how to get there. Few people your age are strong-minded enough to design such a blueprint for their life. Your parents must have been very influential in guiding you toward such self-confidence."

"Yes, my parents encouraged me to think critically and creatively, and those skills empowered me to reach beyond myself and touch the lives of others."

"You are a kind and generous person, Maggie, and I know you'll be successful. Here are a few books I recommend that you read." Clare jotted down some titles and handed the list along with her personal card to Maggie. "I would be interested in your thoughts. Call me and we can discuss them at anytime."

After the course ended, Maggie and Clare kept in touch regularly. Maggie continued to enroll in Clare's classes, even auditing those she could not take for credit. Through cards, letters and occasional lunches they treasured their friendship, and when Maggie was offered the job at WordTech it was to Clare she turned for counsel and advice.

~✿~

Maggie was half way home when she directed a call from her Bluetooth to the Wellness Center where Clare maintained her office. Clare's assistant informed her that Dr. Sebastian was on duty that evening and would return her call after rounds.

"Sorry for the lateness of the hour, Maggie. If you don't mind a late night meeting we could get together after ten in my office." Clare's voice sounded tired but as intent as ever.

"Thanks, Clare. I can't wait to see you again."

No matter how much time had lapsed since they had last seen one another to Maggie and Clare it seemed like yesterday. They hugged and reminisced in the quiet of Clare's spacious office drinking huge cups of hot black tea and chatting like magpies.

"Maggie, I was glad to hear you finished your MBA. Congratulations."

"Thanks, Clare, and thank heavens for online technology."

"So what brings you on a professional visit?" Clare's voice was suddenly serious.

"Clare, I know you'll understand my reluctance to name names but the party I'm going to tell you about has no idea I'm as involved in his life as I am."

"I understand perfectly, Maggie. Please put your mind at ease as this meeting is strictly confidential."

"I really don't know where to begin, so I best start at the beginning."

Maggie began slowly, tactfully painting in large brush strokes a portrait of the person she prudently referred to as "my friend." As the session progressed, her outpourings deluged into greater details regarding Harry's behavior. Her revelations included personal discoveries about Harry that she had refused to consciously acknowledge. Without realizing it, Maggie revealed aspects of Harry's personality that suggested her involvement with him went far deeper then she herself had previously admitted.

As she haltingly described passages from Harry's journal writings she struggled to maintain a sense of detachment and objectivity. She confessed to being both jealous and provoked by the images roused by Harry's words and shamefully admitted that in trying to stop the sensual feelings she had become all the more sexually incited.

"My God, where did all that come from?" Maggie, her face wet with perspiration, was surprised at her passionate outburst.

"You must have been holding onto it for some time," Clare's tone was unmistakably professional. "Maggie, there is no need for you to harbor any feelings of guilt or shame. Harry's discourse, although intensely passionate, would not have affected another reader in quite the same way it did you. Feeling the way you do about him, his words created a subconscious impasse causing an emotional upheaval that triggered feelings you were unprepared to deal with."

"In other words the closer one is to the fire, the more serious the burn."

"That's a good analogy, Maggie, and you'll need time to work through those issues."

"All right, Clare, but for now could we talk about my friend. I was hoping you could tell me more about him from a medical standpoint. I know I've given you only a thumbnail sketch of his personality but I feel he needs professional help and I want to know if my assumption is correct."

"You can hardly call it a thumbnail sketch, Maggie. You seem to know Harry, your friend, quite well."

"My friend, I mean Harry. Oh Clare, this is ridiculous since we both know I'm talking about Harry."

"What is it you want to know about him?"

"I've done some research and I think Harry has a sexual addiction. He did tell me he was going to see his own doctor but all the same I'm worried about him."

"Maggie, sex, gambling and drinking are not new behaviors. People have engaged in and in some cases suffered from them for centuries. What that means is that the scope of diagnosis covers a large area, ranging from behavioral compulsion at one end of the continuum to severely impaired interpersonal functioning or impulse control disorders at the extreme other end."

"Where is Harry on that continuum?"

"Maggie, you have done a good job of giving me a representation of the situation but it would be impossible for me to render any opinions regarding Harry. For the sake of argument, however, we could discuss sexual addiction and the impulsive personality."

"If Harry has a sexual addiction, can he be cured?"

"First of all, that's putting the cart before the horse. Harry may or may not be suffering from a behavioral compulsion. In addition, when and if such a diagnosis is confirmed, it would take time to ascertain to what degree he is suffering."

"Clare, as a doctor you don't want to commit yourself and I understand that but I'm sure he's sick. I just don't know what he's suffering from."

"Maggie, the neurotic lifestyles cover far too large a field to attempt a diagnosis without examination. I think it is important that we talk about traits and styles of functioning. It will give you a better understanding of how individuals adopt their lives to meet their goals, and it may also clarify some points by putting the situation into a proper perspective. You're worried not just about Harry but about yourself as well. Discussing the issues candidly will give you a sense of composure and a reference point from which to draw your own conclusions."

"You're right, Clare, I'm worried and it's the not knowing that stresses me out."

"Let's first consider the impulsive personality issue. This means that the individual's primary style of functioning reacts to irresistible impulse which would be the case whether he or she was narcissistic, an alcoholic or an addict or all of these."

"Or someone with a compulsive sexual addiction," Maggie interjected.

"Correct. Let us begin with compulsive behaviors. These are marked by a repetitive or driven quality. The actions of these people might be passive, for instance drinking, or they might be conspicuously impulsive, such as in gambling or sexual bingeing. The common denominator is that these people don't know why they do the things they do."

"That's Harry. Always making excuses about his behavior."

"The individual wants or desires in the moment and takes action without a clear and complete sense of motivation. They are seized by an impulse which overrides what they really want to do. That's their defense system in play; guilty but without premeditation."

"Impulsive. Harry describes himself as impulsive."

"When an individual's motivation is distorted their defense operation exonerates them of all responsibility and they give in to the irresistible whim."

"But isn't that something we all do at times, Clare?"

"Yes, but in the impulsive person's case this type of motivation is predominant. They cannot sustain wanting. In other words it doesn't just happen occasionally as with a normal person or as a result of a breakdown."

"So it's a regular feature for the impulsive person."

"Yes, and in a markedly interesting piece of research, Shapiro found that the sense of unintentional behavior or what he calls nondeliberatenss was one of the most interesting traits for people of impulse. They have a freedom from inhibition which we see only in normal people when they are intoxicated."

"Harry did say that bad men were more interesting. Even in his journal he portrays himself as very attractive on a sexual level."

"Since you're reflecting on that particular characteristic, you will find it interesting that Shapiro suggests that those who suffer with impulsive personality disorders are typically the fictional men of action that one reads about in the romantic novels. They demonstrate competency and a capacity for quick and unhesitating action which makes them all the more appealing."

"Oh my God, Clare, we're talking about Harry's personality and I don't mean just his journal writings. He said he was only interested in the moment."

"Maggie, stop jumping to conclusions. People never fit into stereotypical molds because each individual is unique and unrepeatable. When I describe impulsive people as adaptable individuals who are often very charismatic and fascinating, you immediately tell me that Harry is charming, engaging and the life of the party."

"Don't you find it ironic that Harry should be so accommodating? What you've told me so far is exactly how he describes himself."

"Granted he may have a pretty good handle on himself, but try and keep in mind that we're reviewing characteristics of the impulse personality and we haven't as yet made any determinations about Harry. We are not discounting the fact that he may in fact be ill but there are more than likely other issues of which you are unaware."

"All right, Clare, I'll try to remain impartial."

"Good. It is true that the impulsive person is short-circuited in the integrative process and has you might say a deficiency of sorts which allows them to be unmindful of the consequences of their actions. There are exceptions but for the most part long range interests, values, and emotional involvements unless specific to their own existence, don't become part of the impulse personality."

"Would this individual hate the past and have no interest in the future? No long range plans?"

"Maggie, we are not speaking in absolutes. For the most part asking self-critical questions, organizing information and considering possibilities all fall into the normal person's process of judgment. This absence of judgment in the impulsive person is impaired and limited. Have you actual proof that Harry demonstrates lack of long range planning?"

"No, not exactly, but he's sure good at short range plans."

"The impulsive individual has a keen practical intelligence suited to immediate aims or what we refer to as short range planning. Their goal is first and foremost to achieve satisfaction and they operate mainly on what they can get out of life. They live for opportunities that reflect their moods and they may even prove to be exploitive."

"A very effective way of functioning," Maggie said sarcastically.

"Yes, and for the impulsive personality it explains how they demonstrate a limited sort of empathy."

"Harry's one of the most sensitive people I know yet his journal entries are riddled with exploits of the moment. And what about loving and being in love?"

"Maggie, let's reassert that I cannot psychoanalyze Harry without his being a patient."

"I understand your reservations, Clare, and I promise to keep this information in perspective, but I need to know if an impulsive person can love and be loved?"

"Then let me say that the person of impulse cannot sustain anticipations within a stable context and unfortunately, without this context, the experience must remain one of sexual impulse. We're talking about a person who does not have an interest in an object but an interest in satisfaction. In other words, deep friendships or love are not much in evidence. These people can appear quite sincere and sensitive but their emotional involvements are limited to immediate gains. But again, these are textbook definitions."

"A normal person would find it hard to accept such a relationship."

"Maggie, be reasonable. Even if Harry were suffering from a sexual addiction we do not know to what degree nor where he is on the continuum."

"Clare, can Harry be helped?"

"Regardless of the diagnosis, with pharmacological and psychosocial treatment interventions, I would say, baring the unforeseen of course, that the prognosis, although long range, is excellent."

"I know this question is hypothetical but could he grow worse without help?"

"Maggie, logically it goes without saying that recovery is therapy-based and is closely related to the individual and the extent to which his or her self-critical process is functioning. If it is strong, then we need not fear that the condition cannot be rectified. Through treatment it is possible to help such an individual regain a sense of objective, independent reality."

"What if he's diagnosed with impulsive personality?"

"Keep in mind that the impulsive person is egocentric and although their awareness is dominated by the immediate without a sense of future planning, it is possible to help the personality reject the immediacy of experience and expression and focus on fact and truth."

"Clare, how would a person suffering from a sexual addiction due to impulsive behavior get to be that way?"

"Research on impulsive behavior suggests that in most cases it comes about at an early age through the individual's personal interpretation of his or her environment, created by a weakened ability to deal realistically with certain situations. Normal children require time to form long range emotional developments and intrinsic core values but with the impulsive person immediate gain to the individual is predominantly the goal."

"I know Harry was orphaned at an early age. Could that be what caused this?"

"Maggie, each mind interprets data differently and we don't know how Harry understood his childhood. There could be a totally different underlying cause which would contribute to a different diagnosis in which case the basis for Harry's illness might be genetic, environmental or neurochemical."

"How severe do you think Harry's illness is at this point?"

"Only through a psychiatric evaluation could the degree of impairment be ascertained. The examination would also determine whether or not the patient had trouble filtering his or her behavior or actions and to what degree. However, based on what you've told me, and remember I'm qualifying my answer because I have made no examination of Harry, I do not think he has trouble filtering his behavior or his actions at this point nor do I believe his judgment is severely impaired."

"In other words, Clare, are you saying Harry is neurotic but may not be an impulsive personality," Maggie sighed with relief.

"I'm offering an educated guess based on the information I've gleaned from you to help you realize that you cannot be judge, jury and executioner before reviewing the details. Presuming to diagnose an individual without comprehensive facts can be detrimental. Try to reserve your judgment, Maggie, until Harry has gone into rehab and undergone treatment."

"Clare, I know people are complex individuals and don't fit into square or round holes but I want to know if I can help him."

"This is Harry's struggle, Maggie, and only if he chooses to fight. Even then there are no guarantees."

"He said he was lost and couldn't find his way out of the darkness. I can understand a little better what an enormous task he's got in front of him."

"As with any illness it takes time to heal."

"I do have one last question."

"And that is?"

"Would an impulsive individual be aware they were asking someone to do something that was not morally right?"

"Strictly speaking the impulsive person does not critically examine such aspects. Moral values such as personal integrity are abstract ideals and require a long range viewpoint. In the true impulsive person it does not exist but again, as we have said, along the continuum there are varying degrees and some patients through treatment can redirect their energies."

"I wonder if I'm a little crazy, Clare, because I still believe in him."

"You are not crazy, Maggie. You're governed by reason and that is why you are seeking help for Harry in a logical manner. Harry isn't crazy either. He needs help to give higher expression to his sense of self."

"I appreciate hearing that, Clare. Just knowing that Harry will benefit from psychotherapy has relieved me considerably."

"On a positive note, Maggie, if Harry has made an attempt to seek assistance, and I say if he has, then he is trying to help himself."

"Why do you say it in that way, Clare?"

"Maggie, keep in mind that in Harry's case wanting to do it and doing it are two different things. He may be uncomfortable with some of the decisions in his life but that doesn't mean he's wants to stop living life the way he has been. Assuming he had specific issues and assuming he really wanted to stop would be very telling indeed."

"What do you mean, Clare?"

"In the impulsive patient we have someone who might say they want to stop, or feel they want to stop or even feel repentant about not stopping but in the final analysis it comes down to the fact that he or she predominately isn't interested in doing so because nothing in life is more important than immediate satisfaction."

"And if Harry isn't willing to change?"

"Maggie, stop assuming. Wait until you have more data and then make your own decision about supporting him. Keep in mind that while you're looking to help Harry, he has his own agenda. It has very little to do with you."

"Thanks, Clare, for giving me hope. I realize how complicated and involved this situation is and I appreciate your trying to help me to understand it. One thing is for sure though."

"And that is what, Maggie?"

"I'm going to find out if Harry is more than the sum total of what he pretends to be."

"You may be disappointed with what you discover. People are never what you expect them to be."

"So I've been told but I've got to find out just the same. I think he needs my help more than he knows."

"That can be risky. Be careful that your generous impulse doesn't get you hurt. We are all vulnerable at levels we are sometimes unaware of in ourselves. I am not trying to dissuade you from your mission but

I would ask you to use critical judgment in all your undertakings."

"Dr. Jeckel or Mr. Hyde, will the real Harry please stand up?"

"Keeping your balance should be your prime consideration, Maggie and whatever your findings, trust yourself. I hope I do not sound too admonitory but you need to realize that you could be putting yourself in psychological danger. You must promise to keep in touch with me."

"Are those doctor's orders?" Maggie asked, touching Clare's hand.

"Maggie, call me without hesitation if anything should happen that proves disturbing to you. Please use my private number." Clare handed Maggie her card.

Maggie stood and walked with Clare to the door. "All right, Clare, but I'm now on a one woman crusade to find out what makes Harry tick. I only hope I can come up with an intervention strong enough to help him."

"With the kind of faith you have in Harry," Clare nodded supportively, "it may work out reasonably well."

"Thanks again, Clare," Maggie said, closing the door behind her.

---

* The author gratefully acknowledges David Shapiro's *Neurotic Styles* (1965) in the writing of this chapter.

Chapter 13

"Hey Mom, I'm going for a drive. My nerves are jumpy and I've got to get out of the city for a few hours," Maggie called to her mother who was lounging on the patio.

Whenever Maggie felt the need to relax she retreated to the countryside, her favorite haunt since childhood. It had been her father who had taught her the importance of getting back to nature whenever stress reared its ugly head. He had used their trips as learning experiences and imparted to his young daughter a world of knowledge, often conferring with her on an adult level. It was on one such outing in the forest preserves during a particularly glorious day that her father extolled the benefits of nature.

"Never forget nature is our friend, Maggie dear," he'd say, "refreshing and uplifting our poor, downtrodden spirits. Nature clears the mind and restores the body. It helps alleviate tension and takes away the punishing thoughts that make us anxious. Go back to nature whenever this world becomes too cruel to comprehend."

Maggie's thoughts wandered back to those happy days as she prepared lunch for her outing. As she added the sweet relish to the tuna salad she smiled recalling how father and daughter had played "piccalilli," a game he had invented just for "their special banquets" together. She finished wrapping the sandwiches and tried to dismiss the pangs of sadness but the tears came anyway. Packing her backpack, she added extra water bottles and Snickers bars, and then went in search of her long-billed running cap and car keys.

"Bye Mom," she called as she scrambled out the door.

"Take care, dear and have a good day." Mrs. Reynolds waved good-bye.

"Hi Maggie," Harry yelled, pulling his convertible up alongside her car in the driveway. "I overheard your mother saying have a good day. Where's this place you're off to?"

"It's no secret, Harry. I'm going out to the country."

"Would you like some company?"

"I only have two tuna sandwiches."

"I'll take my chances."

"Okay, get in. I know where I'm going so I'll drive." Maggie backed out of the driveway and headed the car toward the freeway.

"That sounds remarkably prescient," Harry said, buckling his seatbelt all the while fixing his eyes on her.

"I have been most of my life. As a matter of fact, I was just thinking about you this morning," Maggie commented without turning her head.

"And I show up on your doorstep. Talk about psychic."

"What did you want to see me about, Harry?"

"This is rather embarrassing but to be honest I miss not talking with you. You're the first person in a long time that I've enjoyed conversing with not to mention that your words of advice are what keep coming back to me during the dark, sleepless nights."

"Remember my rain-check? Now it's my turn to ask you a few questions."

"You've certainly got a lot of mileage out of that rain-check, but go ahead."

"Tell me about your daughter?"

"How did you know I have a daughter?"

Although sounding as though he was slightly taken aback by the revelation, Harry did not seem defensive nor did he seem interested in pursuing Maggie's information source.

"I haven't seen her for a long time. Her name is Lisa."

"How old is she?"

"She just turned fifteen."

"Why haven't you seen her more often?"

"It's a trite tale and one I'm sure you've heard before."

"I'm listening."

"I didn't have much of a relationship with her mother. When she died last year I guess I felt guilty. I was busy when Lisa was growing up. I tried a couple of times to see her on weekends, bought her some toys, clothes, you know, but her mom made it tough. Eventually I stopped trying altogether. Responsibility like that is something I can't handle. I see to it that the kid gets what she needs and I have a trust fund set up for her but I can't do more than that."

"Would you mind if I talked with her?"

"Why would you want to do that?" Harry sounded disbelieving.

"I'm interested in your welfare, Harry."

"I'm flattered but curious. You seem intent on investigating me, Maggie. Should I feel privileged or do you have an ulterior motive?"

"I'm taking you on as a personal mission. You need someone who believes in you, Harry."

"If talking to Lisa helps you learn why I am the way I am, sure, go ahead." He took a card from his pocket, scribbled his daughter's phone number on it and handed it to Maggie.

"Harry, what does Lisa know about you?"

"I don't know, Maggie. She probably doesn't want anything to do with me and I don't blame her."

"Maybe you're wrong."

"I kind of hope I am. I'm beginning to realize how important it is to have someone in your life that genuinely cares about you. Let me know what Lisa thinks about her old man."

"I will Harry."

"There is one thing I'm worried about though?"

"What's that?"

"I'm afraid you'll be disappointed in me."

"Why Harry, because you've known so many women in your life?"

Harry looked askance at her remark. "No, not exactly, but suppose you were to find out certain things about me? Would that turn you against me?"

"Harry, that you have feet of clay won't surprise me. You've always been in my corner and whatever happens I'll be in yours."

"I'd like to believe that."

"You trust me don't you?"

"Implicitly but suppose what you discover goes against everything you've ever believed in?"

"Will it, Harry?"

"Let me ask you a question. When you first typed the notes for my journal, didn't it make you sick? You know what kind of person I am, and I know the kind of person you are. Someone like you could never stomach someone like me."

"I admit I was taken aback at first," Maggie said, recalling her recent ordeal in Clare's office. "It's the kind of trash I read as a teenager and hid behind my mother's back. It wasn't your earthy romances that offended my sensibilities as much as you forcing me to type them in the office."

"Sorry, but surely you can see my need for secrecy?"

"Harry, what I see is a man who is desperately crying out for help. Some parts of your journal where you're painfully honest about your shortcomings have merit and I think your doctor will find it a very useful therapeutic tool."

"Would you mind not talking about it? I mean, let's wait till I'm actually in therapy."

"How much longer will that be?"

"I don't know exactly. How long before you finish typing the material?"

"Don't make it depend on that, Harry. A great American general once said that wisdom is nothing more than healed pain. The quicker you begin treatment the better you'll feel."

"Who was that general?"

"Robert E. Lee."

"I might have guessed; a Confederate loser. I wonder if he wished things had turned out differently in his life, too."

"Your life isn't over yet, Harry."

"One can't erase the slate."

"No, but you wouldn't want to. How else can you learn but from your experiences? With a clearer vision you can reshape them into a meaningful whole and use the knowledge to make better choices in the future."

"They're not worth it, trust me."

The car suddenly bumped and jolted as Maggie turned off the main highway onto a country road that stretched through a forest of oak trees.

"Well, here we are. Would you mind, Harry, if we don't talk for awhile? We're heading up that way," Maggie pointed to a distant hill as they entered the park grounds.

"Sure, I'm just tagging along for the ride."

"This is my way of jump-starting my psyche and I need quiet time." Maggie parked the car and took her pack from the backseat.

"Who knows, maybe some of this nature stuff will rub off on me."

Harry walked quietly beside her as they headed toward a field covered in tall grass and wild flowers. After awhile they came to a sun-dappled trail that led them down past an old wooden bridge whose rutted creek bed was dry and dusty. The trail grew pungent and cool as its gentle twists and turns meandered through a massed darkness of dense pine trees until it spilled into a green meadow completely surrounded by a string of knobby hills. It was a flawless day without a cloud in the sky and only the chirping of the birds broke the stillness.

"Does the air always smell like this out here?" Harry asked in amazement as he stopped to take in the view. "It's really something, like a different place."

"This is where I leave you, Harry. I'm going to get a little running in. I'll see you at the top of that hill but take your time because I'm going up the long way." Maggie pointed into the distance before sprinting away.

Forty-five minutes later Maggie watched as Harry struggled up the last few feet of the incline. "It sure took you long enough," she shouted, swallowing her laughter.

"Hill my eye, that was a mountain," he retorted defensively.

"It's called communing with nature, Harry." Maggie, reclining against a large boulder, had set up a small campsite using her backpack as a table.

Harry stood there panting. "I'm out of condition that's for sure. Do you hike like this often?" Although there was a cool breeze, he wiped perspiration from his face.

"Take it easy and relax."

"Now that's something I can handle." Harry plopped down in the grass and closed his eyes against the sun.

"Don't you think makeshift picnics are the best?" Maggie said as she arranged the food into his and her piles.

"It all depends on who's at the picnic," Harry squinted a smile in her direction.

"Harry, I got to thinking that something must have happened to you when you were on vacation. It wasn't until you came back that you started acting strangely."

"Maggie, don't go there."

"But it's a point of departure from your regular behavior and it might be important."

"Playing detective with my life could be dangerous."

"Harry, don't joke. This is serious."

"I'm not joking, Maggie. There are things I want only the doctor to know about me. I hope you understand it's confidential." Harry propped himself up on his elbow and gave Maggie a studied look.

"That's exactly what I want you to do, talk to your doctor but for some reason I have this nagging doubt and don't believe you will. What do you think of that?" Maggie handed Harry a sandwich and a bottle of water. "I've got Snickers for dessert."

"You think I'm trying to con you, is that it?" Harry drank his water and took a bite of the sandwich. "Umm, good sandwich, thanks."

"You're welcome. Harry, don't you want to get well?" Maggie persisted.

"At what price, Maggie?"

"It's your life we're talking about, Harry."

"Somethings are better left for dead."

"Harry, I can't stand by and let you destroy yourself."

"Why do you care so much?"

"I know you, Harry. Perhaps better than you know yourself. Sure, I don't pretend to know what sordid choices you've made in the past or the kind of life you've led but I know that deep down you're a man of worth."

"You could be wrong about that."

"I might be wrong about many things but of that I'm not."

"It's going to take a lot of digging to uncover that core part of me and I'm not sure I can handle it."

"I know you don't like to deal with emotional reactions, Harry, but there are times when it is necessary. It'll be painful but it's a grieving process and you've got to let yourself go through it."

"Are you talking about my divorce from Ellen?"

"Among other things."

"Would it make you happy, Maggie?"

"No, Harry, don't do it for me or anyone else. You've got to do this one for yourself."

"That's something I've got to think about. Hey, where's my Snickers bar?"

"Let's eat them on the way back to the car." Maggie tossed Harry the candy and finished cleaning up.

As they walked down the hill, a young boy was having trouble getting his kite into the air. He raced back and forth without success.

"Wait a sec, Maggie. I use to be a great kite flyer."

Harry ran over to the boy and for a few minutes they stood together deep in conversation with Harry waving his hands in one direction and then in another and the boy nodding his head up and down. Finally the young man took off running in one direction and then in a split second, reversed himself going in the opposite direction. Within minutes the kite was airborne.

"He's got it now." Harry waved at the young boy who waved back smiling.

"Where did you learn that maneuver?"

"Maybe you're right, Maggie, it might be that some of my experiences are worth remembering." Harry kept watching the kite as it flew higher and higher.

Chapter 14

The week that followed was a particularly busy one and while neither she nor Harry mentioned the subject, Maggie knew his journal was still a priority. With job and personal commitments having increased however, she had to fight for every opportunity to work on the project and although less than committed she no longer felt about the task as she had in the beginning. Going through analysis with Clare helped her gain new insights and she was able to view the situation more dispassionately.

After last weekend, I'm getting a better understanding of Harry. I've decided to adopt a new attitude regarding his writings even though they're nauseatingly repetitious. In a way I'm his doctor too, and just as a doctor would view his patient's x-rays, I've got to examine Harry's thoughts in the same vein. Harry isn't well and he needs my help. He doesn't even realize how seriously ill he is. Of that I'm absolutely sure. He was there for me in the beginning and now it's my turn to reciprocate. I know he's going through a terrible soul searching point in his life and I've got to help him make the right decision.

A last minute change of plans with Lisa, Harry's daughter, forced Maggie to rearrange her schedule in order to keep the appointment late Friday afternoon. In an effort to complete the final passages of the last notebook and still get away early, she typed quickly without giving much thought to Harry's clichéd phrases. However, when she looked at the clock and realized how late it was she decided to save time by leaving the saved material on the hard drive.

Harry's latest entry of romantic bilge is thick enough to sicken the most seasoned reader and I'm glad I'm finished with this one. I can't start another piece tonight if I'm going to make it on time to meet Lisa. I've got to get out of here, now. I guess it'd be okay if just this once I save the document to the hard drive. I'll come in extra early on Monday to make a copy for Harry and take this stuff off the hard drive then.

Catching the last express to the garage, Maggie ran into Harry coming off another elevator.

"Hi Harry, are you still here? I thought you left hours ago."

"Had some unfinished work in Production," Harry replied dryly.

"I'm driving to Sorrento Beach to meet with your daughter. Keep your fingers crossed all goes well."

"You're wasting your time, Maggie," Harry said as he walked dejectedly towards his car.

"Harry," Maggie shouted after him, "I hope you get some rest this weekend. You're hanging by a thread." She shook her head sadly as she watched him disappear down a row of parked cars.

What could have happened to him? What an abrupt change. Boy, Harry's mood swings are becoming more prevalent. Only a couple of hours ago we put the finishing touches on the Mercer contract and he was in good spirits. Now he looks at me as though I were a stranger.

As she sat waiting for several cars ahead of her to exit the garage, Maggie replayed Lisa's message on her cell phone and thought about their planned meeting.

She's Harry's daughter all right. The voice has the same cadence, the same inflection as Harry's and they both have that way of commanding attention with the simplest sounding request. Lisa's message asked me to come down alone. I hope I can find her. She's going to be at the end of the boardwalk wearing a bright red jogging suit and a green visor.

Maggie was early. There had been very little traffic on the beach highway and she had made good time. It had gotten cooler and she was glad she had remembered her jacket. Standing on the boardwalk, letting the wind play with her hair, she watched as the unrelenting waves crashed against the rocky shore and quietly tiptoed back into the sea. She breathed in the smell of salt air and stared out beyond the reef where the sky and horizon merged in a blur of muted color. Engulfed in the magic of a midsummer's eve, Maggie found herself indulging in reflections and she did not hear the footfalls behind her.

"Excuse me, are you Maggie Reynolds? I'm Lisa Cooke, Harry's daughter." Lisa extended her hand and smiled.

"Hi Lisa, I was daydreaming."

"That's easy to do out here."

"Thanks for meeting me on such short notice," Maggie said taken aback by Lisa's striking facial resemblance to Harry.

"I look a lot like him, don't I?" Lisa removed the visor and looked intently at Maggie.

"Yes, you do."

"Do you mind if we walk? It won't seem as cold," Lisa proposed as the wind grew gustier.

"Not at all, I could use the exercise," Maggie said, pulling her jacket collar up tightly around her neck.

They walked along in silence for a while. Maggie studied the girl. She was Harry's child right down to the stubborn chin and those beguiling blue eyes. Tall and extremely slender, she looked almost anorexic. Her clothes, although inexpensive, were worn with flare and Maggie wondered if she had ever considered a career in modeling. Her stylishly cut auburn hair framed a pixie face with a flawless completion. Hands in her pockets, she walked with long strides projecting a sense of confidence that belied her age.

"Maggie, how long have you known Harry?" Lisa gave Maggie a

sideward glance shouting into the deafening roar of the waves.

"Seven years. I started working for him as an administrative assistant at WordTech but the position has evolved into a sort of jack of all trades job." Maggie noticed Lisa had no problem hearing her.

"Do you like working for him?"

"Very much, he's a good boss… ."

"…but a fucking father." Lisa's profanity struck Maggie as more theatrical than honest.

"If you're trying to offend me Lisa I've heard about every curse word there is. Let's save the outrage until I know more about you. Tell me about you and Harry."

"Harry left my mother when he found out I was on the way. He didn't want to pay child support until my mother finally took him to court. Are you sure you want to hear this, Miss Reynolds?"

"Call me Maggie, and yes, I very much want to hear it."

"The very first time I remember seeing Harry was when I was six years old. He came over to the house and brought this big brown teddy bear. It had a red ribbon around its neck and he took it off and tied it in my hair. He told me I was beautiful and asked me to stay that way always, and then he whispered in my ear that it was to be our secret. He kissed me on the cheek and left. I loved him at that moment and a thousand moments later."

"Did you see him again?"

"I saw him only one more time. I was seven years old and he promised to take me to the circus. He came into the house with a gigantic package wrapped in blue paper and covered with silver stars. He had to help me unwrap it; it was that big. It was doll and I told him right off her name was Ginger Cooke. He hugged me so tightly I can still recall his wonderful smell." Lisa smiled at the memory. "But while I was putting on my coat, he and my mom started fighting again. He came over to me and kissed me on the cheek. He said he was sorry but that we couldn't go to the circus that day but we would someday soon. He walked out of the house and out of my life."

"I know you were very young but do you remember if your mom tried to contact him?"

"I kept begging her to call him and make him come back but she kept saying the same old things over and over."

"What was that?"

"How he didn't really care about me and never wanted me. She told me he didn't love me because he didn't want kids cluttering up his life. She told me to forget about him; that he wasn't worth it. I started writing him letters and she said she mailed them but she didn't because after she died I found them in a shoebox under her bed."

"I bet your dad would love to read those letters."

"I think my mom loved Harry so much she hated him. She cried a lot and used to say that if it weren't for her bad luck she wouldn't have any luck at all. I guess I believed her about my dad because she said it so often. Does that make any sense?"

"Yes, I can understand that."

"Mom said Harry didn't care about anyone but himself but she had a big picture of him in her room. He looked so wonderful in that picture that sometimes I'd sneak in just to stare at it and pretend to be with him. You know, talking to him and kissing the picture. Once mom caught me and spanked me good."

"I bet that didn't stop you?"

"You're right, it didn't. I just learned to be sneakier," Lisa laughed.

Maggie was laughing, too. "It's funny how things work out in our lives."

"Yeah, like how I wanted my dad to come to school with me so I could show him off to the other kids. I told them he was a big executive who traveled all over the world. I made up all these lies about how he was too busy making money and could only send me presents. A lot of the kids envied me but I used to cry myself to sleep because I was so lonely for him. When my pillow was wet I'd imagine him coming during the night and drying my eyes and kissing me good night."

"How do you feel about Harry now?"

"I don't know. Sometimes I don't care and sometimes I wish he were dead like mom. I really hated him for a long time but now that mom's dead I kind of feel he's the only one I have left in the world, even though I live with my aunt and her family. You know what I mean?"

Maggie nodded.

"My aunt and uncle, they're good people but I feel like I don't really belong there. They've got my three cousins and I'm like an outsider. I know my dad's money pays for everything because his lawyer came over to see my aunt and uncle and they didn't want me to hear anything so they told me to go outside, like I was a dumb kid or something."

"Would you want to see him?"

"I'm not sure I'm ready yet."

"What makes you say that?"

"Do you believe in reincarnation, Maggie?"

"No I don't. I'm hoping to get into heaven on the first try."

"Well, I'd like to come back as a dad and give my kid the kind of feelings that fathers are supposed to give their kids. I loved my mother but it's my dad who left a hole in my heart. Someday I'd like to be able to forgive him but I can't just yet."

"I think Harry would understand. You know, Lisa, my father died when I was ten years old. I can't pretend to know the pain you've felt all these years but I have a pretty good idea about loss and losing someone we love. I missed my father terribly and still do but there was nothing I could do to change things. I just tried to live my life as best I could."

"But Harry didn't die. He just didn't want to see me. He hates me."

"Lisa, I think you know in your heart that isn't true. Blaming him won't help but talking to him and finding out why he did what he did will. It's something only you and your dad together can put right."

"If it wasn't for me maybe my mom and dad would still be together. I believe what my mom said about Harry never wanting kids. He never loved me," Lisa said, rubbing her eyes.

"I've got to tell you something that I learned about your father, Lisa. I spoke to a psychiatrist and she told me that people like your dad can't bring themselves to have relationships. They don't live like a lot of us, thinking about the future. They believe only in the present and live in the moment. Relationships take time. It's like nurturing flowers. You've got to plant them, water them, and take care of them. Unfortunately, your dad can't do that. I'm making this sound awfully simplistic but I could give you the doctor's name and she could help you learn more about your dad."

"Wow, is dad seeing a shrink, too?"

"Not yet but he's going to very soon."

"I've been seeing one for two years. He said I'm a mass of contradictions. One moment I love my dad and the next I hate him. My dad has made my life miserable."

"Don't you think you need to take some responsibility for your own life? Your father and mother gave you life but in a way their responsibility ends there. You've got to make your own way in this world."

"You sound like my shrink," Lisa giggled.

"Do I?" Maggie grinned back at her.

"Do you know why I wanted to meet you?"

"No, but I'm glad you did."

"I've been putting a scrapbook together on my dad ever since I was able to write. Whenever I find someone who knows him or has heard about him, I try to get to meet them. Then I put the information into my scrapbook. I've got a pretty good picture of him. It's not real but it's like that song, "Artificial Flowers." Oh, I got flowers and presents on my birthday and when I was sick but I know it was my aunt who signed the cards. That's my relationship with my dad, strictly phony."

"Lisa, would you like me to arrange for the two of you to meet?"

"No, Maggie. I don't want to see him right now. I don't know if I ever will. I don't even want you to give him any message from me. Except maybe that I hate him."

"That's the child in you speaking. Lisa. You're afraid. The thread of fear runs through all of us in some way or another. In time you'll bridge the relationship with your dad. It won't be easy because it means you'll have to cross the bridge that separates the two of you."

"Maybe we could meet part way."

"What a wonderful idea, Lisa, and I think you're right; he'll probably be waiting for you."

"It hurts too much for me to think about that."

"Trust me, Lisa, I understand how painful the journey is but there will come a time…"

"Don't start preaching at me, Maggie. I've been there and back. I like where I am right now."

"Would you like for us to get together again?" Maggie asked hopefully.

"You mean just the two of us, you and me? I'd like that."

"Lisa, I've got to get back but I do want to see you again. Is it okay if I call you and we make some plans together?"

"Sure, Maggie, I'd like that lots."

"It's getting late," Maggie said, looking at her watch.

"Yeah, I've got to get home, too."

"Do you need me to phone your aunt and tell her you were

with me?"

"Nope, she knows."

"Lisa, I'm going to say just one more thing and then I promise to shut up and not give out any more advice. May I do that?"

"Okay, Maggie."

"For what it's worth, Lisa, you're the one who's suffering. Your dad can't begin to feel your pain and even if he could he wouldn't be able to do anything for you. Once you forgive him you'll be moving in the only direction that gives you hope."

Maggie reached out to give Lisa a hug but she had already turned away. She watched as Lisa walked, almost ran, back towards the boardwalk.

Chapter 15

Maggie came back from the beach with a head cold. She called Paul and begged off from their Saturday night date, telling him instead of her intentions to stay in bed and drink plenty of tea with lemon and honey.

Paul seemed distant and barely responded. He rudely muttered something about Harry which Maggie ignored completely. Not wanting to provoke the situation she thought it better to end the conversation with a promise to call him on Monday but he hung up before she had a chance to say good-bye.

She slept fitfully Saturday night. Along about sunrise she had a dream and with it a premonition. In the dream she saw herself on the edge of a cliff. She had the sensation of falling but at the last minute grabbed hold of a large tree limb that appeared out of nowhere. However, the tree limb, which looked remarkably like a human hand, was not able to support her and she felt herself falling headlong into the darkness. Miraculously she landed on a ledge below the cliff and although safe she had a sense of foreboding.

The presentiment was so real and frightening she awoke drenched in perspiration and shivering with cold. She remained in bed on Sunday feeling so sick she dreaded the thought of going to work. However, on Monday morning she felt better and decided to go in for at least a half day to get some paperwork out of the way.

Even before she sat down at her desk, Maggie sensed something was wrong. She knew instinctively that someone had been in her office but there was concrete evidence as well. Her keyboard had been moved and her desk drawer opened. She recalled leaving Harry's most recent file on the hard drive Friday afternoon in her effort to leave the office early for her appointment with Lisa. She also remembered her plan to get in early on Monday and remove it from her computer after making the necessary copy for Harry.

She knew that someone could easily have called it up if they had gotten her password. Her suspicions were confirmed when she noted the time differentiation between her closing the file and when it was next accessed. Seized with dread, she realized someone had read the file at ten o'clock on Friday night.

In an effort to assess the seriousness of the situation Maggie called David Canyon in IT. When he came on the line she forced the panic from her voice.

"What's the problem, Maggie?"

"David, I need you to come up here immediately. It's an emergency."

"I'll be right up."

When David arrived Maggie relinquished her chair and closed her office door. She had already accepted the worse case scenario and needed only confirmation.

"David, I know this might seem a bit irregular but I need to know on the Q.T. if my computer has been accessed since I logged off late Friday afternoon and if anything has been copied."

David said nothing. He insinuated his tall, lanky frame into the chair and placed a CD into the slot. He began typing. His strong, dark hands manipulated the keys as his tapered fingers flew across the keyboard. Maggie watched as his eyes darted across the screen.

"Yep, someone hooked into it all right." He stopped typing abruptly and looked at Maggie. "Do you want to know what files they looked at?"

"Yes," Maggie whispered hoarsely as she watched the young technician confirm what she already knew.

"It looks as though they searched through quite a few files but the one they opened and copied was named…"

"HICChronicles," they finished the word together.

Maggie, although shaken, was determined to remain calm. She left David in her office and went out to the water cooler for a drink. Except for Denise answering phones at the console the reception area was empty.

She walked back into her office and sat quietly watching David work at her desk. She noted how neatly his thick ebony hair had been braided into tight cornrows and how his soft caramel features pulsated with excitement as his eyes absorbed the information.

"How valuable is the data? Do you want to call security?"

Maggie weighed each of David's questions as she tried to examine her own fears.

Hindsight, what is it they say about hindsight? Who could have hacked into my computer? They copied Harry's file for a reason. I could kick myself for not taking the material off the hard drive as I've always done before. Let me think, although the file contained only a small portion of the journal what was on it would be incriminating. I'm racking my brain trying to remember the exact contents of that last book but then what difference does it make? It was as bad as all the others. Whoever took the material is intent on making a case. Harry's confidentiality has been breached.

"How did they know my password, David? How could it have happened?" Maggie listened halfheartedly as David offered some rudimentary explanations.

"Well, there's not much we can do now. How about a cup of coffee? We could go up to the cafeteria," he suggested.

"Yes, please. I'm going to need your help, David."

Maggie was thinking about Harry. What would he say when he learned what had happened. For some reason she thought of Paul but quickly put it out of her mind.

They took the elevator to the twenty-second floor. As they got off the first bank of elevators Maggie's heart sank. Coming down in the corporate elevator was Paul. She wasn't surprised. Maybe it was a coincidence but somehow Maggie didn't think so. She didn't want to believe it but she couldn't stop her growing suspicions.

I'll have to hear it from Paul. Could he possibly have done it? Was this Paul's idea of revenge because he was in a position to short-circuit Harry's career? Did he think he held the winning hand? Is he congratulating himself on his hard won achievement? What would management say, kudos for Paul but too bad for you Maggie, you're plumb in the middle of it. That's the way the ball bounces. If he's done this, he couldn't have cared much about our relationship? Tell me Paul were you driven to do such a despicable act? I must not have meant anything to you. I still don't want to believe it but Paul is the only one who had both the motivation and the means of entry.

"David, let's sit outside. I need some air," Maggie said, hoping a cool breeze would make her feel better.

"Sure." David led the way to the employee tables on the far side of the patio. He pulled out a wire chair and Maggie sat down without a word.

"I'll get the coffee."

"Make mine tea, please, David. Thanks." While David was gone, Maggie reviewed her options.

It's imperative that I see Harry. He'll know how to handle the situation. I best not think of what Clare said about Harry. Surely he'll come through with a solution at this eleventh hour. After all, the sordid material was his journal work for his doctor and the company will likely consider that in their decision when they realize the reason it was being done in the first place.

"Here you go, Maggie." David put the tea on the table. He had also bought her a donut.

"Thanks, David. How sweet of you. I can't thank you enough." For the first time that morning Maggie managed a smile.

"That's okay. What else do you need me to do?"

"I don't know what to do. I'm really worried about this data being taken. It could mean my job."

"As serious as all that? You still have the data but someone made a copy of it. What would they do with it?"

Maggie trusted David but did not want to embroil him in what could become a company scandal. She told him that the material could be damaging and that she had certain misgivings regarding a few employees. She also told him that the seriousness of the situation could prompt an investigation from Corporate. David listened quietly, occasionally shaking his head in what appeared to be disbelief.

"Wow! It sounds like a movie script," he said after Maggie stopped talking. "How can I help?"

"I need to know who took the copied disc to Corporate this morning. Could you find out for me?"

"Sure, I can try. My connections go all the way to the top," he grinned.

"David..." Maggie hesitated.

"No need to tell me. I know how confidential this is, Maggie. I won't say a word to anyone."

"Thanks, David. I need to know right away. "

"Tell you what, I'll go upstairs and see what I can find out. It may take me a little while but I'll come down as soon as I find out anything." For all his youth David seemed extremely mature and decisive.

Maggie's eyes followed him through the double doors toward the corporate elevators. As she drank the hot brewed tea, she savored its flavor and became aware of the enticing aroma. Inhaling deeply, she felt calmer.

How lovely to have a friend and a cup of tea. The whole ugly scenario seems to have been put in a better light. Thank God I'm able to think clearly again. My faith will ground me. I must remain balanced. I've got to make plans in case Harry fails to come into the office today. I'll have to go to his home. I'll get his address off my computer and drive out to Ridgeway Park. I've got to copy the remaining data onto the flash drive and delete the material from the hard drive. I wonder how long it will be before Corporate calls me upstairs. Surely Corporate will take all the mitigating circumstances into consideration, Harry's illness, his doctor's confirmation, and my duty to my employer. The one thing I don't want to do is to confront Paul today. I wish I didn't feel so lousy.

"Maggie, I'm back."

"David, that was fast."

"My sources tell me that Mr. Keating brought a package to the CEO's office early this morning." David's voice was low and guarded. "Mr. Cummings' secretary told another secretary, a good friend of mine, that it contained a CD and a brief note. Does that help?"

"It's what I suspected." Maggie looked across at David. She had known what he was going to say the moment he approached her. "David, it confirms my worst fear. I've got to reach Mr. Cooke as soon as possible." Maggie stood up but the effort proved more than she could handle.

"Maggie, are you okay?"

"I'm a little dizzy. I think this cold of mine is getting me down."

"Do you want me to drive you out to Mr. Cooke's home? I'll be able to get away from my desk and we could make it there and back within a couple of hours."

"David, you've helped me so much. I can't expect you to do more than you've already done and I don't want to jeopardize your job."

"Don't worry about it. It's cool. Do you need to go down stairs first?" David was already standing ready to go.

Maggie wanted to double check Harry's office before leaving with David. She asked Leeann if Harry had left any messages for her that morning but when she found out he hadn't even called in she knew he couldn't possibly know the complications his journal had caused. She grabbed her purse and headed down to David's car.

They drove the first hour in silence. David seemed to understand Maggie's need for downtime. The traffic was fairly light and the music from David's CD player was soft and mellow. Slowly Maggie began to relax.

"I had the cafeteria fill a thermos with hot tea if you'd like some." He reached behind the seat and pulled forward a large red container.

"David, you think of everything." Maggie unscrewed the lid and poured the liquid into the thermos top. "Do you want some?"

"No thanks, I'm strictly a coffee guy myself, but I'm good."

"David, how long have you been at WordTech? It seems I've known you forever."

"Five years in June."

"Have you heard of other situations similar to the one I've described?"

"The closest one I heard about was some secretary in Purchasing who typed something personal for her boss, like a term paper or something for a college assignment."

"What happened in that case?"

"Hmmm...I think they docked her and reprimanded him. In any case we all got a memo stating that under no circumstances was personal material to be worked on at Word Tech."

"I guess that answers my question. So ends the short but sweet career of Maggie Reynolds. David, I've got to talk to Harry alone. Would you mind waiting in the car when we get to his place?"

"Hey, no problem. Don't worry about me."

It was early afternoon when they turned into Harry's driveway. Maggie got out of the car unsteadily and slowly headed up the walk. It was a stately townhome and Maggie was sure the Mello Roos were quite expensive. She rang the doorbell several times. It never occurred to her that Harry might not be home. The text message he sent her cell phone during the drive up said he was doing work at his home office and would be in tomorrow. For the first time, however, it occurred to her that he might not be alone.

The door opened and Harry, dressed in a blue terrycloth bathrobe with a white towel around his neck, stood drying his face. "What's up, Maggie? What happened?" Harry stared at her. "What are you doing here?"

"I need to talk to you, Harry. May I come in?"

"Sure. Come on in." Harry looked up and down the street as though sizing up the situation. "Is it an emergency? Are you all right?"

"Harry, I'll make it short. Someone made a copy of your journal, or to be more precise, copied the pages from the last book I was working on. I believe it was taken to the CEO's office this morning."

"What the hell?" Harry shouted vehemently.

"Listen, Harry, don't go off the deep end. Please try to control yourself."

"How did it happen, Maggie?"

"As near as I can figure someone came into my office late Friday night and took the data from my computer."

Maggie gave Harry a full accounting of the morning's ordeal including David's investigation. She did not mention her uncertainties regarding Paul's part in the episode and apparently it wasn't necessary.

"Shit. I know who it was. I should have canned that sonofabitch's ass when I had the chance."

"Harry, can't you tell Corporate the truth?"

"What's the truth, Maggie?"

"The truth is exactly what you told me in the beginning. Your doctor needs the typed copy of your journal before therapy can begin. The company will understand the stress you were under and that your health was at stake. We'll get hold of your doctor and with his confirmation I'm sure the company will absolve both of us. It's quite simple, really."

"You're right, let's keep it simple. I couldn't stand it if word got out about any of this. A scandal would ruin me."

"Everything will be kept confidential. That's why I came out here instead of calling you."

"Maggie, remember what you said about feet of clay?"

"Harry, Corporate won't do anything to someone in your condition. When they call me, which I'm sure they will, I'll tell them everything. We'll clear it up and you can go on with your therapy as you originally intended."

"Sure. Sure. That's great, Maggie." Harry sounded extremely agitated.

"What is it you're not telling me, Harry? I get the feeling you're holding something back."

"Nothing, Maggie, nothing I can tell you about now anyway. You look tired. Aren't you feeling well? Do you need a lift home?" Harry reached out for her but Maggie stepped back.

"Just a bad cold but thanks. David from IT is taking me home. He's out in front now."

"He doesn't know anything about this, does he?" Harry asked suspiciously.

"Only that I needed his help," Maggie lied.

"I'll be in the office tomorrow. We'll put our heads together."

"I think it might be better if you called in sick tomorrow, Harry."

"You think so?"

"Harry, I'll call you when I get more information. I'm very tired now and I've got to get some sleep."

"Maggie, I... ." Harry walked her to the door and stopped abruptly.

"What is it, Harry? Can't you tell me?" Maggie got the distinct impression Harry was about to tell her something but thought better of it.

"No, except whatever happens, know that I never intended to hurt you."

"Harry, please don't do anything drastic. Things have a way of working out, you'll see." Maggie tried to keep from looking worried.

"Thanks, Maggie. Take care of that cold."

"Good-bye, Harry."

Standing in his bathrobe surrounded by the shadows of his immense living room Harry looked small and frightened. An overwhelming sadness crept over her. Outside, the warm afternoon had turned cold. She walked to the car without looking back.

Maggie, her head feverishly hot, was quiet on the drive back. David, sensing her pain, said nothing. As best she could, Maggie gave him directions to her home when it became apparent she was unable to return to work. When they pulled up in front of her house, she couldn't seem to move.

"I think I'd better walk you up to the door. You don't look too well, Maggie. If I find out anything more, I'll let you know. Don't worry."

"Thanks, David, for everything. You're right though, this cold has me running a fever. I feel so sick."

David got out of the car and opened her door. She was glad when he put his arm around her waist and almost lifted her up each step. He rang the bell and waited for the door to open. Maggie vaguely heard him explaining the situation to her mother.

She was so very tired. Her head ached and her skin felt hot. She only realized David was leaving when the firm grip supporting her loosened. She watched as he headed for the car.

"Take care, David," she whispered. She didn't think he had heard her until he turned and waved good-bye.

"What a polite and competent young man," Mrs. Reynolds said taking Maggie upstairs.

Her mother's voice was the last thing she remembered hearing before she fell asleep.

Chapter 16

A week went by before Maggie felt well enough to return to work. Paul made a pest of himself leaving messages and texts on her cell phone but when he went as far as calling her mother, Mrs. Reynolds told him in no uncertain terms what she thought of him.

Leeann kept her updated on office projects and she was able to handle the majority from home. However, the twice daily running commentaries on Paul's inquiries into her health made her cringe and she finally asked Leeann to stop relaying his pleas.

Nevertheless, Maggie knew their meeting was inevitable but she wasn't prepared to see him sitting in the reception area when she walked off the elevator the following Monday morning. Although she had been mentally practicing for the dreaded moment, her anger got the best of her and she had to fight for composure.

Oh, no! God, why is he here so early? I can't face him. I have nothing to say to him. He's got a lot of nerve showing up here after what he's done. He betrayed me and I can't justify his behavior. Regardless of his motive, his actions are inexcusable. Paul, get out of my life. I can't stand the thought of talking to you let alone seeing you again. Please, just go away.

Paul shot out of the chair and approached her warily. "Maggie, I know you know what I've done but you've got to let me explain."

"Why, Paul? You got your revenge on Harry. It's just too bad I was in the way. Is there anything more to the story than that?"

Maggie was both surprised and pleased at how civil she sounded.

"No, that about sums it up. I told you already how I felt about Harry. Nothing on earth could have prevented me from getting him. You should have known what a bastard he was. I tried to warn you."

"Paul, let's just say I got the message and leave it at that. There's nothing more I have to say to you."

"You mean you're going to allow what I did to Harry to change our relationship?"

"Paul, if I have to explain that in destroying Harry you've destroyed me then we couldn't have meant much to each other."

"That's crazy. I did it because of the way I feel about you. After all, it's like you said; you were only his administrative assistant. Weren't you?"

"I won't even dignify that with an answer."

"Maggie, I'm sorry but we need to talk. Can't we have dinner tonight? Don't you think you owe me that much?"

"I only eat with friends."

"Then let me buy you a drink. I just want to talk to you."

"You want me to listen to your explanations so I can excuse your contemptible behavior."

"Yes, for the sake of what we once meant to each other."

"Paul, even you can't be that hypocritical." As Maggie pushed past him, he grabbed her arm. "Let me go, Paul, I've got work to do." Maggie walked toward her office, furious with Paul who continued dogging her steps.

"I suppose now that you're dating Harry, I've been cancelled out," he pouted.

"Dating Harry?"

"Sure, I know you've been going out with him. What do you take me for?"

"Is that what this was all about, an adolescent case of jealousy?"

"Listen, Maggie, I'm going to keep on annoying you until you let me explain what happened. After that, if you still feel the same way, I'll get out of your life forever."

"All right, Paul, one drink, but I'm holding you to your promise."

"I'll pick you up at eight."

"No, let's meet here. What's the name of that restaurant on the fifth floor?"

"You don't mean the Black Onyx? But Maggie, that place is so loud we won't even hear ourselves think, let alone be able to talk to one another."

"Does that really matter, Paul? And let's make it around nine, I've got an errand to run and I'll be late," Maggie said, feeling positively triumphant as she turned and walked away leaving Paul standing despondently in the middle of the room.

Her errand that evening was a chance opportunity to meet with Harry's aunt. Maggie had gotten a call on Sunday morning from Hoppy who in his unconventional way had taken to calling her regularly. She couldn't help smiling as she recalled their conversation.

"Hi little lady, I was thinkin' about you the other day. Naw, Miss Maggie, that's a dang awful lie. I think about you everyday and I ain't too proud to say it."

"How sweet, Hoppy. That's a very nice compliment."

"Ain't no compliment, just the truth," he said testily. "Anyhow, I got to recollectin' the good old days and it came to me right out of the blue."

"What was that Hoppy?"

"Well, I had a little address book in my personal papers and what do you know if her phone number wasn't in there."

"Whose phone number are you talking about, Hoppy?" Maggie asked, puzzled.

"Why Harry's Aunt Jessie's of course."

"Harry's Aunt Jessie," Maggie repeated excitedly.

"I thought that might shake your apple tree a wee bit. I figured the number might have changed but the nurse here was kind enough to check it out for me. And yep, it's still a workin' number," Hoppy said with unabashed satisfaction.

"What did she say when you spoke to her, Hoppy?"

"Let me tell you, old Aunt Jessie was mighty surprised to hear from me. I think she thought I was dead and buried. She's still as cantankerous as ever and one to be reckoned with, but I told her all about you and she wants to meet you."

"Why, Hoppy, I'd love to meet her. How nice of you to tell her about me. I'll call her right away. Are you doing okay, Hoppy? You mentioned a nurse. Have you been sick?"

"Well, my ticker kind of acted up, Miss Maggie. It was a small attack last week but nothing to worry your pretty head about. They put me here in the clinic but I'll be up and around, right as rain, before you know it. I was kind of hoping to see you again though, maybe even that rascal Harry. That's why I'm being so pesky lately."

"Why of course, Hoppy, I'll be glad to come up. I want very much to see you again, too. How about next weekend?"

"Sounds mighty fine, Miss Maggie. I'm handing the phone over to Miss Gilda and she'll give you Jessie's phone number. Don't forget now. We've got a date."

"See you, Hoppy. Stay well." Maggie took the number down and asked how Hoppy was doing."

"Why, ever since your visit, Miss Reynolds, he's a changed man. He's got more energy than most of us. This was just a small setback. He's really doing much better."

"Thanks, Gilda. I'll be seeing Hoppy soon."

Maggie dialed the number and waited what seemed to be an interminably long time. Just as she was about to hang up she heard a subdued voice at the other end.

"Cooke residence, Jessie Cooke speaking."

After explaining who she was, Maggie asked Miss Cooke if there was any possibility of their meeting in the not too distant future.

"Why, yes, Miss Reynolds. Hoppy's told me so much about you that I feel I already know you. I'm looking forward to meeting you. If you'd like, we could get together tomorrow evening."

"Thank you, Miss Cooke, tomorrow would be perfect!" Maggie was heartened by the swiftness of the invitation and jotted down Aunt Jessie's meticulous instructions on how to reach her home.

"Come before five, dear, won't you?"

"Yes, I'll be there, Miss Cooke."

Allowing for traffic, she gave herself plenty of time to make the drive to the old but charming section of the city where most of the homes, large picturesque edifices, were still very much in demand. The address was clearly visible as she parked on the wide, tree shaded lane off Maple Court.

The house had been well-built back in the late thirties. Even by today's standards the two-story, brown clapboard mansion boasted a regal air. The grounds were surrounded by stately trees and flowers in every shape and variety, and the primly manicured lawn smelled of freshly mowed grass obviously tended to by a professional gardener. Even the oversized windows, decorated in white gingerbread trimmed shutters, showed signs of a green thumb with framed window boxes literally bursting with colorful blooms.

An enormous front porch, reminiscent of long ago summer days when lemonade was the drink of choice, encircled the house. A green swing and yellow rattan chairs and tables were placed invitingly along the balustrade. Wisteria mingled indiscriminately with climbing ivy and both vines clung tenaciously to the weather-beaten woodwork. Tall plants, in a variety of pots and containers, camouflaged the chipped and pealing paint, and achieved, Maggie thought, the look of an old Southern plantation home.

Before she had time to ring the bell a smartly dressed, elderly woman opened the heavy, wooden door. She was almost as tall as Harry but slight of build and rather fragile in appearance. Her hair, plaited and pinned high on her head, was gray and thin. A red gingham apron covered a stylishly long, black dress.

"Please don't stand on ceremony, young lady, come in."

"Miss Cooke?"

"Yes, I'm Jessie Cooke and you must be Maggie Reynolds. Hoppy said you were very pretty."

She ushered Maggie past a magnificently carved staircase that turned and twisted out of view, and into a very big living room.

"Please sit down," she said, pointing to a turn-of-the-century sofa that had been recovered in a lovely blue and red chintz pattern. "Is Maggie your given name?"

"It's actually Margaret Marie, but I've been Maggie ever since I can remember."

"May I call you Maggie?" Miss Cooke asked, eying Maggie subtly.

"Yes, please do, Miss Cooke."

"And you, my dear, must call me Aunt Jessie. Would you like some tea?" Despite her age, she seemed agile and energetic and disappeared into the kitchen before Maggie had time to respond.

"Yes, thank you, Aunt Jessie," Maggie called after her as she surveyed the surroundings of what had once been referred to as the front parlor.

The high ceiling loomed majestically above the room and was accentuated by six broad, red-hued wooden beams which seemed to be suspended in midair. A boarder of elaborately carved crown molding instantly transported her back to the early nineteen hundreds when houses of this type were undeniably in a class by themselves.

Book shelves and curio cabinets were in abundance, skillfully built from the same rich textured burnished wood that had been used throughout the house. The sturdy, craftsmen-like interior glowed from the warmth of the great fireplace which, although burning only a few logs of firewood, gave off a comfortable measure of heat.

Maggie's eyes were drawn to the intricately carved mantelpiece on which were displayed several large framed pictures of Harry in a variety of poses at a much younger age. She was taken aback by one particular photo in which Harry sat astride a pony directly behind a young boy who could have been his double.

Although the room was darkened by yards of green drapery and a rather threadbare rug of the same color, an air of opulence lingered in the atmosphere. Evoking a bye-gone era, the antique furniture pieces, lamps and well-appointed pictures in gilt-edged frames fashioned an ambiance of welcomed hospitality that was unmistakable.

"This house belonged to my grandparents and I've pretty much kept it looking as they left it. It was their gift to me and I felt obligated to maintain its remarkable beauty," Auntie Jessie said by way of explanation as she placed the heavy tea service on the highly polished coffee table in front of Maggie.

"It's a beautiful house, Aunt Jessie. It's original in every detail."

"I'm so glad you appreciate its beauty, Maggie. For a while, after Harry first got hired at WordTech, he'd bring home his friends. My how the house was alive with music and laughter then. That's how I came to know Hoppy, that dear man. Even after Harry stopped visiting, Hoppy and I remained friends for a long while. He was my lifeline to Harry."

"I wish I had known Hoppy then."

"He was quite a charmer. That's probably why he and Harry got on so well. After he left WordTech I lost contact with him and when his wife Laura died I ...," Aunt Jessie's voice trailed off. "But, my dear, we digress. You've come to find out about Harry." It wasn't a question so much as a statement of fact.

"Yes, Aunt Jessie." Maggie accepted the cup of tea and a cookie from the exquisite china plate Aunt Jessie held out to her.

"They're freshly made oatmeal raisin, and my own recipe," she whispered conspiratorially.

"Mmmm…they're delicious."

"My, my, it's been sixteen years since someone's come to ask me about Harry." Aunt Jessie's eyes, twinkling through her little granny glasses, looked straight at Maggie. "That makes you special, my dear."

"I came because I wanted to know Harry better."

"Well of course, and so you shall. But first, tell me a little about yourself."

During their conversation, Maggie perceived that the frank, outspoken woman sitting next to her displayed a resolute stick-to-it-tivness that was as much a part of her character as her strength and will power. Open and candid about her past, it was clear that Aunt Jessie, in spite of a great many trials and hardships, was a survivor.

She had a unique sense of humor and enjoyed peppering her memories with spicy stories that although funny, seemed to kindle occasional wisps of melancholy. Maggie noticed how from time to time she would stop in the middle of a sentence and turn away, staring forlornly at the flames in the fireplace.

"I'm the Cooke family historian," she affirmed proudly, opening one of the many beautifully bound photograph albums lining the bookshelf. "I've kept these photos right up to date. They're a detailed chronicle of our family and I've always hoped Harry would make use of them someday."

"Why Aunt Jessie, this is a picture of you." Maggie pointed to an attractive woman in a revealing swimsuit standing near a lone palm tree on a deserted stretch of beach. "You're beautiful!"

"Yes, I was quite a beauty in my day, and not that I'm bragging, but very popular as well. That was taken by a very good friend of mine on one of our many vacations," she smiled self-assuredly. "People couldn't imagine that I was happy being single. I'd go out and do things. I'd travel, go to dinner and parties and socialize. I liked having men friends around as long as they didn't live with me."

Maggie saw that Jessie still retained her porcelain completion and well shaped figure, and although she had made it clear she was single-at-heart, Maggie wondered if it was partly because of Harry whose pictures she exhibited with a deep sense of pride and longing.

"Here's one of Harry. Don't you think he looks a great deal like his father? Here's one taken with his mother, Iris. She was such a delicate woman."

Delving into the past seemed to reinforce Aunt Jessie's stamina and with each turn of the page her energy heightened. "No," she said with laughter and "No" and "No" again as each picture evoked another memory.

"Aunt Jessie, who is the other little boy pictured in several of the photographs with Harry? They look remarkably alike."

"They should, my dear. That's Harry's twin brother, Arnold." Aunt Jessie paged through the book and pointed at numerous pictures in which the baby boys were docilely posed between both parents.

"Harry was a twin?" Maggie asked in amazement.

"It's no wonder you're surprised my dear, Harry never mentions Arnold. Of course, he never speaks of either his father or his mother for that matter."

"Aunt Jessie, I'm not sure I understand."

"Harry's kept his family a closely guarded secret, not just from you, but everyone. The only person he's ever gotten close to and confided in was Hoppy."

"Can you tell me about his family?"

"Why certainly, my dear, after all, now that you've met the old maiden aunt it's only fair I introduce you to the rest of the Cooke clan," she laughed quietly.

"Maggie shared her smile and took another cookie. "I feel at home already, Aunt Jessie."

"Good, glad to hear it. Now let's get at it. We'll start with Harry's father, my brother, Harold, or as his wife Iris called him, Hank." She pointed to a picture which Maggie thought looked remarkably like Harry.

"As you said Aunt Jessie, Harry's the spitting image of his dad."

"Yes, good looking men run in our family," Aunt Jessie said matter-of-factly before continuing. "Harold was a degreed engineer who graduated at the head of his class. It's funny how youth can never live in the present but must constantly pursue the future," she mused, "and dear Harold was no exception. He got a good paying job at an international copper firm and dated a lot of girls who were crazy over him, but, as fate would have it he fell for Iris Nelson, a hippy-dippy dropout from the lost generation who thumbed her finger at convention and never gave a thought to anyone but herself. I don't know if her parents knew they were naming her after the goddess of the rainbow but I can tell you Iris was not a happy person. She coaxed Harold, much to my parent's chagrin, into her drug-riddled psychedelic world and he gave up being a responsible young man for a lifestyle devoid of stability."

Maggie sat quietly shaking her head at the revelation.

"Yes, it was a bitter pill for my mother and father, particularly since Harold had so much potential. But he loved Iris so much they finally gave in. My father persuaded them with a monetary gift to tie the proverbial knot and soon after they setoff for parts unknown. Their bohemian existence took them all over the world and for a number of years we didn't know where they were. I must say it put a great strain on my mother not knowing whether they were alive or dead but my father had connections and every once in a while he'd get some news as to their whereabouts. Another cup of tea, Maggie?"

"Yes, but please, Aunt Jessie, go on with your story," Maggie said politely waiting for Aunt Jessie to finish pouring.

"Well, after six and a half years they finally came home one summer. Iris was seven months pregnant. She refused to live with any of her relatives, in-laws or out-laws as she called them, and Harold was forced to rent a small house in the suburbs, borrowing from our parents just to get by."

"Did it get better after the boys were born?" Maggie asked hopefully.

"On the contrary, things got worse. Iris was pretty much relegated to staying at home and she hated it. Harold, faced with two extra mouths to feed, straightened up rather quickly and took a job with a mining company. In the beginning he worked at the plant and was home every night. Although Iris was never satisfied and complained constantly, Harold was determined to give his family a normal life. They joined a church and had the boys baptized but when Harold tried to get the family involved in the community, Iris drew the line and would have none of it. Sad to say, it was when the company sent him to South America that Iris really lost it. She was fit to be tied. She didn't want him traveling without her and even though he needed to support his young family, she was furious that she and the children couldn't go with him. She was so jealous and it was quite soon after that her depression became obvious."

"How was that, Aunt Jessie?"

"I don't think Iris was ever into the role of homemaker and mother. I know for a fact she never lifted a finger to do any housework or cook a decent meal, and perhaps it was wrong of me to bring it up to her but when I did all she said was, 'Come on Jessie, it's only dust and it'll be back again tomorrow,' and then she'd stop talking for days, going somewhere inside herself. It was a private world where she pined for her Hank and reminisced about their past life together.''

"She must have loved her husband very much."

"Yes, I think Harold was the only person Iris ever really loved. If he had let her, she'd have farmed out the kids and followed him in a heartbeat."

"Aunt Jessie, was Harry close to his mother?"

"Strange you should ask that. Arnold died of some sort of congenital defect when the twins were three and Iris, who by that time had alienated herself from just about everyone, became completely unstrung. She use to say that the wrong twin had died and that it was God's little joke. Even though Harry was very young, I'm sure he knew how his mother must have felt about him. She'd make up all kinds of excuses to keep him away from her."

"Like what, Aunt Jessie?"

"Well, for instance, if he tried to sit on her lap like Arnold, she'd push him off saying he was too heavy, or if he tried to hug her she'd tell him to stop it and get out of her hair. "Grow up" was her favorite phrase when it came to Harry. She'd carry Arnold around for hours but if Harry cried and asked her to pick him up, she'd haul off and cuff him sharply. She never really took to him even when Arnold was alive but after Arnold's death her feelings became even more apparent. She'd leave Harry completely to his own devises and never seemed concerned about his welfare treating him like the runt of the litter. Whenever I'd come over to help out a little, I'd see Harry, if you can believe it, eating cereal out of the box or munching on some sweets, and he'd say, 'Help, Aunt Jess, feed mama, she's hungry,' but I couldn't even answer him without crying, I was that heartbroken. He was a baby but a mighty independent one."

"You mean Harry looked after his mother? How could that be?"

"Oh, babyish things like dragging a pillow to her bed and lifting her ankles onto it or spilling a cup of water over everything just to bring her a drink. My heart would break for him and I used to beg Iris to let me take him for weekends but she wouldn't hear of it. She was afraid that Harold would come home and not find Harry there."

"Was Iris an alcoholic?"

"No, she never drank alcohol. She had taken her share of drugs when she was younger but when the depression set in, becoming so severe she could no longer handle it, the doctor prescribed medication. However, she began abusing the pills, preferring instead to live a sedated existence at least while my brother was away."

"You mean she'd change when he'd come back?"

"Harold probably knew she was sick but Iris could put on a good act, becoming the loving wife and mother when he was home, making-over her husband and son like it was an everyday occurrence. Little Harry, who worshiped his mother, took it all in stride, getting kisses and hugs one day, and the cold shoulder the next."

"Poor Harry."

"When my brother was killed in that copper mine explosion in Bolivia, Iris couldn't accept it. She became more and more despondent until she finally took her own life with an overdose of sleeping tablets."

"Dear God," Maggie inhaled a sigh.

"Iris made sure Harry was to come and live with me. Although I was not her favorite relative, she preferred me over her own family members. She was meticulous about settling all the insurance monies and handling the paperwork before she left this world."

"When did Harry come to live with you?"

"Now let me see, Harry was four when his father died in March and his mother passed away in the early autumn of that year. He was almost five. I can still see him standing like a little soldier clutching his suitcase when I went to pick him up at the lawyer's office. He was a lonely little orphan who never smiled or cried. When I came in he took my hand and said, 'Time to go, Aunt Jess,' and we walked out to the car together. It was as though he knew he was leaving one life behind and starting another."

"What was Harry like as a little boy?"

"Harry was never a little boy. From the moment he came to live with me he acted grown up. We were at odds with one another from the very beginning, both cursed with the Cooke stubborn streak and neither of us giving an inch. You'd think a four, going on five, year old child would be easy to deal with but he wasn't. He wouldn't listen to anything I said and deliberately went out of his way to disobey me. I was beside myself, and God forgive me, I even gave thought to putting him into a boarding school although he was my brother's only child."

"What changed your mind?"

"Harry changed. Almost overnight you could say. Just when I felt I could endure no more, he somehow figured it out."

"Figured it out?"

"Yes, that it was easier to get bees with honey than with vinegar."

"How did he change exactly?"

"Harry was smart. Soon after he came here, I found him reading. Not baby books but books that were way above his grade level. He was so young I didn't believe it at first. I don't know who taught him or whether he was self taught, but reading was like magic to him and he soon settled down devouring the books I brought home. When I took him to work with me at the library he was a changed child. He'd sit for hours, content after making his selections as though he were in a candy shop. It was a truce of sorts, and the books were like the glue that held it together."

"Harry was smart but didn't he get into mischief like other little boys?"

"No. He was a constant amazement to me, especially since I had no idea what was involved in raising a child. He'd putter around the house always looking for something like an old toaster or lamp or he'd go out to the garage or into the alley and find some old piece of junk and spend hours breaking it apart and putting it back together. He could size up a situation in a flash and come up with a solution. It got to where he got really good at fixing things and some of the neighbors started showing him their broken appliances and he'd make them work."

"Did he have lots of friends?"

"When he was younger he liked being by himself. It was like he couldn't get information fast enough. He may have been a child prodigy. His father was very smart but I never had him tested. Instead he tested me."

"How did he test you, Aunt Jessie?" Maggie suppressed a smile.

"Harry found out early on that the only thing he couldn't break was my iron will. Nobody could. My father use to say that was one of the reasons I'd never marry. I was too darn inflexible for my own good. I wouldn't give in to anyone."

"What did Harry do?"

"Harry determined to charm his way around me, and if you know Harry, you know how appealing he can be when he wants to be. It was the one thing I never figured on and before long he had me right in the palm of his hand."

"I know what you mean."

"I believe there's a goodness in Harry, way down deep. There's no doubt that he's as manipulative as he is charismatic, but I never found him to be a bad person."

"He does have a way about him."

"After that, for the next ten years or so Harry and I got on and enjoyed each other's company. He was always coming up with some scheme or other trying to invent something or make money in a business venture he'd start up. He'd have garage sales with the old stuff he'd polish and shine, and he was very successful. Harry was a born salesman. He had an irresistible side to his character and you couldn't help liking him. He did well in school and worked part time at a gas station when he was only thirteen. I was so proud of him. Every once in a while he'd come up with an idea for a new enterprise and I'd support him. He put me on a pedestal and made me feel as though I were the love of his life. I adored him, Maggie, and I still do."

"What happened as he got older?"

"Harry was always a now person. When he wanted something, he had to have it right away. He couldn't wait. He couldn't and wouldn't discipline himself. Even with his jobs, he never saved any money. When he got older he had a million friends and he'd buy things for them or treat them to cokes and sweets. I couldn't keep food in the house because he was always having friends over and they'd eat me out of house and home. He and I started having run-ins when he got into his late teens. I had to lay down certain rules and he chafed against them."

"What kind of rules, Aunt Jessie?"

"Well, for one thing, I don't believe in drinking, bad language or rowdy partying that can lead to sin. Harry seemed to drift in that direction no matter how I railed against it. When he started being underhanded about breaking the rules, that was the last straw. I found out he had been drinking in the house when I wasn't home. I told him that if it happened again, he'd have to leave. He said he'd rather not have it hanging over his head and packed up that evening. After our falling out he was gone for about a year. I don't know what he did or where he went, but I heard that he fell in with a bad crowd."

"I thought Harry graduated from college?"

"He did, magna cum laude. One day I came home from the library, and there he was, sitting on the front porch in that big green swing just as natural as though he hadn't gone anywhere since breakfast. He told me that he was wrong and that he figured out if he was going to get anywhere in life, he'd have to have a college education. He asked me if I'd forgive him and take him back on whatever conditions I wanted. That's one thing about Harry, once he made up his mind about doing something, nothing stood in his way. He graduated in three years, and I've never seen anyone so driven."

"How did you manage to financially send him to college?"

"Well, I was executor of his parents' estate. He had been left a good deal of insurance money from the mining company his father worked for and my sister-in-law spent very little on herself. Iris made sure Harry would not inherit the bulk of his estate until he turned twenty-five but she took care of all his financial needs. For all her weaknesses, she had a strong mathematical mind and she knew how to invest money. Her instructions were clear about his education and we had enough money on a day to day basis. I used the money frugally, and combined with the money I made and had inherited from my father and mother, we made do nicely."

"Harry gives the impression he was pretty well off."

"Well, we were, and of course I spoiled him by giving into his whims. I have no excuse except that I believed in him. Harry's intelligent, and I thought some of his business ideas and inventions were really very good. Unfortunately we did spend some money on those enterprises but they didn't work out."

"I hope this question doesn't sound too forward but are you financially okay today?"

"Oh yes, dear. My trust fund is still intact and I have my pension from the library. And of course, after Harry got the job at

WordTech he was pretty much set. I don't know if he went through the monies he inherited when he turned of age, but he's always been very generous and continues to make sure I'm taken care of. He was never one to worry about money and somehow I think that's all tied up with the loss of his family."

"He's really a good person at heart," Maggie said softly.

"Do you love him, Maggie?"

"He is my friend and mentor, Aunt Jessie."

"Oh, for some reason I thought you and Harry had a deeper understanding," Aunt Jessie replied, fixing her eyes on Maggie.

"To be honest with you, I believe Harry needs help. He's got so much potential but he's floundering and I'm afraid he's destroying himself."

"I hope he's not up to his old tricks. I always suspected he got involved in some nasty business because his visits became fewer and fewer until he finally stopped coming altogether. Oh, he'd call and promise to come over but I haven't seen him for ever so long." Auntie Jessie put her hand to her mouth and stifled a sigh. "I'm glad to hear that you're helping Harry fight his demons. That says a great deal about you, Maggie."

"My reasons are my own but I do think we need to follow through on what we believe in."

"You're the new generation, Maggie. You want nothing less than to change the world. You remind me a lot of myself when I was young."

"What were you like when you were young, Aunt Jessie?"

"My generation wanted to make a difference and improve society. We were socially aware and concerned about the needs of others. I was always into causes and worked with the poor and needy. I was interested in spiritual objectives rather than materialism."

"It's wonderful to find someone who believes in people as much as I do," Maggie said unreservedly.

"Helping people can make a great deal of difference in their lives and ultimately in our own. Unselfish acts are the closest we come to true happiness."

"Do you believe that we can help people change, Aunt Jessie?"

"Change can happen only if a person wants it but first they need to see and believe they are good and worthwhile human beings. No one is ordinary, Maggie, everyone is extraordinary and they need to hear that."

"I believe that, too, Aunt Jessie."

"When someone has faith in you, it gives you a reason to live. It's like love."

"How's that, Aunt Jessie?"

"Maggie, people don't love people because they're perfect. It would be a pretty unpopulated world if that were the case. If you love someone, you don't give up on them because they have problems."

"Suppose they can't or won't be loved."

"Oh, nonsense, I don't believe there is a soul in the world who wouldn't respond to the power of love. You practice patience, and keep on loving them no matter how rough the going gets."

"Wouldn't you need some proof that they could respond?"

"That's the strange part. I believe the proof's in the gut feeling you either get or you don't get."

"Isn't love a two-way street?"

"Yes, both parties have a stake in the success of the relationship and need to take responsibility if the love is to grow. But it has struck me that it's usually one person in the relationship that loves the other a little more and is happy is make a few extra sacrifices. I think that person is the luckier one."

"Why is that, Aunt Jessie?"

"It's because being loved by someone is wonderful but giving love is something immeasurable that fills the very essence of our souls." Aunt Jessie looked away, sighing at a memory long gone.

"Thank you, Aunt Jessie."

"I'm so pleased it's you who's helping Harry, Maggie. After that woman visited me I must say I had doubts about Harry's friends but you're so sweet and kind." She reached over and touched Maggie's arm encouragingly.

"Is that who you meant when you were talking about your last visitor?"

"Why, yes. She was the most obnoxious person I have ever met. I wanted her to go almost as soon as she got here. You know how you get a feeling about some people. They just don't strike you as right and I was sorry I let her into my home."

"What exactly did she want?"

"That was the strangest thing of all. She wanted a picture of Harry. She said he told her to come here and get one but I knew that was a lie. When I told her no she got very angry. She said she could tell me things about Harry that would curl my hair, of all things. I just wouldn't listen to her. I asked her to leave. I don't even like talking about her now."

"Aunt Jessie, do you remember her name?"

"Funny, but I remember it because the name was in one of my favorite Miss Marple movies. Margaret Rutherford, she played Miss Marple, recited a poem in one of her movies about 'Dangerous Dan McGrue' and that was her name…McGrue, and believe me, she was dangerous, too. I think she did something to Harry. I don't recall what her first name was, but I certainly didn't entertain any thoughts about her when she left. She was bad for Harry, and I knew it."

"Did Harry ever mention her name to you?"

"No, but as I said, Harry doesn't communicate with me anymore. But this woman had an evil streak running through her a mile wide. I could feel it. I had to threaten to call the police to make her leave. She probably put a curse on Harry. He was dumb about women like that if you know what I mean."

"A lot of men are, Aunt Jessie."

"What Harry needs is the love of a good and determined woman," Aunt Jessie, a diminutive smile on her lips, looked straight at Maggie.

"Aunt Jessie, this is important," Maggie said, ignoring Aunt Jessie's comment, "do you remember anything more about the McGrue woman?"

"Goodness, that was such a long time ago and I wanted to forget it. But one thing happened that I was never sure about."

"What was that?"

"I have pictures of Harry over there," Aunt Jessie nodded nostalgically toward the mantel, "and the day she left, one or maybe two, I can't be sure, were missing. They just disappeared. I looked high and low, but I never found them. I know she wanted the pictures and when I refused she got fuming mad but I never left her alone so I don't see how she could have gotten the pictures out of my house."

"But you still think she took them?"

"I don't like blaming people, Maggie, but yes, I think she took them. I don't want to talk about it anymore, dear, it makes me nervous."

"Harry's lucky to have you in his life, Aunt Jessie."

"I miss him so much, Maggie. Your mother is lucky to have such a wonderful daughter."

"I don't want to wear out my welcome, Aunt Jessie, so I think it's about time I went home. May I come and visit you again?" Maggie got up to leave.

"Please come soon, my dear. I don't know when I've had such an enjoyable evening. Perhaps you can persuade Harry to come, too? " Aunt Jessie's eyes glistened as she kissed Maggie's cheek.

"Thank you for everything, Aunt Jessie. I promise to call."

As the door closed, Maggie walked out into the chilly night

pulling her hood over her head. Her cheek felt wet and she realized it was because of Aunt Jessie's tears. Somehow she knew they were as much about her as they were about Harry.

Chapter 17

"Drinks were a bad idea, weren't they?" Paul looked tired and unhappy.

"Paul, I'm no good at pretending. Let's just say good night."

"But its good-bye you're thinking."

"Paul, I won't deny it. I told you there's no point in our seeing each other. Maybe in time, when the hurt's not as raw, I'll come to see things differently but not now." Maggie couldn't keep the anguish out of her voice.

"I'm sorry for the pain I've caused you, Maggie, but not about anything else. I know you don't want to talk about it but do me a favor and read these documents." Paul handed Maggie an envelope.

"Paul, I…"

"Don't say anything now. Just read them and my notes, too. If you want, call me and we'll talk. But you're right, Maggie, it's about time we get going. After all, there's no point in prolonging the end."

~❦~

When Maggie pulled into the driveway the patio lights were on and her mother was standing in the doorway.

"Mom, you shouldn't have waited up. It's late."

"I made some hot cocoa like I used to when you were little,

remember Maggie? Come and have a cup."

"Thanks, Mom," Maggie said as she sat down at the kitchen table and cautiously dipped her tongue in the frothy concoction. "Mummm, it's good and hot."

"Maggie, tell me the truth. You haven't fallen for Harry, have you?"

"Mom, I can't say whether it has anything to do with the kind of love you're talking about but I do know I care about him."

"What he's done has put you both in jeopardy."

"Mom, Harry's a sick man and if my typing his journal helps him in even the smallest way to get better then I'm glad I did it."

"I must admit, I would have questioned his motives, but not you, Maggie. Harry can do no wrong in your book."

"Mom, you're forgetting that this whole mess happened because Paul hates Harry."

"Yes, I know Paul was wrong going behind your back the way he did, but he loves you. Men are strange creatures, Maggie, especially when it comes to love."

"Please stop sticking up for him, Mother. Anyway, I'll say good night. I've got some reports to read."

"Now you're mad at me, Maggie. I only say the things I do because I love you and I'm worried about you."

"I know that Mom and I love you, too, but really, I do have some things to read." Maggie gave her mother a hug and headed up to her room where she spent the better part of an hour going over Paul's documents.

At first glance, she saw how organized Paul had been in detailing the material with names, dates and explanations but the confidentiality of the personnel records concerned her. She thought about putting them back but her inquisitive nature got the best of her and she decided to read them in spite of her apprehensions.

How did Paul get these? Will I be compounding one offense with another by reading them? Paul paints Harry as some tyrannical dictator who either fired or transferred any employee who transgressed against him. Is there any truth to this or could there be another explanation?

Maggie noted the dates documented the past twenty years of employee records at WordTech and could only guess at the devises Paul had used to secure the information.

If these ever got into wrong hands there's no telling how much damage could be done.

As she read through the files, she could find no tangible evidence of Harry's having persecuted any of the employees that worked under him. She was sure that Paul's personal experiences had colored his objectivity and convinced him of Harry's guilt.

What was Paul's motive in giving me these files? It's obvious he wants to destroy my faith in Harry, but to suggest that Harry victimized those who fell from his favor is monstrous. It's true, Harry's a micro-manager without a lot of people skills but the documents show that he followed all the proper channels in disciplining his staff. Perhaps Paul wants to frighten me but whatever his reasons, the whole idea is preposterous. These aren't the Dark Ages and Harry has only as much power as the company allows. Paul's grasping at straws to save his own inflated vanity and I truly don't think there's any truth to his inferences. If I did, I'd have to admit it regardless of my feelings for Harry.

As Maggie sat fighting with herself over whether or not to make the phone call to Paul, her eyes suddenly fell upon a name she had heard before, McGrue. Kate McGrue, the infamous KM. She picked up the file and began to read through the material. It was a detailed report beginning with Kate McGrue's start date and ending with the last day worked. The words "**NOT ELIGIBLE FOR REHIRE**" were stamped boldly across several of the documents in red ink.

Kate McGrue's position was listed as head secretary to several salesmen in both the Advertising and Marketing departments. A generic work history followed with information on annual performance appraisals that included several negative write-ups. Maggie was about to dismiss the information when she noticed a document stapled to the final entry. It was signed by both Harry and the assistant manager.

It is our recommendation that Kate McGrue be immediately terminated. She has admitted falsifying credit card accounts which the company interprets as tantamount to thievery. Miss McGrue has confessed to both the assistant manager and me that she, as sole perpetrator of the fraudulent scheme, used the WordTech billing system to deliberately defraud and mislead customers out of monies they had used for advertising purposes.

During her ten years of employment, Miss McGrue has admitted that she began this fraudulent operation over eight years ago and continued to charge clients an inflated sum on their ad placement when in actuality the cost was less than she proposed. The clients were never made aware of the actual difference, which although nominal, added up to sizable amounts over the years. Miss McGrue admitted transferring the overage into personal bank accounts. The Accounting department brought this incident to the department's attention. The city attorney is now involved in the case. A copy of this recommendation has been sent to the corporate office.

Maggie reread the personnel file with new found interest. In examining the performance appraisals, write-ups and management comments she was particularly interested in the dates Harry had signed the documents. Copies of several newspaper articles, probably inserted by HR, revealed that Kate McGrue had been convicted and sentenced to prison and was currently serving a two year term.

On a hunch, Maggie copied the personal information on Kate including several old addresses and phone numbers. She noticed that on the final document someone had scrawled a different phone number on the side and she took that number down as well. Then she picked up the phone and called Paul.

"Paul, it's me."

"I've been waiting for your call. Can we meet somewhere?"

"It's so late."

"It's only a little past one."

"Where?"

"I'll pick you up in twenty minutes. We can decide then."

"Paul, I..."

"Don't say anything, Maggie. I'll be right over."

It was a sleazy all-night café and they were the only customers. Paul ordered a pot of tea for Maggie and a cup of coffee for himself. However, when the waitress returned she sat a pot of steaming coffee and two mugs between them.

"I'm sorry but the order was for a pot of tea." Maggie looked questioningly at the waitress.

"We ain't got no tea or teapots," she responded indifferently.

"I'll just have a glass of water." Maggie saw the annoyance in the woman's eyes but a minute later she returned with a half filled glass of tepid water.

"We're still charging you for the pot of coffee," she said defiantly, turning on her heels and walking away.

"Not the kind of place we're used to," Paul said, staring regretfully at Maggie from behind his coffee cup.

"No, that's for sure."

"For God's sake, Maggie, look at me. I'm not the devil incarnate."

"Aren't you, Paul. I can hardly believe what you did, let alone the lengths you've gone to trying to prove your case. What impels you? You're out on a limb and for what?"

"Hatred, sheer hatred, that's what. I'm mad as hell and I'm going to make sure that snake in the grass is found out. Too bad, Maggie, but I think you're already a victim."

"Paul, you don't get mad unless you're hurt. In your case, terribly hurt. Isn't it possible you could be wrong? After all, every one of the employees listed in those files actually did commit a wrongdoing of some nature, regardless of how petty. True, some managers might have made light of it and let it go but Harry choose to discipline those staff members and brought HR into the resolutions. As far as I could tell, he did nothing out of the ordinary."

"You can't see it, can you, Maggie? Harry's tyrannical hold over everyone who works for him."

"Paul, you and I both know that in the corporate world there are managers who might have made it a lot worse for those people than Harry did."

"There you go again, justifying Harry's behavior."

"I'm not doing anything of the sort but whether you realize it or not, we're all part of the corporate game. Surviving is one thing, but betrayal is another."

"That's really hitting below the belt, Maggie."

"Yes, Paul, but can you deny it?"

"Harry's led you to believe you had a job that was open and above board, and now you're facing a reprimand for a transgression which could lead to termination. And you're calling me disloyal? What will it take to wake you up?"

"Paul, I wish I could come up with an answer that would satisfy you."

"Maggie, I really think God broke the mold after He made you. Your mistake is being too nice to people who don't deserve it. You look for the good in the other guy but not everyone sees life through such rose-colored glasses."

"What do you mean, Paul?"

"Simply this, you don't for one minute believe it was his wife that Harry took to all those out of town conventions, do you?"

"You must have learned a lot from those card playing chums of yours, Paul."

"So you know about that, too. Well, sure, we talked."

"Gossiped is more like it. Is that what you based your research on?"

"I wish you believed in me half as much as you believe in Harry."

"Paul, try to understand that what we had together is over."

"I guess I knew it was coming but hearing you say it hurts like hell."

"Paul, did you really expect me to see it your way and that everything would be like it was before? You don't care who you destroy. You're so consumed by hate you're no longer thinking straight."

"I wanted you to know what damage he's done to other people's lives. How he's manipulated the system to his own advantage. He distrusts anyone who argues with him, and if he harbors the least suspicion about you, you're history."

"Paul, you're not being objective. Your argument is based on how you perceive Harry and what he did to you. You've got parts of the story but you don't see the whole. I've worked with this man for seven years and I've seen him do the best he could for the people in his department. Granted, there are those who are not happy with him but I for one could never betray him."

"You don't have to worry about betraying him. He'll take care of that, Maggie. Everything is fine as long as you don't cross his path or way a red flag in front of him. Once he's discovered that the prey has strayed, either deliberately or by mistake, it's over. Harry devises a plan to which only he is privy and subtly and slowly obliterates his enemy. Once he's locked horns on his victim, he's tenacious, intractable and merciless. He cunningly intertwines the web, and little by little tightens it until the victim perishes."

"Oh Paul, that's rubbish. You're just being dramatic. No one in your file was killed or hurt in any physical way. People make mistakes. They lose their jobs, but they move on. At least most people do."

"That's just the point, Maggie. It's psychological terror. By the time Harry finishes, the prey no longer presents any danger, to itself or anyone else. He or she is usually discharged for some vague shortcoming, driven to anxiousness or with any luck, able to get out of the department, like me."

"That really tears it, Paul. I've witnessed how Harry handles personnel problems. Sure, there are times when he's opinionated, unreasonable, and perhaps overly dogmatic about infractions but what you're suggesting is hideous. HR has always been made aware of the situations, and if people disagree they have recourse to take their disagreements there. Sometimes things get ironed out favorably, and sometimes not. I won't listen to anymore of it, Paul. You're so full of hatred and jealously, you're no longer being realistic. Painting abhorrent pictures of Harry and defaming his reputation all because he chastised you."

"It's good to see you're finally letting your hair down, Maggie."

"My God, Paul, you've carried this sack of hatred for such a long time. It's childish and beneath you. I can only hope you come to your senses and get help before you destroy not only Harry but yourself as well."

"Now who's trying to convince who?"

"Paul, listen to me. Even if there were a modicum of truth in what you say, which there isn't, hate like yours is poisonous and you're killing yourself. The papers are filled with stories of employees who wait for years and then take revenge. For your own sake get rid of this file." Maggie took the envelope out of her purse and pushed it across the table.

"Maggie, as I said, Harry is subtle. Most of his victims never realized what was happening. Remember when we use to play hangman? It was fair because every time you missed, another piece of the scaffold was drawn in. Harry doesn't play fair. He makes up the rules as he goes along. Maybe I am trying to frighten you, but I don't want you to wake up one day and find the noose around your pretty neck."

"Paul, I do have one question. Why have you been able to skirt the revenge of Harry? What magic do you possess that permits you to have waved the red flag and yet managed to avoid Harry's maniacal retribution?"

"I haven't Maggie. I'm number one on his hit list. But he knows I know, and he's more circumspect in my regard. I'd love to have seen his face when he realized I'm the one who got him on this ethics investigation charge."

"Paul, this situation no longer involves just you and Harry. You've taken it upon yourself to include the entire company. You've exposed me to a corporate investigation that could easily cost me my job. I'm beginning to doubt my own ability to make judgments. I've been put in a position that requires me to defend even minor decisions where before I never had to qualify my actions. The company trusted me, Paul, and you destroyed that trust. I wish you had believed in me enough to know that I would never have compromised my ethics or belief system for anyone. It's regrettable, but in doing what you say you had to do, you've shattered our friendship."

"I warned you but I can see there's no point in trying to convince you, Maggie. I want you to remember one thing. If you should ever need me, I'll be there for you. Like you said, we are both true to our friends."

"It would've been nice, Paul, if you had remembered that before taking matters into your own hands. You never once thought of including me before walking your evidence up to Corporate."

"I did write a note but I didn't leave it. I don't suppose it would do any good to show it to you now?"

"No, Paul." Maggie didn't even try to keep the bitterness out of her voice but her eyes began to sting. "Perhaps it would be better if you left now. I'll catch a cab." She watched as Paul picked up the envelope and paid the tab before walking out the door.

Maggie returned home exhausted. She was beginning to wonder if these late night confrontations were taking a toll on her health. Almost asleep on her feet, she was halfway up the stairs when her cell phone rang. She and Paul had parted in silence and she was glad it wasn't him.

"Hello Harry. Why so late?"

"Maggie, you were right. The CEO called me today. He wants me to come in tomorrow and talk about the situation."

"What did you tell him?"

"I told him exactly what you and I decided to tell him. I told him I was going to take time off and work through the health problems I was having. I told him if he had any questions to contact you."

"Thanks a lot, Harry."

"Listen, just stick to our story. You have nothing to worry about."

"Story?" Maggie repeated the word incredulously. "That story as you call it was what you initially told me this was all about. As far as I'm concerned I can't see why Corporate would make an issue out of this when it involves your doctor's participation in your health issues."

"Sure, Maggie, that's right. I don't want to say anything more right now, but I'll phone you later."

"Harry..." but Maggie knew they were disconnected.

Another week ended without a call from Corporate. As she waited for the inevitable, the strain played havoc with her nerves. She was jumpy and irritable and on more than one occasion Leeann remarked that it was like working with a time bomb. Several times Maggie was tempted to send out her resume but under the circumstances felt it was better to wait and see the difficulty through to its proper conclusion. Instead she spent hours in the gym working off excess energy and taking long walks in the country on weekends.

Harry was officially on disability and had been out of the office for three weeks. The workload piled up and Maggie worked overtime to keep on top of the projects, grateful for the opportunity to forget her problems. She was filing in Harry's office when she heard her office phone ring.

"Corporate's on your line, Maggie, do you want me to transfer it in there?"

"Yes, Leeann," Maggie said, taking a deep breath.

The conversation was brief. She was expected in the CEO's office tomorrow morning at eight. Reawakened fears now became troubled thoughts.

Perhaps it's not as bad as Paul has led me to believe. I've kept to myself and said nothing to anyone about the situation, the fewer people who know about it the better. Paul's been true to his word and has made no attempt to contact me. David knows but he's been great. He realizes how much stress I'm under and he's a good friend. And Leeann's kept me as calm under the circumstances as she could with her vigil of nightly phone calls. I'll tell Corporate the exact truth and hope they see the logic in my making the choice I did.

"Leeann, thanks for being there for me. In a way I'm glad it's almost over," Maggie said, watching as Leeann calendared the early morning meeting on her computer.

"Are you going to be okay, Maggie?" Leeann looked worried.

"I think so. Could I ask a favor?"

"Name it, kid."

"Is there any chance you could run a little interference for me and find out what happened to a Kate McGrue? She worked at the company about eighteen years ago."

"McGrue? Why does that name sound so familiar? Let me see what I can find out.

"Thanks, Leeann."

"Keep a positive thought, Maggie. It'll all turn out okay." Leeann gave her a thumbs-up.

Maggie smiled. "See you tomorrow after the meeting, I hope."

Gloria Preston

Part Two

Chapter 18

The rewind tape sputtered to an end and Maggie slowly emerged from the past. It was like coming out of an anesthetic. Everything at first was blurred and unrecognizable but piece by piece the puzzle began to fit together. She could hear Leeann's voice off in the distance.

"Maggie, Maggie, snap out of it."

"I was thinking about Paul. I was sitting in front of the office window, reminiscing about meeting him years ago, and suddenly I got so tired. I only closed my eyes for a moment."

"You okay now, kid?" Leeann asked as she placed a wet paper towel on her forehead.

Maggie took the compress and put it against her neck. "I'm okay, Leeann, thanks."

"I thought you were unconscious, or dead or something."

"My journey through time caught up with me, Leeann. The years melted into minutes. I've got such a headache."

"It's probably due to looking back on your muddled life. I knew you were exhausted when you came back from that lousy meeting but you scared the shit out of me when you started mumbling all that stuff that didn't make any sense."

"I was just overly tired." Maggie opened her water bottle and took a sip. "I feel fine now."

"Maybe you should go home and get some sleep, Mag. Stress

can kill you."

"God, is that the right time? I'm supposed to be meeting Harry right now. Can you call me a cab, Leeann? Tell them I'll meet it downstairs at the south entrance."

"Sure, Maggie, but take it easy. Nothing Harry could say would be that important."

❦

In the cab over to the restaurant Maggie reviewed the day's events and knew she had made the right decision. Regardless of what Paul and the others in the company might think, a man's sanity was at stake and she had chosen to help him.

As she approached the table in the tiny bistro Harry was staring at the bottom of his empty glass. In the dimly lit room the candles on the tables cast shadows across his tired face. His disheveled appearance reminded her of a broken down character actor in an old movie.

"Hi, Harry. Sorry to be so late."

"C'mere."

Maggie went round to Harry's side of the table and bent down to his level. "What's wrong, Harry? Are you sick?"

He looked up into her face and brought her chin close to his mouth. "This will have to last me forever." He kissed her gently.

"Harry, you look awful. I've never seen you like this. Have you been drinking all afternoon?"

"Sit down, Maggie, and have a drink. You'll need it when I tell you what I've done." Harry signaled the waiter for another round.

"Harry, you're talking nonsense."

"There'll be a scandal, Maggie. I'll be ruined. My career at WordTech's finished. I won't be able to hold my head up anywhere on the street. And I can only guess what will happen to you."

"What are you talking about, Harry?" Maggie grew quiet.

"WordTech will find out the truth. Then the shit will hit the fan."

"Oh, Harry, are you still worried about that silly drivel you wrote in your journal. It's all right. I spoke to Cummings and the corporate attorney and told them the truth. The good news is that they've accepted it and they're in your corner. They want you to get well and the sooner the better." Maggie sipped her drink and smiled.

"Maggie, Maggie, what you told them wasn't the truth."

Harry's hand was visibly shaking. The glow from the candle exaggerated his bloodshot eyes.

"What do you mean, Harry? Not the truth?" Maggie was trying hard to remain calm.

"I don't know how to tell you."

"Try hard, Harry."

"I lied to you. The reason I gave you about writing the journal was a damn lie."

"For God's sake, Harry, what are you talking about?"

"None of it was true, Maggie. I used you. I wanted to write a book. It seemed like such a small thing at first. This friend of mine gave me the idea and said a publisher would pay me for the memoirs."

"Are you kidding, Harry?" Maggie felt the color drain from her face.

"No, I wish I were. I'm sorry, Maggie. I told you once I was a no good sonofabitch. Maybe now you'll believe me. What hurts most is that I've destroyed us and anything we might have had."

"Harry, I don't believe it. What could you have been thinking?"

"The stuff I wrote sounded good to me. I thought with your skill at editing, I'd have a best seller. I thought it would be a slam dunk but you put up such a fuss I had to make up that crap about seeing a doctor."

"Harry, let me get this straight. You used me to type a personal novel on company time just to get a book published? I guess I should be flattered but instead I feel utterly devastated." Maggie took a gulp of her drink and sat back.

"I had my friend look up this producer and he said I had a good shot at a reality TV series. Looking back at it now, I must have been crazy but when they proposed it, I believed it. I even put up money to finance it. Nobody's ever too stupid or gullible, huh Maggie?"

"Harry, you put our jobs on the line for something as crazy as that?" Maggie was incredulous.

"Once WordTech finds out there was never any doctor, they'll never believe you knew nothing about the book."

"Harry, how could you? You set me up. The therapy journal, the doctor, your nervous breakdown, it was all a ruse? You couldn't be that despicable." Maggie shook her head in disbelief. "You made up the entire thing just so I'd type your dime store romances. I just can't believe it."

"Maggie, stop looking at me like that. Why don't you get mad, really mad! Tell me I'm a bastard. Tell me to go to hell."

"Oh, Harry, shut up. You know, I knew you were sick before, but I didn't realize how very sick you really are."

"Maggie, what are we going to do?" Harry put his head down.

"We don't have a choice, Harry. Look at me, damn you, and listen carefully. Ironically, it's your journal that's the only thing true about you. Somewhere in that tapestry of lies you've woven is a part of your authentic self and I believe with a doctor's help you'll find that truth. Anyway, in your state it won't take much to prove that you needed and sought treatment."

"But, Maggie, what happens when they find out there never was a doctor?"

"Oh, but there will be a doctor, Harry. And you will be in therapy. You've been running on empty for some time, Harry, and you're fresh out of options."

"Okay, Maggie. What do we do? Just tell me how I get myself out of this."

"Get us out of it, Harry. I'm in this just as deep as you."

"Of course, sorry, Maggie." Harry sounded spent.

"I'll call the doctor tonight and let her know you'll call her first thing in the morning to make an appointment. After you see the doctor, call Corporate and tell the CEO that you're working with her on your treatment sessions."

"Will she go along with it? What about the journal?"

"You'll actually start therapy with her and you can ask her about the journal. Tell her the truth, and who knows, she'll probably want to see the bloody thing. After all, it's a very telling part of your life."

"That's makes sense. Corporate has your word that the whole thing was true, and you're so damned principled no one would ever believe you'd be unethical."

"Oh no you don't, Harry. The price you'll pay is sticking to the plan and making it true. You'll keep your appointments with the doctor and take time off on disability until you get a clean bill of health, otherwise there's no deal."

"You mean you really want me to see this shrink?"

"It's the only way I'll stand by you."

"Sure, whatever you say, Maggie."

"Harry, don't try to placate me. I've had it up to here and I won't take it anymore. I'm tired of trying to sober you up. I'm tired of trying to cover for you. I'm tired of hearing you say one thing and than turn around and do something else. Whether you believe it or not, you really do need help. I want you to get well. This is your last scheme. Do you hear me? You either pull yourself together or else."

"Is that an ultimatum, Maggie?"

"Yes, Harry. I have no intentions of playing the patsy for you, now or ever."

"I'm sorry for the mess, but nobody needs to know about it."

"Harry, your secret life is safe but only if you go through with the program. One slip or any excuse about missing a medical appointment and I walk straight to the CEO's office."

"Maggie, I..."

"Don't say anything more, Harry. Strangely enough it's your secret that will save your sanity, provided you cooperate fully with the doctor. It's up to you." Maggie pressed Clair's business card into Harry's unsteady hand. "Put this in your pocket. You're not too drunk to remember to call her tomorrow morning. Do you hear me, Harry?"

"Yes, Maggie, but how will the doctor know about me?"

"Don't worry, I'll call and tell her everything. She's a great person and I know she'll help you if you really want it. She's also my friend, so don't think you can bluff your way out of this one."

"I've finally painted myself into a corner, Maggie. It's the end of the line." Harry drained his glass, dribbling the last few dregs over his chin.

"Remember Harry, nothing happens by chance, only by choice."

"You mean you think I wanted this to happen?"

"Not on any conscious level but somewhere inside you called for help."

"What have I done?" Harry kept shaking his head.

"Harry, let's go. Remember, take no calls from Corporate and don't talk to anyone until after you've had your initial session with Dr. Sebastian."

"Got'cha, Maggie. Just pour me into a cab and send me home, honey."

When the taxi arrived, Maggie helped the driver get Harry inside and then gave him the address.

"Harry, call me after you make the appointment."

Harry nodded as the driver slammed the door shut.

As she stood on the corner waiting for another cab Maggie

thought about Harry and the events whirlpooling around her.

I was warned, but went ahead, eyes wide open. I have no one to blame but myself.

⁂

As her taxi made its way through the darkened streets, Maggie felt as though Harry's confession had robbed her of the last vestige of hope she had in him. The immediacy of a call to Clare was upper most in her mind and she was both relieved and thankful when the doctor answered her private line. In between sobs, Maggie blurted out what had happened and Clare advised her to come straight away to the clinic.

"Clare, you were right after all. Harry had no intentions of seeing a doctor. I'm the one who got caught believing in him."

Clare said nothing but listened as Maggie disclosed the events of the day. After an emotionally charged hour, Maggie regained her composure and sipped at her tea.

"Now that I've dumped all this on you, what's going to happen?"

"Maggie, that's why I'm here; do not trouble yourself."

"What about Harry, Clare? Will you be able to see him?"

"One can see you are still very much involved in Harry's life. And yes, I will see him, but you understand that my working with him is contingent on his making the first call. I need to hear from him that he wants to take responsibility for his own welfare. After that, we will see. The results of the initial examination are important but much depends on Harry and his willingness to accept treatment whatever the diagnosis."

"Thank you, Clare. It's such a relief to hear that Harry will get the help he needs. There were moments when I thought this convoluted journey of his would destroy us both."

"What about you, Maggie?"

"After tonight, I'm not sure of anything anymore. I don't know what I would have done if I hadn't had a chance to talk to you."

"You'll need to stay in therapy, Maggie."

"I know that, Clare. The whole thing makes me feel out of control. I feel like I'm in a circus sideshow. I know you warned me but honestly I never thought he would do something like this."

"My friend, you are like Joan of Arc, heroically leading the charge in the face of adversity but fortunately you've recognized the need for caution before... ."

"...being burned alive," Maggie interrupted cynically. "Well, of one thing I wasn't wrong. Harry does need help. I think realizing he was as sick as he was scared me."

"Maggie, call me as soon as you can make another appointment for yourself."

"Thanks, Clare, for everything. I'll get back to you in a few days," Maggie promised.

After leaving Clare's office, she slowly made her way down the dimly lit clinic walkway toward the exit. As she passed the crowded waiting room overflowing with those who had come seeking help, her heart sank. The depressive, dispiriting atmosphere was dismally pervasive and she turned without thinking into an unmarked corridor.

The narrow passageway was dark and deserted. She could hear her heels echoing against the steep stone floor as she descended into a shadowy lower level. It was clammy and reeked of antiseptic. Massive, double-bolted security doors framed gray, dungeon-like walls from which low, muffled cries and indistinguishable voices seemed to emanate. Her heart began racing as she hurried her pace, desperate to find a way out of the tomb-like labyrinth. Overwhelming darkness enveloped her vision and distrust in her own reflexes increased. Fear gnawed at her insides as she pushed to no avail against several locked doors. It was silly she tried to tell herself even as her panic swelled. A scream caught in her throat and she heard herself shouting into the blackness, "God help me." Seeking vainly for an exit sign she at first discounted the twinkle of blue light in the far distance but as it grew larger, giving her a sense of direction, she began running toward it. Dashing down the hallway toward the tiny beacon she was overjoyed to discover a door that showed a crack of light. It opened into a pleasant, little chapel. Emotionally spent, she entered quickly and took refuge in the comfort of the cozy room.

It was as though she had entered another realm, redolent with the fragrance of flowers and shimmering with the warmth of candle light. Overcome with a sense of peace, she thought suddenly of Tony. For as long as she had known him his level-headedness had been a source of strength and understanding. Calmed by the reflection, she became aware of a deep feeling of reassurance, so compelling she knew that whatever happened, she and Harry would make it through this awful time.

She began to cry. Hot, salty tears poured down her cheeks in blessed release. Minutes slipped by as she embraced the solitude. Her mind, desperate to retreat, focused on the quiet, tranquil silence and the only sound she heard were her whispered prayers for Harry.

Dear Lord, help him. He has so much potential yet he cannot find peace. Please help him to help himself. May he find the courage to believe that he is a good person and that You, dear God, will give him the power to change his life.

Chapter 19

With Harry in rehab Maggie again took on managerial responsibilities. This time, however, she had no idea for how long. With virtually no opportunity to reflect on personal dilemmas, she buried herself in contracts and presentations, gradually regaining a life of normalcy. By the end of the month, she was pretty much on top of things and decided to catch up on her promised visit to Hoppy.

Calling the rest home to check on visitation hours she was delighted to hear that Hoppy was out of the clinic and back in his bungalow. However, when Mrs. Kemper asked her to speak directly to Hoppy to arrange the date, Maggie noted a decidedly protective tone and realized the director did not want to risk further disappointment for her client.

"Hoppy, I'm sorry I had to postpone our last few visits but I'll be there at ten thirty this morning, if that's all right with you?"

"I'm counting on you this time, Miss Maggie. I'll see you when you get here," Hoppy said impatiently.

She had barely hung up when her cell phone rang.

"Hi, Maggie, got a minute?"

"Harry?" Maggie had not heard from Harry since he had gone into rehab and she was at once startled and concerned. "Harry, how are you? Is anything wrong?"

"No, everything's okay." Harry sounded hesitant. "It's just that

I've been allowed out of isolation for a couple of days and it's the first chance I've had to call you."

"You sound so, so different. Are you all right?"

"This past month has been hell, but Dr. Sebastian says I qualify for a weekend pass. I needed to talk to you so badly, Maggie, you don't know."

"Harry, it's good to hear you're doing better. I was so worried about you."

"The doctor's got me on meds but she's letting me out on my own recognizance as long as I promise to be a good boy and be back at the clinic Sunday afternoon." Harry's voice was raspy.

"Harry, I'm so glad."

"She's a good doctor, Maggie. Thank you seems so lame but maybe with both of you helping me I can make it. I'm just beginning to realize how important it is to have something to look forward to. Is there any chance I could see you today?"

"Harry, I'm sorry but I've got an appointment that I can't reschedule. I was just leaving the house."

"Sure, sure, I understand." Harry sounded let down.

"As a matter of fact, I'm going out to see a friend of yours. Would you care to join me?" Maggie recalled Hoppy's request.

"I don't have many friends left. Who is it?"

"Hoppy Dixon." Maggie waited for a response and then asked, "Harry, you still there?"

"Yeah, what makes you think he'd want to see me? It's been a long time."

"I think he would, Harry. He talks a lot about you and it might do you some good to see him, too."

"I'm not sure if I'm up to it, sober and all…"

"Let me pick you up. But you'll have to be ready to go in thirty minutes. I promised Hoppy I'd be there at ten thirty and I can't disappoint him."

"I don't know, Maggie. Maybe you'd better go by yourself."

"Be ready, Harry, and no excuses. I'll be there at nine."

"Okay, as long as you think it'd be all right."

When Maggie drove up she saw Harry sitting on the stoop in front of his house. It was precisely nine o'clock.

"Hi lady, could you spare a ride to the old folk's home?" Harry laughed his old familiar laugh as he looked in through the open car window.

"Get in, silly."

As he opened the door and slid in next to her, Maggie was encouraged by what she saw. Clean shaven, well dressed and smelling only of aftershave, Harry looked like his old self.

"I'm impressed, Harry. You look human again."

"Yes, I'm stone cold sober, too."

"A far cry from when I saw you last."

"After that meeting I didn't think you'd ever want to see me again. What changed your mind?"

"Harry, let's just say you weren't yourself and leave it at that."

In a loquacious mood, Harry did nothing but talk for the duration of the ride. He was impressed with Clare, the rehab clinic, and what was involved in the intake process. Sounding like a medical student, he spoke but didn't dwell on some of the less than pleasant treatments he had endured. He seemed upbeat for a guy who had been cut off from his favorite pastime but knowing Harry as she did, Maggie recognized the con artist bravado that hid his fears and doubts.

"How are you, really, Harry?"

"I thought I was well enough to make this trip but maybe this wasn't such a good idea. Want to stop and get a cup of coffee?"

"We've arrived, Harry. There's no turning back."

As Maggie turned the car into the Mount Abbey driveway she

noticed Harry fidgeting with his seatbelt and squirming in his seat.

"What's wrong, Harry, got cold feet?"

"Yes, I'm having second thoughts. What if the old man sees me and has a heart attack or something?"

"Harry, don't pull a guilt trip on me. Hoppy's pretty strong and it would do him good to see you again. Stop thinking of yourself and think of someone else for a change."

"Okay, okay. Let's get it over with. I just wish I had a drink."

"We'll order you a nice, big glass of tomato juice as soon as we're inside," Maggie said chidingly as she parked the car and led the way toward the entrance.

"That's not exactly what I had in mind," Harry mumbled under his breath.

"Welcome back, Miss Reynolds. Hoppy has done nothing but anticipate your visit. It's about all we can do to keep him from getting overexcited," Mrs. Kemper said frankly. "And two visitors in one day; won't that surprise him?" She smiled, genuinely pleased to see Harry.

"I appreciate you letting me come on such short notice, Mrs. Kemper. Hoppy and I go way back," Harry added nervously.

Mrs. Kemper led them to the lanai where they waited for a nursing assistant to walk them across the grounds to Hoppy's.

"Pretty plush," Harry whistled softly as they were led to one of the detached bungalows nestled off a private cul-de-sac.

"It's charming, like a quaint English cottage," Maggie said admiringly as they strolled through an exquisitely manicured garden and up a cobblestone path.

After the aide rang the bell and departed, Harry grinned at Maggie. "I sure as hell wouldn't mind retiring here myself."

The door opened and a short, squat man in a white orderly's uniform invited them in. "Mr. Dixon's awaiting you in the sunroom," he informed them. "This way, please."

He led the way through several rooms tastefully decorated in mahogany and cowhide furniture. The western motif, Maggie noted, was exact, down to the famous cowboys whose pictures decorated the walls.

"Hi Hoppy," Maggie yelled as she entered the room.

Although taken aback by Hoppy's appearance, she did not let on. He was seated in a wheelchair and looked much weaker than when she had seen him last. He beckoned her over and kissed her on the cheek. It was then that he saw Harry.

"Harry, is that you, you old son of a gun?"

"You recognized me, Hop, after all these years? Hope it was okay for me to come up with Maggie to see you?"

"Harry, Harry Cooke," Hoppy said croakily, the words catching in his throat.

It seemed it was all Hoppy could do to keep from howling out loud. The change in his demeanor was phenomenal. In a matter of minutes, he looked younger, stronger and more alert.

"You look great, Harry. Just like old times."

"Thanks, Hop. I can't say the same about you, old timer. What are you doing in that contraption?" Harry eyed Hoppy's wheelchair with disbelief.

"The same old Harry. Damn but it's good to see you, son. I've thought a lot about you. Wondering what you were up to, and how things were going for you." Hoppy suddenly stopped talking and looked at his caretaker. "Quincy, don't stand there dawdling. Let's get these folks some refreshments. What would you like, although if memory serves me, it's scotch for you, right Harry?" His eyes locked on Harry almost as though he expected him to disappear.

"Coffee and tomato juice would be fine, Hoppy." Maggie was quick to answer giving Harry a sharp glance of disapproval.

"Sure Hop, like Maggie said, coffee and juice would be fine."

"A little too early yet, huh, Harry? I can remember back when you'd think nothing of hoisting a couple before breakfast," Hoppy said chuckling.

"Those were the days, Hop." Harry sat down on the leather divan next to Hoppy. "So this is where you've been hiding out? It's a pretty swank place, Hop."

"Yep, Harry, this is probably my last stop before cashing in my ticket. You look a little ragged young fellow. What've you been up to? Has our Maggie been giving you a hard time?" Hoppy's eyes twinkled under the familiar cowboy hat.

"Don't give him any ideas, Hoppy," Maggie said, returning his smile.

Hoppy didn't seem to notice but reached instead across his chair and good-naturedly slapped Harry's arm. "Harry, I'm glad I didn't die waiting for you to come for a visit."

He said it teasingly but Maggie saw the pain in his eyes and knew Harry had seen it too.

"Hoppy, I don't know what to say. It's been so long...I, I." Harry looked apologetically at Hoppy.

"Do you fellows mind if I take a little tour of the garden? I think you guys need some catch up time."

Maggie walked out onto the lawn before either man could respond, hoping the reunion would be beneficial for both of them. She headed toward a secluded bench by a small fountain near a mass of yellow rose bushes that filled the air with a heavy scent. Amazed to find her favorite flower in such abundance, she sat quietly, taking in the beauty around her. Thirty minutes later she started back to the bungalow but was almost sideswiped by a run-away wheelchair.

"Watch it, Maggie." Harry had shoved Hoppy's chair in her direction and was now running after it.

"What happened? Did you fellows settle your old disagreements or start new ones?"

"Maggie, we're escaping." Hoppy sounded thrilled by the turn of events. "Run for it, girl!" His cowboy hat slung low over his eyes, Hoppy was dressed like a Texas oilman, sporting a leather jacket and expensive western boots.

"I suspect Harry's behind this kidnapping, Hoppy. He can be very persuasive when he wants to be," Maggie stared at Harry and frowned.

"Maggie, Hoppy wants to get out of this joint for a little while, and we're going to spring him."

"Harry is that wise?" Maggie looked at Harry and then at Hoppy. "Don't you think the staff will worry about you, Hoppy?"

"Oh, shucks, Maggie. It's my money that pays for all this service. If I want to go for a joy ride with you and Harry, it'll be perfectly fine with them. Don't you want to go with us?"

"Sure I do, Hoppy, as long as you're feeling up to it." Maggie searched Harry's face for a clue as to why he would have proposed such an outlandish scheme.

"Come on, Maggie, we've cleared it with Mrs. Kemper, and Hoppy's houseboy packed a few of his personal medications. Let's get going." Harry handed Maggie a small leather valise and continued pushing Hoppy toward the parking lot.

"Come on, Maggie, my dear. Harry's taking me on a cook's tour, get it?" He was still chuckling like a schoolboy at his own joke as they approached the car.

"Comfortable, Hop?" Harry put Hoppy in the front passenger's seat and secured the seatbelt around the old man's bony frame.

"Sure, Harry. I feel like a million. We're together again, boyo. Where're we goin' first, Harry?"

"Yeah, Harry, where are we going?" Maggie made sure her voice accentuated her disapproval. "Here you go, boyo, you drive since it was your idea," she mocked as she threw Harry the car keys and got into the back seat.

"Okay gang, here's the plan. We take a tour of the town. First, we head out to the zoo. Then lunch, maybe a picnic. After that we'll play it by ear." Harry was in his element, whimsically arranging the day's schedule obliviously to any of Maggie's arguments.

The day went by in a shimmering Indian-summer haze. Their brief excursion had led to a quick game of miniature golf, a look-see at the town's old western museum and finally down to the waterfront for a riverboat ride. Their outing progressed pretty much as Harry had planned although most of their experiences had been spur-of-the-moment. It was, however, pretty late in the afternoon before they were able to picnic; something Hoppy had set his heart on having. They parked the car and walked to the river's edge, setting up camp on a table that was within a stone's throw of the water.

In spite of her earlier reservations, Maggie had been having a wonderful time. "Thanks guys for a great holiday. You two are my best beaus," she kissed each of their cheeks as she handed out plates and napkins.

"You're going to spoil me beautiful lady with all those hugs and kisses but keep it up, I'm enjoying myself," Hoppy grinned unpretentiously.

"Me too," Harry said, holding Maggie in a bear hug that nearly took her breath away.

"Harry, you're squeezing me to death. Get back to your hotdogs," she joked as she pushed Harry toward the picnic table.

"I hear and I obey your majesty." Harry bowed and began doling out the hotdogs and sodas they had purchased at the local Dairy Queen. "Get'em while they're hot, folks," he hollered as he filled their plates.

"It can't get any better than this," Hoppy said, relishing each bite as mustard slid down his chin. "Just look at what a fight that sun is putting up before she sets." Hoppy looked contentedly out over the river at the blazing sky.

"What a glorious day, Harry. You should be planning vacation packages." Maggie was stretched out on the grass with Harry's jacket for a pillow. "I don't think I've ever enjoyed a picnic as much." She was sorry she had reacted so vehemently to Harry's plans and plaintively looked at him for absolution.

"I can remember another one that was pretty darn good." Harry winked in her direction.

"Yes, sir, that's what I call food." Hoppy, munching on the Twinkies his man Quincy had packed in his valise was pleased with his contribution to the meal. "I always bring these little cakes with me but who knew they'd turn out to be our dessert," he said, consuming the last few crumbs.

"Hop, you must have been some kind of hungry," Harry said as he took Hoppy's empty plate off his lap.

"It was great, Harry. The whole day was grand and I spent it with my two best friends. This day has really been special for me. I got a chance to put my boots on and see a little bit of this great, old world again," Hoppy added nostalgically.

Harry threw the trash into the dumpster and walked languidly back toward Maggie. "Come on lazybones, let's take a walk before you fall asleep," he said, pulling her to her feet.

"But we can't leave Hoppy," Maggie protested halfheartedly.

"You two go and have some fun. I'd like to sit here for a little while." Hoppy grinned contentedly.

"You made his day, Harry. He worships you. I wish I had trusted you more but I was afraid." Maggie held Harry's hand as they walked along the riverbank.

"Sometimes fear can keep you from enjoying life. It's the difference between a picture postcard and the real thing."

"I'm all for having fun, Harry, but within moderation."

"Maggie, you're afraid I'm too reckless, too wild. You're all for orderliness and responsibility but I have such a thirst for life, no pun intended, that I'm afraid I won't have enough time to savor it all if I don't go after it now."

"Harry, I'm not confusing one with the other. I just believe that we have to put thought into what our life's about, otherwise, before you know it, it's gone and then there's nothing to show for it. Time isn't our friend, Harry. It's a thief that steals before we even know it."

"Talk about stealing..." Harry drew Maggie close and kissed her quickly.

"Harrrrrry."

She tried to shy away but was fluid in his embrace. Her arms instinctively reached out and encircled his neck as he lifted her skyward. Her feet dangled off the ground as she clung tightly to him, laughing gleefully.

"You sound like a little girl when you laugh like that. I wish I had known you when you wore pigtails."

"I never wore pigtails. I..." Her words were stilled by his lips.

They kissed, gently at first like strangers unsure of one another; then long and hard, swallowing each other's breathlessness. He guided her down onto the soft bank as though her body was an extension of his, pillowing his jacket beneath her as his fingers softly pushed back her hair. When his lips touched hers they turned to fire.

"Harry." She heard herself whimper against the roaring in her ears.

"Maggie, Maggie."

He held her head braced in his hands as his mouth covered her face. She felt his fingers move slowly down to the pulse of her throat and trembled as they brushed against her breasts.

"Harry, Harry," she pleaded after each tender agony.

She pulled his head to hers and kissed him hungrily. Her body ached for his touch. As he caressed her, enfolding her in his arms, she could think of nothing but him. She wanted him inside her. Unappeasable, she drew him to her, breathing him in and longing for everything there was about him. Impatiently she nibbled at his lower lip until he groaned and lowered his open mouth over hers. With each kiss the warmth of his breath caused her body to shiver uncontrollably as the firestorm of fervor heightened.

Then, from somewhere deep within her, she struggled to regain her senses even as every fiber in her body insatiably craved his tenderness. There was an element of madness in her passion and it frightened her. Like a sea diver pressed into the rapturous fathoms with a single-mindedness that eliminated all thought, she gasped for breath and fought her way to the surface with an inborn determination known only to her.

"No Harry, no, no, please stop. Please don't kiss me anymore." For a minute, she wasn't sure she wanted him to acquiesce but he adhered obediently.

"What's wrong, Maggie?"

"It's not fair to either of us."

She felt his body stiffen. He didn't say a word but only kissed her nose and shifted to the side all the while holding her closely.

She knew by the look in his eyes he understood. They laid there in silence watching the sun slide like a fireball into the river.

"Harry, I couldn't let… ."

"I know. You don't have to say anything, darling. It's all right."

"But I want you to know… ."

"Yes, I do know and you're right, dearest, so don't worry. We'd better get back to Hoppy," Harry said as he knelt and put his arm around her waist, lifting her up.

"Grab my jacket, Maggie, will you, honey?" He bent slightly, hovering lower until she had it in her hands.

"Harry, you silly, put me down."

Wrapped in his arms, she laughed as Harry made a game of stopping and kissing her along the way until they arrived back and he tenderly put her down in front of their picnic table.

"Maggie," Harry whispered her name almost as softly as he kissed her. His hands, strong around her waist, held her tightly as if he were afraid she would vanish.

Maggie did not know how love was revealed to other women but it came to her in that moment. Looking up into his eyes, it was as though in the whole of her life she had never felt as she did now. "I love you, Harry." Maggie did not utter the words out loud but saw from Harry's expression he understood.

I love him. It seems so simple but it's such a revelation. I wonder if my expression has changed or if anyone will notice. I feel as though a veil has fallen from my eyes and I can see clearly. My heart is so full it may burst at any minute.

"You kids have a good time?" Hoppy looked at her and grinned. "Boy, howdy, that was some sweet sunset."

The three of them looked out to where the sun was setting and said nothing. Harry reached for her hand and held it in his. As they gazed at each other, she saw her love mirrored in his eyes. Wordlessly they squeezed each others' hands.

"We'd better start heading back," Harry said quietly.

Hoppy was reluctant to leave but when Harry promised one more special stop, his energy seemed recharged.

"What you cookin' up, Harry? Get it, Maggie? Cookin' up?" Hoppy was in high spirits.

She watched as the lights blurred past the window as the car headed downtown. "Where are we going, Harry?" Maggie asked but didn't expect a reply.

"For a drink, right old timer?" Harry nudged Hoppy as he pulled in front of a rather run-down establishment called the Golden

Nugget. It advertised itself as having the best beer in town.

"Harry... ." Maggie knew there was no point in protesting. Harry had already lifted Hoppy out of the car and was pushing him toward the entrance.

"Maggie, this is Hoppy's last request for the evening. Don't spoil it."

"Thought I'd have a little nip, if you don't mind, Miss Maggie? You know, one for the road so to speak. Harry knows how I love C&W music."

"Hoppy, you're on medication and Harry, why you're just out of the... . I just don't think it's a good idea." Maggie stopped objecting and shook her head. She knew when she was licked.

"Let's go Harry. Don't mind Miss Maggie," Hoppy said, as indifferent to her pleas of resistance as Harry. "Yippee," he whooped as they entered the bar.

The Golden Nugget was jammed with patrons. It appeared to be the only watering hole in town and the clientele, mostly dressed in western attire, were a lively, rowdy bunch. Although the band had finished playing, colorful floodlights from the stage remained glaringly focused on the room as county and western music wailed loudly from a booming jukebox.

Harry wedged them around a table covered in a red-checkered oilcloth as he and Hoppy began munching on the fresh peanuts and pretzels contained in bowls so large they were almost meals. Maggie found the high-backed, spindled chairs hard-as-nails, but the grating sound of empty peanut shells under her shoes was far more annoying.

Although the place was a rumble of deafening noise, the crowd seemed to take it in stride. Everyone seemed to be enjoying the camaraderie including a horde of drunken cowboys who hugged the bar boisterously ordering rounds and a tangle of reeling line dancers who stomped their boots into the linoleum floor as they whirled past the other customers. Harry managed to get the attention of one of the waitresses. He ordered three steins of beer and whispered something to the short-skirted cowgirl before she wrote the order down.

"Here's to my friends," Hoppy shouted, lifting his glass.

"To the three of us," Maggie toasted as she looked first at Harry and then at Hoppy, trying to envision them as young men out for a night on the town.

"Anything else, sir?" The waitress grinned flirtatiously at Harry as she politely laid the check on the table.

"No thanks," Harry shook his head and smiled as he put the money on her tray.

"Thank you, sweetie," she purred.

Although Maggie got only a scowl, she was able to read the words "non-alcoholic" on the check before the young woman sashayed onto the next table.

For a couple of hours they rolled back the years, laughing, joking and reminiscing until Harry broke the spell. "Well, Hop, what do you say we call it a day?"

"I suppose we've got to get back." Hoppy begrudgingly allowed Harry to push his wheelchair toward the exit. "Wait, Harry, turn me around one more time," Hoppy begged, tugging at Harry's coat sleeve.

"Listen, Maggie," he said, looking back at the crowded bar room. Amid the raucous sounds, Maggie heard the strains of Eddie Arnold's voice crooning from the jukebox.

"Make the world go away, take it off of my shoulders... ." Hoppy mimicked.

"You had a good time, Hoppy?" Maggie could see the answer in his face.

"Mighty fine, Miss Maggie," Hoppy said, repeating the words again. "Yes sir, mighty, mighty fine. That Harry sure knows how to throw a hell of a party." He took off his cowboy hat and waved it in the air, shouting "Good-bye, folks," as though the words were a final salute.

Harry was unusually quite as they drove back to the city that night after they had safely entrusted Hoppy back into Mrs. Kemper's care. Maggie, content with her own thoughts, said very little except for a few observations about the day's events.

"Harry, you made Hoppy's day. I suspect just seeing you again made all the difference."

"As Hop would say, it's a lot of water under the bridge, Maggie. Years of laughter and heartache go by so quickly. It's hard to believe it's the sum total of a man's life. I didn't think seeing Hoppy again would be so god-awful hard. Geez but I hate good-byes."

Chapter 20

Maggie found the CD on her desk when she got back from lunch. Attached to it was a blue envelope on which her name had been cursively written in a handwriting she recognized immediately as Paul's. Although her first inclination was to toss the whole thing into the trash, she decided instead to open the letter.

Dear Maggie,

I found this old Glenn Miller recording and I thought you might enjoy it. The song's called Perfidia. *I've listened to the words again and again and I'm overwhelmed by the new meaning the song has for me. Maybe if you get a moment you could listen to the words and who knows, you may even understand me a little better. God knows I'm trying to understand myself.*

Maggie, as I told you, I did leave you a note on that Friday I stayed after to copy the stuff you typed for Harry, but at the last minute, I decided not to leave it. Not that I was trying to hide my actions. I just wanted you to hear it from me rather than read it. How ironic that in the end, you'll be reading it anyway. It's a little the worse for wear since I've been carrying it around for a while. Remember, if you ever need me...

Maggie smoothed out the crumpled sheet attached to the letter and read:

Maggie,

By the time you read this, you'll know what I've done. I have no excuse because I believe in what I'm doing. Corporate needs to know what Harry's done and what he's done to you. I love you very much but I can't let Harry get away with it. I know it's going to implicate you and that's my only regret.
Paul

Maggie put the CD into her purse along with the letters. Although she tried to be objective, Paul's explanation of his side of the issue left her unmoved.

Paul's right. I don't understand him, and I doubt I ever will. He says he loves me and yet he betrayed me. I'll never trust him again. He gave no thought to what his actions would do to me, and never considered my feelings. Now he asks that I empathize with him and see his point. It was none of his business, and I wish to God he would have stayed out of it.

On the way home she popped the CD into the player. As she listened to the plaintive melody, Paul's message became obvious.

To you my heart cries out perfidia for I found you, the love of my life, in somebody else's arms: Your eyes are echoing perfidia...*

In the weeks that followed, however, she found herself haunted by the tune, constantly playing and replaying it. The words intrigued her as did the definition of perfidious and she realized she was no longer as angry with Paul as she had been.

Perfidious means betrayal. Paul thinks of me as the perfidious one. Somehow it doesn't surprise me that he's the one who feels betrayed. Men so easily turn the tables, especially when it involves another man. Paul doesn't even care about the computer issue or what his personal involvement could do to my reputation. He just blames Harry for everything.

*Copyright: Glenn Miller Orchestra

All the hate he's ever felt has now grown inside him to where he can no longer rationalize it. He thinks Harry stole my love away from him even though what we felt for each other had ended long before. I can forgive him because I understand him.

With Harry it was a different story altogether. Clare had called after Harry's brief weekend of freedom to report that he had suffered a minor setback. Although she in no way suggested it was because of Maggie, Clare was adamant that neither of them have further contact with one another until he completed the next phase of therapy.

"Maggie, Harry has put his wellbeing into my hands and as his doctor I am concerned about experiences that might prove detrimental to the curative procedure."

"Clare, what do you mean by experiences? Is it something I've done?"

"No, it is simply Harry's inability to process encounters which could endanger his ability to handle certain situations."

"You're talking about a sexual encounter, aren't you? Clare, I swear to you nothing happened between us."

"Maggie, I am not here to play God, and it is certainly not my intention to make you feel responsible. Harry has told me everything that happened. It is simply that I am being cautious where my patient is concerned. Therapy at this stage is extremely sensitive to outside issues and requires discretion. It is difficult for me to estimate a timeframe but suffice to say he will probably be able to talk to you within a few months. Trust me, Harry will be fine."

After the conversation with Clare, Maggie worried incessantly about Harry. Although she no longer worked on his journal, having turned back all his materials and deleting permanently any remnants from the hard drive, she was constantly reminded of him by the WordTech projects they had created together. She was anxious to hear how his treatments were progressing but the confidentiality issue kept her from inquiring and each day brought her another night in a limbo of uncertainty.

Like a schoolgirl pulling petals from a daisy, she spent her evenings assessing her feelings, vacillating from one emotion to the next. Over and over again she reflected on the rapturous moments she and Harry had shared with one another, and although a tiny voice somewhere in the back of her mind warned of impending doom, she couldn't stop the winds of obsession from fanning the fire in her soul.

While her own sessions with Clare seemed ineffective, it was at the doctor's insistence that she agreed to continue her analysis. Thoughts infiltrated her every waking moment and she found herself growing desperate for the sound of Harry's voice.

I'm in love with Harry but I can't bring myself to even think about it. It's so painful it hurts my heart. Sometimes when I say the words out loud I'm afraid the fates will hear. Paul's already guessed it. He knew before I did. I don't think I can endure not hearing from Harry much longer. I don't know what's happening to me. The thought of losing him wreaks havoc in my soul; arousing my senses in the waking hours and keeping me from sleep in the darkness.

Late one night the ringing of her cell phone woke her from a restless sleep but even before she picked up she knew it was him.

"Maggie, it's me." Harry was barely audible.

"Harry, how did you know I've been frantic to hear your voice?"

"Me too yours, darling. I'm disobeying doctor's orders but I couldn't stand it any longer."

"How are you?"

"I can't talk long, Maggie. The real pain in this treatment is not being able to see you. I'm afraid my recovery is going to take longer than I realized and ..."

"Don't say it, Harry. Everything will work out."

"It's tough but I'm hanging in there. The hard part is realizing I'm not in charge; I'm not in control anymore. I've had to let go and let others take care of me and it's taken awhile to sink in. Doctor Sebastian says I'm shaping up as a model patient. This isolation sucks but I'll be an outpatient in another month. By the way, we're using the journal as a therapy tool and Doc's agreed to use it in my defense in her report to the committee."

"Are you all right with that, Harry?"

"I guess so. I'm pretty disgusted with myself but I can handle it. With Corporate it will be a pretty humbling and humiliating experience but I'm the one who wove this web and I'm the one that's got to extricate myself from it. I'm just sorry I got you involved. I have nothing but regrets but the Doc says it's a sign of healing. God, I hope so."

"I'm glad to hear you're doing better, darling. I worry so much about you."

"Would it be okay to tell you that I miss you terribly and that I feel like jumping ship and coming out to see you right now?"

"Harry, you mustn't. You promised. Just work on getting well." Maggie tried to keep her voice impersonal for fear of unduly influencing him but the sound of his voice made her acutely aware of how deeply she cared about him.

The next few weeks were easier. In her mind, Maggie replayed the late night call again and again as a defense against the doubts that plagued her. On Friday she left work a little early to work out at the gym and was surprised to see Paul coming out of the men's locker room.

"Hi Maggie."

"Hi Paul."

"I didn't plan this or anything."

"I know, Paul. I've been meaning to thank you for the CD. It's lovely and I'm enjoying it."

"That's okay. I'm glad you like it."

"No, it's inexcusable of me. Lately, I've been so preoccupied."

"Could you use a cup of tea?"

"That would be nice."

"How about our yogurt shop?"

"Sounds good."

"Look, it's the old booth. Is it okay with you if we sit here?" Maggie knew Paul was trying to sound upbeat.

"Sure, Paul."

"You look tired, Maggie."

"You look fit and healthy, Paul."

"Okay, okay, I finally get it," he laughed. "I promise not to pry but how are things going?"

"As well as can be expected."

"I hear you've been promoted. Congratulations."

"Only until Harry comes back. I'm getting anxious about testifying at that final ethics committee meeting but then I expect you must be looking forward to it." Maggie saw the crestfallen look on Paul face. "Sorry, Paul," she apologized, "that was a nasty crack. How are things with you?"

"You mean other than missing you? Well, I've put in for a transfer. I don't know if I'll get it but I do know it's time for me to move on."

"I hope it goes well."

"I just wanted to say, Maggie, that you were right. I've been working with an anger management support group and doing a lot of work on myself trying to let go of all the hate I had for Harry. It isn't easy. I can see how damaging it was but when that poison gets into you, nothing seems to matter."

"I'm glad for you, Paul."

"Don't you hate small talk?"

"There's nothing much we can talk about but just seeing you again is a good thing."

"You're not angry with me anymore?"

"No, I've let go of my anger, too."

"I wish …anyway, what I said still goes. I'll always be there for you, Maggie. I know I shouldn't ask but any chance we could see one another again?"

"No, Paul. It wouldn't be a good idea."

"You love him, don't you?"

"Yes."

"I guess that's pretty clear."

"Here's my share of the bill, Paul." As Maggie handed him the money, their fingers touched.

Paul bent and kissed her hand. "Regardless of your decision, I'll always cherish our friendship, Maggie."

Maggie reached for her gym bag. "Thanks, Paul. Well, if I'm going to stay in shape I'd better get down to the gym. See you." She hurried from the shop without looking back.

❦

"Hi Mag. How about brunch at the Beachcomber? It'll be my treat." Leeann seemed unusually excited.

"Sure, what up?"

"I had my snoops working overtime and boy did we ever hit a jackpot. I know you're going to love it."

"Great! What time do you want to meet?" Maggie was already pulling a dress from her closet.

"Noon."

"See you then."

It was a bright, breezy day and Maggie decided to drive out to the beach by way of the scenic highway along the coast. Others apparently had the same idea and as she pulled into the restaurant's parking lot and saw Leeann's car she hoped she hadn't kept her waiting long.

"Hi slow poke." Leeann, sitting out on the patio, looked cool in a yellow tank top and big straw hat.

"Sorry, Leeann, I couldn't help it. It's such a glorious day I had to savor every minute."

"I'm just kidding you. I just got here myself," Leeann confessed, absorbed in the menu.

"Okay, stop torturing me. You know I'm just dying of curiosity."

"Let's order first and then get down to the nitty-gritty," Leeann proposed with a glint in her eye.

"This is the life," Maggie said sipping her strawberry lemonade after they had ordered salmon steaks, Cajun style, "but I'm going to scream if you don't tell me what you found out."

"Here it is, kid." Leeann opened the envelope and began extracting several sheets of paper. "For starters, let's just say she was a real b-i-t-c-h," Leeann said bluntly as she handed a stack of papers to Maggie. "Take a gander at these."

"Wow! Where'd you get this stuff?" Maggie, her glasses popped on the edge of her nose, finished reading the report and looked at Leeann. "So she was the department's tattletale who spent all her time running to the manager reporting hearsay on the staff."

"Yeah, a lousy spy who used her position to destroy a lot of people on trumped up charges without proof. Now I know where Harry got that story about me and the racetrack. For some reason I didn't remember her name, but I do remember her," Leeann said, tossing Maggie an ID picture.

"Is this Kate McGrue?"

"None other than the witch herself," Leeann's voice quivered.

Maggie stared at a thin face with a rather sharp, prominent nose. Large almond eyes with long black curly lashes stared back at her from beyond the years. A steel helmet of premature grey hair crowned her head. Her lips were full and suggestive, and Maggie thought, quite provocative.

"Have a look at page five. It's feedback from a number of people still at WordTech who remembered her well, for one reason or another. Get my drift?"

"Do you think Harry believed everything she told him?"

"He must have. Let's face it, she knew a lot of people when he took over as manager and he probably counted on her for feedback. A ready made snitch system and for whatever reason he believed her. She was in the driver's seat with other people's careers." Leeann was fuming.

"In a way Paul was right about the department but he got the wrong person."

"And here's the clincher. The dame was way into a destructive lifestyle. Apparently she bragged about it. Some of the people I talked with said half the time she was strung out. A few of the guys said she lived well beyond her means. She drove a fancy car and wore designer clothes. They got the idea that somebody was paying for it, even an apartment on the riverfront. They guessed they knew the guy."

"What do you mean?"

"They thought it was Harry but nobody knew for sure."

"You mean Harry saw her personally, outside of work?"

"Yes. Several of the old staff remembers Harry and Kate seeing each other regularly. They were both wild in those days. I didn't get wind of it because I was only an underling then. They said Harry was a changed man when he was with her, like crazy, you know. She was real possessive and apparently watched him like a hawk."

Leeann shook her head. "Sorry kid, but you wanted the truth."

"Hoppy said something about that and Aunt Jessie, too. She even believed that it was Kate who stole Harry's pictures. She seems to have had a lot of influence in Harry's life."

"Let's not get carried away, Maggie. Lots of people at WordTech have affairs but not everyone goes off the deep end. Harry could certainly take care of himself. He's no victim and anything he did he was responsible for."

"You're right, Leeann. I'm not trying to justify Harry's actions but I know something happened in his life that changed him. I've got a funny feeling that this Kate McGrue knew about it, too."

"Maggie, I say don't get involved. It was a long time ago and Harry probably has lost contact with her, particularly after she was terminated from the company."

"Yes, that's true Leeann, but I can't help wondering if Harry's personality changes are somehow linked up with her."

"Hey, here comes our food. Let's forget this crap and enjoy ourselves," Leeann said, cutting ravenously into her salmon steak.

"Thanks for digging up the research, Leeann. It's another piece of the puzzle in Harry's life. But you're right I'm too hungry to talk about it anymore."

Still, for a few minutes more, she lingered over the shadowy picture of the woman she now considered her nemesis before finally putting the envelope in her purse.

～✽～

That night Maggie had a nightmare. She dreamed she was in a courtroom surrounded by strange looking people, none of whom she recognized. She cringed when she heard her name called out by the court clerk and felt the urge to run and hide. Looking down she saw a thin, frayed blanket covering her lap, and realized she had no legs. She was wheeled to the witness stand where someone placed her hand on the bible.

"Do you promise to tell the truth, the whole truth and nothing but the truth, so help you God?"

In her dream, the judge, who seemed miles away, was unable to hear her response and accused her of being too submissive.

"Your meekness is your weakness," he growled, and Maggie saw the jury members nod in agreement.

Suddenly, Maggie saw Harry. He was sitting in the front row. His eyes were like steel gray targets that fixed on her like magnets. She searched his face for a hint of a smile but there was none. The lips, once warm and loving, were now drained and bloodless. Then she looked at the figure sitting next to him. It was a grotesque caricature with the large red letters KM painted in where the mouth should have been.

"Harry," she heard herself calling futilely. "Harry, Harry." She wanted to run to him but she couldn't move.

"Maggie, Maggie dear, wake up. You're dreaming." Her mother was shaking her gently but Maggie was unable to respond.

"Mom, Mom," she mumbled faintly.

"Here dear, this should help." Mrs. Reynolds spoke in a quite, reassuring voice as she put a warm compress on her forehead. "My but that must have been some dream."

"It was a nightmare, Mom," Maggie said still shaking. "It's as though I'm being warned not to trespass further if I know what's good for me."

"That's never stopped you before, Maggie dear," her mother said shrewdly.

Chapter 21

The ethics committee meeting convened at precisely ten in the morning. It was the final chapter for Harry, Paul and Maggie who were called at different times to testify separately. Maggie dutifully answered the same questions she had been asked at the first meeting. This time, however, she knew the committee had Dr. Sebastian's report on Harry's condition in front of them and regardless of their bias would be forced to rule in Harry's favor. Paul's outrage and Harry's humiliation not withstanding, the outcome could not be altered.

Maggie listened dutifully as Mr. Granger read the committee's ruling regarding her involvement in the situation.

"Ms. Reynolds, your complicity in the entire affair will be ruled a non-issue as we believe you acted in good faith in support of a WordTech employee whose illness prevented him from making a proper judgment. As such, Ms. Reynolds, you are held blameless and the said issue pertaining to you is considered resolved." Granger sounded disappointed with the verdict.

"Gentlemen, thank you for your time."

Maggie rose from the chair and walked to the door without looking at any of the faces seated around the boardroom table. She made it past Irene's desk without a word, and it was only after she reached the corridor that she uttered a sigh of relief.

She saw him then, standing in the shadows. He had lost weight and looked thinner. She wanted to call out to him but thought better of it and continued on to the elevators. After all, she reasoned, he'll be coming back to WordTech soon.

Two weeks later, after almost six months on disability, Harry was back in his office. With the dust having settled, Maggie was finally able to relax. Although she noticed that Harry was hesitant in making several decisions, she attributed this to his long absence. Within a week he seemed to have reverted back to his old, brash, irreverent ways, qualities of his that had first attracted her to the job.

She did, however, began to notice little changes about him. They were subtle and fleeting at first, but before long the transformation became obvious. Ill mannered and bad tempered, he condescendingly embarrassed not only her but other staff members as well. Having consulted with Clare, she continued to excuse his behavior because of his recent illness and the underlying anxiety involving both of them in the corporate melee, but she couldn't keep the seeds of apprehension from growing within her.

In July, the weekend before her twenty-ninth birthday, she and Harry celebrated with a quiet dinner at Les Champs. He seemed distant and complained of an awful headache. They made an early night of it with Maggie relegating Harry to the passenger's seat on the drive back to her house.

"Come on in and have some coffee, Harry," Maggie offered as she parked the car.

"Don't go in just yet, honey," he coaxed, "let's talk."

"You sound so serious, darling. How about sitting on the patio for a few minutes?" Maggie took his hand and they walked in silence to the backyard.

"Maggie, I love you. I love you more than anything in this world. You believe me, don't you?" Harry asked haltingly.

"Yes, Harry, of course." Maggie touched his cheek which was

unusually warm.

"You're the one constant in my life. Promise me you'll never forget that no matter what." He held her in his arms for a long time without saying a word. Then he raised her chin and kissed her gently, whispering, "Thank you, darling, for helping me find what real love is all about."

"Harry, what's wrong? There are times when you're unapproachable and down-right mean and then, like now, sensitive and gentle. I don't know what to make of you any more."

"Maggie, it's like I've got this hole in me that nothing will fill up. It scares the hell out of me. I can't explain any better than that. Just remember what I told you."

"Harry, you're under a doctor's care and you've been through a lot. Clare says …"

"Don't let her fool you. There's no excuse for my sickness."

"Harry, I know you love me and I love you, but you're scaring me. It almost sounds like you're saying good-bye. You know I hate good-byes, too."

"I'd have given anything to make it work, darling, but let's face it I've given you nothing but grief and a lot of words. I know words hurt, sometimes more than physical pain, but try to believe in the good ones and forget the ones I've said that are ugly and cruel."

"I believe in you, Harry. That's enough for me."

Maggie pressed her lips impatiently to his, her limbs growing limp as she felt his heart beating against her breast. For a minute Harry's response was reassuring but his impassioned kisses abruptly subsided and he released her quickly.

"Harry?"

"I've got to go, honey. I'll see you Monday."

"Harry, can't you tell me what's going on?" Maggie begged as she watched him walk to his car without turning around as he usually did. "Harry, Harry, you're tearing me up inside," she cried out loud, half expecting him to answer but he had already driven away.

In the dark hours of early morning Maggie had a premonition. It was a feeling of foreboding the likes of which she had never experienced. She went into her mother's room and shook her awake.

"Mom, I can't sleep. I'm so worried about Harry. I think he's in trouble."

"Say a prayer for him, Maggie, there's nothing you can do. Call Clare in the morning and maybe she can shed some light on his behavior."

"No, she'll only tell me what she usually tells me about patients taking steps backward. She'll also go on about how all patients tend to lie to their therapists when the going gets rough. I don't know what's happening with Harry but he's in trouble, I can feel it."

"I'm not in Harry's corner but I am in yours and you need sleep. You've got a busy day tomorrow, so please go back to bed and get some rest."

A happy birthday banner was stretched across her office door when Maggie walked in that morning. Her desk was filled with cards and packages but her eyes were drawn to an elegant vase holding two dozen, long-stemmed yellow roses. She knew they were from Harry. She read the card and quickly put it out of sight.

All my love, all my life.

~H.

Reflecting on it later, it was the week after her birthday that things really got bad. By then, Harry was altogether a different person. There was not a glimmer of humanity in his new persona. He was distant and aloof and acted toward her as though he were punishing her for something. Maggie didn't know what.

From a supportive mentor who went out of his way to alert her to imperative assignments and schedules, he became a thorn in her side. Constantly criticizing, his negativity played havoc with her nerves. There were days when she was desperate to quit. She wanted to walk away from the whole mess but she knew she couldn't do it. Maggie made excuses for his obdurate behavior but others weren't as understanding as Leeann mentioned at lunch one day.

"What the hell's the matter with Harry? He's turned into a carbon copy of the Harry Paul's always railed against. I said something to him the other day and he nearly bit my head off, and you poor kid, you got the worst of it. He treats you like shit."

"Please Leeann, he's been sick. We'll just have to give him time."

"You're sure a glutton for punishment, Maggie. I just hope none of us has a nervous breakdown before he gets better."

On Friday, Harry came barging into her office a little before noon and insisted they go to lunch. Maggie hesitated to accept the invitation at first but decided it would be better to know just what tricks Harry had up his sleeve.

The restaurant he chose was far removed from the extravagance they had indulged in a week before her birthday. The tiny eatery was sweltering from the heat of bodies crowded into a lunch line queue. The delicatessen type menu offered only sandwiches. Harry ordered two pastramis on rye and beers for both of them.

"Harry, since when did you start drinking again? Won't it interfere with your medication?"

"You can stop worrying about me, Maggie. Don't you think you're carrying loyalty a bit too far?"

"Harry, why go through this charade? You don't even want me to be here with you. You're leading up to something. Let's have it. I personally don't have time to waste on this theatrical nonsense."

"I wanted to explain my actions this past week."

253

"Go ahead, explain."

"I've got problems, Maggie, and they don't concern you. You'd be better off without me. Staying too close will only take you down."

"Meaning what? I should quit my job? Is that what this is all leading up to?"

"I didn't say that."

"You didn't have to. Now that the ethics committee has made their decision, there's really no reason to keep me around, is there? I know a little too much about you, don't I, Harry?"

"Maggie, I don't want you to quit but I was thinking your skills could be better served in another department. Production has a job opening for an associate content producer," Harry said, picking at his sandwich without interest.

"Hardly a promotion, Harry. If you want me out of your life why not just say it?"

"You're a valuable commodity, Maggie. You could get a job anywhere in WordTech. I'm just looking out for your interests," Harry said ingratiatingly.

"Harry, I'm not going to argue with you because you seem to have made up your mind, but I think you're afraid of something or someone."

"Don't try using your psychic skills on me, Maggie," Harry said, growing suddenly agitated.

"Harry, whatever happens I'm in this for the duration. I have no intentions of quitting on you regardless of what you say or do."

"I always said you were tenacious, Maggie."

"Only in your case, Harry."

"You've been seeing Paul Keating again. I think that's a wise decision."

"A cup of tea in a yogurt shop can hardly be construed as seeing Paul. Besides, I'm perfectly capable of directing my own life. I hardly need you to tell me who I should or shouldn't be seeing."

"Are you and Paul conspiring against me?"

"What?" Maggie asked in disbelief. "Harry, you're beginning to sound paranoid. I'd almost prefer you drunk." She regretted the words as soon as she had said them.

"I don't like double dealing behind my back, Maggie. I have too much at stake to risk your betraying me. Stay away from that SOB or else."

"Now who's giving the ultimatums, Harry?" Maggie stood up and walked away from the table without saying another word.

Harry didn't return after lunch and Maggie decided to use his office to finish up a contract she had been working on. She was sitting at his desk drinking a ginger ale and mulling over the luncheon fiasco when the phone rang. Leeann was not back from lunch so she answered it.

"Harry Cooke's office. No he's not in Mr. Tyler. Yes, I'll have him call you back in the morning. What was that number, sir?" As she reached for the pen, Maggie accidently knocked over the pop can.

Hanging up quickly, she grabbed some kleenexes and began to blot up the mess. The liquid had spilled onto Harry's desk, saturating his files and seeping into his personal organizer. She opened the book and began wiping off the pages. All at once she noticed hidden inside the cover was a scrap of paper with the same number scribbled over and over. It was the phone number that had been in Kate McGrue's file.

"Bingo!" she said out loud as she hurried back to her own office.

Why would Harry still be writing down Kate McGrue's phone number? And to have written it so many times means it's important to him. How important, Harry? Does this have something to do with your radical behavior? The first thing to do is make sure it's hers. Well, I wanted to be a detective, now's my chance. I'll have to play it by ear to find out anything. Here goes nothing.

Trusting a hunch, Maggie punched in the number on her cell phone and waited while it rang on endlessly. Finally a thin, reedy voice answered.

"Hello?"

"Is this Kate McGrue?"

"Who wants to know?" The voice was suddenly loud and belligerent.

"I'm Maggie Reynolds and I believe we have a mutual friend."

"Like who for instance?"

"Harry Cooke." Maggie listened to the silence.

"What do you want?" The voice was now breathy and insistent.

"I'd like to talk to you."

"You must be crazy. Who the hell are you?"

"It might be worth your while to talk to me."

"Go to hell."

"Listen, in case you change your mind, call me." Although apprehensive, Maggie gave out her cell number and hung up. She walked over to Leeann's desk and told her what she had done.

"That's pretty risky, kid."

"Curiosity killed…"

"Exactly, and you could be one dead cat. But if you're determined to go, I'm going with you. As soon as the witch calls, let me know. Remember, I've got a bone to pick with her, too."

"Thanks Leeann, I was hoping you'd say that. I've got to get to an ATM for some cash. This gal's going to need some incentive."

The call came at eleven the following night. Maggie knew it was deliberate but she had no intentions of allowing Kate to intimidate her.

"Yes, this is she. What do you want, Kate?"

"Listen, if you still want to meet, I'll be at Foggy Eddies in an hour. If you're late, don't bother to come. And if you expect cooperation, you'd better have the right denominations with you, otherwise forget it. Understand?"

"Understood."

"How will I know you?" Kate hissed into the phone.

"I'll know you, Kate," Maggie hoped she sounded tough.

"Remember, I said midnight." The phone went dead.

Maggie put the money in her purse and called Leeann. "She just called. Are you still game?"

"Only if I can do the driving, Maggie, since I'm not half as nervous as you are. I'll pick you up in twenty minutes. Don't worry we'll get there on time."

True to her word, with ten minutes to spare, Leeann pulled up in front of a dilapidated building on Locust Street. It was one of the poorest and most crime infested sections of town, and Maggie could tell Leeann was worried as she parked her brand new Mazda on the dimly lit street.

"Hurry up, Leeann."

"I'm saying good-bye to my car. I hope it's still here when we come out."

"It'll be all right," Maggie said without much confidence as she opened the tavern door and stepped into a room that looked as though it had been condemned years ago.

"Gee, this is the foulest smelling bar I've ever been in and believe me I've been in a few." Leeann held her hand over her nose.

"It's so dark in here we probably won't recognize her." Maggie hoped her courage wasn't waning. "Stay close, partner."

"Yeah, it would be easy to lose each other in this joint. Let's sit over there where we can see who comes in." Leeann ordered a couple of beers and led the way to a booth near the front of the bar.

"I'm getting itchy," Maggie said, scratching at her arms. "I don't like not being able to see anything."

"We're probably lucky we can't. I'd love a cigarette right about now, and I don't even smoke," Leeann said as she began to pour some of her beer into a glass. "On second thought we'd better drink out of the bottles. It's probably safer."

Maggie's eyes were glued to the doorway. "Leeann, I think that's her," she said, poking Leeann fiercely when an older version of Kate McGrue walked in.

"She looks ancient," Leeann said, raising her arm and beckoning Kate over to their table.

"Which one of you is Maggie Reynolds?"

"I'm Maggie Reynolds."

"What's she doing here?" Kate pointed a boney finger in Leeann's direction.

"Either she stays or I walk," Maggie asserted with conviction.

"What the hell, it's no skin off my nose. If you don't care, I don't care. What's this all about anyway?"

"I want to know what you have to do with Harry Cooke."

"Old Harry put you up to this?" Kate signaled the bartender and ordered a beer as she lit up a cigarette.

"I don't think you can smoke in here," Leeann advised.

"Shut up and mind your own fucking business," Kate screeched, her voice ratcheting up several notches.

For a split second before the match flickered out Maggie saw the weather-beaten face, tired around the mouth and old beyond its years. The hair, long and greasy, lay unflatteringly on top of thin, scrawny shoulders.

"Harry doesn't know anything about this meeting and I'd prefer you keep it that way."

"Take it easy, sister. Harry and I go way back and we're as thick as thieves but before I say anything more I want to know how much is in it for me?"

"I hope the information you have is worthwhile?" Maggie took out a large, overstuffed envelope and removed a one hundred dollar bill.

"For openers, that gets you my name."

Maggie took out two more bills. "Let's hear something or the party's over right now, she threatened."

"Harry and I worked at WordTech together. There was no love lost after he had me canned."

"Tell us something we don't know," Leeann piped in.

"Who the devil are you anyway?" Kate gave Leeann a contemptuous look.

"Just someone you lied about years ago," Leeann sneered back at her.

"So join the club. I told lies about lots of folks back then. Don't take it so hard, toots."

"Did you and Harry have a relationship?" Maggie's stomach was tied in knots.

"You might say of sorts. He and I saw a lot of each other in those days. Harry was crazy and really into sex, a real sicko."

"What did he have to do with you?"

"Why I was Harry's pimp, don't you know? It was my idea. He wanted women and I had a hundred dollar a day habit so I came up with a switch on the oldest game in the world. I'd get close to a few women and promote him. Next thing you know, they'd want to meet the hunk and I'd collect and set him up."

"A gigolo? Are you saying Harry was a gigolo?" Maggie was stunned.

"That's one I never thought of. I called him a male escort. What's wrong, sweets, can't take the truth about your precious Harry?"

"Keep talking."

"Harry never took any of the money. He didn't need it. What he wanted were the dames. He'd let me introduce him to these broads but it wasn't my take he was interested in."

"How long did that go on for?"

"That was before Harry climbed to the top. He and I didn't run around in the same circles after that. He got squeaky clean, sort of, after he got married."

"Then why does Harry have your number in his book?"

"Like I said, I wanted to get even with him."

"How?" Anger displaced the queasiness in Maggie's stomach.

"That'll cost you big time, sister."

"It had better be worth it," Maggie said menacingly as she laid a few more bills on the stack.

"Keating contacted me and wanted to know the whole story."

"Paul Keating?" Maggie and Leeann asked simultaneously.

"Ladies, that response will cost you another two hundred big ones." Kate took a drag on her cigarette and smiled.

Maggie pealed off the bills. "Did Paul know about the journal?"

"Sure. I told him Harry was having you type it. Ain't that a kick?" Kate snickered into her beer.

"Why would Harry get back in touch with you after all these years?" Leeann's question seemed to throw Kate off balance.

"Well, I… I saw a picture of Harry in the paper. He looked good and rich. I could tell he was doing a hell of a lot better than I was, being an ex-con and all, so I called him up. I threatened to tell everything I knew about him and ruin him if he didn't play ball. I swore I'd make him the laughing stock of WordTech. He said something about not having anything to lose."

"Blackmail," Leeann spit the word.

"If you open your fucking mouth again so help me I'll shut…"

"What happened then?" Maggie interrupted Kate's tirade.

"It was like old times for awhile. Then he told me he was through, wouldn't do it anymore. Said he wanted to change or something like that. Go straight, you know. That's was when I came up with the idea of the memoirs. I told him if he wrote it and I could make some money on it, I'd call it even and walk out of his life forever."

"What did he say to that offer?" It was an answer Maggie needed to hear.

"What could he say? He knew if he didn't do it I'd talk to Corporate and squeal my head off. I figured he'd write'em and I'd sell'em and we'd be on the gravy train. After all, Harry lived every one of those moments but he had me to thank for them. One of my friends promised to sell the book to this producer he knows who does reality shows." Kate sniffed loudly. "How the hell did I know Harry was such a lousy writer?"

Maggie took a sip of her beer. "How did Paul get into this?"

"He got my number the same as you I guess. I told him everything I'm telling you."

"Why did he want to hear the story?"

"He said something about it being the last part of the hangmen's noose for Harry. I liked hearing that. I didn't even charge him as much as I'm charging you guys."

"Why are you telling us?" Maggie inquired suspiciously.

"Now that Harry's seeing a shrink it doesn't matter to him anymore. And with WordTech knowing there's nothing left in it for me."

"Why did he ask me to type that trash?"

"That's the crazy part. He told me some cock-and-bull story about wanting you to find out what kind of a sonofabitch he really was. Said your knowing about him would make it a whole lot easier or something like that. He also said it was the only way he'd ever break free of me, short of killing me, which believe me he wanted to do."

"What about all those people who worked for Harry? Was he really as underhanded a person as Paul claimed?"

"Listen, I don't know what you heard but Harry never ruined anyone but me and himself. Sure, he may have put the screws to the people in the department, especially after I got finished with them but that was only to keep them on the straight and narrow. He was a bastard but he did 'em all a favor. He actually protected the slobs."

"How can you say that? He believed your lies."

"They weren't exactly lies, just exaggerations."

"So that makes everything okay?" Leeann shot back at her.

"Knowing what you were, why on earth would Harry believe you?" Maggie asked mystified.

"Listen, in my position I used the gossip I heard around the department. It was usually enough to start Harry wondering if it were true or not. He'd make his own investigation and put the person on the right track regardless. He didn't want Corporate or HR coming down on anyone in his department."

"It was all about office gossip?" Leeann shook her head.

"Harry was a control freak. He kept on top of the people in his department. He wanted things done his way and most everyone found out it was the only way. He's not a people person, he's strictly corporate. He fired me when he found out I was pilfering from the company till. He was a rough manager. He made money for the company and that's what the big shots wanted. Listen, that was years ago. Who gives a shit about history?" Kate rubbed her nose violently.

"Why did you take Harry's pictures off his aunt's mantel?"

"Did that old broad tell you about that? I took two lousy pictures that night, both good shots. God, he was gorgeous. I used 'em in the business. You might say it was a calling card advertising Harry. Boy, the women really dug him. He's awfully good looking and I guess you know he's even better in the sack."

Maggie was glad her face was hidden in the darkness. "If I ever hear from you again, I will go to the authorities and to WordTech security. Is that clear?"

"Crystal," Kate said as her broken nails scratched up the cash, "but don't worry, sweetie, Harry told me he was planning on doing that himself. The game's over. He's washed up," Kate sneered as she licked her fingers and counted the notes.

"What do you mean? Who does he plan on telling?"

"I don't know. He said something about not being able to live with what he had become and not having what he wanted most in life."

"Does Harry know that Paul knows everything?"

"I suppose so."

"I don't want you telling him that I know," Maggie insisted.

"Sure, it's no skin off my nose but I think he thinks you and Paul were in on it together. I just happened to mention to Harry that Paul said it was because of you that he wanted Harry's hide nailed to the wall," Kate laughed as she put the money in her purse and got up to leave. "By the way, sweet cheeks, the same goes for you. Don't anybody call me again because I'll just deny everything."

Maggie and Leeann watched as she opened the door and slid into the night.

"Now that's someone you wouldn't want to run into on a dark street corner. She gives me the willies. Do you believe her, Maggie?"

"I don't think she had anything to lose by not telling us the truth. The fact that Harry believed I was part of Paul's scheme really hurts."

"Yeah, here he is dictating to all of us when he's the one with the crappy, corrupt life." Leeann finished her beer. "What a scumbag. Can you believe anyone could be that rotten?"

"The whole thing is so sick, so terribly, profoundly sick." Maggie rubbed the wetness from her eyes with the back of her hand.

"Yeah, like reading someone you know's obituary, Harry's for instance."

"He's like someone who's become a stranger. Someone I never want to see again." Maggie rose from the table using every ounce of effort she possessed. "Let's get out of here, Leeann. I want to forget this whole thing ever happened."

"That's right, Maggie, bury him deep. He's not worth it."

Chapter 22

When Leeann dropped her off, Maggie went straight to her room. Exhausted, she fell prostrate onto her bed feeling drained of every human emotion. It was as though all her energy had been sucked from her body. Suddenly she needed to throw up. She barely made it to the bathroom. Retching violently, she seemed unable to find release from the tormenting thoughts that assailed her.

Needing something to settle her stomach, she went downstairs for a glass of milk but felt faint and barely made it to the couch before passing out. She made no attempt to hold onto reality and felt herself slipping into the peaceful world of illusion. As darkness descended she entered the mirrored valley of dreams.

It was a strange house. Wandering through its corridors Maggie entered several large empty rooms filled with ornate, cascading fountains before she came to the staircase. It was a large, circular staircase and resembled those from the antebellum era. She heard her name and looked up. Harry stood looking down from the top of a high tower. Maggie knew he was waiting for her. He beckoned her forward.

Although she tried desperately to hold back and resist his provocative commands it was useless and she was compelled to obey. An icy coldness prodded her forward and she found herself moving effortlessly toward the top. It was as though she were flying.

When she looked down at her body she was clothed only in a gossamer gown. The delicate fabric had a life of its own. It whirled about her like a cyclone, propelling her toward the shadowy heights, irrespective of her fears.

Almost like magic, he was there before her. His hands encircled her waist and he lifted her high above his head. Her diaphanous gown fell away exposing her breasts and trembling limbs. They climbed higher and higher into the tower. He carried her in his powerful arms unmindful of her resistance.

She was at once cognizant of his thoughts as though their minds had become one. His rage and bitterness empathically entered her being and she felt his fright and helplessness. His emptiness was unbearable. He was an impotent shell carrying his fantasy to inaccessible heights without satisfaction. She tried to drive the feelings of self-revulsion from her mind but it was impossible and she was forced to emotionally identify with his pain, an unquenchable longing that was excruciating. How could she help someone so filled with despair? A captive within his own body, he was fated to remain in desolation for all eternity.

The cold specter of terror crept into her heart and she knew at once Harry was lost to himself. Unable to love or be loved, he faced a void of nothingness that would eventually consume him without mercy. From somewhere deep within the inner recesses of her soul, she suddenly felt a strength that consciously willed him to awaken.

She heard herself cry out, "Love me, Harry," but he was incapable of understanding her words.

She was desperate. She wanted to save his soul from the darkness he had always feared but she couldn't fathom why he remained deaf to her entreaties. As they climbed still higher, it became clear to her. Filled with jealousy and bitterness, he resented her unending capacity to love. He would rather see her destroyed than be unable to love her himself.

As often happens in dreams, she realized she had the answer. The only way to save Harry was by giving him her love, for it was only through her that he would find release. Aroused, and no longer able to contain her desire, she felt her instinctual impulses plunging her forward into a whirlpool of passion.

She heard herself calling out to him again, "Love me, Harry, or let the emptiness consume me, too."

In that instant, when she finally acquiesced, totally and completely, he heard her. It was as though her willingness to give him life had freed him from his demons. He was like a man starving for that which had been denied him his whole life. She listened in anguish to his tormented yowls reverberating against the walls as he flailed about as though he were being reborn.

Suddenly he was quiet and when he came to her it was with a trust so complete they were as one body. She wanted to unbind his troubled soul but more than that, she wanted him. She felt his powerful hands grasp her hips as his lips moved slowly across her nakedness suckling her flesh into agonizing bliss. She heard herself wail as pleasure merged into madness.

"Please, please, Harry," she pleaded in absolute surrender.

He was hers then, unable to deny her anything. She opened herself to him. He nudged her legs apart and entered her. Their bodies shuddered convulsively as he penetrated deeply; his plummeting strokes forcing an intake of breath so rapturous it was all she could do to whimper, "Harry." He released himself into her, shouting her name; her name the only sound that escaped his lips. He was whole again, and at peace with his completeness. No longer afraid, he had been freed from the terror of his monstrous self.

"Truth is eternal love," she heard him whisper.

They lay together intertwined without beginning or end. He cupped her breasts in his hands and kissed her upturned lips. She wrapped her arms around him feeling every beat of his heart against hers. They clung to one another without restraint, tremulously, in speechless pleasure.

Maggie awoke. Her skin was damp with perspiration and she was shivering in her nightgown. She had sweated during the night as though she had melted. She wasn't sure where she was but the dream remained vivid.

⁓✲⁓

Maggie sat on the edge of the couch like a nervous cat. She had retreated to the security of Clare's office in an attempt to unburden herself but her confession did nothing to lessen the unrelenting emotional pain.

"Clare, I'm cracking up. I don't know what's wrong with me. It feels like I'm going to pieces," Maggie shouted in desperation.

"Calm down, Maggie," Clare said, handing her a mug of tea. "Why are you so upset?"

"After that vile dream last night, I was sure I was having a nervous breakdown. It makes me cringe to think I'd have anything to do with Harry. Why would I have a sensual dream about someone I despise?"

"Maggie, on one level your dream was a conscious wish stimulated by bodily desires. Your repressed sexual needs were gratified in the safety of your dream state. It is quite common and natural. More importantly, however, it was a very telling dream, filled with unconscious symbolism. In it you realized your own solution but because transitioning states can be disturbing you were not able to recognize the illumination. The very fact you empathically identified with Harry's needs means you are in full control of the situation. We will talk about the dream in detail later but for now,

267

remember, dreams tell us things that we need to know to function more effectively when we are not dreaming."

"This thing with Harry has me so messed up. I find myself wishing I had never known him. He's a cruel and vengeful monster and I absolutely hate him."

"Maggie, you at once both love and hate this man. In one respect you feel he goes against every principle you believe in and yet you cannot let go of that part of you which cares for him. That is why you feel torn in half. Your confusion stems from your inability to make a decision. You need to assuage the rupture by mending the split."

"In other words if I don't want to have a nervous breakdown I've got to make up my mind once and for all."

"You and I both know it is not as simple as that. Vacillation, nonetheless, can prove vexing."

"Clare, you're in the business of dealing with disturbed people; people who don't make sense, but I've gotten in over my head. After hearing Kate McGrue's story, I don't feel I should have any more dealings with Harry. I just want to get as far away from him as I can."

"Maggie, your personal experiences have engaged you in the complexities of people that are struggling with extreme difficulties, and your own emotional upheaval has caused you to doubt yourself. Unfortunately running away is no solution."

"What am I going to do, Clare?"

"Maggie, our increasingly complex world requires all of us to work at maintaining a balanced sense of identity. That means looking at the whole picture and facing it truthfully. You took on this task but I warned you of your own vulnerabilities. Now you must find the inner resources to cope with what you have learned. Only then can you come to a determination and maintain your own mental health."

"I doubt that looking objectively at Harry's sordid experiences will make me stronger or give me any additional insight. Besides, it's a moot point since I no longer want to involve myself in his rotten life."

"The answers must come from you, Maggie. You can only be one person and that person must clearly assess her strengths and weaknesses before she can demand that she give fully to what she believes in."

"Clare, I told Harry about my meeting with Kate. I hadn't intended to but in light of his accusations, I felt it needed to be said. We quarreled violently and I haven't seen or spoken to him since and that's fine with me."

"What happened to that dogged determinism you initially had when you decided to help your friend Harry? Did you think it would be easy to help someone who has broken down? Broken psyches need time to mend just as broken bodies do."

"Clare, how can you say that after what I've told you about him?"

"Of course you feel repulsed by the messiness, ugliness and disorder of the situation. Mental illness is untidy and confronted with it unpleasantness it is only natural that you recoil in fear, but your humanness and desire to heal are what Harry needs most. I will handle his medical condition but he will need someone to understand that he is a human being who has made mistakes."

"Clare, he's even drinking again."

"Maggie, Harry is a reactive drinker. He's been honest with me."

"What's a reactive drinker?"

"They are people who suddenly start drinking too much seeking relief from mental pain, like we take aspirin for a headache. It usually happens following a loss, accident, or some type of trauma from which they can't escape. This change is a temporary one and once we work through his emotional disturbance he will discard the pain killer because the pain will be gone."

"He's Mr. Hyde and Kate McGrue was his mentor. How

deplorable is that?"

"She is but one entity in a myriad of quandaries. Harry is a complex person, as we all are, and he must learn to examine each facet of his personality. From what you have told me about this woman, she too has endured a life of disorder and chaos. We cannot feel their pain, and we are not here to judge. Suffice to know that they used each other and acted the way they did because they could not act otherwise. People get caught in this vicious circle from which extrication is nearly impossible without psychotherapy."

"One thing I noticed is the change in Harry. He seems more interested in the future, you know, those long range plans we talked about, rather than immediate satisfaction. Isn't that a sign he's getting well, Clare? Perhaps I shouldn't have antagonized him. He warned me not to mettle in his affairs. You don't think he'd do anything rash, do you?"

"Harry has enough guilt for both of you, Maggie. I'm not minimizing the situation, but he is resilient and determined to come to grips with his inner demons. He told me of your quarrel and of course he's sorry he reacted so vehemently toward you. I am happy to say he has experienced extreme remorse from the confrontation. It was a good thing. You, however, need to rest and regain a sense of composure."

"I get the message, Clare. By the way, did you know Harry resigned from WordTech?"

"Yes, but even though he's written out his list of crimes as he calls them, the committee won't act on his request because he's under a doctor's care. He's been given additional disability time."

"Yes, I know. Corporate has asked me to take over his job in the interim. He trained me well." Maggie sat shaking her head in disbelief. "I don't think I can help him, Clare. There's too much I can't forget."

"Maggie, if you didn't have so much mental anguish you'd be the first person to suggest forgiveness. When your pain eases then you will be able to move forward."

"That doesn't seem to be enough."

"What is it that's really bothering you, Maggie?"

"To think I could have ever loved someone so depraved. It frightens me."

"Harry was primed and ready for the influences that he encountered. His illness was his weakness and it made him an ideal candidate for his own concupiscence."

"That still doesn't excuse him."

"He knew you'd feel that way once you found out. That was why he tried to get you to transfer out of the department. He at once wanted you to know the truth about his life but at the same time he was afraid of losing you. It was then that he came up with the idea of having you type the journal. He wanted you to know what kind of person he was. The things he did were inexcusable but in the unstable state he was in, it made sense to him. What are you thinking, Maggie?"

"I'm remembering that you said that to Harry the only time that matters is now. The future means nothing and the past is forgotten. These so called changes could be just another trick from Harry's magic hat."

"You're right to be suspicious, Maggie. Harry himself knows that he resorts to these masquerades in his efforts to self-cure but he is learning that they are nothing but delusions. The journey he has consented to take will progressively move him through his infancy and forward, and he will relive the happenings in his life in relation to me, his therapist. This requires much courage and he will want to quit when it gets rough. There will be times when he'll be indecisive and not show the self-confidence he once did. These regressions, however, are all temporary."

"He'll be transferring his feelings onto you?"

"Exactly, that is part of the therapeutic process. Harry's loss of both mother and father at such an early age aroused a cold hatred in him which he never consciously acknowledged. Through lack of maternal love he has managed to wreck the lives of those around him including his own. He has to grow up all over again. That means mourning his parents by learning to care for someone else. He's got to mourn for the loss of his dreams and only then will he emerge as the whole creative person he has the potential to be. He can resolve these conflicts in his own life when he finds himself. It is not going to be an easy road and he knows it."

"Funny, it's almost like my dream. His pain was awful—I could feel his loneliness devouring him."

"Yes, Maggie. Try to understand that sexual addiction is a secretive and shameful behavior and it has been incredibly painful for Harry to admit to and take responsibility for his actions. He also has had to accept that others know about him and that is extremely humiliating and disturbing for him. He has made progress but as your dream suggests, transformation involves a rebirth, and to someone who has avoided introspection his whole life, it can be a particularly agonizing process. In the world of mental illness, one day is sunshine and the next a torrential downpour."

"I feel used up, Clare. I know what you're saying but I've already given him what I thought he needed; obviously my trust, my faith and my love weren't enough."

"Remember the dream in the courthouse? You said you were wheeled to the witness stand and found you had no legs. What do you think that dream meant?"

"I thought it meant that I needed more courage. I thought that faced with all that I've learned, it wouldn't be easy to stand up and face the truth."

"You're a very honest person, Maggie. In your dream the very principles in which you've always believed were cut from underneath you, leaving you vulnerable and in a weakened position. But even that has not stopped you from finding the truth and the truth has moved Harry to try and save himself. In that respect, you were successful."

"Yes, I was willing to move heaven and earth to help Harry but he's twisted what mattered most to me and that I can't forgive," Maggie said, knocking her purse off the couch.

Among other things, a card fell onto the floor.

"All my love, all my life. H," Clare read out loud before handing it back to Maggie. "Do you believe he was sincere when he wrote those words, Maggie? If you do, you need to allow yourself to walk again and not be crippled by fear."

"He's led such a self-indulgent existence, Clare. I no longer believe he can change."

"Stop finger pointing, Maggie. I'm not suggesting you continue your relationship as before but you must examine your own feelings if you don't want to be swept away by emotional storms."

"I understand what you're saying but I don't have the strength to weather those storms."

"Try understanding that the road will be long and arduous for both of you. Human betterment is a gradual, two-steps-forward, one-step-back effort. Harry asks only for your friendship. Take some time off. We will continue to meet and talk and you will heal."

"Yes, Clare. Sort of like maintenance therapy in small doses."

"In your case we must make it a large dose." Clare smiled.

"You're my guardian angel, Clare," Maggie said.

"Never discredit your judgment, Maggie, because you're one

person I know who stands behind the decisions you make."

"I don't want to judge him but I wonder if I could ever trust him again."

"Maggie, you have doubts and questions and that is good. We can only be responsible for our own quality of life. Right now you are torn by indecision and as we both know it's the choices we make that set us free."

"And Harry has made his and I'm not going to excuse him because of his illness."

"Maggie, Harry has had an idea that you may or may not want to involve yourself with but he asks you to consider it."

"I doubt seriously if I'd want to involve myself in anything he'd come up with but for the sake of argument, what is it?"

"Harry wants you to sit in on a session and hear where he's coming from. He wants you to feel free, as he puts it, to distinguish the truth from the lies."

"I'd almost be willing to take him up on it."

"What's stopping you?"

"All right, I'll do it. No holes barred regardless of how sick he is?"

"As Harry's doctor, I reserve the right to make those judgments, Maggie, but I have agreed to Harry's terms."

"How soon can you arrange the session, Clare?"

"Harry has agreed to tomorrow evening, if that is good for you?"

"I'll be there."

Chapter 23

Harry was sitting in Clare's office when Maggie arrived.

"I thought we said seven o'clock." Maggie could not hide the anger in her voice.

"Please sit down, Maggie. We have only been waiting a few minutes. However, there has been a change in plans."

"I might have guessed." Maggie unseated herself abruptly.

"Maggie, the only change is that Harry has consented to take a drug which will release his repressions. Although I am not in favor of it, he believes it would give you a more objective view of his life." Clare nodded in Harry's direction.

Maggie looked directly at Harry and saw the outline of a faint smile. "Is it safe, Clare? I thought that only through transference would he be able to work through his problems."

"It isn't a safety issue nor is it a therapeutic short cut. Harry knows and understands that he will still have to remain in therapy even after this session but he believes it will offer a more truthful and less biased inspection of the situation. It is in essence a revelation of his life as heretofore been hidden from both himself and the world."

Harry, looking drawn and tense, spoke for the first time. "It's my decision, Maggie, and I've already made it. Please don't worry."

Clare directed Harry to the couch and rang her intercom. A nurse carried in a sterile tray covered with a thin, cotton cloth. On

Clare's recommendation she lowered the blinds and then left the room. Maggie watched as Clare filled a syringe with a colorless liquid from a small bottle.

"Take off your jacket and roll up your sleeve, Harry. This is sodium pentothal."

"Isn't that truth serum?" Maggie asked in alarm.

"There is no such thing as truth serum. This drug simply releases fears and inhibitions. It is perfectly harmless, Harry. It will only serve to relax you and free your mind."

"Go ahead, Doc."

Clare tied a rubber tourniquet around Harry's arm and rubbed the area with an antiseptic cotton ball. "I must be able to administer the drug slowly as need dictates so this part of the procedure is necessary. Relax, Harry. Flex your hand. Hold it like that," Clare ordered as she inserted the needle.

"When do we start?"

"We have already begun," Clare said as she undid the tourniquet. "You may count backwards from one hundred if you wish." Clare signaled for Maggie to come closer.

"One hundred, ninety-nine, ninety-eight, ninety-seven, ninety, ninety... ." Harry's voice trailed off.

"Listen only to my voice, Harry. You are perfectly safe and very comfortable. You will remember everything that is said."

"Yes, comfortable, very comfortable. Remember...yes..." Harry's body seemed to stretch forward on the couch and his facial features relaxed.

"Tell us your full name."

"Harry Ian Cooke."

"How old are you?"

"Forty."

"Where do you work?"

"WordTech Incorporated."

"How long have you worked there?"

"Eighteen years."

"What was your father's name?"

"Harold Cooke."

"What was your mother's name?"

"Iris Cooke."

"Where are your parents, Harry?"

"They left me."

"What happened to them, Harry?"

"They left me behind."

"Yes, I know Harry, but where did they go?"

"I don't know," Harry seemed to wince in pain.

"Yes you do, Harry. Why weren't they in your life?"

"I can't tell you. Please… they left me alone. I was bad and they left me." Harry began to cry.

"Harry, why are you crying?"

"They went away and left me cause I was bad."

"No Harry, you weren't bad. You were a good boy. But your mommy and daddy had completed their journey and had to die."

"No, no, no. They didn't die. They didn't, they didn't. They left me cause I was bad and mean and made mommy angry." Harry began to sob uncontrollably.

"No, Harry, they didn't want to hurt you but death separated you from your mother and father."

"I don't understand. Didn't they love me enough to stay?"

"They loved you very much but they did not have a choice. We must all die and leave our loved ones."

"Mother left me. She didn't love me. She loved Arnie, not me."

"She was in pain Harry and it was hard for her to show you her love."

"Why didn't she love me? I wanted her to love me. I loved her sooo… much." Harry tried to wrap his arms around himself as his facial features contorted.

"She loved you as best she could."

"No, she wanted me to die like Arnie died. She didn't love me. I hate her, too. Hate, hate, hate you Mommy." Harry's voice was choked with tears.

"Harry, try to remember that when you spoke, your mother listened. When you waved, she turned and saw you. You were her beloved child and she took care of you. She gave you life. Your mother loved you and did not want you to be hurt but she was very sick. You know how it is to be sick, Harry. Our mind sometimes plays tricks on us. She didn't mean to hurt you, Harry. Forgive her."

"Mommy, Mommy, I need you. Why don't you wake up Mommy? Don't leave me, Mommy. Please don't leave me all alone in the dark," Harry pleaded as he tried to hurl himself forward.

Clare restrained him. She pushed the plunger forward injecting more of the fluid into his vein.

"Don't leave me, Mommy. I'm so scared."

"Harry, time is passing. Someone else loves you."

"Who loves Harry? Nobody loves Harry."

"Aunt Jessie loves you."

"No, she doesn't love me. I'm bad."

"What does Aunt Jessie want?"

"She wants me to be a good boy or she'll send me away. I want my mommy. I don't want you. I hate the pain and sadness. It comes every day and never goes away. It hurts me so bad. No one notices Harry or cares about him."

"Harry, Aunt Jessie cares. She loves you. Your mother asked Aunt Jessie to take her place when she died."

"She didn't care for Harry. Only my mommy would care for a

naughty boy like me. Aunt Jess tells me everyday how bad I am. And I know that mommy didn't care because she sent me away."

"You're a good boy, Harry. You didn't die. Your mommy wanted you to live and be well."

"I'm not going to die?"

"Harry, listen carefully to my words. When you lost your mother and father you didn't want to go away like them. You needed to prove that you really did exist. You turned your anger inward upon yourself. You can let go of the anger, Harry. You can forgive your parents for leaving you. They loved you. Aunt Jessie loves you. Say that with me, Harry. I am loved."

"I am loved. I am loved."

"Love cannot be destroyed. You have it in you and it cannot go away."

"I have love." Harry tried again to hug himself.

"Harry, time moves on again. Kate McGrue is here."

Again Clare pushed the hypodermic plunger forward.

"Kate. Kate. I don't want to tell."

"Tell us, Harry. It is all right for you to tell. Nothing can hurt you now."

"Harry needs love but can never find it. Must keep looking for someone to love little Harry. Kate knows."

"What does Kate tell you?"

"Kate says anyone can find love. You make love. You make love happen again and again."

"Why do you do that, Harry?"

"I get them to love me. I make them love me with my body. I am baby Harry. They love the baby. I get inside them and hide. I am safe inside them. They are happy and I am safe. They don't push Harry away. They want Harry and love him."

"Why are you safe inside, Harry?"

"I'm loved. No past, no future. I'm inside, it's good inside. It makes me feel good. I'm satisfied. I want to be swallowed up."

"Sex makes you feel loved, Harry?"

"Sex? Yes. Love, yes, sex. Love is touching. They touch me. I want my mommy to touch me and hold me. Hold me, too, Mommy like you do, Arnie. I don't want to grow up without you. I won't leave you, Mommy. Love me, please love me." Harry suddenly smiled.

"Why are you smiling, Harry?"

"Mommy is touching my face and hugging me like she does to Arnie. I'm happy to be in her arms."

"When you make love, Harry, do you think of your mother?"

"Yes. Love feels good. Harry is a good boy. Pain if Harry is a bad boy."

"What kind of pain, Harry?"

"Endless longing, nothing ever fills the hole. So much pain and loneliness," Harry said, his head drooping to one side.

"The pain will pass, Harry, and you will grow strong. Say with me, I am perfectly healthy in body and mind. I am loved."

"I am perfectly healthy in body and mind. I am loved." Harry seemed at peace with the phrase and repeated it again. "I am perfectly healthy in body and mind. I am loved."

"Time is moving forward, Harry. You are not afraid. Your mother loves you very much but she wants you to know that it is enough for you to be yourself. The love you feel for yourself is good. You are a good person."

"No, no, lies, all a pack of dirty lies. It's black and dark in the night. I'm afraid of the dark. You die in the dark. Mommy died in the dark." Harry's body twisted violently.

Clare depressed the hypodermic's plunger a final time. "Listen to my voice," she directed. "Not lies but the truth, Harry. See the light. Bring the light to you. Your father and mother want you to have the light. It brings you truth. You must live in truth. Say after me, I am loved. I am no longer afraid."

"I am loved. I am no longer afraid."

"Do you believe those words, Harry?"

"The words are tears. Who will hear Harry crying in the dark hole?"

"I hear you, Harry. You are not alone anymore. You are loved. You are not in the dark but in the light. Feel the light, Harry and remember."

"I will remember," Harry said, touching his face.

"You can sleep now, Harry. Know that you are safe and loved. Sleep, Harry," Clare instructed, gently covering his eyes with her hand.

"Harry is loved. Maggie, Maggie…," Harry called, as he drifted into a deep sleep.

"You are at peace, Harry. Sleep and relax," Clare said again. She retracted the needle and swabbed the area with alcohol. "He will sleep now." Clare wiped the perspiration from Harry's forehead and covered him with a light blanket.

"Oh God, Clare, I didn't know. He's suffered so much pain." Maggie's eyes were wet with tears.

"He's a very sick man but with time he can resolve these issues," Clare affirmed quietly. "Harry's life was ruled by the loss of his mother and the feelings she could not give him."

"It's so hard to believe."

"We none of us know what triggers the mind to interpret events. When a child is deprived of love, the pain is unbearable. For that child it is very difficult unless he or she has some direct guidelines. Apparently Harry was not able to make the transition with his aunt. She probably did not have a clue as to how to meet his needs. He created the outlet that best served him."

"We all need love in our lives and Harry was so desperate to have that love he took whatever avenues he could to get it."

"Yes, and it was that need, that particular compulsion that set him off on a vicious cycle. The body and mind create whatever we need. He believed he was saving himself and the ideas he constructed as a child were false, delusional if you wish, but to him they were real. Now we must work to correct those ideas. He must return to his infancy, correct the misapprehensions and start again."

"Clare, I don't want to be here when he wakes up. I don't think it's fair to him. You're right though, I understand now that I cannot judge him. I guess he wanted me to know just how badly his early life had disillusioned him."

"Harry will deal with his past and put it in perspective. I believe he has the determination to work towards his health and well-being."

"I believe that too, Clare, but I think we both need time to heal. I'm taking a month's holiday. Maybe then I can fit the pieces together. When I get back perhaps I'll have some answers. Right now, I don't even know the questions. Please tell Harry for me. I couldn't bear to say good-bye."

Chapter 24

Maggie scanned the skyline as the plane banked and prepared its descent onto the runway at the Leonardo da Vinci/Fiumicino International airport. Rome. It has been ten years since she had last visited her favorite city, the Eternal City.

Before she got into the taxi she inhaled deeply. "That's what I've missed most, that wonderful aroma of Roma," she said, sighing pleasurably.

"Where does the Signorina wish to go?" The taxi driver, his tattered fedora hanging lopsidedly to the back of his head, smiled genially as he struggled to place her luggage inside his small trunk.

"The Penzionne Doria. It's near Doria Pamphile Park close to the gallery," Maggie directed.

"Si, Signorina, I know it well. The Signorina, she is an Americani, si? My English, she is very good, no?"

He pulled into the traffic without waiting for her response and narrowly missed hitting another car. Maggie watched as he shouted and made hand gestures at the other drivers, all the while keeping up a running conversation. She sat in the taxi and shook her head in amusement. Undeniably, she was back in the land of her forefathers.

After a short introduction, wherein he discussed his five bambinos, three dogs, two cats and last but not least his beautiful and adoring espousa Gina, Giuseppe the driver turned out to be Maggie first acquaintance in Rome. He was a pleasant, middle-aged man who continually chomped on his cigar while pointing in a variety of directions. Maggie learned he had been driving a taxi for thirty-five years and had always accommodated his out of town passengers with an informal sightseeing tour at no extra charge.

Expertly steering his well-worn vehicle at breakneck speeds down tiny one-way streets and narrow boulevards off the beaten path, Giuseppe somehow magically re-emerged almost on the very doorstep of such glorious splendors as the Coliseum, the Spanish Steps, the Villa Sciarra, Trevi Fountain, the Borghese Gardens and the majestic Basilica of Santa Maria Maggiore. Each was breathtaking and offered her not only a feast for the eyes but made her homecoming all the more special. Gazing at the lush colors of the landscape and the softened hues of the architectural splendors through the warm, golden light of the city, Maggie felt privileged to have come back again.

Afterwards, Giuseppe drove to a quiet tree-lined avenue and promptly stopped in front of a little hotel. "We are here, Signorina," he said, handing her his card with a promise to be at her beck and call while she was in the city.

A bellboy came out and loaded her luggage onto a small dolly. As he slowly made his way to the reception desk Maggie heard the wooden floor creak under the weight of the worn wheels.

"Welcome to Roma. Welcome to the Penzionne Doria. We are most happy to be of service, Signorina Reynolds." The manager's greeting was said with such gusto that his smile looked as large as his handlebar moustache.

"Grazie, Signore." Maggie handed him her passport and signed her name to the oversized register.

"We have been holding a few letters for your arrival, Signorina," the manager said, handing Maggie a small packet. "We hope your stay with us will be most pleasant."

"Grazie mille, grazie," Maggie said, smiling graciously as she hastily deposited the mail into her travel bag but not before she recognized her mother's handwriting.

Maggie looked around the tiny lobby as she and the bellboy waited for the elevator. Sparsely but exquisitely furnished in rich, well-designed pieces, the room appeared comfortable as well as stylish. Even the lift, although extremely small, was charming. A relic of the past, the rustic machine clattered up to the third floor accommodating her luggage and only the two of them.

The room did not disappoint her. It was a spacious apartment with the walls a warm, peach-colored stucco. The lovely, oversized furniture pieces were covered in rich floral tapestry and the sumptuous bed, piled high with thick down comforters and pillows, looked delicious. Light from the balcony window flooded the room and Maggie caught a glimpse of the piazza below.

"It's enchanting, grazie," Maggie said, handing the bellboy a tip after he unloaded her suitcases.

"Grazie, Signorina."

"Prego, prego."

"Un momento, Signorina," the young man unbolted the balcony window and gestured at the cool breeze which suddenly blew across the room.

"Grazie mille, grazie," Maggie nodded in appreciation.

Once he had departed she indulged herself in peaceful seclusion. Everything was exactly as she had pictured and with few tourists to disturb the quiet she felt completely at home. A hot bath did wonders for her psyche, rejuvenating both her spirit and appetite. She wrapped her wet hair in a towel and called the hotel's room service to order dinner.

When the food arrived, it took only a few whiffs of the delicious creation to convince her she was ravenous and she sat and devoured the fresh salmon and zucchini, sipping at her wine in-between bites. She decided to take her tea and dessert, an exquisite custard fantasy, out onto the enormous balcony and languidly reclined as she watched her fellow tourists saunter past the fountain below.

How wonderful to be here taking in the pleasure of the remains of the day. What a glorious feeling to be alive and at peace in such a tranquil setting. Perhaps I'll even sleep through the night for the first time in weeks. But before I can stretch out on that beautiful bed I'll have to read those letters I've managed to avoid all afternoon.

The first letter Maggie opened was from her mother.

Dear Maggie,

I hope this letter catches up with you in Rome. I wanted to write and let you know that Dr. Sebastian called and asked for your address. It appears that Harry asked for it so that he could write you a letter. I really didn't want to give them your hotel address but with the doctor requesting it, I thought I'd better give it to her and you could decide later if you wanted to read the mail or not.

Dearest one, please try and get away from all your problems and rest up on your trip. I hope you have time to visit your father's grave and say a prayer for me while you are there.

I don't pretend to know what is best for you, but I am praying that you make the right decision. You are so young and unselfish that I fear you will be used by those who wish to take advantage of your generosity.

Whatever your decision, I will respect it. I love you very much.
Love,
Mother
P.S. Daisy and Shadow miss you and send their paw prints.

Clare's note was next.

Dear Maggie,

Harry has asked my permission to write you. He was upset when he learned that you had left on your trip, but understood your desire to get away from the situation as soon as possible. I have told him that under no circumstances, short of a letter, is he to contact you. Apparently there is something he wants very much to tell you, and he didn't want to wait until you returned.

I deemed sending you a brief report on Harry's condition a sound idea, and he concurs, so please bare with me while I put forward these particulars.

Harry is making good progress. He is aware that continuance of therapy is essential to his recovery and that the time frame, although indefinite, will eventually promote longer lasting benefits. Psychologically he is of sound mind and body, and is patiently and stalwartly working through his impulsive behavioral issues.

Although he contends constantly with feelings of depression and hopelessness, I have noted a glimmer of optimistic change in his demeanor as he becomes more accepting of his condition. I have great hope that eventually he will successfully complete his treatment.

Maggie, I felt this information would prove invaluable toward your efforts in maintaining a balanced perspective, which I hope, regardless of adversity, you continue to sustain. In the meantime, rest and mend yourself, dear friend. Time can be a wonderfully healing agent. If I can be of any assistance, you need only contact me.

Take care,
Clare

Maggie didn't want to read Harry's letter but decided that the miles between them would made it easier.

Dearest Maggie,

I got permission from Dr. Sebastian to write you this letter. I understand why you left so abruptly and I don't blame you. The doctor told me that she would write you a brief evaluation of my progress but I wanted you to know from my heart how I felt.

I come to you knowing that my deplorable actions do not deserve your forgiveness, but I humbly plead for it all the same. I apologize for all I've done to you, particularly for having exposed you to my wantonness in a most despicable fashion.

Words do not seem to be sufficient and I make no excuses for my behavior except to say that I am a troubled scoundrel who thought he had all the answers. I despise what I was and what I have become and I curse myself for what I have done to you. I hated the past until you entered my life seven years ago, bringing a semblance of reason into my tangled, chaotic world. You even made the future seem hopeful. The tragedy is that I failed to recognize what you offered me and instead slipped further into the quagmire of disillusionment.

Your faith in me has led me to this moment. We are all products of those we meet and you have made it possible for me to salvage whatever I have left of this earthly existence. To say that I am grateful for your kindness and support is an understatement, and I can only hope you know how sincerely I value your friendship.

At last I know what real love is, and I believe in its power to conquer that which seeks to destroy it. I do love you, Maggie, and for as long as I live I shall think of you, wishing you the best of everything, always. I wanted to tell you this in person, but I know this is the better way. You helped me find the light in the darkness and now I hope you find the happiness you so deserve. I am content to know that for one brief moment you were part of my life.

All my love, all my life,

H.

Maggie folded the letters and put them in her bag. She was

determined to let nothing spoil her holiday, yet it was Harry's words that gnawed at her, distressing her to the point where she was desperate to escape their bewildering implications. Wanting sleep, she capitulated and took two of the tablets Clare had prescribed. She soon drifted off into a world devoid of dreams.

Rome awakened her early. She felt refreshed and eager for the day to start. She ordered breakfast and ate it unhurriedly, savoring both the delights of the city and the superb meal from the hotel's kitchen. On the privacy of her balcony Maggie contemplated the next step of her journey. She had come thousands of miles to find and visit her friend. She spent very little time unpacking, preferring instead to locate and ask the concierge for directions.

"Mi scusi per favore, Signore, can you tell me where is the Chiesa de Santa Maria della Pieve?"

"Si, si, Signorina," the concierge, smiling indulgently produced a map and circled the location of the church. "I will call Giuseppe and be assured Signorina he knows the way," he said, beaming at her as he placed a call from behind his counter.

Giuseppe appeared within minutes of her request almost as if he had been camped down the street. "The Signorina needs her Giuseppe, si?"

"Signore Giuseppe, so good to see you again," Maggie said appreciatively as he held open the car door and listened as she repeated her destination.

"Si, si, Signorina, so good to see you, too. I make the trip for you quick, yes?"

"Grazie, Giuseppe," Maggie agreed and got into the back of the taxi. Once again she made herself comfortable on the well-worn leather seat.

Giuseppe, true to his word, did indeed make the journey in record time. As Maggie later recalled she spent most of the journey with her eyes closed, hanging tightly to the tattered strap which dangled from the taxi's roof.

Once they left the city, Giuseppe threw the taxi in gear and pressed the accelerator to the mat. The engine coughed and wheezed as they made their way up the twisting roads into the mountains. Maggie heard the tires scream for traction as they churned up gravel along the narrow passageways.

At one point, nearing the precipice, Maggie saw an old man with his donkey. As the taxi careened toward them, man and beast hugged the mountainside in terror. Battling for control, Giuseppe turned the steering wheel reflexedly from left to right as he waved his hands and bellowed curses out the window. The car swerved dangerously close to the edge, avoiding what could have been a terrible accident and miraculously righted itself near the peak's top.

The last part of the journey was relatively calm. The taxi made its way down the mountain going at a good clip and soon reached the valley junction where the road became wider. Giuseppe's heavy foot prodded the vehicle over the last few miles of the trip which was a series of jolts and jerks on a pockmarked road filled with ruts and gapping holes. Maggie felt every bump as the car bobbed and buckled up the steep lane until finally, its tires screeching beseechingly, it turned into a small courtyard.

"Does the Signorina wish for me to wait for her?" Giuseppe asked hopefully as he helped her out.

"No, grazie, Signore Giuseppe, my friend will drive me home." Maggie put several bills into Giuseppe's hand and smiled graciously.

"Grazie, mille grazie, Signorina." He pressed his card into her hand and asked somberly, "Signorina Maggie will call Giuseppe if she has need of him again, yes?"

"Yes, Giuseppe. Grazie, mille grazie."

Maggie watched as Giuseppe and his old brown taxi raced down the hill, disappearing in a cloud of dust. She was glad she wasn't a passenger on the trip back to the city.

Maggie went into the church hoping for directions to the rectory but was instantly enthralled by the stone edifice. According to the cornerstone the church had been built in 1350 A.D. and here, deep inside its cavernous chambers it was cool and inviting, its architects having discovered the lasting secret hundreds of years before the advent of air conditioning.

Her eyes were drawn to the beauty of the exquisite stained-glass windows but as she approached the altar the statue of Saint Anthony took hold of her attention and she knelt in prayer. She never understood how anyone could not have a sense of God but here in this wonderful old church the truth of it was all the more poignant. The bells began pealing for the noon Mass and Maggie looked up to see a young priest lighting candles.

"Excuse me Father, but do you know where Father Anthony might be?"

As soon as he turned to face her, she recognized him.

"Maggie, is that you?" Hoisting up his black cassock, Father Anthony came down the steps two at a time. "What a surprise! It's been so long," he said, embracing her fondly.

"Father Anthony, I'm so glad to find you here," Maggie cried, burying her face in his robe.

"Maggie, Maggie, it's great to see you again. Sit down and tell me what brings you back to Rome?"

Maggie sat back in the pew and fought to regain her composure as she stared into the fine looking face of the man she had almost married.

"Father Anthony, I needed to see you. There's no one else on earth who could understand what a terrible predicament I've gotten myself into," Maggie wept into her handkerchief.

"Maggie, please call me Tony, after all we've known each other for a long, long time."

"Father, I mean, Tony, if you're sure it's all right."

"Certainly, I'm a priest but still a good friend. Let's go into the rectory and talk. It's more comfortable there. I'm lighting the candles today but Father Carlos is saying Mass."

"Tony, if you can't help me, I don't know what I'll do."

"Calm down, Maggie, and tell me what it's all about," Tony said, pouring scalding water from the copper kettle into the teapot.

Maggie blurted out her story, unburdening herself of the pent-up emotions she had carried across the ocean. Occasionally stopping to sip her tea, she talked non-stop for hours until the young priest interrupted her.

"Maggie, I've got to get ready to say the evening Mass. Afterwards we'll have supper and talk more. Would you like to attend Mass?" Tony asked, as he walked back into the room dressed in his religious vestments.

"Father, it's as I always pictured you. And yes, I very much want to attend Mass."

"God bless you for your kind words, Maggie."

Maggie noted that Tony's youthful informality had changed into a more formal manner. He had grown far more serious with the years and although he occasionally lapsed into Italian to address her, even to using hand gestures, there was a distinct aura of solemnity about him.

"Will you hear my confession first, Father?"

"I will, gladly."

Later, her head covered in a white lace mantilla, Maggie watched as Tony, Father Anthony, said Mass. She marveled at the radiance of his countenance and listened with rapt attention to his sermon, the words of which transcended the language. When he stood at the altar blessing the bread and wine, she knew in her heart he had made the right decision, and, as she received the sacred host and cup from his hands there was an unutterable sense of contentment she had not realized since her First Communion Day.

At supper that evening he was his old convivial self, showing her how to rub chunks of raw garlic into hot bread and directing the pouring of olive oil over the golden crusts. It was a veritable feast of lamb, fresh vegetables, and deep red Chianti. For dessert she ate the sweetest grapes she had ever tasted. Picked early that morning Maggie swore they were still warm from the sun. She could not recall having savored such a sumptuous meal and she was astonished to learn from the other priests that the entire repast had all been produced right there on the premises.

While waiting for Tony to finish vespers, Maggie walked contemplatively through the gardens under stars so bright there was no need of lights. When he finally rejoined her they talked through the night, and only as dawn illuminated the sky was he able to persuade her to take sleep in the little guestroom off the kitchen. For the first time in months, she slept soundly, naturally, in a dreamless sleep that seemed to wash away her cares and concerns.

Maggie chattered like a schoolgirl through their mid-morning breakfast of fresh fruit, biscotti and hot cocoa, and afterwards, as they climbed the hills into the church vineyards Tony remarked that he had never seen her so filled with joie de vivre.

"It's true. I haven't been this happy in a long time, Tony. This must be what you feel everyday."

"Yes, it's a good place. The earth is rich and the air is pure. And look," he pointed in the distance, "God's bounty."

"You mean as far as the eye can see? All those vines, Tony, and they belong to the church with you in charge as the master vine keeper?" Maggie beamed with pride at his accomplishments.

"Yes, you could say that. The village and the church have a cooperative wherein we share the profits earned from the wines and preserves."

"Tony, it's a wonderful life you've chosen. You look happy," Maggie said as she hungrily consumed a hunk of cheese and some of the bread Tony had brought for their lunch.

"God's given me peace."

"You never hesitated when He called you into His service."

"May I tell you something, Maggie?"

"Yes, please do."

"The night we said good-bye was the hardest thing I've ever had to do. I admit I was torn and in doubt but when I laid the decision at His feet, all my uncertainty disappeared and I knew it was the right choice for me. I've never looked back and each day of each year my heart's been filled with happiness for all God's given me. Working and serving Him and His people, it's what I want to do. It's hard to explain in simple terms, but when I'm saying Mass, especially during the Consecration, it feels as though my soul were on fire with His love," Tony said, a look of inexpressible joy on his face.

"Tony, how I wish I could find such peace instead of this confused and jumbled mess of misery."

"You'll sort it out and I promise when you leave Italy it shall be with a light heart and a firm decision."

"I'm holding you to that promise, Tony."

"You know Maggie until rational thought is linked with purpose there can be no intelligent accomplishment. From what you've told me about Harry I believe his problems lie in the futility of his having led a life of utter disappointment in himself."

"Tony, can he extricate himself from such a prison?"

"When you choose the wrong road, you must travel it twice. I gather from your description of the situation that his aimlessness stems from his insecurity and inability to find meaning in his life. He'll have to find his own answers. Remember Christ said that to those whom much is given, much is expected."

"But how, Father?"

"Only a wise man can make the journey through the winds and storms of the soul. If he sacrifices little, he'll accomplish little. Right now he's risen to heights in the business world but he's descended into personal wretchedness. Only by giving up on his old self can he expect redemption. The gate into heaven is going to be a pretty tight fit for all of us."

"Tony, his selfishness and corruption frighten me."

"Those are the outward signs of his disease, Maggie. Inwardly, it is much worse. He's got to resolve the conflict that torments him, otherwise it will destroy him. Harry is an intelligent man and he knows that in order to experience the calm he has first to make it through the tempest."

"He's been searching for the light all his life and it has somehow eluded him." Maggie shook her head.

"Until you appeared in his life and become the one person able to help him find it, is that it? Sorry to disillusion you, Maggie, but in reality the journey from self-discovery to self-transformation is a personal quest and each of us must do it alone. It's never easy, no matter what our age. We either let life's situations defeat us or we rise above them."

"Tony, in the beginning I was filled with confidence that he'd see the truth, a bit naively I admit, but I don't believe it's possible anymore."

"Maggie, Harry is first and foremost the only person that can change his life. Man is always the master, even in his weakest state. When Harry begins to reflect and self-analyze himself by directing his efforts toward intelligent solutions he'll find the answers."

"What do I care what he does with his life. He's not the man I thought he was. You can't imagine, Tony, how I believed in him and looked up to him."

"Tolerance fosters understanding, Maggie. When you come to

terms as to how you feel about Harry, and you will, you can offer him the solace of friendship. He's surrounded by shadows of grief and guilt and helping him disperse those sorrows is what a good and patient friend can do."

"Father, how can I bring peace and comfort into his soul when I can hardly help myself?"

"Maggie, you've already made a difference in his life. Your words of encouragement have already helped Harry try for a second chance. You may not realize it but you've given him hope for a future he never believed in. People underestimate the power of kind words and don't realize their importance. When we hear them, particularly from those we love, they can turn us inside-out. The wonder is that in helping others we help ourselves, just as you've managed to do."

"Suppose he never gets better. Suppose he regresses into the depraved life style he's known for so long?"

"That's a great deal of supposition. Don't expect him to respond overnight. He may in fact regress as I'm sure Clare has told you. Stop expecting big outcomes and settle for small improvements. After all, we humans understand failure a lot more than we do success."

"Harry says he loves me but that's something I could never come to terms with, knowing what he's done in the past."

"The one thing I heard was the word past but what I'm not hearing is that you're prepared to walk away from him now."

"That would be quitting on him."

"No, that would be forgiving him."

"Maybe I could start in the minors and work up toward the majors," Maggie smiled feebly.

"Yes, and keep your relationship at a level you are both comfortable with. Your friendship is all that both of you need at the present."

"Do you still think he wants me to help him?"

"People gravitate to what they need in life. Harry admires your strength, will power and your vision but it's up to him to develop a set of ideals that will alter his condition and hopefully come up to your level. From what you've told me, that's important to him, and ultimately to you."

"Tony, if it ever comes to his asking me to be more to him I don't know if I'd be able to give him what he needs?"

"Maggie, all you can offer is the gift of perfect love."

"Perfect love…I don't understand. What is perfect love?"

"Perfect love sees the suffering and does not condemn. Perfect love embraces the oppressed with compassion. Perfect love does not belittle but seeks to uplift and encourage."

"Father Tony, even if I offered him such a love, I doubt if I could help him?"

"Maggie, love is a friendship that has caught fire. Perhaps you need to step back from the flame and let go of your own desires."

"Father, it's easier said then done. I can't tell you how ashamed I feel every time I think of how I… felt about him." Maggie confessed, biting her lip.

"Maggie, if God is for us who can be against us? Don't be so hard on yourself, and as for Harry, he's got to muster up his own courage. God help him, he's got quite a challenge on his hands but from what I've heard you say it seems like he's taken some steps in the right direction."

"Father, the soul may be willing but the body is weak."

"I understand that, Maggie, but to accomplish anything we've got to be willing to sacrifice. Isn't that part of this whole process? Harry's working with Clare to right himself. He got to struggle against his weakness by facing the pain of unpleasant thoughts with mental courage. Courage that takes place in the head is just as heroic as physical courage. It means admitting we're wrong and that we've made mistakes. No one will have to tell him when he's accomplished it. He'll know it. Sure, he might fall back into failure, but none of us are strangers to sorrow and regret. The key is to keep trying."

"Father, up until now I have truly loved only once in my life," Maggie smiled at Tony knowingly, "and it seems I'm doomed to have my heart torn apart again. How can I find the truth?"

"Love requires risk, Maggie. The stakes are high but if it's real the end reward is worth it."

"I'm not much of a gambler, Father. I'd need more of a guarantee than that."

"Maggie, your father is buried not far from here in the village of Palombara Sabina. I could drive you there tomorrow. There is an inn near a little lake that I think would make a charming place for a retreat. If you wish, I will call and let them know that you'd like to stay for a few days. I believe that if you make this pilgrimage you may find the answers you seek."

"All right, Father, please call for me. Maybe there I'll find what I'm looking for."

"The answers are within you, Maggie. All you need is quiet solitude to hear them."

⁂

Just before dawn, Maggie and Father Tony got into the church's jeep for the drive to Palombara Sabina thirty kilometers further up into the mountains. The morning air was cold and Maggie wasn't sure if it was the weather or the prospect of returning to her paternal family home that gave her the shivers.

It certainly wasn't Father Tony's driving skills. As she watched him deftly maneuver the vehicle around the corkscrew turns taking them higher and higher up the craggy cliffs she was reminded of the spine-tingling ride she had experienced with Giuseppe. Now even the sound of the tires grating against the gravel on the hairpin turns along the steep ledges didn't alarm her.

Her thoughts were suddenly interrupted by Farther Tony's hand-waving gestures as he called her name into the wind.

"Maggie, look! Isn't it everything I said it would be?"

Rounding the bend, Maggie gazed at the panorama unfolding below them. In the early morning light, the tiny, picturesque town looked like a scene out of a painting. It was a sight that literally took her breath away.

"It's beautiful!" She shouted back at him.

By the time they entered the village the late morning sun had blanketed the valley, and the temperature change forced Maggie to peal off several layers of clothing. Except for a few stray dogs lying contentedly on the warm cobblestones, the town was virtually empty. As they pulled into the parking lot of the half-timbered two story hotel, Maggie saw the words, 'Bella Fortuna' printed on the side of the building.

"Beautiful fortune, or as we would say, good luck," Father Tony translated as he jumped out of the jeep and helped Maggie with her backpack. "Maggie, sorry to be in such a rush but I've got to get back to the church. I've borrowed one of the two means of transportation we have and Father Carlos needs a ride to the doctor's this afternoon."

"Of course, Father. Thanks so very much for all your help."

"Here's the private number of the rectory. Call me when you're ready to leave and I'll pick you up. May God go with you, Maggie, as do my prayers," he said, embracing her warmly.

She felt her eyes well with tears. "Father, I'll call you Wednesday," she said, forcing back the urge to cry.

Father Tony, his cassock skirt swinging freely out of the well-worn vehicle, waved good-bye as he flew full tilt down the road.

"God bless you, dear friend."

It took Maggie very little time to register at the quaint hotel's lobby desk and to refresh herself in the small but well appointed room. Within the hour she set out on her quest to find her father's grave. She had been in the little town years before and figured it would be fairly easy to retrace her steps with a few directions from the local residents.

Walking down the narrow streets of the village, Maggie inhaled the delightful fragrances of home cooking and her mouth began to water as she passed several little sidewalk cafes. One particular establishment was just opening and Maggie sat down on the charming outside patio and ordered saltimbocca for lunch.

Her father had made the savory veal dish many times and as a child she had learned that it literally meant to "jump into your mouth." The bittersweet memory, however, robbed her of her appetite and she sat forlornly people-watching without touching her food.

"Mi scusi per favore, Signorina, you do not find the saltimbocca good?" A young waiter stood asking, a concerned look on his face.

"Si, si, it's delicious. It's only that I'm not very hungry," Maggie tried to explain but stopped speaking when she realized the young man might not understand English.

"I understand, Signorina, I speak English very well. I must say this not to offend the Signorina but as a compliment. The Signorina, she is molto bella, yes? Bellissima Signorina, sei molto bella," he repeated kissing his fingertips. "Perhaps the Signorina would do me the honor of escorting her this evening to the dance in the palazzo, yes? It is a night of festival in Palombara Sabina."

"No grazie, Signore. Ho un appuntamento." Not wanting the young Italian to think she was returning his flirtatious exchange, Maggie gave him a diminutive smile, paid her check and darted out onto the crowded marketplace.

After purchasing a small bouquet of wild flowers from a

street side vender, Maggie made her way up the steep hill walking contemplatively past the silent fields of the open countryside. It was a land of olive trees and quiet beauty. She stopped often, meditating on each lovely vista that caught her eye and it was late afternoon when she finally reached the cemetery entrance.

There was no one around, and except for a few birds and the calls of far-off animals, she was alone. The sun was already beginning to set and had cast a hazy film over the ground as she approached the wrought iron gate. A thicket of dried copse lay across the graveyard's entrance making it difficult for her to open the rusted relic and she had to push at it several times before it began to move. Cringing and crying for lack of oil it finally gave way, depositing her in a thick, weed strewn enclosure.

Following an untended path overgrown with thistles along the far edge of the grounds, Maggie worried she might not even recognize the grave after all this time. It had been years since she purchased the granite headstone and watched its placement next to the graves of her grandmother and grandfather. The monuments took on a surreal quality as her eyes searched for the three pronged key design she had commissioned the stonemason to cut. Then she saw it. Gleaming in the sun, it beckoned her approach. Falling to her knees, she read the inscription.

Robert (Roberto Renoldazzi) Reynolds,
beloved husband of Patricia
and loving father of Margaret.
1955-1990.
LET THE MORNING BRING ME WORD OF YOUR
UNFAILING LOVE. Psalm 143

Even before the flowers fell from her hands, Maggie became inconsolable.

"Papa, why did you leave me?"

The tears streamed down her face as uncontrollable sobs wracked her body reducing every breath to a spasm. Still she could not stop crying.

"Papa, please help me," she pleaded, as weak and weepy she laid her grieving body down on the roughhewed grass. "I've lost my way and don't know which way to turn. Please help me."

Consumed in grief and anguish, she was unable to extricate herself from the predicament which now threatened to send her over the edge. Feeling as though a dam had burst in upon her she was immersed in desolation so profound she wept herself into a deep, fathomless sleep into whose silence she at last surrendered.

Time became indiscernible and she was unaware of the day's passing. As night approached, she was oblivious to the cold rain which poured down on the parched ground. Somewhere in her subconscious, voices tried desperately to rouse her but she was far beyond acknowledging their frantic calls. Shadowy arms lifted her aloft as she barely clung to her earthly ties. Banishing her encroaching fears she was content to rest in the warmth and tranquility of her father's presence.

Chapter 25

She saw him from her vantage point high on the hill.

"Papa, Papa," she called after the tall, solitary figure walking briskly across the green meadow. She had recognized him immediately but when he showed no signs of stopping she hurried down the hill after him.

"Wait for me, Papa," she pleaded breathlessly.

He was already far off in the field. Maggie knew he was heading toward the river that ran through the valley but at the pace he was traveling it would be hard for her to catch up to him. Her skin felt hot to the touch and she longed for the coolness of the water. The blazing heat from the blistering sun made it all but impossible for her to run but she was determined not to let him get away from her.

"Papa," she said, catching her breath, "I should be very cross with you. You didn't stop and wait for me." Maggie grabbed at her father's hand and began to walk with him, trying to keep up with his long strides.

"Maggie, dear, I didn't want to wait for you. It's not your time, yet."

"I love you so much, Papa, and I need you so desperately. I've gotten lost and I need you to help me find my way."

"Dearest, you know I will help you, but I was hoping you'd remember what I taught you and come to find the answers on your own."

"It's too hard, Papa. I'm never going back. I'm staying here with you forever. Please promise you'll never leave me again."

"That's not possible, Maggie." Her father stopped and looked down at her. He smiled as his fingers brushed against her tear stained face. "My dearest child, you must go back and live your life."

"Look, Papa, it's a white-tail deer. Isn't it magnificent?" Maggie deliberately interrupted her father's reprimand as she had done so many times in her childhood.

"It's a buck, see the antlers?" Her father pointed to the large animal's huge horns. "Let's go rest by the stream, Maggie. It will be cool there this time of day."

"Yes, I could use a drink of cold water. All this running has made me feel hot and tired." She bent low and drank the cool, clear liquid, splashing her face with the shimmering drops that evaporated as soon as they touched her feverish skin.

Her father dipped his fingers into the stream and touched them against her forehead. The icy coldness made her throbbing head feel better.

"Look, Papa, a spider spinning her web," Maggie exclaimed, looking intently into the dense shrubbery at an almost transparent maze. "That's what Harry's done, twisted our love just like that old spider. Everything's so mixed up. What shall I do, Papa?"

"Things do get muddled every once in a while, dear, but if you give them time they usually work themselves out. Take that web for instance. It's quite a remarkable feat of engineering skill and creativity. I imagine it's a lot like your own creative force of silver threads."

"What do you mean, Papa, my creative force?" Maggie asked, sitting comfortably against a rock and wiggling her toes in the cool water. She watched as her father lit his pipe and waited for the familiar tobacco scent to reach her nose all the while eyeing the smoke-puffs that curled around his head.

"The Indians believed the spider was a creative force that gave energy to our dreams. You've spun your own lovely web, dear one, the dream of your life's design. It was never a tangled web of illusion but rather a web of solution; a pattern of love with interconnecting lines perpetually meeting. It touched Harry and helped him unlock his world of fear and limitations. The threads of love are never easy to weave. Sometimes they do get tangled but if we're going to face life's challenges then it's up to us to learn to disentangle the cords and reweave them when necessary."

"Will I ever be sure, Papa?"

"Maggie dear, no one can ever be sure of anything. We make the best choices we can because we all want to be proud of the chapters we create in our lives. You've woven something beautiful, a design of courage and determination. You've used your creative force, your love, to help you find your way through the silver strands."

"Harry isn't going to be part of that new chapter," Maggie said petulantly. "I loved him so much but I don't think I could love him again. I don't believe it would be wise of me to love him. Does that sound terribly mean, Papa?"

"It sounds to me as though you're afraid to give him your love."

"Yes, I think you're right, Papa. I knew you'd understand."

"Why are you afraid to love him?"

"How can I take such a risk after the awful life he's led? Even if I gave him my love, it would probably mean nothing to him."

"Wounded pride can sometimes cause a great deal of pain, daughter."

"Papa, can't you see that he's not the man I thought he was?"

"So, he'll use you up, spurn your love and when he walks away you'll be left with nothing. Is that it? Is that what you're afraid of?"

"Oh, Papa, yes, yes," Maggie's put her opened palm to her mouth to stifle her sobs. New tears glistened in her eyes.

"There are no guarantees in life, my darling. You will have to trust yourself that you see not the man he was, but the promise of the man he hopes to become. That's what faith is all about."

"What about love, Papa? How can I love such a man?"

"Maggie, Maggie, do you remember when you were very small and asked me what I thought love was?" Her father gently wiped her cheeks with a great handkerchief he had pulled from his jacket pocket.

"Yes, Papa, I was so little and I remember seeing you and mother holding each other and telling how much you loved one another. I was jealous because I wanted you to hold me like that and I didn't understand."

"Do you recall what I told you?"

"Tell me again, Papa." Maggie snuggled closer to her father as he put his arm around her shoulder. She loved the feel of his rough textured corduroy jacket against her skin.

"Love is goodness, Maggie, plain and simple."

"I've always felt your love, Papa, no matter how far away you were."

"Yes, honey, because love always puts the other person first. Not time, nor distance nor even death can retract one drop of love once we've given it to another. It becomes our legacy and it lives forever."

"Why is that, Papa?"

"Because when we love, we don't think of ourselves. We're always thinking of the other person. We're worried about that person's well-being. Are they happy? Do they need a blanket? Could I give a cool drink or a warm hug? Did I say something hurtful?"

"We think of the other person and want the best for them, right, Papa?"

"Yes, Maggie. People today so often use the word love they've forgotten the real meaning of the word. I love a certain movie or a favorite food. We meet someone and it's love at first sight, but real love is so much more. We will the best for those we love. We want it so much for them, we will it to happen. That means from the very core of our being we want them to have all the goodness in the world. Love doesn't take but gives, generously, openly without constraints or contingencies because it can only exist in that form. Once it's redefined or put upon, it's no longer love."

"That's why we say love's unconditional, just like you and mother gave me when I was a little girl. I remember you called it love without strings."

"Yes, my darling, parents love their children above all. They are the future, our legacy to life, and, like all of life's gifts, require sacrifice. Parents don't love their children with the idea of getting something out of it. Instead, we only want the best for them. Sometimes it requires showing a tough love but it's all from the heart, there is no malice."

"Why is love between a man and a woman different, Papa?"

"There is no real difference, Maggie, if we truly accept the real meaning of love. We still will the goodness from the bottom of our hearts to the person we love. When you love someone, you want them to have all the happiness you feel. You accept their frailties and weaknesses and love the whole person."

"It's like being on the same wavelength with each other. You both want the best for one another." Maggie so wanted to hear her father's words but her eyes felt heavy and she yawned in spite of herself.

"Yes, dearest, that's why in many cultures, letting the person go rather than hurting them in any way is the respectful way of showing how much you care. Again, it's sacrifice, for we have to be willing to totally give everything and expect nothing in return. The very act of loving exudes its own joy."

"Listening to your words, Papa, I feel as though I've already made a decision. Is that possible?"

"Yes, Maggie, it may well be that in your heart, you never called it love, but you've given so much of yourself to your friend, you can now put a name to it."

"I love Harry."

"Do you, my dear?"

"If you love someone, you can forgive them anything. Isn't that right, Papa?"

"You're right about that, Maggie."

"I want so much for him to get better. I want him to be happy and find himself in this life, and I know it doesn't have to be with me, as long as he's whole again in body and soul. Every fiber of my being wills for goodness to be his and when I know he is no longer suffering, I'll be content. And I'll go on willing his happiness for the rest of my life."

"What a miracle love is," her father said, kissing her teary eyes.

"It's such a glorious and uplifting feeling, Papa, and that's how I've always felt about you. My love's transcended time and has no boundaries. The more I give the more complete I am."

"It wasn't such a secret after all, was it my darling? When you love deeply anything is possible."

"Papa, why is it when I'm here with you it all seems so simple. It's as though all my problems have vanished and I've finally found peace."

"Unfortunately, Maggie, you've only taken a brief hiatus and you must soon return to complete the tasks of your life."

"No, Papa, I no longer want that part of me, I'm satisfied to let it go. It was my yesterday and today is all my tomorrows here with you. I'll never let you go again, never," Maggie cried, hugging him tightly.

"There are times when we have little to say in what happens to us, my dear. That's when we must be our bravest and trust the Lord to make those decisions. Remember, He is our heavenly Father, and He will take care of us." Her father fingered the small three-pronged key that hung from her neck. "You remember, Maggie?"

"Yes, Papa, I remember everything you taught me."

"Good, I'm glad, but there were times when I thought you needed an extra little push." Maggie's father winked knowingly.

"Papa, I'm afraid I don't have enough courage to make it through this life."

"Maggie, don't you see, darling, if you live by the principles you believe in you'll have nothing to fear. Only people who have no central purpose in their life fall easy prey to worries, troubles, self-pityings and all the weaknesses that lead to failure, unhappiness and loss."

"That's what Harry needs to know."

"And you my sweet angel will help him learn."

"Papa, this is the nearest place to heaven I have ever been and I've waited ever so long to be with you again. Please don't talk about my leaving you."

"It's time, Maggie, for both of us to go back."

"If you loved me you would never submit me to such torment, Papa," Maggie shouted in terror. "I can't make it alone any more."

"You're not alone, darling, not as long as you have God and those around you who love you, and you keep on giving that love back. Take care, my sweet Maggie, till we meet again."

He kissed her gently, stood up and began to walk away. She followed him with her eyes as he made his way along the riverbank but she was so tired she was unable to run after him. When she could no longer see him in the distance she buried her head in the soft, green grass and wept.

"Papa, I love you so much. Please don't leave me."

Chapter 26

Maggie opened her eyes slowly. It was cooler now and she was not as tired. Engulfed in darkness she was at first terrified but as her vision adjusted she was able to see shadows and shades of light.

Cautiously she looked around and discovered she was in a small room. She could make nothing out distinctly except for the huge bed which seemed to have swallowed her up. Lost amid the sheets and covers, her body was tucked in so tightly it was difficult to withdraw her hand from beneath the thick feather-tick quilts. Once freed, she moved her hand to her forehead, touching the cold compress lightly with her fingertips.

She wondered if her eyes were playing tricks on her as she watched what appeared to be an apparition coming as though through a misty fog. As she willed all her powers of concentration she made out a figure sitting near the fireplace. Fully dressed, and in the same corduroy jacket her father had been wearing, Harry was sound asleep in a large wooden rocker.

"Harrrr...," she tried to call his name but her voice was a mere croak.

"Maggie, Maggie darling," he called out as he rose at once and knelt beside her. "You're doing fine, no matter how you feel. Everything is okay. Don't worry about anything, I'm here with you."

"Harry, where are we? Where did you come from?"

"Don't try to talk now, dearest. Please try to sleep." He kissed her gently and she closed her eyes obediently.

"Harry. Harry."

It was easier waking up this time but Maggie was disappointed that her voice remained only a feeble utterance. Harry did not stir and it seemed an eternity past before she could rouse herself from the sleeping stupor that had left her so weak. However, the exertion proved too strenuous and she again slipped into unconsciousness.

When she awoke it was darker than before. The streams of light which had punctuated the interior of the tiny room had disappeared and in their place was a blazing fire in the hearth. She realized the day had gone and night had come. He was still there, exactly where she had seen him last. His hair was tousled and his face unshaven but it was him.

"Harry, Harry, is that really you?" Maggie's throat was dry but her voice sounded stronger.

For a minute she thought she had dreamed the whole thing but seeing him asleep she was content to know he was flesh and blood and a few feet within her reach.

"Harry," she intoned again.

This time he heard her.

"Hello, sleepy head. It's about time you put in an appearance," he said as he removed the compress and gently kissed her forehead. "I think your fever's pretty much gone." He smiled as he replaced the compress with a much cooler one.

"What is this place, Harry? How did I get here?"

"Don't overdue it now with questions," Harry said as he held a glass of water to her dry, chapped lips. "I'll give you a quick overview and then you've got to promise me to go back to sleep."

"Deal," Maggie said with some disappointment as Harry allowed her only a small amount of the water she had been thirsting for.

"Some village people found you a week ago. You were in the cemetery. I know you came all this way to visit your father's grave but apparently you suffered some kind of fainting spell and fell unconscious. It rained real heavy, like sleet they told me, and when they finally found you, you were soaked through. You developed a bad fever and you were lucky it didn't turn into pneumonia."

"It felt like I was dying."

"The village doctor said you had a close call but he pulled you though. Father Tony contacted your mother and she called me, God bless her. I got the first plane I could. Now, young lady, you promised. Close your eyes and sleep."

"You've been at my bedside all this time?"

Harry nodded. "I'm so scruffy looking, I probably scared you."

Maggie pointed to the glass of water again and Harry lifted her head as she drank greedily.

"Easy does it, Maggie. I don't think you appreciate the seriousness of all this."

"You thought I was going to die, didn't you Harry?"

"Yes, when Father Tony gave you the last rites, I thought I'd lost you."

"My father sent me back; it wasn't my time."

"Try not to talk, Maggie." Harry seemed concerned about her ramblings.

"Don't worry, Harry, I'm not delirious any longer, I'm fine." She reached out for him and he came into her arms. "Harry, I know and understand so much more. It was like an epiphany, a real eye-opener."

"I love you, Maggie, but it's unfair of me to say that to you now. When you're feeling better we'll talk."

"Don't worry, darling, I won't say anything I'll regret later.

I'm here and in the now, and I know that I love you." Maggie wanted to remain in his arms but sleep overcame her and she drifted into nothingness.

The wafting fragrances interrupted her dreams. Maggie opened her eyes and breathed in the aromas.

"I'm ravenous. What's on the menu?" She called out to no one in particular.

"Maggie, just because your temperature's back to normal doesn't mean you're out of sickbay. Take it easy," Harry chided gently as he carried in her dinner tray.

"Where is this place, Harry?" Maggie asked as she sat up with the help of several large feather pillows and ate a little of the soup Harry spoon-fed her.

"It's the home of Maria and Marilla Compallie. They've volunteered to take care of you while you've been sick. They're friends of Father Tony and he can tell you more when he comes to see you later today."

Father Tony had been making the trip up from the church several times a week during Maggie's illness and was genuinely pleased to see her sitting up in bed when he arrived that afternoon.

"Hi, Maggie, you look wonderful. How are you doing?"

"Fine, Father. It's good to see you again."

"That Harry of yours is some guy. He's had to put up with the Compallie sisters and believe me that's no easy task," Father Tony said, smiling indulgently at Maggie.

Maria and Marilla Compallie were actually widowed sisters-in-law who had lived together in the small cottage since both of their husbands had died years before. They generously gave of their time to the church and community, asking for little and living a relatively simple life. They religiously made the trek down the mountain every Sunday for Mass, and it was there they learned of Maggie's ill-health and kindly offered to see to her recuperative needs for as long as necessary.

Maggie was feeling almost normal toward the week's end but the doctor ordered continued bed rest. Under the watchful eyes of her two nursemaids Maggie found she could do nothing but comply. However, once she got back her color and appetite, she used her charms to coax Maria and Marilla into allowing her to have her meals in the dining room with Harry. Even though the rains continued day and night, Maggie's health improved and both Tony and the doctor were encouraged by her progress.

The young priest's visits were continually heralded with shrieks of joy as Maria and Marilla sought to make him comfortable. They were, however, not fond of Harry and from the moment he arrived they had been unduly vigilant in his presence with one or the other maintaining a wary observance of his every action.

Although they gave him a room in their home, they were not accepting of the situation and with their patient's welfare upper most in their minds they made clear their suspicions vociferously whenever the couple tried to be alone. Harry, for his part, was a model of gentility, accepting amiably Maggie's guardians' attentiveness, knowing it was in part their ministrations which had saved her life.

On Saturday morning, Father Tony came to the cottage with a young man in tow. The brawny teenager, his muscled arms glazed with sweat and dirt, hung back shyly, kicking mud from his boots before cautiously entering the house.

"Maggie, this is Umberto Cipollini, the good Samaritan who found you and brought you to the doctor's home."

"Grazie, grazie, Umberto," Maggie gently shook the youth's calloused hands as he beamed with pleasure at the mention of his name.

"Umberto had apparently been bringing home his cows from the pasture that night when he discovered you lying in what by that time must have been a drainage ditch," Father Tony said as he looked from Maggie to Harry translating the dairy herder's words. "He said he heard you shouting to someone in the cemetery and it was lucky you were so loud or he would never have heard you. He said it sounded as though you were talking to your Papa and it was a good thing he didn't believe in ghosts."

Maggie looked at the young man and smiled. "I'm so glad you were there for me that night, Umberto. God bless you."

As the weeks progressed the weather turned warmer and when the doctor came he found his patient quite able to be up and about. He continued prescribing a great deal of tea, something Maggie found quite enjoyable, and although she was not to excite herself, she was allowed outside for a few hours each day when there was sufficient sunlight.

"The doctor thinks you'll be fit to travel soon, Maggie," Harry said as they lounged in the sun outside the tiny apricot painted house.

"I don't care if I ever leave, Harry. I could live here forever. What about you?"

"I like being wherever you are, honey. But sure, it's possible as soon as we sort out a few practical matters," Harry reminded her thoughtfully.

"Great! How about six months here and six back in the states," Maggie was quick to suggest.

"Okay darling, sounds good to me." Harry lifted the wide-brimmed straw hat off his face and smiled in her direction.

"Harry, do you remember when Clare called a couple of weeks ago and said I was fortunate to have gotten well so fast. Well, I think you and Italy made all the difference in my getting better."

"That may well be, Maggie, but according to Clare you were lucky not to have suffered a more severe emotional breakdown."

"Harry, let's buy a little house and fix it up," Maggie said, ignoring Harry's reference to Clare's comment. "I can just see you working in your vegetable garden or just laying around in your hammock like you're doing now." Maggie, covered from head to toe in a blanket, looked dreamily over at Harry.

"Okay by me, darling, but right now how about getting a little shut-eye. You still need your rest."

The day was languid and balmy and soon they were both fast asleep. It was the sound of Maria's voice that jolted Maggie awake.

"Harry, wake up, Maria's coming."

"Oh no, it's time you were getting back to bed, young lady." Harry checked his watch and looked skyward toward where the sun was setting. "That's all I'd need is for you to catch a chill and those ladies in waiting of yours would have my head on a platter."

"Harry, I want us to spend all our days like this, sitting in our yard and chatting about nothing more then the weather. I know you think I'm still recuperating and that I'm being sentimental but having you all to myself these past weeks has been the best medicine for me." Maggie reached out for him as he picked her up to carry her back inside.

"I've never been happier, Maggie. I realize I didn't even know what love was until you came into my life. You knew me better than I knew myself." He kissed her tenderly.

"Harry, since I've improved so much, don't you think I warrant a less conservative kiss?"

"Maggie, don't make it any tougher on me than it is. I've got to be on my best behavior." Harry's voice strained as he struggled to keep his voice below a murmur.

"They're coming," Maggie teased as they cautiously approached the bedroom door only to run into the outstretched arms of the two nurses.

"Il Dottore no like Signorina Maggie not to be resting," Maria Compallie shouted as both women shook long, pointed fingers in

Harry's direction.

"Scusa, mi scusi, Signora Maria and Signora Marilla," Harry apologized as he hurriedly laid Maggie down on the bed and retreated from the room.

"See you later, darling," Maggie called, her eyes following him out the front door.

Minutes later, she heard a car pull up in front of the house and watched from her bedroom window as Harry affectionately greeted Father Tony with a firm handshake and a friendly slap on the back. The two men then went and sat in the garden under a grape arbor engrossed in conversation for the duration of the afternoon.

Hours later, Maggie heard Tony calling her out of the deep sleep into which she had fallen. "Maggie, how are you feeling? I didn't mean to wake you."

"No Father, I was just napping. I'm fine, really I am. Father, I hope nothing's wrong with Harry. I saw the two of you earlier in the garden and you were absorbed in discussion."

"In other words, Maggie, you want to know what Harry and I were talking about." Tony's smile was gentle and uplifting.

"Is it confidential?"

"Maggie, this isn't the first time Harry and I've had a chance to converse. He and I have been chatting a great deal lately, and I think he has finally come to terms with what has haunted him his whole life. But that's something you'll have to ask him about. As a matter of fact, he's asked me to sit with the two of you while, as he says it, he bares his soul to you. Would you feel up to it now if I went and got him?"

"Yes, Father."

"Before I get Harry, I thought you'd like to read the prayer that helped him with his decision. He handed Maggie a little holy card which she took and read:

There is no darkness or evil so profound that it cannot be penetrated by the light of Christ. There are no burdens beyond bearing when we are supported by Christ's love. There is no sin so serious that Jesus will not forgive us if we but turn to Him with contrite hearts. No suffering so excruciating, no death so agonizing that it can destroy us because Jesus passed from death to life. Nothing ever again can be hopeless.

When Harry came in he was in good spirits. "I see Tony's already given you the prayer card, Maggie. Those words had such a profound affect on me. After I read it, it was as though the darkness I feared all my life was shattered by the light. I owe so much to Father Tony. He and I have been doing a lot of talking and I've come to the conclusion that although I rejected God, He never rejected me."

"Harry, I…," Maggie was speechless.

"Somehow," Harry continued, "that thought has given me hope and I know in my heart I can change. I can do all things in Christ, isn't that how Saint Paul put it?" Harry looked toward Father Tony.

Maggie pulled at Harry's sleeve and he sat on the edge of the bed. "Harry…," was all she could manage to say.

"I know, honey, I've a long way to go, but now I know that God's in my corner and I feel as though I can make it. Father Tony has promised he'll keep in touch with me to guide me over the rough spots." Harry leaned over and kissed Maggie gently on the cheek.

"I'm so glad, Harry. My heart's so full, I can't express it. When I got your letter, I wanted to forgive you but something inside held me back. Like Father said, when I forgave myself, I was able to forgive you."

"Maggie, do you recall my telling you about the hole inside me that I couldn't fill. I don't have the hole anymore. It's been filled up. It's like I've found my secret faith. I feel like a new person. It's my affirmation," Harry grinned.

"Love is miraculous," Father Tony said as he got up to

leave the room.

"I know you can make it Harry and I want to be with you, always." Maggie reached over to him.

"Do you, love?" Harry moved to her and put his arm around her, hugging her tightly.

"Yes, dearest. Father, before you go, may we have your blessing?" Maggie held Harry's hand in hers.

"Of course," Father Tony said as he made the sign of the cross over them.

The three of them talked a while longer until Maggie grew tired and fell asleep in Harry's arms.

A month passed before the doctor pronounced Maggie well enough to return home. The cloudy, rainy weather outside matched her mood as she prepared to leave. Harry had made the airline reservations and they were to fly out of Rome in the late afternoon.

"Arrivederci, Miss Maggie. You take good care of yourself." Maria and Marilla covered her cheeks with kisses as she finished packing the last of her luggage.

"Thank you for everything. I love you both." Maggie hugged them tightly and promised to write when she returned home. She laughed delightedly as they pulled Harry down to their eye levels and pecked his cheeks in unison.

The rain was coming down in torrents as Harry lifted her into the front seat of Father Tony's jeep. With a final wave, the vehicle sped away from the little crowd that had gathered to say good-bye. As they drove past the cemetery road on the way down the mountain, Maggie felt a reassuring sense of peace as she thought about her father.

"Dear Lord, take care of my father and give him eternal rest."

She had no sooner finished her prayer when the sun peaked

through the black clouds sending a shaft of light through the windshield. Suddenly a rainbow appeared in the distance and when Harry, sitting in the back seat, gripped her shoulders tightly, Maggie knew he had seen it as well.

Chapter 27

"Harry, could we have lunch today?"

Maggie called Harry the day after she was discharged from the hospital. The trip back to the states had proved fatiguing and Maggie agreed with Harry and Clare that it was best to check into the hospital and make sure everything was all right.

"Sure, honey, but take it easy. A week in the hospital is enough to weaken anyone," Harry said with a chuckle.

"Let's just say it wasn't my little Italian cottage. Harry, don't plan anything. Just pick me up at noon and let's play it by ear."

"You must be feeling pretty good."

"Being able to put on a dress and step into heels has done wonders for my morale," Maggie confessed.

"Not to mention what it's going to do for me."

Harry drove to the embarcadero with one hand on the wheel and the other holding Maggie's hand. She sensed he had something serious on his mind and was glad Leeann had recommended the out-of-the-way beach shack which according to her served the best fish tacos in town. Harry asked for a secluded table on the patio and quietly held her chair as she sat down.

"Harry, what have you been doing with yourself while I've been laid up?" Maggie asked as she turned her head and looked up into his eyes.

"Thinking of my beautiful Maggie," he said, gently kissing the nape of her neck before sitting down at the table.

"Harry, let's take a solemn vow to never blame one another for anything ever again," Maggie said, after the waiter had taken their order.

"It's a deal, but what brought that on? Are you're still worried about what Clare told you?"

"Not really, darling," Maggie said fetchingly, watching him react to her invisible caress.

"You know, you hadn't aught to look at a guy like that, Maggie, I can't think straight. Anyway, Clare's probably right about us not seeing each other until I've had more time in treatment."

"Harry, how do you feel about that? You were fine in Italy so it's really up to you."

"To tell the truth, honey, I'm scared. I'm a regular humpty dumpty. Italy was one thing but back here it's a day to day struggle. I've got a lot of work to do before I can put myself back together again and I don't want it to impact your life."

"Harry, Clare's evaluation gives you an excellent prognosis but she's afraid both therapy and a relationship might prove too stressful."

"It can't be much fun for you, either," Harry said, squeezing her hand.

"If it makes you more comfortable let's not see each other until Clare says you can handle it better."

"The upshot is I'd still be in therapy most of the time and it's the backsliding she knows I'm scared of."

"It won't be forever, Harry."

"No, I guess not," Harry said without conviction.

"Darling, are you still afraid of the dark?"

"No, thanks to you and Father Tony I've refocused my life. Our sojourn in Italy helped me find myself and gave me a sense of peace I've never known before." Harry's smile picked up where it had left off.

"I can see it in your eyes."

"What you see sweetheart is your light shining in my eyes. It was your faith that made me believe I could change. Like Father Tony said it's my second chance, and I don't want to foul it up."

"The peace that surpasses all understanding," Maggie whispered.

"I didn't get knocked off my horse like Saint Paul but I sure know what it feels like to have the bottom drop out from underneath you. We both got the message though; you've got to believe in someone stronger than yourself when the going gets tough. Everyday I count myself lucky to have survived the hopelessness. I know that God will get me out of this, maybe not today but someday."

"What about your bouts of depression?"

"Not quite as often but they come on quicker. Doc says I don't need as many meds but what happens if I turn into a tired, frustrated old man. I couldn't stand if that happened to us. If I wasn't already a certified nut case, I'd go mad," Harry said, making a comical monster face at her.

"Harry, you're incorrigible," Maggie shook her head. "Clare says the medication is temporary and I know you won't have any side effects."

"How do you know? We're talking platonic relationship here for God knows how long."

"Are you feeling sorry for yourself?"

"Damn right I am."

"Harry, I happen to be in love with all of you and there's a great deal more to you than sex. If I was in some accident and this happened, you wouldn't stop loving me, would you?"

"Of course not, honey, but…"

"And besides, I repeat, it won't be forever."

"I bet Clare made it clear though that I come without a warranty."

"You know Clare. She said on one hand a relationship would be good for you but on the other it might prove detrimental. She wants us to understand all the consequences."

"Well, that said, what did you decide?"

"I don't want to endanger our friendship."

"Leave it to you to have such friends."

"I have a great many wonderful friends and I intend on keeping them all in my life," Maggie said, smiling at Harry.

"Thanks Maggie. Speaking of good friends, could I ask a favor?"

"Sure, Harry, what is it?"

"It's about Lisa. I want to talk to her. Dr. Sebastian agrees that I've got to start mending my fences."

"I'll call her Harry. We've been talking about you for a long time and I think she's beginning to understand you more."

"Let her know whatever she decides is okay with me."

"All right, Harry, let's call her right now," Maggie said, reaching for her cell phone.

"Hi, Lisa. I'm with your dad. He wants very much to see you. Yes, I'll tell him," Maggie laughed and looked at Harry. "She says she's tired of being a badass and won't you please forgive her?"

"Only if she forgives me first," Harry offered.

"Yes Lisa, but he wants you to know he's sorry for being a badass, too."

Maggie handed the phone to Harry and listened as he made polite conversation with his daughter. "She asked us to drive down and meet her today?" Harry looked bewildered and handed the phone back to Maggie. "I don't know what to say," he added nervously.

"Yes Lisa, we could be there in an hour. Are you sure? Your father doesn't want to rush you into anything. Yes, I remember the boardwalk. We'll see you there." Maggie stared at Harry. "Well, as Hoppy would say, it's now or never, boyo. It seems like she's been thinking about you all this time and really wants to see you."

"Maggie, are you up for such a long drive?"

"Of course, I feel great."

"I hope Lisa's not disappointed with her old man."

"She won't be, Harry, trust me. She's knows what you've been through and she's quite a mature young woman."

"It's funny, Maggie, but you know more about the people in my life than I do."

"They all helped me find you, Harry."

Harry paid the waiter and waited as Maggie finished putting on her lipstick.

"I never grow tired of seeing you do that." Harry, his elbow resting on the table, held his chin in his hand and smiled as he watched her.

"You're silly Harry, but I love you for it." Maggie blew him an airmail kiss.

"Try and catch a few winks, honey, so you don't get overtired," Harry suggested as they walked arm and arm toward the parking lot.

"Okay, I'll try." Maggie slid into Harry's convertible, tied a scarf around her hair and closed her eyes.

They drove north along the coast highway surveying the small beach towns alive with crowds and merrymakers. Lisa's seaside resort was no different. Swarming with people when they arrived, Harry and Maggie had to drive blocks before they found a parking space. They moved unhurriedly toward the boardwalk, holding hands and talking until Maggie saw her. Standing by herself on the pier, a loner among the masses, she looked more childlike than ever as her auburn wisps blew across her pint size face.

"I don't think I would have recognized her if you hadn't pointed her out to me," Harry said as he and Maggie approached the young girl.

"Harry, you go by yourself. I'll walk along the beach and you can catch up with me afterwards."

Maggie watched as Harry picked his way along the planks walking briskly toward the daughter he hadn't seen in so many years. For a few moments she stood and watched the two figures standing motionless like gleaming bronze statues in the sunlight. Then she blessed them in her heart and walked on.

I wish I had brought my own car. Then Harry and Lisa could have had as much time as they needed with each other and not have concerned themselves with me. I'll just rest for a few minutes before I start walking back as it will take me time. I wish I didn't tire so easily but being sick has really set me back a bit.

Maggie found a bench and was resting in the sun when she saw them running down the beach toward her. They ran neck and neck like two graceful gazelles until Lisa sped up and reached her first.

"Hi Lisa," Maggie said as she held open her arms.

Lisa sat down and gave Maggie a big hug. "Maggie, my dad wants me to live with him. Can you believe it? We can be a family again after he gets well."

"I'm glad, Lisa. I'm happy that you've got your father back in your life."

"I'm glad for you and Harry, too, Maggie." Lisa hugged her again.

"I told her about you and me, Maggie. I hope it was okay?" Harry grinned.

"That's fine with me." Maggie smiled at them both.

"How about we grab something to eat?" Harry suggested.

"Can you guys give me a rain-check? I sort of promised someone I'd meet them, if it's okay with you Harry, I mean, D… D… Dad." Lisa sputtered happily as she kissed her father. "Boy, I've got to practice that one," she said, departing in laughter.

They watched her sprint along the beach until she disappeared into the crowd. Maggie kept Harry's hand in hers as they stood looking out at the blue water sparkling in the sunlight.

"Maggie, there's another favor I'd like to ask you for."

"Aunt Jess?"

"Still reading my mind?" Harry kissed her on the forehead.

"Well, I figured that since you were fence mending, she'd be next. I like her and I know she loves you very much."

"I do miss her and I want her to know about us. She put up with me big time and it's taken me all this while to realize it. I guess I'm finally growing up."

"Harry, you're not afraid anymore of the past or the future, are you?" Maggie asked, the reality of it just beginning to dawn on her.

"No, I guess not, and I …" Harry was interrupted by the sounds of blasting horns and coughing motors. "Speaking of the future, honey, look how that traffic's piling up."

Maggie looked toward the highway. "Harry, maybe it would be easier if we drove back now."

"Are you all right, darling?"

"Of course, Harry. Why?"

"I just wouldn't want to think of you as not being all right, that's all."

"You know you're a lovable guy," Maggie said, squeezing his hand.

As the car sped along the highway they drove in silence. Watching the unremitting waves crashing violently against the rocky shore, Maggie occasionally looked over at Harry who seemed far away.

"What's worrying you, darling?"

"Maggie, I hope you can put up with me. This damn depression comes on pretty fast these days, and like I told you even the medication sometimes doesn't help."

"It'll be okay, Harry. Let's be positive and look at all the progress you've made these past months. Try not to worry," Maggie said quietly as she moved closer to him.

"I was thinking what a lousy mess I've made of our relationship. I've got so many regrets and I'm scared to death of myself. I've hurt you so often, Maggie, and I couldn't stand to hurt you again. I can't bring myself to ask you to stick with me when I've got nothing to offer you."

"Harry is that what's worrying you?"

"Yes, Maggie, and it's got to be said. Nothing can ever be the same between us. I know that I love you, Maggie, and I want you desperately but I've destroyed us. My life right now isn't worth a plug nickel. I wouldn't blame you if you said good-bye."

"You know how we both hate good-byes, Harry, but it's true, I'm not interested in our current relationship."

"I can understand that. We need to take time and not rush into anything. The sooner you distance yourself from me, the better off you'll be." Harry voice was barely audible.

"Harry, that's not what I mean. I did some thinking while I was waiting for you and Lisa and I've come to the realization that I need you just as much as you need me. Both of us will get better a lot sooner if we cement this relationship permanently."

Maggie watched as Harry speechlessly turned the steering wheel sharply to the right and pulled off to the side of the road.

"You mean get married?" Harry turned off the car motor and sat quietly staring at her.

"Yes, and providing we agree on our new relationship, we should be able to come to terms rather quickly."

"At this moment you could ask me anything."

"First of all, I want us both to realize that marriage is going to be a challenge for us. We both bring our own backgrounds, our own wills, personalities, preferences, and passions into this union, and it's important that we know beforehand that there will be times when we'll have to renounce ourselves to love one another. Are we up to such a sacrifice, Harry?"

"Maggie, you'd be the one that would be sacrificing. You're young and you'd be handicapping yourself with me, my past and my health issues to boot. "

"I love you, Harry, but we each must make a choice. I choose you, and God willing, I'll never be sorry."

"I know that I love you, Maggie, and I know that I wouldn't want to live this life without you. It won't be easy but I want to learn how to grow in love as a couple. I want you more than anything in this world and whatever challenges there are out there, I know I could face them if we're together."

"Thank you, darling, that was a beautiful proposal, and I accept," Maggie said, kissing Harry's cheek.

"Honey, are you sure this is the right decision, especially after all we said this afternoon. I can't promise you anything except that I love you, but is that good enough to build a marriage on? You'd be taking me when I have nothing to give you."

"Harry, I love you. I knew it when I woke up and saw you sitting there by my bedside. You and my father were part of the same dream. I don't want to wait around and hope that all goes well while you're facing the hardest struggle of your life. I want to be there with you. You need me to light up the darkness, darling. Call it a leap of faith because it has to be all or nothing for me." Maggie pulled Harry's arm around her.

"Maggie, I…" His voice tapered off as he brought her hand to his lips. "You name the date, darling."

"Harry, if you don't mind driving a while longer we could be married today. The Mission San Pietro is just across the border. The padre could marry us and it would mean so much to me."

"Sure, honey, it's still early enough but let's make a quick detour to a little jewelry shop I know so you can pick out your wedding ring."

"I like that idea." Maggie stared up into his eyes.

"Maggie, I'm so afraid of losing you. I know you should be marrying someone lots better than the likes of me but to be honest

I know I couldn't live without you." He brought her close and held her tightly, kissing her gently.

"Harry, don't forget I'm tenacious, the sticking kind. Let's not be afraid. I'm not underestimating what's in store for us but with the Lord's help we'll make it worth the effort." She traced along his cheekbone with her fingertip and kissed him again but her kiss was not as gentle and she felt his body stiffen in response.

Warmed by the sunshine they indulged in an unbroken movement of shared affection until the shadows of late afternoon forced them back onto the road. They drove leisurely, making good time even after shopping for her ring, and it was not yet dark when they arrived at the mission.

As the last rays of light streamed through the chapel's stained glass windows, Padre Philippe performed the brief ceremony to the satisfaction of the newlyweds. Having taken their vows, Maggie watched as he blessed her ring with holy water and handed it to Harry.

"With this ring, I thee wed," Harry said solemnly, placing the simple gold band on Maggie's finger.

"May God bless you both and give you a happy married life. Remember my children, when you make your marriage a triangle with God as the center nothing or no one will ever come between you."

They signed the paperwork and Harry pressed an envelope into the Padre's hands with repeated thanks.

"Gracias, Padre, gracias."

"Vaya con Dios, my children. I must go and make ready for Mass. Stay and pray as long as you like."

After Padre Philippe left, they moved closer together, their arms tightly wrapped around one another in the darkness. The white marble altar and the red sanctuary lamp were all they could see as night fell across the tiny church.

Harry whispered in her ear. "Do you realize, Mrs. Cooke, we're an old married couple of twenty-five minutes?"

"Yes, Mr. Cooke," Maggie answered softly, "and this is the first day of the rest of our life together."

They watched as several altar boys came forward and began lighting the myriad of candles throughout the church. The glow seemed to radiate all around them.

"Harry, look at how much light there is now."

"You've made the darkness disappear, Maggie."

Epilogue

The renewal of their wedding vows was a formal, catered affair with friends, co-workers and family members in attendance. Since Hoppy's health did not permit his leaving the premises, Maggie and Harry decided to hold the ceremony at the Valley View Retirement home in the garden of his bungalow. Hoppy, his wheelchair pushed along the red carpet by Mrs. Kemper, held Maggie's hand in his as he escorted her to a beaming Harry who patiently stood under an arbor of yellow roses.

Resplendent in an ivory lace gown, Maggie smiled as she looked upon the face of the man who had been her husband these past seven years. Looking very formal in his tuxedo, Harry appeared as handsome as when she had first met him fourteen years earlier. Although his hair was a great deal grayer and he carried a few extra pounds, he was still her Harry, and Maggie attributed this to the peace and love they had found with one another.

She looked over at her mother who was holding their thirteen-month old daughter Laura in her arms, while keeping a watchful eye over their four-year old son, Robert, who for a few minutes at least seemed content to sit and play with his toys.

As Maggie listened to Harry repeat his wedding vows, she thought of how things had changed during these years and how kind God had been to her little family. It had not been easy, but firmly grounded in their faith they had taken each day as it came.

Harry had left WordTech and opened his own consulting business. Tremulous at first, the business had finally taken root and Harry was building a successful company. When he was on disability, she had taken the reins of the department, and within the year had permanently been promoted to the head of Marketing with Leeann as her assistant. Clare was still Harry's therapist and although pleased with his progress had advised him of the need for continued analysis which was fine with him as she was his friend as well as his doctor.

Lisa had come to live with Maggie and Harry and was almost finished with college. She and David had discovered one another at one of the family gatherings and had been dating ever since. Aunt Jess was a regular visitor at Hoppy's and had helped Maggie's mother decorate their new home with the promise of visiting their summer cottage outside of Rome once it was finished.

Paul, who declared himself a good loser, had been offered a vice presidency in Accounting at WordTech's Hong Kong office which he took without fanfare. Within the year he married Kim Lee and became a member of a wealthy Eurasian dynasty. Ellen had taken a page from Harry and gone into therapy, eventually turning her life around.

Suddenly Maggie's turn was upon her.

"I take thee Harry, for my husband, to love, honor and obey till death us do part."

She finished the words and watched as Harry put the ring on her finger, the same plain gold band he had given her that day in the mission chapel. Harry, who had wanted his own gold band after they were married, kissed Maggie's hand as she slipped his ring on his finger and echoed his words.

"With this ring, I thee wed."

"God's blessings upon you both Maggie and Harry and may you

and your family continue to receive an abundance of His grace and love." Father Tony, who had made a special trip to officiate at the celebration, gave his blessing to the couple as he had years before.

"Ladies and gentlemen, please join me in wishing the very best to Mr. and Mrs. Harry Cooke at the renewal of their wedding vows. You may kiss your bride, Harry," Father Tony put forward encouragingly.

Harry took Maggie in his arms as she reached out for him. They kissed amid the cheers of the well-wishers surrounding them.

"Thank you for being my wife, Maggie. Thank you for your faith in me. All my love, all my life," he whispered in her ear.

"I love you, darling." Maggie could say nothing more for Harry had said it all.

About the Author

Born in Los Angeles, Gloria Preston grew up in Chicago and resides in San Diego where she is completing work on a children's book entitled, *Yonyo and the Magic Thimble.*

Having earned her Doctorate in Clinical Psychology and Masters in Education, the author has interwoven psychological aspects into the framework of her novel providing a unique insight into the clinical process.

www.gapreston.com